The Stars Plot Revenge

L.J. Kerry

The Fallasingha Chronicles
Book 1

The Stars Plot Revenge

L.J. Kerry

The Stars Plot Revenge © 2022 L.J. Kerry
Editor:
Dianne M Jones
Map Illustrator:
Z.K. Dorward
All rights reserved. No part of this book may be reproduced, transmitted or stored in any form or by any means, electronic or mechanical, photocopying, recording, scanning or otherwise, without permission. It is illegal to copy this book, post it to a website or distribute it by other means without permission.

This novel is entirely a work of fiction. The names, characters and incidents portrayed in it are the work of the author's imagination. Any resemblance to actual people, living or dead, events or localities is entirely coincidental.

L.J. Kerry asserts the moral right to be identified as the author of this work.

This book has been professionally typeset on AtticusText © 2022 L.J. Kerry

First Edition

Paperback:
978-1-80068-173-6
Hardback:
978-1-80068-174-3

To all the people
who feel like they're locked in their towers.

OTHEREAL

LHANDAHIR

KARSHAK CASTLE

HARANSHAI

KARSHAKROH

TSUNAMAI

YETNALOUI
NALLAVAGHN
AKORNSONIA
TRODORE
TORWARIN
CLERAVORALIS
NAVAWICH
OLD
LIATNOGARD
ALSAPHUS
CASTLE
FALLASINGHA EMPIRE
CARDENK
LAKE
BRALOAK

Note to Reader

Despite working hard, through multiple rounds of edits, to give you
the best product possible some grammar and spelling issues may have slipped through the cracks.

Please direct any concerns to:

ljkerrybooks@outlook.com

Content Warning

This book contains scenes which depict violence and sexual harassment.

ONE

The walls of the castle still held the ghosts of Orison's screams.

After a month of being in the Othereal, Orison was still scared to set foot in the throne room.

That was where her captor King Sila Alsaphus—Fae King of the Fallasingha Empire—turned her into a Fae. Although she didn't remember all the details, she could still remember the immense pain and the screaming. Now she was stuck here, unable to return to the mortal realm, and being paraded around as a princess for King Sila's benefit.

Joyous orchestral music filtered out of the throne room door and into the main body of the castle, in celebration of the king. Orison stood before the open door, watching partygoers dance in dizzying circles, trying to pluck up the nerve to cross the threshold. All she wanted to do was pick up the skirts of her heavy green dress and run back to bed. No... Orison couldn't give Sila that power. Pushing her shoulders back, she put on a brave mask and took the step that she had dreaded all day.

Music swelled to a crescendo, then dived into quietness; dancing like the people on the dance floor, in the throne room of Alsaphus Castle. It was a sight to behold for the celebration of King Sila's 550th birthday. Large stone archways flanked the dance space, the grey stone lit up in a warm glow. In the left central archway was a table of food and drink, manned by a pale servant with tree bark on the side of their face, their fire-red hair tied up in a bun.

Amongst the procession of dancers, Orison tolerated dancing with King Sila Alsaphus. His glowing yellow eyes burned into her soul as he held her hand and spun her around in circles. Sila had his shoulder-length red hair tied back, with a silver crown on his head. It was a simple crown that looked like flowers and thorns mingling together.

When the music and dance changed, he moved her hand to his shoulder. Sila's velvet royal blue tunic felt soft under her fingers. Orison let out a gasp when his icy hand held her waist; the touch burned through her heavy green ball gown. Her thoughts drifted to how many different ways she could punch him, if he tried to touch her anywhere else. The music resumed to a slow tune and the pair swayed ever so slightly in time.

"Princess Orison," he drawled. Her attention turned to Sila. "You need to relax to dance efficiently."

Usually, Orison loved her name. Spoken like horizon—without the H—it was fitting to the fact she always sought the sunrise. However, when her name came from Sila's mouth, it grated on her like nails on a chalkboard.

She smiled sweetly, "How many times, I'm not a princess."

He pulled her into his chest, "Hush now, we have guests."

After celebrating for three days, each move for Orison was an effort; especially with how numb her feet felt in her heels. Yet Sila didn't look tired in the slightest, even though he had been taking various courtesans back to his chambers for another kind of party.

He pushed her away from him and spun her around again. Orison stumbled slightly. When he pulled her back in, his eyes narrowed. Nevertheless, they continued with their movements, which now included more swaying.

"I'm tired," Orison told him for the hundredth time as the music died down.

Sila spun her around again, only this time he extended his foot. Orison tripped and fell hard onto the throne room's stone floor; her golden hair falling out of the braided bun from the sudden impact. The procession of dancers around the pair gasped to see the fallen princess. Sila tutted as he crouched down to her level. She looked at him through her hair, which he brushed back with the metallic scent of his magic.

"You're an embarrassment to my empire," Sila snarled. "Guards!"

Orison's eyes widened as two guards forced her arms behind her back. She cried out as one of them bound her wrists with a rope of fire. They hauled her up with a forceful grip on her upper arms, she struggled in their grasp, but they were too strong. Tears glazed over her eyes, her lips trembled as she looked at Sila.

"I'm sorry," she breathed, as she let the tears fall. "We've been dancing for three days..."

He grabbed her face in his hands. "I don't want to hear it. Get her out of here."

"No!" Orison pleaded when he let go of her. As guards dragged her away, she thrashed in their grasp, only to cry out when they tightened their grip.

The procession of dancers parted to let the guards pull Orison towards the doors into the rest of the castle. She continued to struggle and let out a scream, until her voice was muted by the metallic scent of Sila's magic stinging her nose. Double doors opened on a phantom wind, two guards flanked Orison, dragging her into the corridor that opened to a circular stone room.

They yanked Orison down the corridor towards the West Wing. Their path was illuminated by the Othereal lights that lined the wall between the arched windows. The sound of Orison's feet scraping on the floor, along with the guards' footfalls echoed around the stone walls. She had given up fighting as they hauled her up the winding staircase; and even more so, when they shoved her into her chambers and slammed the door.

Elsewhere, in a small, thatch-roofed cottage, Saskia rocked in a creaking chair, knitting a blanket. At her feet was a small black dragon, asleep in front of the crackling fire. Lining one wall of the cottage was Saskia's collection of dresses in varying styles. Between the collection was a full-length mirror with tutorials etched into the seams on how to do hair and make-up.

The attacks are getting worse. Move in now before it's too late, a voice warned within her head.

Her feet were planted on the floor after she received the message from her spy. Saskia's blue eyes fell onto the sleeping dragon snoring loudly like a cat. The dragon's fur was an obsidian colour and had small horns and wings. Placing her knitting needles into the basket at her side, she leaned over towards it.

Extending her hand, she softly touched the dragon's back. The dragon opened his eyes and shook his tiny body. He stretched with a yawn, showing rows of razor-sharp teeth. "It's time. Go to the castle and protect the princess."

Saskia's chair creaked as she stood up, pulling her pink robe around her body. Her slippers scuffled along the floor as she crossed the threshold. She opened the front door for the dragon that was close behind her. Moving out of his way, she watched him run off into the night and take flight.

Despite her servants getting her ready for bed, Orison was restless. She sat curled up on her royal red sofa. She bit her thumbnail as she read over the note that had been placed underneath her pillow while she was at the celebration.

'Princesses don't deserve to be locked away in towers. The door can be opened if you speak my name.'

It was the fifth time she had read it. Once again, she turned over the note several times, expecting it to be different from the last time; but no name presented itself. Something told her it was a trap, if she did figure out who the sender was. Maybe the sender's intentions were malicious, intending to move her from this glorified prison and into a worse one.

Throwing the note in the fire, Orison wiped her hand down her baby-pink nightgown as she stood up and paced in front of the ornate marble fireplace. She rubbed her neck with a groan, biting her nail again, she regarded the mysterious note as it went up in flames. *It's a trap,* Orison told herself. Her hair, styled in soft waves, swayed with her erratic movement along the royal red rug.

Her meeting rooms were extravagant, disgustingly so by Orison's standards. The fireplace had two mermaids carved into the marble that reached up to the ceiling. Wood-panelled walls had occasional breaks in them, depicting oil paintings of war; it was this simple detail that showed this wasn't a princess' room yet. At the end of her room was a semi-circular section for her dining table. Such extravagance continued into her bedroom where a four-poster bed sat in the middle, in front of a tapestry that depicted the bloodiest battle Fallasingha had waged.

Even though her servants had tried to force her to decorate, Orison refused; on the slim chance she could find a way to escape from Alsaphus Castle and return to the mortal lands. It was a foolish plan, given the fact she was no longer mortal. Orison's ears were now pointed at the tip, and her eyes glowed a purple hue; the colour was unnatural for a human, but normal for a Fae.

Unable to tolerate the roaring in her head, she approached her chamber door and tugged it open. To her relief, no guards were posted outside. Taking a step into the corridor, she glanced to her left where the noise of the celebration travelled up the stairs; people laughed and roared over the music. Wanting to avoid any attention, she made a right turn to a servant's staircase, where she started her descent.

With each hurried step, her nightgown billowed behind her until she came to a stop at each servant's door; in case anyone came through. Orison was relieved that no one made an appearance. At the base of the stairs, she pushed open the wooden door that led outside, towards the stables. She inhaled the crisp night air that settled some of the roaring in her head; it wasn't enough.

As Orison entered the stables, the stench of sewage overwhelmed her. She ignored it as she said hello to each creature she passed, locked up in their pens; they were trapped, just like her. Peggy, one of the three unicorns in Sila's arsenal, poked her head out of her enclosure, ready for Orison to pet her. She obliged, kissing Peggy's muzzle. When Peggy gently nudged Orison's shoulder, she wrapped her arms around the unicorn's neck and held her close. Orison had always thought of Peggy as a splendid creature. She had a good temperament, never biting or rearing up on her hind legs like the other unicorns, when Orison came to visit. After a couple of moments, she pulled away and continued further into the stables.

The hellhounds barked as she passed, globs of saliva surrounded their lips and dribbled down into the hay at their feet, Orison wouldn't dare pet those things; even if somebody paid her. She passed other animals that were sound asleep. The luminescent eyes of an owl in the shadow of its box almost scared her to death.

Unbeknownst to Orison, somebody lurked in the shadows; their face darkened by the hood of their purple velvet cloak. They reached a hand towards Orison and grabbed her by the arm. "Boo!" A warm feminine laugh bounced around the stables.

Orison jumped and whirled around, placing a hand on her heart when she recognised her pursuer. "Thank Othereal!" She sank against the wall of the griffon enclosure. The griffon, Hypnos, immediately poked his head out and nipped at Orison's hair. She quickly tugged it back into her possession. "Kinsley!"

Kinsley laughed again as she pushed the hood away from her head. Black hair cascaded down just past her shoulders. The cloak revealed the silver ball gown that she wore to the party, which accentuated her curvy figure. "I see he finally let you flee the ball!"

Kinsley and the rest of the Luxart family were the only true friends Orison had made since arriving in the Othereal. Having Kinsley as a friend was like having a sister she never had. Finding some semblance of a family in such bleak times made it much more tolerable.

The griffon nipped at her hair a second time. "You could say that." Orison turned to Hypnos and glared at him. "Will you stop eating my hair?" Hypnos ruffled his gold and brown feathers with a squawk of protest.

Since the first day she met Hypnos, Orison had thought of him as beautiful. He had the head of an eagle but the body of a horse, except having talons for feet. He was magnificent, yet terrifying to look at, he was a beast with a hearty appetite. With a sigh, Orison ran her fingers through his soft brown and gold plumage. He ruffled his feathers and squawked, nipping at her hair a third time.

"Are you hungry?" Kinsley crooned.

With a shake of her head, Orison used her magic to unlock the metal box of food that was outside of his enclosure, to grab a dead rat. He stomped his claws while tossing his head in silent warning to hurry up. Orison threw the rat to him, which he caught in his large beak and devoured it, as she locked the box of food again.

That's when something soft came out of the shadows and brushed against her ankle. When Orison looked down, she was overwhelmed by the cutest creature she had ever seen. It was obsidian black, with tiny horns and wings, boasting the largest purple eyes that had twinkling stars in them. It was no bigger than a Labrador puppy back in the human lands.

"Othereal above, it is so cute!" Kinsley squealed at the sight of it, covering her mouth with her hands. Orison threw her a warning glare.

Turning back to the creature, Orison extended her hand. "Hello, what are you doing out of your cage?"

Both women laughed when a powerful sneeze threw the creature backwards, resulting in purple flames barrelling out of its nostrils and setting fire to some hay. Orison instantly knew it was a type of dragon, but what kind; she couldn't put a finger on it.

All the things in the Othereal were new to her. In the human lands, none of this existed—even the thought of magic alone was impossible—but there were rumours it did exist. The faerie tales she'd heard when growing up were just fiction; a way to keep children in line. She grew out of them eventually, only to realise at twenty years old, they weren't fiction at all. Yet, she still had to learn about the Othereal from books in the library. Anything outside of the castle was strictly forbidden, according to Sila's demands.

The dragon jumped into Orison's lap and snuggled into her. Cradling it in her arms, she stood up and realised it had fallen asleep. Kinsley dared a step forward and stroked its soft fur, awe written all over her face. The pair did a few rounds of the stables, only to realise there were no empty enclosures for the strange creature. With no guards around, they both returned to the castle with the dragon.

Orison watched the dragon trot around her meeting room. It made noises like a cat and sniffed every piece of furniture that it could. It pawed at the plush rug a few times, ruffling its fur as it proceeded to do a large stretch, showing off its claws and yawning. It disappeared behind the sofa, where Kinsley watched it by hunching over the arm. She straightened up when it approached the fireplace and began sniffing. Laughter bounced off the walls when it sneezed and lit the logs with purple flame.

"We'll have to figure out how to control that fire," Orison told the dragon.

When her chamber door burst open, Orison froze. Kinsley grabbed hold of their new companion and threw it into Orison's bedroom. She held the door closed with a forced smile on her face; especially when sounds of scratching and whining came from the other side. Orison paled as she stood next to her friend. Her stomach did somersaults as Sila entered the room with his hands on his hips, his infamous scowl on his face.

"Where is it?" Sila snapped.

Orison audibly gulped. "What?" A meow came from the other side of the door. "Shut up," she hissed.

"I think you know what I'm talking about," Sila replied with a flare of his yellow eyes, pushing his red hair away from his face.

Faking a laugh, "I really have no idea." Orison swore to herself. She forgot about the traquelle he had forced upon her. The tracking spell let Sila watch her every move through a mirror. She swallowed her fear and faced him.

"Really? So, why is your bedroom making noises if nobody is inside?" Sarcasm laced his words and the smirk he gave was pure rage. It was obvious that he'd seen.

"Wind? The windows can get a draft," Orison stammered.

The metallic scent of magic filled the air and stung their noses. Like a sick puppeteer, Sila controlled both of their movements, separating them from the door like it was nothing, Kinsley staggered into a nearby dresser and Orison into an end table. Orison cast him a glare, which he ignored as he forced his way into her room without permission. He emerged seconds later with the creature in his large hand, its little ears flicking back and forth.

"Happy birthday!" Orison squeaked, tilting to the side with her arms in the air.

Sila sucked on his tongue and sighed. "Why the fuck have you brought a baby Nyxite into the castle?" His authoritative voice bounced off the walls. Sila turned the creature over to inspect it with narrowed eyes. Orison petted its fluffy head and it meowed in response. "Kinsley, I'm telling your uncle about your careless behaviour. Especially one that puts my daughter in danger!"

"He is not my uncle; he is my father!" Kinsley shouted. "We are not careless; it was lost and lonely!"

"I don't give a shit if it was lost and lonely, it does not take away the fact it's a Nyxite!" He waved it around like it was an inanimate object. "You could have burned down the entire castle! If that was the case, I'd have made you two alone rebuild the castle from scratch for your entire recklessness!"

"Well, it didn't!" Orison shouted back. He stalked towards the door with the Nyxite in hand. "Wait, can it stay? It has no enclosure in the stables."

Sila turned to the women. The Nyxite growled as he held it on its back. "Oh, Sila, can he stay? But he's so cute!" he replied in a mocking tone, trying to imitate her voice. He approached Orison until his nose pressed to hers. "Do you hear how pathetic you sound? This *thing* does not deserve sympathy." Standing up and returning to the door, he looked at them. "Now, if you will excuse me, I have a celebration to return to."

"You are excused, King Asshat," Orison spat.

The room shook from how hard Sila had slammed the door behind him. Orison jumped from the sound. Collapsing against the wall, she looked at Kinsley, who shook her head and glared at the door. Kinsley knew what a tyrannical asshole Sila was; everybody in the castle knew. Especially when he refused to acknowledge the fact Kinsley had two fathers, preferring to call them her uncles instead.

Once they calmed down, the pair approached the dining table, where Kinsley pulled up a chair. With a click of her fingers, a pot of tea, two cups and a bowl of sugar cubes appeared in front of her. Orison sat nearby and allowed Kinsley to fill her cup, an awkward silence settled in the room, like a thick suffocating blanket.

"Did I tell you what Aeson and Eloise did today?" Kinsley asked Orison, cleaving the silence in two. The sound of the spoon rang like a bell as she stirred her tea. Orison shook her head and leaned back in the chair, as she listened to her talking about her boyfriend and girlfriend. "Well, he did my chores for me, so Eloise could make me fit for the ball; she picked out this dress."

They descended into gossiping about relationships over their tea, such as the guard who Orison occasionally took to bed with her. As time wore on, it turned to various other subjects, like activities outside the castle that Orison was forbidden from. Or Kinsley's twin brothers pranking the guards and resulting in them being grounded. Some subjects were rumours from guards and various other topics that made Orison forget her predicament for a little while. Until Orison's personal assistant—Aiken—arrived at midnight to take Kinsley home.

Two

Through the mirror, Kiltar watched as Saskia narrowed her eyes when reading the hair tutorial that was etched into the mirror while she braided a black wig. He caught his reflection in the mirror; it felt good to be Fae again after another night of enduring the Nighthex curse. He didn't think he'd ever get used to the pain of his bones snapping and repairing themselves, as he was forced to turn into a Nyxite at sunset—enduring it all over again at sunrise when he returned to being Fae.

His shoulder-length black hair swallowed the sun. Stars danced in his purple eyes—though they weren't his original eye colour; they were yellow before the curse. So much of him had been lost to the curse that he sometimes forgot who he was beforehand.

He turned back to Saskia when she swore under her breath. The braid that she had been working on for two weeks had become lopsided on the left side. She ran her fingers through the wig with a frustrated groan.

"You're doing fine, Grandma," Kiltar reassured her. "Fallasingha wasn't built in a day."

Saskia turned to him; her natural short brown hair was in small curlers. Her face was already adorned with make-up—red lip colouring, eyes lined with black eyeliner and blue eyeshadow. "The girls in the village look beautiful with this hairstyle. Mine looks like I rammed this mannequin through a hedge backwards."

He bit back his laugh. "Try again."

"How is Orison?" Saskia's chair creaked as she stood up for another go at the wig. Her blue tunic dress came to her knees. "Did you put the Desigle on her?"

"My Nyxite form isn't that powerful yet. Maybe I should befriend her first," Kiltar suggested.

With a nod, Saskia continued to braid the wig. Before the Nighthex took hold, Saskia was his second-in-command; until announcing her transition into womanhood a month ago. Hence, the king banished her from the castle with the archaic belief that only men could fulfil such a position. Around the same time, Kiltar had been banished as well; after making the fateful mistake of trying to stop the bargain that put Orison in her current predicament. Remembering the night of her arrival made him flex his hand so tight that the nails dug into his skin, as anger boiled the blood in his veins.

The only good that the Nighthex brought to them both was the fact it changed Kiltar's appearance enough to wander the castle grounds without recognition. Protecting Princess Orison was much easier because of it, though they had to maintain discretion.

They both knew what harm the king could do to Orison, the girl who came from the mortal lands on a fateful bargain. His gaze fixated on the guard uniform in the centre of Saskia's collection of dresses. It was the only way to get close to the princess without raising suspicion; it was the only way to ensure her safety before it was too late.

Orison cast a discreet glare in Sila's direction as she ate some toast loaded with scrambled eggs. She would have felt like a princess today, if it wasn't for the chain wrapped around her ankle; he had to ruin everything. Her personal assistant, Aiken, had braided her hair in a fishtail style before giving it a splattering of pink, white and purple flowers. The same colours as her floor-length empire dress with baby-pink slippers.

The dining room could have been mistaken for the throne room—part of King Cervus II's design; on the off-chance that any thieves tried to enter the castle. The same stone archways framed the dining table in the centre. Instead of small windows, several doors led to a large stone balcony; two were open to let in the warm spring breeze.

The king slouched in his chair at the head of the table, slurping from a goblet of wine, despite being early in the morning. He chortled as he talked about diplomatic issues with Emissary Taviar Luxart and King Idralis of the Akornsonia Elves, with his Elven emissary—Nazareth.

It was Orison's first time meeting the elves; they looked like the Fae with their pointed ears and unnatural beauty. The only difference was that their eyes didn't glow with the power in their veins. Both elves before her wore animal hides from their many hunting journeys and had blonde hair. Their uniqueness was their eyes—Idralis' were deep-set blue, like the deepest parts of the ocean; Nazareth was a beautiful female with amber coloured eyes.

"Is your kingdom so boring that your elves have to infect Fallasingha?" Sila drawled to Idralis, his yellow eyes flaring.

Orison watched Taviar fake a laugh, the chains threaded through his earlobe shifted with the movement. He had three earrings at the top of his other pointed ear. His shoulder-length black hair brushed against his black tunic—the royal crest of a stag over his heart. A snort came from Idralis as he smiled.

She made the mistake of taking a drink as Idralis retorted, "No, but it's nice to have exotic women every once in a while." Orison spat her coffee back into her cup, smacking her chest as she began coughing. Idralis smirked as he ate some eggs, giving her a wink.

Sila sat forward, slamming down his goblet. "Don't look at her," he snapped. "The women of Fallasingha don't like dirt or tree fuckers, Elf King."

"The women of the brothels say otherwise," Idralis drawled.

"We don't fuck trees; splinters are awfully painful things," Nazareth stated, sitting back in her chair as she drank coffee, flicking her blonde hair over her shoulder.

"And may I add, I do have a name you know, all you have to do is say it," Idralis muttered.

"Take your elves back to Akornsonia or I'll make sure Emissary Nazareth loses her other leg."

Orison gasped loudly at the threat, making her put her head down when Sila's gaze fell on her. After a few mouthfuls of food, she looked at the elves at the table, placed her elbows on the wood and rested her chin on her interlocked hands. "What is Akornsonia like?"

A deliberate move made the chains around her ankle clank together. She bit her lip when Sila winced from the sound. Orison brought the strawberry jam closer to her, making Taviar smile. It was reassurance that his husband, Riddle, had continued to teach Orison how to use her powers while he was away.

A wild smile grew on Idralis' face. "There are a number of places you'd love to see, Princess, especially…"

"Get your elbows off the table before I get the executioner to cut your arms off," Sila snarled as an interruption.

Knowing it was an empty threat, Orison's posture remained as she took a bite of toast. "Emissary Luxart told me Akornsonia has lots of trees," she mumbled. Her chains clanked together again as she crossed her ankles. Taviar gave a nervous glance at Sila. "And there's a place where I can see a festival, but I can't remember where off the top of my head."

Nazareth nodded with a glance at Sila. "Correct, there is the city of Irodore where we host something called the Irodore Lanterns each night, are you interested in seeing them?"

"Of course, I'm interested in anything that isn't these four…" she began, but the metallic scent of magic stung her nose. Her elbows were forced off the table and when she tried to resume her conversation, no words passed through her lips. Idralis' and Taviar's jaws fell open; they both looked at Sila. The table shuddered when he rested his booted feet on top of it.

"Silence is much better than a headache first thing in the morning," Sila muttered as he laid back and drank from his goblet. "Taviar, please teach Orison and Kinsley about the creatures of our world. You would think they'd know better by now, clearly not."

Taviar's grip on his fork tightened. "What has my daughter done, Your Majesty?"

"Last night they brought an oh-so-cute Nyxite into the castle. Have you taught your niece anything in the ten years you've been babysitting her?"

His jaw tightened as he weighed up his answer. "May I remind you; she is my daughter and we have had plenty of talks about why Nyxites are bad news—while raising her." Sila waved his hand in dismissal. "Fine, I accept my duties," Taviar retorted.

"Good, you shall begin within the hour."

Orison rolled her eyes. She thought Sila would have more respect regarding Taviar's family life; especially with the amount of spying Taviar did for Sila. She drank her coffee, glaring occasionally at the king; he glared back every time that he caught her.

What followed this conversation was an utter awkward silence, with a sporadic taunt at Orison from Sila for being a disrespectful child. Taviar kept giving her glances before returning his gaze to Sila; Idralis had his head down. She knew Taviar felt bad for her situation. She just hoped that one day they would both get freedom.

The noise of books arranging themselves filled the silence of the golden library. Their pages sounded like the flapping wings of a bird as they moved between the four levels. The books landed on their shelves with a dull thud. All this was under the watchful eye of the stars painted on the ceiling. Each of the golden pillars that held up the spiral staircases were carved with Fallasingha creatures.

The Visyan Mountain Range that the castle was built upon could be seen outside the large window in the centre of the library. Beyond the Visyan Mountains a sea of trees stretched out for miles. The only evidence of towns were the clouds of smoke lingering over isolated spots.

Kinsley huffed out a breath as she sat sideways in the red leather armchair, her brown peasant dress pooling around her. Her hands rested on her lap, and she twiddled her thumbs. She glanced briefly at Orison in the adjacent armchair, curled up with her nose stuck in a book; blonde hair in a fishtail braid falling off her shoulder and into her lap.

The sounds of doors opening echoed through the library, making Kinsley turn her head and watch her father approach them both with a stern expression. The third leather chair creaked as he sat down. His muscular arms rested on his legs and he clasped his hands together.

"What have I said about angering the king?" Taviar asked Kinsley, his green eyes flaring.

Kinsley dipped her head. "Sorry, Father."

He looked between the two women. "Orison, please, stop reading."

"Just let me get to the end of the chapter."

Taviar accepted it; he knew how stories could be gripping. Kinsley loved reading just as much as Orison and both devoured as many books as possible. He waited until Orison slipped a red ribbon into the book and closed it. He looked at his hands as he tried to come up with the words that he wanted to say.

"Why did you bring a Nyxite into the castle? Orison, I can understand. But Kins, you're twenty, we've had the talk about how dangerous these types of dragons are."

Kinsley looked at her hands. "I didn't realise it was a Nyxite. We just thought it got lost."

Orison adjusted in her seat and hugged the book to her chest. "It's my fault. I carried it in."

"I'm really disappointed in you, Kins. You should have known that it was a Nyxite and warned Orison to leave it alone," Taviar said. Kinsley knew that he was upset with her; but whenever she was reprimanded, she appreciated her father's authoritative tone that warned not to do it again.

"But I've never seen a Nyxite in real life; especially a baby. It was an easy mistake to make," Kinsley spoke up, playing with the string on her bodice.

Taviar sighed; he couldn't blame his daughter. Muttering something under his breath, he sat back, taking in his daughter and Orison. "Yes, it is understandable, especially how incredibly rare these creatures are. The last one was spotted twenty years ago; it burned down the entire village of Cleravoralis."

"Cleravoral-what?" Orison asked, leaning forward. She placed her book on the coffee table between them.

Clearing his throat, Taviar clicked his fingers in the air. One of the books flew from its allocated shelf and onto the coffee table. He swiped his hand in the air; the book opened with a groan. "These are old texts, so it's best not to touch them." Taviar kept his hand over the book as the pages flipped through; only stopping when it showed a hand-drawn picture of an enormous dragon as dark as night, setting fire to a village. "Cleravoralis, known as the Lost City, was a victim of the Nyxite two decades ago. To stop its wrath of terror, they had no choice but to surrender the land to the creature, now Fallagh has reclaimed it as her own."

Orison gawked at the picture; the beast was about the size of a two-storey home, with fluffy fur. Nothing like the cute thing she found last night. Her heart raced when she saw the picture of all the people running out of the village. She reached out to touch it, but her hand slammed into a shield. Orison looked at Taviar who gave her a smile. A puzzled look crossed over Orison's face and she blinked a couple times.

"You didn't use magic on me," she said quietly.

When Taviar shielded the book and didn't use his magic on Orison it was like a breath of fresh air. It felt strange to be treated with respect.

"I have no reason to use magic on you," he reminded her. He turned back to the book. "The Nyxite is a type of dragon. Weaknesses—enchantresses, sunlight and Fallasingha blades."

"Fallasingha blades?" Orison asked, head cocked to the side as she leaned in to Taviar.

He nodded. "They're made from a particular ore of metal which can only be found in the Fallagh Mountains. It's lethal to our kind as well, if hit in the right spot like the heart or neck."

It was a piece of information he shouldn't have told Orison. She raised her eyebrows and lifted her head to look at him. "Where can you obtain a Fallasingha blade?"

Taviar cleared his throat. "Strengths, unknown." She restrained herself from swearing under her breath, cursing him for changing the subject. "A Nyxite diet consists of raw fish, meat and vegetables."

At some point, the lesson turned into a discussion between Taviar and Kinsley about water nymphs and sirens, who resided in somewhere called Lake Braloak—a place Sila would probably never let Orison see. Then they moved on to the Firepolke elves, wicked things that set fire to objects out of spite. By the end of the lesson, Orison felt more familiar with the creatures in the Othereal; and she didn't feel quite so scared.

Gravel crunched underneath her feet. Her hand vibrated and sizzled as she ran it along the shield that Sila erected to prevent Orison from leaving the castle grounds. She often walked along the edge of the courtyard, trying to find a weakness in the invisible wall; each time, it was impenetrable. Why couldn't she have been made into Tearager, the type of Fae able to tear down shields? Instead, she was a Mindelate, the type of Fae who could read minds and manipulate them if she wanted to.

Orison bent down and picked up a rock, which she threw at the shield out of frustration. Just like the other times, it sailed through like a knife in warm butter. All Orison wanted was to see anything that wasn't the stone walls of Alsaphus Castle. She wanted adventure—something different. The hairs on the back of her neck prickled, telling her she wasn't alone.

"I wish you wouldn't do that," Sila snarled.

Casting a glance at him, Orison continued to walk. Her hand fizzled against the shield on the slim chance this time would be different. "Do what?" she asked.

"Throw things through the shield." Stifling a smile, Orison kept her back to him. "You won't get through it, no matter how many rocks you throw at it."

This conversation was always the same—Sila was annoyed that she tried to tear another hole in the shield and proceeded to lecture her about its indestructibility. Orison knew he could feel a dip in his magic each time she threw something through the shield; it made her do it more out of spite. Their footsteps crunched on the gravel.

"I formally request to leave the castle," Orison announced. Another part of the conversation that was exactly the same.

Sila cleared his throat. "Request denied. You are not allowed outside of the castle; you know the rules." She crouched down and threw another rock through the shield. Orison wanted to make sure this conversation was different from the one before, "Stop that!" Sila demanded.

"No!" she screamed. "According to you, I am not your prisoner, yet you treat me like one!"

Sila backed Orison into the shield; it sizzled against her skin as it tried to hold her in place. She fell backwards when Sila let the shield drop. Her hands stung as they scraped against the gravel that was normally out of bounds for her. Orison saw her opportunity. Without hesitation, she pushed herself up, lifted her skirts and ran. The king called out to her, making her skin crawl; like she was being touched by a phantom, but she ignored it. The ground shook as he roared in protest.

The castle gates came into view. She couldn't let Sila catch her, she grimaced while trying to run faster. Just a few more steps to freedom. She kept telling herself that it was her destination—past the castle gate to Fallasingha and beyond. No sooner had she worked out where to go, when a purple flurry of night and stars wrapped around her body. Wind tore at her hair. She felt weightless as she was lifted off the ground, then carried through a dizzying whirlwind.

Within the blink of an eye, Orison landed face-first in the gravel. Pain enveloped her and she groaned loudly; her hands and knees stinging. A wave of nausea slammed into her. Orison's stomach rolled so violently that she threw up with a cough, as her entire body started to shake.

The crunching on gravel told her Sila had approached. "I let my shield down once and you try to run."

"Can you blame me?" Orison spat.

Orison screamed when he grabbed her hair and pulled her backwards. Sila's breath was warm against her cheek as he snarled. "I am your protector; can you not see that?"

"No," she spat. "You kidnapped me!"

Through heavy breaths, she took in her surroundings. She was surprised to see that she was on the opposite side of the castle gates. A plan started to formulate in her head of ways to escape Sila's clutches. All she had to do was repeat what she did to get outside the castle gates. Mustering up all her strength, Orison slammed an elbow into Sila's ribs. He let go of her hair as he staggered back, with a groan. It gave Orison enough opportunity to resume running. She wracked her brain for travel stories that Taviar had told her. Cardenk! She could go to Cardenk, the town that this road led to.

She visualised the picture that Taviar had sent to her mind, back when she first learned how to use her Mindelate powers. She thought about going there many times. Another purple flurry of night and stars spun around Orison. Wind tore at her hair as it carried her, until the night was replaced by roaring fire.

Orison smashed into a piece of stone, sending pain flaring through her ribs. Pain in her spine made her cry out. Every part of her body hurt; she groaned and struggled to move. The smell of roasting meat hung in the air. Moving her hair out of her face, Orison was eager to see her first glimpse of Cardenk. Her heart sank as she found herself face to face with Sila in the fucking throne room of Alsaphus Castle.

"A valiant effort to escape. However, you underestimate my abilities. If you try to Mist out of here, I can manipulate your power to come right back to me," Sila snarled as he tapped her cheek.

Orison cringed and inched away. "Is that what I did?" she asked, her brow furrowed. "I Misted somewhere?"

There were numerous times that Taviar and his husband Riddle had tried teaching Orison to Mist but hadn't been successful. Knowing that she had achieved it today made her giddy with excitement. She wanted to run to their little shop on the castle grounds to tell them.

Sila scowled as he looked around the throne room. "Guards!"

"No!" Orison cried out; her hopes of running to the Luxarts diminished.

Grabbed violently from behind, Orison was forced to stand up as two guards flanked her. Orison struggled against their tight grip, screaming as she tried to fight them. Her scream was reduced to nothing more than a squeak when their hold tightened. Tears rained down her cheeks as she gave up the fight.

As they pulled her to the double doors, Orison's attention was fixated on a singular guard. He hid in the shadows, isolated from the others. Though her vision was blurred from crying, she could still make out the stars in his glowing purple eyes.

Three

Orison winced as Aiken ran a brush through her damp hair that evening. She kept looking at the Viren through the mirror. Most servants in the castle were Virens of the Nemphi Forest. All their faces were adorned with tree bark that bloomed flowers, depending on the season. When Aiken's eyes met Orison's, they glowed like a cat's eyes.

Peeling her attention away from Aiken, Orison watched her other servants turn down her bed, ready for her to sleep in. Her mind wandered to the mysterious note she had found there. She had temporarily forgotten about it until earlier, when she had a taste of freedom; the taste was so sweet that she was now yearning for it. If she knew the sender's name, she'd be screaming it right now.

Playing with an ornate stick barrette between her fingers, Orison stared at the stranger in the mirror; they stared back with an empty expression and dark circles under their dull eyes. Tearing her gaze away, Orison fixated on the infinity symbol in the barrette's centre; set in the deepest emerald gems that she'd ever seen. She placed it back on the vanity and looked down at her flowing white nightgown.

People in Burla are saying the Princess is a bad omen. Orison looked up when she heard a servant talking about her through their thoughts. Looking in the mirror, she realised it came from the servant watering a plant; judging by their paranoid glance around the room.

Aiken simply nodded as she ran the brush through Orison's hair. *I've heard of that.*

"Why am I a bad omen?" Orison asked. The servants gasped and busied themselves. She went to turn to them, but Aiken moved her back to the mirror. "I'm a Mindelate, I can hear your thoughts when you don't isolate them."

The first servant sighed. "You arrived on the night of the prince's disappearance. The people of Burla are very superstitious and they think something will happen to the Empire."

Orison tried to turn again, but Aiken held her in place. "Wait, what do you mean there's a prince missing? Which one?"

"Prince Xabian Alsaphus, he was second in line before you arrived," Aiken explained. "He vanished without a trace, and nobody is looking for him. Sila forbids it."

The announcement sent chills down Orison's spine; this time Aiken let her turn around. "He's the king's brother, is he not?" The servants all nodded. "Please tell me they didn't use his brother's corpse to turn me into a Fae."

Giggles echoed around the room from the servants. Orison tensed when Aiken placed her hands on either side of her head. The tree bark on Aiken's face began to glow in a soft yellow light, like the sun's rays when it hit the trees in the forest.

Images started to fill Orison's head; it was like looking through somebody else's eyes. She saw herself chained to a stone altar, struggling against the bindings—nothing more than a mere mortal against monsters. Tears streamed down her face and she kept pleading to be set free. A guard was thrown before the altar, forcing him onto his knees; he too, was begging for the same thing. What followed were two henchmen forcing iron masks onto Orison and the guard. An enchantress began to chant, and the masks glowed as red as a fire. Screams of agony tore through the air. It felt like the screams prevailed for hours; until both fell silent, until only one was still alive.

Orison cried out as Aiken removed her hands. "The king didn't use Xabian to turn you into the Fae," she blurted. Turning a trembling Orison back around, she continued to brush her hair.

"If I'm not him, then this is probably his old chambers," Orison suggested after a few moments, trying to compose herself after what she saw.

"No, he had an entire floor of the East Wing," Eyam pointed out, as she dusted the curtains. "West Wing is usually reserved for guests."

The room fell silent when her meeting room door slammed shut. Servants busied themselves with various positions around the room; trying to look more hard-working than they were, before the conversation. As the servants who were turning down the bed finished, they left the room to find other chores. Orison had zoned out enough that when something cold ran against her face, she flinched. Aiken applied cream to her face; the mixture smelled like various herbs that she couldn't name.

"The thing I just saw, was that what happened?" Orison asked, lifting her chin for Aiken to apply cream there. She couldn't remember being turned into a Fae, just the pain that followed. "Was that how I became Fae?"

Aiken shook her head. "That, Princess, is not important." She dabbed on more cream. "I heard about you finding a Nyxite. You risked everybody's life in the castle. If you see it again, make sure it leaves."

"I know, Taviar told me," Orison grumbled.

"Good. Hopefully he teaches you better," Aiken replied.

A cough made Orison turn her head to see Sila leaning against the door frame. "Oh, if it isn't King Asshat. To what do I owe the displeasure?"

Sila glared. "I don't appreciate you distracting the staff."

"Distracting the staff?" She scoffed. He nodded. "Making small talk while my maid prepares me for bed is distracting the staff?"

"Why do you insist on fucking about? I'm addressing the conversation before that," Sila snarled. His yellow eyes flared.

Orison rolled her eyes and grabbed her hairbrush from the vanity. She paused briefly as she caught herself in the mirror; the cream Aiken applied, did make her look more alive. The Viren was a miracle worker at times. Orison knew that Sila had been watching in the traquelle. She had always planned to smash that mirror but couldn't—not without alerting the guards.

"Considering this is *my* chambers, I can do whatever the fuck I want. You can go and fuck yourself with the traquelle mirror," Orison retorted. She squared her shoulders but jumped when Sila punched her wall. He pushed off the door frame and approached Orison. "Don't act like these are your chambers, you foul beast. Now get the fuck out!" Sila's face was turning red, like his hair. A deep satisfaction filled her as she watched Sila's eyes widen at her defiance.

Pain slammed into Orison before she had time to blink. She fell to the stone floor with a thud. The sound of the slap echoed around the room, followed by choruses of gasps from the servants. Sila grabbed her by the hair and dragged her towards him; Orison trembled in his hands.

"Learn your place, Princess, that is no way to talk to your Father," he snarled, letting go of her hair with a shove. Sila straightened up and looked at the servants. "If any of you mention Prince Xabian's name again, you will be hanged at my next council meeting."

Sila turned and left Orison in a trembling mess on the floor. The room shook when the chamber door slammed. A hand on her back made Orison flinch, only to relax when reassured that it was Aiken trying to offer solace. The Viren held her close as the other servants hurried over. She felt too numb to even cry, even though her face burned from the force of his slap.

"Are you alright, my lady?" Eyam asked, concern had darkened her face.

Orison nodded, wincing from the burning sensation in her cheek. "I will be."

The servant who started the Xabian conversation crouched on the floor. "Nothing good comes out of a man who lays a hand on a woman."

Aiken looked around at the group of women. "She spoke like a true queen," she stated. Orison huffed out a breath and laughed, sucking in a breath out of pain. "Come on, let's get you to bed."

The servants helped Orison stand on wobbly legs and led her to the bed. Once she was underneath the blankets with her head resting on the soft pillows, the scent of flowers in spring wafted into her nose and drove her into a light slumber.

Kiltar's power thrummed in his veins. The bastard hit her; the bastard would pay.

Climbing down from the gargoyle that the Nyxite was perched upon, Kiltar landed silently on Orison's balcony; claws clicking as he approached the large double doors.

Being in the Nyxite form had its benefits, though the negatives did outweigh them. Having to stand on his hind legs just to reach the door handle was currently one of them; his only relief from it was the knowledge that the Nyxite would grow exponentially over time. When pulling down on the handle, it squeaked from the movement; if Kiltar was in his Fae form, he would have winced.

As the door swung open, the Nyxite trotted into Orison's room. The mass on the bed trembled, along with the sound of sobbing; it shifted sometimes with heavy breaths. Scurrying along the floor to the empty side of Orison's bed, the Nyxite gripped the mattress and pulled itself up. Orison paused her cries to look at her companion.

"Hey bud," Orison said with a sniffle. She wiped her eyes, forcing a smile. He nuzzled her hand, knowing she needed comfort. "Sila and Aiken said you can't be here." Orison ran her fingers through his soft fur. "But you can stay."

Not knowing how else to dry her tears, the Nyxite licked her face, sending Orison's sobbing into a fit of giggles as she petted its fur. She kissed the top of its head, coaxing the Nyxite to curl up next to her. Once it was in the correct position, Orison pulled the Nyxite into her chest, like a child with a teddy bear and closed her eyes.

"Goodnight," she said. Resting her head on Kiltar's back, just above the wing.

The Nyxite made a noise in response, feeling his ears wiggle. She held its massive paw and let sleep pull her into the abyss, as the darkness closed in around them.

Riddle Me This Antiquities was a small shop with a timber-framed structure. The wooden floors creaked under Riddle's footsteps, as he walked in the aisles of timber shelves to take down the inventory of his stock. His golden waistcoat complimented his dark complexion. His brown eyes glowed as he approached the iron chest of enchanted antiques that beckoned him to set them free. If he gave in to their wishes, Fallasingha would have hell to pay for.

To Riddle, the iron chest emitted a purple glow, but to any other Fae it would just be a chest. He was the type of Fae known as a Charmseer. Riddle would see enchantments on people and objects in various hues that they emitted. When he married his husband, he also gained the Mindelate ability, which made him extremely powerful.

"Last night, Aiken touched me and I swear I saw the night when I arrived." Orison chewed meat from a turkey leg that she was eating. Riddle's curiosity was drawn towards her. "What was it like that night?" asked Orison.

Moving his attention to his daughter who was seated behind the cash register, Kinsley's brow furrowed. "That was a very strange day. At one point, night turned to day momentarily, and Father came home looking like he'd seen a Rokuba."

Riddle tensed when Orison's purple haze turned pink. A sign somebody was watching her traquelle. Clearing his throat, he said to their minds; *the king is watching, drop the subject.*

"What's a Rokuba?" Orison asked regardless.

"A Rokuba is something that looks like a snake, but it has the head of a beautiful woman. It'll lure you in by its song, and once you're in its trap, it'll suck your blood," Kinsley answered with a strange passion in her green-coloured eyes. Riddle stifled a smile when seeing the colour drain from Orison's face at the explanation.

Drop the subject, he persisted as he picked up a brass monkey.

When the pair became silent, Riddle turned to them. Though they were trying to appear like they were busy doing menial tasks, he could tell they were communicating with each other through their minds. He had been married to Taviar long enough to identify the signs. Orison tore off more meat from her turkey leg, looking deep in thought at Kinsley, who pretended to write things down in the logbook.

Riddle pressed on, writing down numbers and dusting some antiques on which spiders had made mansions. If the king wasn't watching, he would have let them talk. Also, if he wasn't sworn to secrecy about that night, Riddle would have told Orison everything. Taviar had broken the vow of secrecy by telling Riddle, and he had paid heavily for it. One day she would know the truth, he vowed to himself. One day she would be free.

The smell of bread and cakes drifted through the air. Orison sat at the door to the kitchens, where servants busied themselves with baking for tomorrow's meals. Their voices travelled up the stairs. All of the kitchen walls were stone. A large table was in the centre of the room, with a roaring cast iron oven in an old fireplace. Strings of herbs hung from the ceiling rafters. Orison would have gone down to the kitchens to help them if it wasn't for the shield preventing her.

She remembered when she was a baker with her boss, Bara. On market days, there was always a long queue at their stall; they always went home with pockets weighed down in gold and copper. A smile tugged at her face from the memory.

"Are you a peasant?" Sila spat. He had been spying on her through the traquelle again.

Orison jumped at his sudden appearance. Pushing herself to stand up, she curtsied. "Not anymore. I just love to bake; it was one of my favourite activities at home." She pushed her hair behind her ear, avoiding eye contact. "If you would be so kind, I would like to bake with the servants and... and present you with a cake that I made."

"You *are* home." He looked her up and down with scorn. "If you want to act like peasantry scum, be my guest, but you'll be glad of the position *I* gave you."

When he walked away, Orison returned to the kitchen door, watching the servants talk while kneading the dough. Something pushed into her back that nudged her forward. Her heart skipped a beat when she realised the shield was down. Looking around, Sila was nowhere to be found. Placing her hand on the stone wall, she took a step down into the kitchen. The servants fell silent when they saw who was coming down the stairs.

"Hello," she said with a curtsy. "Can I join in?"

A curvy servant looked her up and down. "This isn't a princess's place."

"I was a baker until... until..."

A servant with white hair pointed to an isolated bowl. "I suppose you can start there with a loaf of bread, even though we have more than enough hands."

Orison shrugged as she approached the bowl. Inside was some dough that had risen. After washing her hands, she sprinkled flour on the table. She took the dough out and got to work kneading it. It felt liberating to be allowed this opportunity. She thought that she had reclaimed a bit of normalcy in such bleak circumstances. Orison broke off pieces of dough, placing them on a baking tray with a butter glaze. The servants were watching her diligently, and some of them seemed satisfied with her capability.

Orison was enthralled in the baking; helping to make bread, cakes and pastries for hours. It filled her with immense joy. The servants were more than impressed, some were even shocked at what she had achieved. Orison was covered in flour and her ponytail was limp. She had a smile on her face that she didn't think she could remove any time soon, feeling satisfied for the first time in a long while.

The servants had all retreated to their chambers at one point, that told Orison to do the same. She began to ascend the stairs, her smile quickly faltering when she slammed into a shield. Pounding her fists against the shield, her breaths came out in wheezes as panic set in—Sila had set a trap and she'd fallen right into it. Walking back down the stairs, her heart raced in her chest, she crossed the threshold and tried the other entrance; only to get the same result. Turning to the kitchen, she clutched her skirts and looked around.

"There's no other beds left," the head servant—Dusty announced. Orison jumped as the servant emerged out of the shadows. She placed a straw mat in front of the oven with a pillow. "We'll wake you at dusk," she told her.

Sitting on the stairs, Orison buried her head in her hands. How had she been so foolish? She had slept in the kitchens in the mortal world, especially in winter; but in the Othereal, it felt degrading. If only she didn't give in to her desire for normalcy.

FOUR

Water trickled against the rocks in the stream near Saskia's small cottage—on the outskirts of Cardenk. She knelt by the riverbank, smiling as she sank the clothes into warm soapy water, before rubbing them against a washboard. Saskia hummed as she dipped the clothes into the water a couple of times and wrung them out. Pixies surrounded her, jumping from one lily pad to another. Wind rustled through her brown hair as Kiltar appeared at her side.

"Any updates?" Saskia asked, without looking up. "My spies have gone quiet on me."

Kiltar needed to be quick with placing a Desigle on Orison, but she could understand why it was taking so long. For one, the princess was seldom alone. Also, the first month of the Nighthex nullified powers. This was a secret project that nobody should know about.

"The bastard locked Orison in the kitchens last night because she wanted to bake," Kiltar announced, sitting next to Saskia and placing her laundry in the river. "Called her peasantry scum for it."

Saskia swore under her breath as she scrubbed clothes against the board. "Egotistical brat. If those servants weren't around, he'd starve, mark my words."

She watched as Kiltar nodded with a grim look. The wind whipped his black hair around his face, and he smiled when a pixie landed on his shoulder. "Orison cried herself to sleep last night. He saw how much happier she was while baking, but he wanted her miserable; got a kick out of it even," Kiltar told her. "She cried herself to sleep the night before, as well. I need to check if she's okay." Saskia looked up from her washing as he stood up.

"Go, and make sure she's safe. Even put a temporary shield around her for all I care, just don't let her down," Saskia instructed.

He stretched a couple of times before exhaling a heavy breath. With a flurry of purple smoke, he Misted to the castle.

With trembling hands, Orison cut a portion of chimera steak; piled her fork with mashed potato and forced herself to eat. She was still feeling the humiliation of last night's punishment for doing something she loved. Orison still smelled like fire and her bath water had been black. The chains on her ankle rattled as she moved her foot to cut into the steak. Taviar gave her a smile from across the table. She made herself return the smile, before taking a sip of wine. The atmosphere was suffocating with nobody talking.

Sila ate a roasted acquaenix leg. Aquaenix were a rare speciality of bird from the phoenix family; but instead of fire, they possessed water. Only royalty could eat such a delicacy in the Othereal.

Cutlery clattered on Taviar's plate, making Orison look up. He wiped his mouth with a napkin and looked at Sila. "Your Majesty, I would like to request something."

Sila's yellow eyes slid from his plate to look at his emissary. "What is it you desire?"

"My sons have made the honour roll at school, and we're celebrating in Cardenk tomorrow. I would like to take Princess Orison with us so that she can see some of the empire," Taviar announced.

He set his cutlery down. "Did you set him up to this?" Orison flinched and shook her head; she was unaware that he was planning this. "She's not going to some silly party. You can have it here if you intend for Orison to go."

Orison knew that would be Sila's answer. It was a pointless effort to get her out of the castle, even if it was for just one day. According to Sila, it was unsafe to go beyond the castle walls. He had even refused to teach her how to use her powers; making her grow sick and weak from not using them. That's when Taviar and Riddle stepped up. It was the Luxarts who were keeping Orison alive, they taught her whenever they had a spare minute, and treated her like their own child.

She looked at Taviar as her guardian, throughout this dismal change of her life. She had long dismissed Sila as a guardian in any sense of the word. Instead, she sought out the Luxarts for any queries she had—they always responded accordingly, without asking a single question. In her eyes, Sila was no king or father.

"With all due respect, Your Majesty, you're making Fallasingha look weak," Taviar said, drawing Sila's interest. "Your intention is for Orison to be queen, yes? How can she be one when she is incompetent of our lands and creatures? She doesn't know our customs; she'll make the empire descend into chaos."

Sila slammed his hand down on the table, making everybody jump. He glared at Taviar as he tore meat from the aquaenix. "You think the empire is weak?"

"It will be if you don't give Orison an opportunity to learn about it," Taviar persisted.

Shifting in her seat, Orison kept her head down and continued forcing herself to eat. Taviar was crossing boundaries. If he pushed too hard, she'd get punished for it. If she tried to pretend she wasn't listening, Sila wouldn't think she was in on it. Though she would love to be allowed to go with Taviar to celebrate, there was no way Taviar could persuade the king.

"Fine. I suppose she can go with your niece and nephews to the silly party," Sila grumbled.

Orison rolled her eyes. "Daughter and sons."

"I beg your pardon," Sila snapped and looked at her. "Do not back-talk to me when I have made an exception regarding your safety."

Her cutlery clattered on her plate. "I won't sit here and have you disrespect your emissary. Please unchain me so I can go back to my chambers."

Sila sighed. "Fine. Apologies, Taviar. I suppose Orison can go with your daughter and sons to Cardenk to the celebration." He glared at Orison, but she relaxed in her chair.

From the shadows, Orison's attention snagged onto the isolated guard with stars in his eyes. He was a strange guard who stood out from the other guards. She rarely saw him out of the shadows, but an invisible tether drew her to him. Something that told her she could find safety if she went with him. If she wasn't chained to a table, she'd go over and ask him to free her. Could that guard be the one sending her the cryptic notes? The thought made her lose focus.

The king clicked his fingers in her face. "Sorry?" she asked.

"What a waste of fucking money," Sila snapped under his breath. He forced a smile. "Are you happy now?"

"Yes, thank you, Father."

They returned to eating in awkward silence. Orison kept glancing at the shadows, but the guard had gone; she was certain that he was the note sender. At the end of the meal, she was freed from her chains and escorted out of the dining room. While walking back to her chambers, she kept looking for the guard, wanting to ask his name so he could take her far away. The guard was nowhere to be seen.

After Orison got ready for bed, she curled up with a book. When she checked under her pillow, it left her feeling deflated; no notes had been left. She was certain that she had found the sender, she just had to confront them. Shaking her head, she snuggled down on the pillow and opened the book that flicked to the page where she had left off. The book was a faerie tale that she strongly related to—a princess trapped in a magical land. The only thing she couldn't envisage was herself falling in love with a prince and living happily ever after. It wouldn't happen with Sila's restrictions; he was the only royal she knew and she hated his guts.

When her balcony door opened, she nearly threw the book across the room. The Nyxite came trotting in without a care in the world. Orison relaxed significantly, watching as it climbed onto her bed. She ran her hand through its warm, soft fur and allowed it to place its head on her lap. Up close, in the light of a flickering candle, she could see stars in its purple eyes—the same as the mysterious guard who she had seen, the potential sender of the notes.

"You look... familiar," she mumbled. Running her fingers over its wings, she continued to contemplate why a dragon looked like the mystery guard. "What's your name?" A rich, deep voice filled her head; *Kiltar.* It hadn't spoken to her before like this. "Alright, nice to meet you Kiltar."

Orison felt its warm breath on her hand as she opened the book. She stroked its ears before petting its head, as she read. It was like being back at home with her dog—Morty. Back then, she curled up with books and Morty would lay just like this; wanting to know the story. She missed him deeply, wondering what he was getting up to now.

After a while, she read out loud to the Nyxite; it listened intently. Snuggling down so they laid next to each other, she showed it the oil paintings inside; the princess with her prince. The Nyxite held its attention all the way through the story, giving occasional blinks of approval. As the night wore on, Orison's eyes grew weary as sleep pulled her in. She eventually fell asleep while holding her newly found friend; the open book discarded between them.

Five

Grandma Jo's Restaurant was a quaint, small place in the heart of Cardenk; it was bustling with patrons during the lunch rush hour. On an outside veranda, Orison sat at a large table, surrounded by the Luxart family with Aeson and Eloise, to celebrate the twins' achievements. While taking a sip of water, Orison watched two shifters at the nearby bar and stifled a laugh. They had drunk so much they were no longer in control of their powers; both slumped over their drinks, half Fae-half animal, laughing about a joke that nobody could understand.

Her attention then went to the pixies who navigated their way through a maze of tables, carrying trays weighed down by food. The pixies had either blue or green skin, some had pink hair—others had green. Seeing all different types of Fae and Fallasingha creatures was taking some getting used to. Orison was only familiar with the Fae and Virens, who were permitted in the castle. However, in Grandma Jo's Restaurant, all of the patrons were a variety of creatures;

some had coloured scales and ate with their pets that Orison couldn't even name.

Aeson sat between Kinsley and Eloise. The twins burst into laughter when Aeson's nose shifted into a pig's snout. When he snorted, tears streamed down their faces, as they banged the table. Both of his girlfriends gave him warning looks. Eloise flicked her light-brown hair over her shoulder. Her blue dress complimented her brown complexion with stunning green eyes. She cleared her throat loudly to get Aeson's attention. Picking up on her cue, he changed back, forcing a smile at Taviar and Riddle, who were watching. Unable to hold it in any longer, Orison began laughing.

Aeson's yellow eyes glowed as he scanned the table, his auburn hair waving softly in the wind as he drank. He was the third Shifter in Grandma Jo's—he could change into any creature that he chose, even replicate people when necessary.

"Ew!" Zade and Yil exclaimed when their fathers kissed.

"Oh, grow up. Fathers were just kissing, it's what people in love do," Kinsley scorned. She rolled her eyes when the twins giggled.

The patrons at the table fell silent as somebody approached. Taviar stood up and gave air kisses on either side of their face. Smiling, Orison looked past him to see somebody wearing a floral peasant dress. They had heavy make-up and black curly hair framing their face.

"Grandma Saskia!" Yil shouted, pushing away from the table and hugging her leg.

"Poppet, how have you been?" she asked, looking down at him, ruffling his black hair. "Sorry I'm late, I had business to attend to with my grandson."

Another person approached the table. Orison's breathing hitched when the guard with stars in his eyes appeared in the doorway. She noticed that Riddle stiffened slightly. Taviar greeted him, air kissing either side of his head, laughing as they exchanged greetings. Grabbing her alcohol, Orison chugged it down and winced, jumping when Eloise placed a hand on her arm.

"Are you alright?" she asked Orison.

She forced a nod, but she wasn't okay. That was the person leaving secret notes in her room. She couldn't admit that to Eloise, as she was one of the castle healers who dealt with Sila's nonsense daily.

He bowed before her. "Kiltar Sarling."

The name rang a bell, but she was too flustered to think straight. "Orison Durham," she said without thinking. Realising her mistake, she cringed. Sila forbade her from using her mortal name. "Sorry—Alsaphus. Princess Orison Alsaphus."

A server with green skin appeared at the table and distributed plates. Orison looked down at the dragon nuggets on her plate; she'd never eaten dragon before. Everybody at the table said it was Grandma Jo's famous menu item. Picking up a nugget, she took a small bite. It was perfectly spiced, tasting like chicken, with the slightest hint of fish. When everybody had their meals, except for Kiltar and Saskia, the table fell silent.

"Orison," Yil said, his green eyes glowing. "I have a surprise for you!"

She raised an eyebrow as she chewed on one of the fries on her plate. "What is the surprise?"

"I can't say, or it wouldn't be a surprise."

His brother, Zade, smiled. The twins were identical, except for a scar that Zade had in his hairline. He shifted in his seat as he watched his brother. Taviar and Riddle glanced at each other nervously as they tried to work out what their son was up to.

Propping her elbows on the table, Orison continued to eat while waiting for the surprise. Hearing screams from other patrons, she straightened her back, trying to see what was wrong. A bird resembling a live flame was barrelling towards them. It had a long tail that reminded her of a peacock. Orison reeled back in shock when it took flight and dropped a pouch in her lap, before flying off into the distance.

Taviar dropped his cutlery on the plate. "Yil Aarush Luxart! We have told you countless times not to use your Animunicate powers in crowded places!"

"But... Father," Yil whined with a pout. Orison caught Kiltar smirking while drinking a beer.

"No buts, it scares people," Riddle interjected sternly.

Picking up the pouch, Orison opened it to glance inside. Her eyes widened to see gold coins all clanking together. "Did you get the bird to steal these from a merchant?" she hissed.

Yil shook his head with a smile. "The king's vaults."

"No! Take these back right this minute."

"He's loaded, he won't miss a pouch of coins. Plus, he gave you no money to paint Cardenk red," Kinsley drawled as she drank alcohol with a smile. "You are his daughter, are you not? His vaults are your vaults. Am I okay to go drinking tonight with everybody?" It surprised Orison to see Riddle and Taviar agree. If it was Sila, he would refuse.

After some hesitation, she pocketed the coins. For the rest of the meal, she tried to forget about the heavy pouch at her side; and the fact that the man sending her cryptic messages was right there, ordering food. Then the reason why Kiltar sounded so familiar struck her—the Nyxite. But that was a dragon, and this man was Fae. It was an impossible thought.

She tried to act like she was part of a family outing at a restaurant, to forget the strange events with the man who had stars in his eyes. Orison forced herself to enjoy the moment, pushing all her worries to one side: taking in this rare opportunity of a lifetime outside of the castle. At the end of the meal, the staff gave free cake to the patrons at the table; for the twins getting into the honour roll. For the first time since arriving in the Othereal, Orison felt at home.

Laughter echoed around the courtyard of Alsaphus Castle, just after midnight. The guards on duty exchanged glances and watched the group of four friends. They were drunk on Faerie wine, spinning in circles and stumbling into the fountain; or having a water fight. Realistically, they should report it to Sila, but they had never seen Orison smile so much.

The four of them had indeed painted Cardenk red before returning to the castle. After watching a performance at the amphitheatre, they attempted the Cardenk Run. When Fallasingha children came of age, they tried to drink at all eleven pubs that were within the city of Cardenk. Tonight, the four of them only conquered five pubs before returning.

Aeson hiccupped as he held up a frog that he had found in the fountain. "If I kiss this, will it turn into a prince or a princess?" He looked at it. "For you, my precious, it shall be a handsome prince."

"Don't kiss that..." Eloise fell out of the fountain and onto the gravel. "Bad. Poison. Stay away!"

Orison clapped her hands. She was sitting on the gravel, laughing. "Is that how I turned into a princess?" She giggled, her cheeks a rosy shade of pink. "Sila made me kiss a frog, ew!"

Everybody laughed, then Kinsley emerged from the fountain, hanging over the side with dripping wet hair. "Are you coming to Parndore with us tomorrow?" She hiccupped with a cringe and looked at her boyfriend. "We're seeing Parndore Castle."

"If only the frog lets me," Orison slurred. She giggled and fell back on the gravel. "The frog doesn't let me do anything."

As she stared at the constellations above her head, a dark shadow blocked out the stars. Maybe that was the mysterious Kiltar. She would love to see a different castle, even if she knew nothing about it. If, by some miracle, Sila gave her permission; the upcoming weekend would be one heck of an adventure.

Voices roused Orison from her slumber.

"It's almost noon," one said.

"The king isn't happy," said another.

"I told him the princess is sick, but he watched her traquelle."

She snuggled into her cold, hard pillow as she tried to return to her slumber; but her head was pounding like a drum and the light was too bright. Lifting her head with half-opened eyes, she realised she was on the floor of her meeting room. Orison couldn't remember how she got there. Most of the previous night was a blur.

Sitting up, she rubbed her eyes to see Kinsley slumped over her sofa, fast asleep. The dining table had been pushed up against her bedroom door, where Eloise was asleep on her stomach. Orison could have sworn Aeson was with their party. She groaned as the world spun like she had twirled in a thousand circles.

A scream came from the bathroom, making Orison's instincts kick into high alert. "Call a healer!" somebody cried.

Orison pushed herself to stand up, forcing the dizziness away. She stumbled through the meeting room in a half-asleep stupor and pushed open her bathroom door. In the entrance, she gasped to see Aeson floating in her bathtub face down. Some servants placed their hands on the stone walls for balance as they reached out for him. Her heart raced as she climbed up the marble steps to assist in dragging him out; pausing when she saw gills on the side of his neck.

He flinched and his eyes fluttered open. "Wha-what?"

"We thought you drowned!" Orison yelled.

Aeson winced, his auburn hair stuck to his face. "Don't shout, my head hurts." The servants let him sink back into the tub. "I'm fine. Are we going to Parndore then?"

"Riding a horse with my head feeling like this would be torture," Orison groaned, sitting on the steps to the tub. He nodded, glancing up when Kinsley stepped into the room.

"I'm not feeling Parndore today, another time," she announced before disappearing into the room where the toilet was located.

Both groaned in agreement. Orison rested her head on the side of the tub, looking at the tiled ceiling and crystal chandelier. Now that the fear had worn off, her head was a heartbeat of pain and her limbs felt weighed down. The servants carried on cleaning around them, going into the meeting room and the second door to the bedroom; not wanting to wake Eloise. They all had a heavy night last night.

"Ori," Aeson said quietly. She groaned. "I'm sorry we couldn't go."

She waved him off. "I wouldn't have been allowed anyway."

The sound of snoring filled the bathroom. She turned and saw that he had fallen back to sleep. Kinsley came out of the bathroom and stumbled to sit next to them. They weren't going to do much today, especially feeling like this on the morning after.

Merchants Row was a street on the castle grounds for the guards and their families to reside. It was a little village in its own right. All the buildings were timber-framed and no more than two storeys high; a requirement that they were not to be taller than the castle. People bustled about, moving from one shop to the next or selling goods from wagons. In the centre of them all, Kiltar walked silently; he'd stolen a guard's cloak to conceal himself. As he passed Riddle Me This; a place he knew that Orison was fond of, he wondered what the Luxarts thought of her antics.

"You there!" somebody bellowed. "Stop!"

Kiltar tensed as he came to a stop and slowly turned around. Did somebody recognise him even under the Nighthex's guise? One of the guard captains was hurrying towards him with a large trap hanging off his shoulder, the chain rattled against his legs.

"How may I be of assistance, captain?" Kiltar asked. "I was just on my way to my post."

"Ignore your post, you need to set up these traps around the castle grounds. Special orders from the king."

The guard captain extended the trap out to Kiltar who took it in both of his arms. It was so heavy that he had to avoid cringing just to lift it up. He knew that he was out of shape, after not being on guard position for so long. Looping his arm through and securing the chain around the frame, Kiltar smiled at him.

"What are the traps for?" Kiltar asked.

"There's been a Nyxite spotted on the castle grounds. The king wants it eliminated," the guard captain explained. It took Kiltar everything not to gasp. "Please take that to Princess Orison's chambers and see to it that the others are secured too."

With a nod, Kiltar turned in the opposite direction towards the West Wing of the castle, towards Orison's chambers. The mere thought that these traps were meant for him, made his stomach roll like a storm. He wouldn't actually set the traps but secretly remove them, if Orison didn't order it first. He knew she had the power.

On the way there, Kiltar was handed several more traps from other guards. The weight of the traps made walking nearly impossible. He set the majority of them inside a bush, carrying a couple of the remaining ones up the stairs towards Orison's chambers.

Six

Sunlight lit up Orison's bedroom. The walls were the same as her meeting room, paintings depicting war, except one picture facing her four-poster bed was turned around. One wall displayed a large tapestry of war hanging from the ceiling. Propped up against pillows, Orison rolled a pair of die on the board of Rokubas and Ladders. She was playing with Zade and Yil, who had joined her with a plate of stolen cookies from the kitchen.

Zade moved his piece ten spaces while munching on his cookie, having to go back some spaces after being eaten by a Rokuba. "Ah, this game cheats!"

"I'm going to beat you!" Yil crooned as he shook the dice in his hands. Letting the dice go, he moved the piece seven places. "See."

"Don't argue please. I'm not feeling well," Orison warned.

She rolled her eyes when Zade stuck his tongue out at his brother. Orison played her turn while eating a cookie. She moved her piece five spaces and sank back on her pillows. Casting her gaze outside, she wondered what she was missing at Parndore, and if she would be allowed to go one day. Her reverie was torn apart by the sound of clanking metal in her meeting rooms. She sat up again, blonde hair falling over her shoulder. Orison wasn't expecting visitors.

With a flurry of green smoke, Zade Misted to the chamber door, crouching down as he looked through the keyhole. *There's a guard with a trap*, he said to Orison's mind. *What do we do?*

Orison shifted to the end of the bed. *Yil?*

He climbed from the bed, approaching the chamber door slowly; Orison stood up and followed close behind. With a wave of his hand, the door swung open and Yil entered the meeting room. When Yil yelled, Orison jumped and fled to the meeting room, her heart racing. A flock of ravens in the formation of an enormous bear were in her chambers. When she realised who they were facing, she gasped to see the guard with stars in his eyes—Kiltar. He was frozen in place, kneeling in front of her fireplace, Kiltar wore the guard's uniform and in his hand was a bear trap.

"It's Kiltar. Let the birds go," Orison hissed, jumping when Zade held her hand. "And seriously, Yil, a bear made of birds? What is wrong with you?"

With a click of his fingers, the birds disappeared out of the window. "Sorry, you needed protection."

Kiltar looked at the twins and Orison. "That was a scary trick, little guy."

"What is that thing in your hands and why is it in my chambers?" Orison asked, motioning to the trap in his hand.

"Captain Chester told me to place Nyxite traps in your room," Kiltar admitted.

Her eyes widened. "Get that *thing* out of my chambers!" She let go of Zade's hand and hurried to the chamber doors, turning to the guards stationed outside. "I demand you remove all the Nyxite traps away from my side of the castle."

"But... Princess, we have orders from the king," the guard said.

"I don't care, get those wretched things away from my side of the castle!" Orison ordered. "Now!"

The guards bowed and hurried down the stairs. Orison returned to her chambers where the twins were sitting on the sofa. A flurry of purple smoke appeared in Kiltar's hand and the trap disappeared, replaced by daisies. He extended them to her. "For you, Princess."

Orison took the flowers from his hand and sat on the red sofa beside the twins. She smelled the flowers with a smile on her face. She raised an eyebrow, noticing the twins glaring at Kiltar.

"I don't remember you being a guard," Yil announced.

"Yeah," the twins said in unison.

She straightened up, watching Kiltar stand to full height. "How do you know I'm not?"

"Our father knows all the guards; he's never mentioned you," Zade said.

"I'm a new recruit," Kiltar said casually.

Pushing herself from the sofa, Orison stood in front of Kiltar and looked up at him. His chiselled facial structure reminded her of Sila in a strange way; though Sila's face was morphed into permanent disdain for anything beneath him.

"You are to report to me if the king requires you in my chambers, do I make myself clear?" Orison told him. "This is my territory."

Kiltar swallowed and forced a smile. "Yes, Princess."

"Alright." Orison gestured for the twins to take her hands and she walked them to her chamber door. "I need to speak to the king. Please vacate my premises."

Kiltar stepped towards the three of them. "I can escort you to the king's chambers, if you wish."

"Though I don't require it, you may still escort me," she replied.

They all left the room, pausing briefly as Kiltar shut the door behind Orison, Zade and Yil. They walked down the stairs and began their journey from the West Wing to the East Wing. Orison was determined to get to the bottom of Sila's plan.

Moans radiated out of Sila's bedroom door. Orison was just glad Riddle had taken Yil and Zade while on the way over. She squeezed her eyes shut, ready to knock as loudly as she could, but she couldn't do it. Orison turned to Kiltar, rubbing her arm as she looked around the king's meeting room. Two reflection pools sat in the centre that extended onto a large seating area, before the balcony.

"I guess, I can come back later," Orison said quickly, turning to the chamber door.

"Do you want to go for a walk instead?"

Orison nodded, wrapping her arm through Kiltar's. They crossed the threshold and stepped back into the corridor just as the courtesan, who the king had in his room, screamed with pleasure. Orison's cheeks heated as she smiled from the awkwardness. Kiltar took a step towards the stairs that went up to another level of the castle, but Orison pulled back.

"I'm not allowed up there," she blurted out.

He raised an eyebrow. "What do you mean?"

"There's a shield, I'm not allowed up there."

"Good thing I'm a Tearager then," Kiltar said.

He guided her up the stairs that were usually forbidden to her. Passing several floors, they eventually stopped at a section of the castle that was made of marble. A white sofa faced two arched windows, showing views of clouds that stretched on for miles. Orison gasped, letting him guide her to the sofa and sitting her down with a smile. A giggle escaped her.

"Defying the king is so fun," Orison said with a smile.

"Nobody comes up here, so it can be our place to talk. How are you feeling?"

Orison shrugged. "Aside from the hangover, I'm good." She shifted on the edge of her seat with a smile. "I know about the notes you've been leaving me. So, if I say your name, will you get me out of this glorified prison?"

He frowned. "I've not been sending you any notes."

"Wait, so the notes about princesses locked in castles weren't from you?" Kiltar shook his head. She felt heat rise in her cheeks from embarrassment. Burying her head in her hands, she groaned. "Please ignore me."

"Have you been receiving notes from somebody?"

"Yes, asking for me to say their name so they can help me escape, but the name is never signed." Her eyes widened at who she was telling this to. Turning to Kiltar she put her index finger up. "Do *not* tell Sila."

"I won't." Kiltar inched closer to the edge of the sofa. "You seemed pretty upset about the Nyxite traps."

Orison nodded. "I have a pet one, that's coincidentally named Kiltar as well."

"Interesting choice of pets you have," he commented. She scoffed out a smile.

Leaning back on the sofa, she looked at the clouds. Orison had been foolish to admit to somebody, especially a guard, that she had been receiving the cryptic notes. They stayed on the sofa until the clouds turned pink, as sunset rolled in. That's when she bid Kiltar farewell.

Night had fallen by the time Orison entered her favourite retreat in the West Wing. It was a room in the tallest tower, each stone wall adorned with floral tapestries and a pale pink chaise in the centre. At the foot of the chair sat a trunk of books that she had borrowed from the castle library. Glassless windows at the top let in a warm breeze. This room was the only haven she had allowed for herself in Fallasingha and she had created it without any persuasion.

Every piece of furniture in the space was recycled. She'd taken various pieces of furniture out of the other rooms in the West Wing. Sila refused to buy her anything new unless she decorated her chambers. But this was her escape from the castle. Orison was pleased with her domain and proud that she had decorated it from scratch.

Her feet shuffled against the ornate carpet. She grabbed a blanket out of the trunk and curled up with the book that she was reading. The pages fluttered to where she had left off. That was one of the benefits of being in the Othereal—she didn't need a bookmark because the book remembered her page.

She settled down, tugging the blanket up to her chin; as the page transported her mind from Alsaphus Castle to a land far away. Gone were the stone walls of her prison, the weird notes and the overbearing king. Instead, she made friends with adventurers, voyagers and more.

A loud bang tore her back to the castle. She dropped the book with a scream; it skittered across the floor as she looked around the empty room. Sitting up, her hair fell over her shoulder. Her eyes darted around the room, trying to figure out the source of the noise. She tore the blanket off her legs and swung them off the chaise, clutching the edge of the seat. Nothing was out of place until the trunk moved with a thud.

Her heart skipped a beat as the trunk rocked in all directions. Through the cracks between the lid and base, she saw a glowing purple light. Orison inched back and grabbed a fire poker when the trunk growled angrily. With an apprehensive wave of her hand, she used her magic to open the trunk. She yelped when something as dark as night shot out from the trunk's depths, crashing into the ceiling before landing on the floor with a thud.

Pieces of stone rained down on her. Only then did she realise it was Kiltar. The Nyxite rolled around on the carpet growling, shaking pieces of debris out of his fur. It was much bigger than the last time she saw it a couple days ago; now it was the size of a large dog.

"What the fuck?" Orison exclaimed and looked at the ceiling. She winced at the huge chunk missing out of it, with cracks; Sila would make her pay for that. Her attention returned to Kiltar when he whined loudly. "You're going to get me in trouble."

Kiltar stomped his paws and flopped onto the carpet. She laughed as she laid back down, tugging the blanket back over her legs. When Orison picked up the book, it flicked back to her lost page. Settling back down on the pillow, she continued to read until Kiltar meowed.

"Do you want to join?"

He flicked his ears back and forth; Orison tapped her lap. Kiltar climbed onto the sofa and snuggled into a ball.

She continued to read while lazily stroking Kiltar's warm fur. Without even looking, Orison knew he had fallen asleep. the weight on her legs had increased significantly, plus he began to purr. Everything that the textbooks said about the Nyxites were false—this wasn't a terrifying beast in Orison's lap; it was like a cat but had horns and wings. Orison smiled as she returned to the magic world trapped in the book.

The more Orison stayed away from her book, the more agitated she became. Reading gave her a small distraction from Sila setting up Nyxite traps, when he knew she had befriended a Nyxite. Also, how she humiliated herself with the guard; she needed more distractions.

Getting to the last few steps back to her chambers, she noticed one of the guards—Edmund was posted outside. They had bedded each other on more than one occasion, but there was no love there. The relationship was nothing more than sex when they needed it; Orison didn't get romantic feelings towards people without a strong connection. She looked at Edmund's brown hair and his glowing green eyes, heat rising in her body. Just like Taviar, he wore the black uniform with the Fallasingha Crest over his heart. Edmund looked incredibly bored while standing there doing nothing. She quickly realised she could get what she wanted, while providing him with some fun.

Flicking her hair behind her back, she pushed her breasts up higher, to show off her cleavage as she approached him. His eyes instantly went to where she wanted them. Orison leaned against the pillar of the stairs. "Hello, Edmund."

He cleared his throat. "Is there a problem, Princess? Are you in distress?"

She let out a flirtatious laugh. "No threat, but I may have a job for you." Orison gestured to her chambers with a wink.

"I'm on duty," he whispered. The other guard, with blonde hair, glanced at them.

Orison approached him with a smile, rubbing his chest. "Alioth can take watch." She looked at his lips. "Besides, you'll be protecting me from losing my mind."

"Carry on, and I may be a very bad guard," he groaned as he held her waist, giving her a kiss. She giggled. "But you want that."

Alioth turned to them. "Just go. Have fun."

"Thank you," Orison said with a smile.

Taking her by the hand, Edmund led Orison into her chambers. For the second night in a row, she would piss Sila off, and she knew that. But she needed this. Orison already knew how Sila would react. He had expressed his disapproval several times, with the other nights that she had taken Edmund to her bed. Neither of them cared.

Seven

The dining room was quiet, apart from the sound of cutlery hitting plates or of people eating. Orison dipped a piece of toast into some freshly boiled eggs and ate in silence. Out of the corner of her eye, she noticed Sila and Taviar watching her. She stared back at them as she chewed on toast before cutting up the turkey sausage on her plate. Last night, her needs were deeply satisfied. Although she woke up alone this morning, she always knew where to find Edmund again.

Sila's cutlery clattered on his plate. "How many times do I have to say this? I wish you wouldn't mate the guards, they're there for safety and security. Not for you to ride."

"Don't say *mate*, it's weird." Orison ate some of the sausage on her plate with a smirk. He glared at her and leaned forward. "Did you *mate* yourself while watching me in the traquelle?"

Taviar spat out his coffee, sending a spray of liquid across the table. He began choking and grabbed a napkin to clean up. She smiled as she dipped some ham into an egg. A snarl tore through Sila, his yellow eyes burned into her. Orison looked at him with cool indifference.

"No, I did not *mate* myself, I turned it off when I saw your behaviour," Sila bellowed. "*Again.*"

Shifting on the seat, Orison grabbed her coffee and drank. Her attention was on Taviar who had continued to eat rather than be a part of this conversation.

Taviar cleared his throat. "Can we please stop saying the word *mate*?" he squeaked.

"Alright," Orison said while eating, a smile on her face.

Sila muttered something under his breath and pressed a hand to his forehead. "You're giving me a headache."

"You give me a headache every day, you don't see me complaining," Orison grumbled.

She used a spoon to get the egg out of the shell, as the entire dining room fell into an awkward silence. Sila kept watching her with a glare. Despite his gaze burning into her soul, Orison carried on with her normal routine, using her magic to bring the jam closer and spread it over her toast.

"Just to let you know, Edmund or Alioth won't be stationed outside of your chambers any longer," Sila snarled as he ate porridge.

She gave a shrug. Edmund was usually in Merchant's Row somewhere. If he got the urge, he would seek her out in a few moments; it wouldn't stop them. Pushing her hair over her shoulder, Orison continued to avoid eye contact with Sila.

Once again, the room descended into silence, and stayed like that for the rest of breakfast.

Merchant's Row was heaving with guards and their families. Merchants called out for deals in their shops, entertainers performed on makeshift stages and children scurried in and out of the crowd. Within the throng of people, Orison walked beside Kiltar. To her surprise, he didn't mind talking about her night with Edmund and the nights before that—he was silent while he listened with his hands behind his back.

"Have you ever had a princess, Kiltar?" Orison asked with a laugh, as she dodged somebody with a cart of baked goods.

Kiltar cleared his throat. "Are you offering?"

"No, I'm just curious."

"Then the answer is no, I haven't had any princesses," Kiltar replied.

Orison's face lit up when Kinsley ran up to her. "Hi, are you feeling better?" Orison asked.

"Much. I heard you and Edmund did it again last night. You seriously need to take it to the next level; how many has it been now? Five times?" She stopped talking when she noticed Kiltar standing nearby. Her eyes narrowed before a smile appeared. "My brother told me you're a newly assigned guard."

Kiltar nodded. "I've been assigned to protect Princess Orison under her jurisdiction."

"He arrived yesterday," Orison interjected.

Kinsley wrapped her arm around Orison's and tugged her down the street. *I know every guard on this street and I've heard of nobody new moving in*, she said into Orison's head.

She looked at Kiltar who followed behind them. *I don't know all the details of his placement yet. He seems genuine.*

"Where are you staying while assigned to the princess?" Kinsley dared to ask.

Kiltar cleared his throat. "I have a home in Cardenk. I prefer to reside there than in rooms within the castle. I'm only assigned to protect Orison during the day."

That's not uncommon, just keep your eyes open, Kinsley warned Orison.

They left Merchant's Row soon after their introduction, walking the grounds for a few moments. They crossed the stone bridge towards Sila's orchard and the West Gardens. Approaching one of the apple trees, Orison plucked off an apple and handed it to Kiltar. Then she approached an orange tree for an orange, Orison's favourite fruit in the Othereal; they were sweeter and more addictive than in the mortal lands. Kinsley grabbed an apple while looking at the other fruits around the orchard.

With fruit in their hands, they climbed up a hill where a tree grew near the shield's edge. Orison loved sitting in this tree as it gave her a perfect view of the Fallasingha Empire. She envied the tree's ability to reach beyond the shield tying her to Alsaphus Castle. The trees outside the shield waved with the wind, making Orison smile. Kinsley sat in the grass, bunching up her green dress in her lap. Orison slid down the tree and sat next to her with a thud. Both glanced at Kiltar when he remained standing, biting into his apple while looking out into the distance.

"I want to look for Prince Xabian," Orison announced suddenly, licking the juice off her hand from peeling her orange. The announcement made Kinsley choke on her apple. Kiltar merely glanced at her. "Nobody else is looking for him. What if he's hurt?"

Kinsley stretched a leg out. "Ori, you have your work cut out for you. How can you possibly look for a prince when you can't leave the castle?" She glanced at her. "You want us to look for him?"

"We have to try," Orison said.

Kiltar let out a nervous laugh, which made both women turn to him. "You're biting off more than you can chew." He waved his hand, and Orison's orange started rocking in her lap. Orison looked up at him as a pile of seeds appeared in the palm of his hand. "Best not to be spitting these everywhere."

Orison was taken aback with horror when he placed the seeds in his mouth and began eating them. If memory served her well, consuming orange seeds were poisonous. Shifting on the grass, Orison continued to eat her now seedless orange.

"Why are we biting off more than we can chew?" Orison asked. The wind picked up and a strand of her hair fell into her mouth; she spat it out. "He needs help."

The guard waved his hand before biting into his apple. "All guards are sworn to discretion. The king will keep everything related to the prince under wraps, with enchantments. If the king doesn't want you to find it, you won't."

"You know the king watches her in the traquelle. He probably heard you say that," Kinsley pointed out and folded her arms over her chest.

"I've blinded Princess Orison's traquelle. I can talk openly without consequence," Kiltar responded and shifted on his feet. Her eyes widened to know he had the ability. "You shouldn't pry into the castle's secrets, Princess."

Kinsley stretched her hands out. "We should still try finding him."

The conversation changed to discuss the possibility of Orison ever leaving the castle. Without the king's watchful eye, they could talk about all the places she wanted to visit—all the places that Taviar had told her about that were in reach, but so far away. Orison wanted to see all that Fallasingha had to offer and more. But she couldn't, with the shield keeping her bound to the stone walls of the castle.

The sensation of somebody watching her sleep made Orison awaken with a jolt. She was still underneath the tree; the clouds moved slowly across the blue sky and the birds sang. Orison's nose stung with the scent of metal. She froze. Turning her head, she saw Sila leaning against the tree, glaring. Kiltar was nowhere to be seen, but Kinsley stirred and sat up.

"Enjoyed your sleep?" Sila asked.

Orison sat up with her heart racing. "Yes."

When she looked around, the fruit she had picked with Kiltar and Kinsley was around her, half eaten. Orison looked around the garden for Kiltar, but he must have been stationed somewhere else. She backed away from Sila as he picked up the pieces of fruit and snarled.

"Do I have to enchant my orchard to make you both stop eating it?" Sila snapped.

"Apologies, Your Majesty," Kinsley responded.

Orison rolled her eyes. "It's a tree, it'll keep growing."

"You should have the same politeness as Miss Luxart," he drawled. He waved his hand towards Kinsley. "Leave us."

Kinsley looked at Orison for reassurance, who nodded to tell her it was okay to leave. She used the tree to balance herself, then she Misted away in a flurry of green smoke and trees. Orison stood up and grabbed the orange from his hands.

"Where I come from, people would be proud to see somebody enjoying their harvest, not reprimand them." His yellow eyes flared. "Seeing as this is supposed to be my *home*, that orchard is rightfully mine as well, and I can use it how I see fit. But go on, put another shield up, take even more of my freedom away."

Out of anger, Orison threw the orange at him. Sila's features turned feral when it bounced off his head. Her eyes widened as she started taking steps back. Turning around, Orison picked up her skirts and broke into a run as fast as possible; thankful for her new Fae speed to get away. The ground shook as a loud roar ripped through the air. Orison thought about her chambers as she ran, wanting to get there immediately. Relief flooded through her when a purple flurry of night and stars consumed her, and the grounds disappeared.

Landing in her chambers, Orison stumbled for a moment before righting and locking herself in her bedroom—despite it being no use if Sila entered the room. Dropping onto the floor, Orison crawled under her bed and squeezed her eyes shut. She felt like her heart would leap out of her chest. She bit down on a scream when her bedroom door burst open, shattering into a million wooden pieces as sharp as a knife. Some pieces clattered across the stone flooring.

"Get out here right now!" The room shook at Sila's roar. It was so loud that she had to cover her ears. She bit her lip to stop making any noise. "Orison Aurora Alsaphus!"

Her scream tore out of her when her bed lifted into the air. With a rumble, the bed flew across the room and shattered against the wall, her mattress exploding into a flurry of feathers that rained down like snow. Orison crawled backwards away from him, using one arm to shield herself; her hand trembled. Nobody had taught her how to shield herself. The king tried to approach her but slammed into a shield—not of her making. As he tried to tear into it, burns covered his arms and hands. He roared again.

"You deserve *this* for defying your father!" he shouted before turning and walking out of the room. Orison could hear some commotion before the chamber door slammed.

Orison's breathing came in heavy pants and wheezes. Her hands trembled violently against the stone flooring. Looking around at all the debris in her room, she inched away from a large shard of wood and wiped the tears away from her cheeks. Orison pushed herself to stand up on shaking legs and approached her balcony door; she needed fresh air. Pushing open the door, she stepped onto the stone balcony; taking deep breaths, trying to calm down. Taking another step, Orison tried to lean against the handrail but she bounced back against a shield, her eyes widened. *No!*

Turning and running from her chambers, the guards shifted as she ran past them, down the servant's staircase towards the stables. She took two steps at a time, having to hold onto the wall to stop from slipping; the guards followed close behind. Servants pressed themselves into alcoves in the door, gasping as Orison passed. When she got to the bottom, Orison opened the door which led to the stables and tried to take a step forward but an invisible shield pushed her back. Her eyes widened as panic set in.

She fell to her knees as more tears stung her eyes; her breathing hitched but she couldn't get air into her lungs. Holding her hands to her chest while rocking back and forth, her lip quivered as she looked at the world that was now forbidden to her. Footsteps came closer to Orison; she was frozen on the spot from what Sila had done to her now. Trying to reach the stables again, the shield held firm. With an intake of breath, she released an ear-splitting scream at the top of her lungs, as her emotions reached boiling point.

The Othereal lights around her pulsed and exploded as she curled up into a ball and continued to scream. Her magic sent cracks of lightning through the grooves in the stone floor, followed by purple flames and wind. Orison continued to scream, even as the guards forced her hands behind her back with manacles made of fire and dragged her back up the stairs to her chambers.

Eight

Days had passed since the shield came closer. Each night the Nyxite—Kiltar, appeared to comfort her while she cried herself to sleep. Another note from the mysterious sender appeared on day three, this one saying, '*Let down thy hair, call my name.*' Once again, no name presented itself, frustrating Orison. She thought she knew who the sender was, but alas, it was a dead end. If she knew the sender, she'd be screaming their name at the top of her lungs to help her escape this prison, even if the sender had malicious intentions.

On day seven, Orison awoke in Edmund's arms, who snored lightly behind her. The night of pleasure made her feel better about the mess she was in, but the distraction was temporary. She had to get out of this bed; it had been too long. Edmund's arms moved as she sat up, holding the blanket close to her bare chest.

"Are you well?" he grumbled, rubbing sleep from his eyes.

She looked at him. "Yeah, you should probably get to your station."

He looked at the clock through the open chamber door and swore. The bed shifted as he sat up and tugged on his uniform that was scattered over the floor. Orison clicked her fingers and the once crumpled uniform was soon pristine. Edmund checked himself in the vanity mirror, licking his hair flat once before kissing her cheek as he hurried out the door.

Climbing out of bed, Orison grabbed her robe and tied it around herself. She had yet to master how to make things appear in her hand, like Kinsley and the Luxart twins could. When she checked the vanity mirror, she looked rejuvenated. It made Orison smile to herself as she disappeared into the bathroom to freshen up for a day of exploring her prison.

Horse hooves clicked on the wooden floors of the library. The servants were reluctant to give in to Orison's ridiculous request, but eventually they prevailed. She had mounted an 18 hands high chestnut horse, named Beakbul. It was her favourite horse when she could ride her; and the horse appeared to like her as well.

"Which book do you think is best?" she asked Beakbul, running her fingers over a shelf she hadn't been able to reach before. The horse huffed out a breath as her hand lay on a black leather-bound book. "I don't think Guidebook for the Mortal Realm is a good choice."

Laughter broke off her conversation. Turning her head, Kinsley and Eloise emerged out of the shadows in a fit of giggles, looking directly at her. They had visited her frequently while she was in bed and too upset to do anything. Kinsley shook her head at her.

"The king is going to kill you. What the fuck?" Kinsley said, looking Beakbul up and down.

Orison shrugged. "He won't let me outside, so I brought the outside in."

"Please get down before you injure the horse," Eloise suggested with a smile.

Kinsley brought a chair over and guided Orison down from the saddle. A servant appeared out of nowhere to take Beakbul. Orison waved bye to her companion before facing Kinsley and Eloise, who both started laughing.

"Come on, I have something to show you," Kinsley said.

The three women walked by the library's many shelves. They heard a distant harp playing itself from an unknown location and the sound of flapping pages as books rearranged themselves. They became a distant memory as the library became older. Wood gave way to stone, with the temperature dropping significantly. After a while, they passed a metal archway reading, *'Alsaphus Family Archives',* and Orison instantly knew why Kinsley guided her here.

This section of the library had an oppressive aura, a far cry from the light and inviting section at the entrance. No books moved in this section; all lay dormant. Stone walls pressed in on Orison, even as the candles lit themselves. Spread out before her was a maze of leather-bound books on dark wooden bookcases.

"What are we doing here?" Orison asked, running her finger over the golden lettering of the TA-UA section of the mysterious shelves.

"Looking for Prince Xabian's tellages," Kinsley mumbled out of concentration while scanning the shelves; she frowned.

Orison paused and raised an eyebrow. "What's a tellage?"

"They're like journals, but instead of text they hold memories. I thought if we could find Prince Xabian's tellage from the week of his disappearance we could find a lead." Kinsley turned into a corridor and started to run her finger over the leather-bound books. She pulled one out and grunted while adjusting to the weight. "Here we are."

With a quick scan around this section of the library, Eloise pointed to a table. "We could look at it from there." All three women made their way to the table; Kinsley grunted as she carried the tellage over to the table. It landed on the wood with a heavy thud.

"This contains his memories of that day?" Orison asked.

"No, the entire week he disappeared, that's why it's so thick." Kinsley pressed a hand to her stomach and exhaled a breath.

"How do they put entries in?" Orison asked with eagerness as she sat down in a creaking chair. She held onto the edge of the table. "Do I have one?"

Eloise used her magic to open the tellage and flick through the pages. Each page had a golden frame with a black void in the centre. She pouted. "I'm not sure how they gain their entries, only Fae royalty has them. Maybe look in the OR section to see if you have one."

"Later. I want to see if we can get answers about Prince Xabian first," Orison replied.

Upon further inspection, the black void in the middle of the pages weren't black voids at all but moving pictures. As the pages turned, more and more of the pictures revealed Prince Xabian and King Sila arguing in various sections of the castle. Despite the images being in black and white, Orison could see they looked scarily similar. Xabian had a much softer facial expression that would make him easily approachable, whereas Sila always looked at people with disdain. As they flicked to the last picture, Orison cried out when she saw the page was torn out.

"Well, that's anti-climactic," Kinsley grumbled, her shoulders slumped as she sighed. "If we put our hand to the black void, we can go inside the memory. Do you want to try?"

There was no hesitation from Orison. She extended her hand out and dived into the memory.

They were in Sila's chambers, debating over their political issues with a country in the Southern Isles—useless for what she required.

Over the next few hours, Orison devoured most of those sections in Prince Xabian's tellage. While some of the memories were about political issues with other countries in the Othereal; others were surprisingly about her.

But all information regarding why King Sila and Prince Xabian fought over her was irrevocably destroyed.

She tapped her foot on the plush carpet of the library floor, placing her chin in her hand as she tried to piece together the puzzle. She didn't know how she hadn't been caught by Sila yet.

Footsteps made Orison break the connection to the latest tellage she was devouring. Even Eloise who sat beside her looked up from the book she was reading. The footsteps grew closer until Kinsley appeared—in her arms was another tellage.

"Which tellage is that?" Orison asked, shifting to the edge of the armchair.

"Yours," Kinsley said. She set down the tellage on the table between the trio and gave Eloise a kiss before curling up next to her. "I tried to get King Sila's, but his tellage is locked in a cage."

Orison blinked a couple times and stared at her own tellage; it wasn't as heavy as Prince Xabian's, but it was still there. She still couldn't place a finger on how they gained entries.

Bringing the tellage towards her, Orison opened the book and the bindings groaned. Her eyes widened in awe when she saw that her entries were all about her little adventure outside of the castle—it was of the Cardenk celebration with the Luxart family. A laugh escaped her when she watched the entry where Kinsley, Eloise, Aeson and herself painted the town red.

"That shows you're a real Alsaphus," Eloise said.

Orison's head shot up. "What? I've never been a part of the Alsaphus bloodline." She looked at the spine of the tellage. "It says Orison Durham on the spine—my name before I came to the Othereal. I'm the daughter of Mark and Georgea Durham."

"That wasn't in the Alsaphus family archives," Kinsley piped up and sat down. "It had its own shelf outside of the archives and looked new."

Shifting on the seat, Eloise smiled. "Interesting. The library is making another family archive. Only royal bloodlines have tellages."

Frowning, Orison set the tellage down, not wanting to look at it. It confirmed something that she didn't want to face—recognising herself as a royal. Shaking her head, Orison returned to Prince Xabian's tellage. She cleared her throat while trying to stop the adrenaline pumping through her veins, wiping her clammy palms on her blue dress.

There was a particular entry she kept staring at, one where Sila and Xabian were in a heated argument. They were talking about breaking a bargain with Orison in particular. It puzzled her; she hadn't made a bargain with a Fae. She never knew they existed until Sila tore her away from the mortal lands.

The tellage disappeared with a click of a finger. Orison blinked a few times at the table where only her tellage remained. When she looked over at Kinsley, she pointed to a nearby table. Orison stifled a gasp to see Sila settle down at a chair with a book, his hair illuminated an orange colour from the candlelight. Servants Misted in with tea and food, setting them down at his table.

"Do you think he saw?" Orison whispered.

Eloise glanced over her shoulder and shrugged. "Probably in your traquelle."

Sitting back in her seat, Orison shifted uncomfortably as servants approached her with the cart of tea and cakes. Aiken smiled at her as she poured tea from a pot. If Sila had watched Orison in her traquelle then she was royally fucked.

They passed cakes around their table. With a bow, the servants left as quickly as they came. Eloise paused reading; holding her brown hair back, she took a bite from her cake before reading again. Kinsley nodded in approval as she ate and listened to Eloise. Orison dipped a fork into her chocolate cake and took a bite. A sour taste filled her mouth and she looked around the table. Maybe it was just a new ingredient the cooks were trying out.

"I want to know more about Xabian..." She paused when her head started to spin as the sour taste intensified. "Does anybody else's cake taste funny?"

"Ori, are you okay?" Kinsley asked, casting a nervous glance at Eloise.

Pressing a hand to her forehead, Orison felt like she had just passed through the gates of hell—she felt like she was on fire. Breathing had become a marathon. It felt like she had just Misted for the first time again; she wanted to throw up, but her body refused to. Kinsley looked at Eloise as she approached Orison and cupped her face in her hands, concern darkening her green eyes. Orison's nails dug painfully into her hands as her muscles seized up.

"Help me," Orison managed to say, although her jaw refused to move.

Tears streamed down her cheeks, illuminated by Eloise's hands as she worked her Healengale powers to rid Orison of the poison thrumming through her veins. Crouching down beside Orison, Kinsley held her hand, wincing at the vice-like grip. During the dilemma, Sila continued to read while sipping on his tea.

Eloise's hands stopped glowing as Orison slumped forward. She knelt on the ground and caught her. She looked over her shoulder. "Your Majesty, something is wrong with the princess."

"The weakling is just being dramatic. Lay her down on the sofa and she'll be fine," Sila drawled with a smile as he sat back on his chair.

Eloise rolled her eyes, cradling Orison in her arms. "Stay with me."

Squeezing her eyes shut, Eloise's hands glowed as she Misted herself and Orison to the infirmary with a flurry of grey smoke and snow. Kinsley followed shortly afterwards.

NINE

Sunlight streamed in through the floor-to-ceiling windows of the infirmary, lighting the stone walls in a golden glow. Beds were lined in formation as nurses worked diligently. Orison was recovering in one of the beds; sunlight lit her bed with an iridescent glow. By her side, Kiltar sat in a plush chair. Since the poisoning, four days ago, Orison had lost a significant amount of weight. She still looked like she had been kissed by winter. Her lips had a strange tinge of blue; dark circles lined her eyes.

A shadow passed by Kiltar's peripheral vision, making him turn his head. Eloise set down a jug of water. She was in her nurse's outfit—an all-white dress with a white veil covering her head. Pouring the water into a glass, she handed it to Kiltar; he guzzled it down generously.

"Will she wake up soon?" he asked quickly.

"It depends how long her body takes to rid itself of Hogrite. Changelings heal slower than full-born Fae, so it could be a while. The paralysis may still be persistent.

We'll give her an extra dose of Shingalt tea before sleeping tonight."

Eloise curtsied and walked to the desk where the head nurse was filling out the forms. Kiltar inched closer to Orison's bed, her blonde hair limp against the pillow. He was going to kill Sila for this. All she wanted was to do the right thing and he'd poisoned her with Hogrite. Orison's eyes shifted; his heart leapt to his throat as her eyes fluttered open with a loud gasp. After settling, she looked around the infirmary as she snuggled into her pillow.

"Hi," Kiltar said.

Her dull gaze drifted to him. "Where am I?"

"The infirmary. Eloise and the others fixed you up. They've done an amazing job," Kiltar said with a smile. She was awake after four days of unconsciousness. "How are you feeling?"

"Heavy."

"That's normal." Kiltar jumped when Eloise appeared next to her. "As long as you're awake, it's a good sign the poison is leaving your system."

Orison began to finally remember what the king did to her. She winced as Eloise sat her up and pressed her ear to Orison's back to ensure her breathing was okay. She stayed there for several moments, making Orison more uncomfortable; her breathing was heavy. Laying her back down, Eloise gave a look of satisfaction before fishing out a thermometer from her apron. She placed it in Orison's mouth, while smoothing her hair down.

"What are you checking for?" Kiltar asked.

Eloise removed the thermometer. "Well, your heart rate is slightly fast, but you are still colder than average. A vast improvement from the first night you came in. You'll have to stay one more night to be on the safe side."

"I'm hungry. Am I allowed some food while recovering?"

Eloise smiled. "Of course, we'll send for some porridge to be sent up to you."

Once again, she hurried off, disappearing behind a servant's door. Kiltar knew Orison was in the best hands with Eloise. Before the Nighthex, she had patched him up countless times after battles or bar fights that he got into as a reckless teenager. Eloise knew her craft and did it so well that she was the king's favourite nurse. If he ever got sick or had any ailment that prevented him from doing what he set out to achieve, she was called to him. The only thing she couldn't do was work miracles.

"You were right," Orison said quietly. "I shouldn't have pried into the castle's secrets."

He shook his head. "Don't talk like that. You're being really brave, standing up against the king and looking for the missing prince when nobody else is." Kiltar took her hand; to his surprise, she didn't pull away. "Just tell me when you're doing the searches, so I can blind your traquelle long enough for you to look."

A smile spread across her face. "I like that idea."

It took only a few moments before a bowl of porridge was brought up to Orison on a tray; Eloise placed it in her lap with the spoon. The porridge smelled of blueberries, with little slices of apples cut up. Kiltar knew that would be the perfect combination to get her back on the road to full health and not make her look so fragile and empty.

The Othereal lights flickered on as Kiltar pushed Orison's wheelchair into the castle's art gallery. Orison gasped and covered her mouth to see the maze of oil paintings before her. The wheelchair creaked as she leaned back. It was a war of different colours. With her eyes still sensitive from the poison, Orison had to squint while her eyes adjusted to them all. As Kiltar pushed her deeper into the gallery, she pointed to a picture where a siren was looking out to a stormy sea; fear written on her face of eternal beauty. The next one they stopped at was of a female who blended into a tree. Orison instantly knew she was a Viren. Another painting was of a creature that looked like a phoenix, except it had blue scales instead of feathers—aquaenix.

"This place is amazing!" Orison exclaimed. Her teeth chattered as she tugged her blanket around her.

Kiltar knew her shivering was the poison leaving her system—the room was a comfortable temperature otherwise. The wheels of the wheelchair creaked as he delved deeper into the gallery. Orison pointed out the painting of the Nyxite burning down Cleravoralis. It concerned him to see her veins through her snow-kissed skin. Hogrite was a nasty poison to bestow upon somebody. The king was a heinous beast for doing it.

Turning a corner, Kiltar said, "I want to show you something."

Another gasp left Orison as they passed through a section of the gallery that was full of paintings of Fire Singers. They were the type of Fae who could wield fire and bend it to their will, with just a flick of the wrist. The paintings of the Fire Singers became Ice Singers and so on.

"Zade is a Fire Singer," Orison said with a smile. "He likes to make magic lions out of fire, scaring Taviar and Riddle half to death." Her memory made Kiltar laugh.

As he pushed Orison down the central aisle, she stiffened in the wheelchair and was aghast when she saw a large painting of Sila. He was slouching on the throne with a smirk on his face, his infamous goblet of wine in his hand. Orison didn't want to see him. His painting ruined the escape that this room could have provided.

He guided her to a painting of a prince who looked like Sila, but kindness lit his glowing green eyes; fire-red hair sat on his shoulders. "This is Prince Neasha Alsaphus. He died in battle twenty years ago."

"Neasha is a unique name," Orison pointed out.

Kiltar paused, wanting to make a comment about how great Neasha was, but he shoved the thought away. He was silent as he pushed her to another painting. Orison instantly recognised Prince Xabian from the tellages. Unlike the black and white images, the prince had fire-red hair and yellow eyes, like his brothers; except he had a splattering of freckles on his face. A soft smile was painted on his lips—a stark contrast to Sila's smirk. He looked like a king, despite not being awarded the title.

Something creaked, making Orison look around. It was Kiltar with Xabian's tellage in his hand. He sat on a bench next to her. "Thought this would be a better place to try and get answers," Kiltar explained. Orison tried to push herself out of the wheelchair, but the poison still had control over her legs. She collapsed against the backrest with a groan. "Best to just stay put."

Orison tried to pick up the tellage, but her strength had diminished; it fell from her shaking hands. Kiltar grabbed it in mid-air and placed it on her lap. Knowing Kiltar could blind her traquelle, she wasn't fearful about looking through the tellage. She flicked to the entry that most baffled her. Orison tapped her finger to the black square in the centre of the page and looked at Kiltar.

"Could you help me make sense of this entry?" she asked and leaned closer.

"I can try."

Kiltar extended his hand out, which Orison took; they both placed their hands to the black square. *The gallery slipped away, and they were suddenly in Sila's meeting room. Everything was in black and white, but the black abyss outside of the window indicated that night had fallen. Shouting bounced around the marble walls. When Orison turned around, she saw that Sila was slouching in his favourite chair nursing a goblet of wine. Xabian stood over him with his hands on his hips, shouting. She had heard this argument countless times.*

"Just get a wife and conceive a child, don't take one from an innocent mortal family!" Xabian shouted, rubbing the stubble on his chin.

Sila rolled his eyes. "A bargain is a bargain."

When Orison turned her head, Kiltar was looking particularly uncomfortable to be in that room, watching this situation go down. Maybe he was just as scared of the king as she was. Xabian took a step back from the king. Even though it was nothing more than a memory they were watching—it was too real, too painful.

"They paid back the payment; you don't have to take Orison Durham anymore."

"I think you find that I can. She turned twenty today..."

Kiltar removed his hand from the tellage; both of them snapped back to reality. His breathing was heavy, and he shifted uncomfortably on the bench. Orison straightened up when she reached out to him. Kiltar flinched. Shrinking back in the wheelchair, she placed her hands in her lap.

"Somebody must have made a bargain for you to be here if you didn't," Kiltar admitted. "Fae bargains are dangerous, especially in the hands of King Sila."

"But... they mentioned something about paying back a debt to the king, yet he still took me anyway," Orison stated, looking down at her lap. "I'm not supposed to be here." She sucked in a breath.

"Fae bargains don't require payment," Kiltar said. "Sila must have said that to trick whoever made the bargain. I know the king keeps a logbook of who he makes bargains with. Maybe we can find it and see who bargained for you."

He took the tellage from her. Orison looked up at the picture of Xabian. The prince was out there, possibly injured; fighting something she couldn't fathom. Butterflies waged war in her stomach, at the thought of what he was fighting for. She had to gain access to Sila's office to find that logbook. Orison knew it had a shield around it. Kiltar was the only Tearager she knew; maybe he could help her.

For the rest of the day, Orison was in a daze from the information Kiltar had told her—about a mysterious bargain and how Sila had tricked somebody. Most people didn't question her quiet state or staring off into the distance, knowing what Sila did to her. Despite feeling like she got trampled by a horse, the Hogrite was beneficial for making people avoid her.

Kinsley pushed Orison's wheelchair down the South Wing corridor; sunlight streamed through the windows. She hummed a song to herself, making Orison smile. Even though Orison wasn't allowed outside, Eloise had insisted that her friends took her out of the infirmary to get some fresh air—as much as she could with her predicament.

"What's going on in your head, Ori?" Kinsley asked as she pushed the wheelchair to an archway leading to a courtyard; Orison sucked in the crisp Spring air.

With a sigh, Orison told her everything about the Fae bargain that she had discovered between Sila and an unknown person. Kinsley's jaw fell open as Orison explained how Xabian was trying to save her. Orison also talked about the logbook and the mysterious occurrences whenever she tried to look for the prince. She refrained from mentioning the strange notes about princesses locked in towers, in case she made a fool out of herself again; she didn't feel well enough to do so and her traquelle wasn't blinded.

Their conversation was interrupted by a high-pitched screeching sound. Looking around the South Wing, there was black smoke barrelling down the corridor, like a tidal wave—along with the strong stench of burning. Kinsley stepped up to the wheelchair and pushed Orison towards the smoke; towards the chaos where the screeching was getting worse. Orison's heart skipped a beat as she clutched her blanket on her lap; that's when she realised the screeching was coming from the library.

Orison covered her mouth as she choked on the black smoke blocking their path. Kinsley used her magic to dissipate the smoke and push forward; the smell of burning so strong that it felt like a hand of death smothering her. The pair froze at the open doors to the library. Flaming books screeched as they threw themselves out of the open doorway. Tears made Orison's eyes glaze over and she covered her mouth. Squeezing her eyes shut—despite being weak from the poison; she conjured up enough water to douse the books, to put them out of their misery. They soon fell silent on the still-smouldering pile they had made for themselves.

As the pair entered the library, it was difficult to hear anything over the deafening screeches of books on fire; trying to fly away from the inferno but dropping like flies. What kind of magic was placed on the books to give them feelings? Orison shuddered as she looked up at each level of bookshelves, where flames continued to climb higher—like a spider creating a web.

Conjuring up more water, Orison threw it towards the flames; her hands trembled from the exertion. Behind her, Kinsley doused the other side with water. A lump formed in Orison's throat and her eyes glazed over. She knew she was responsible for the extinction of Fallasingha history; destroying these texts broke her heart. The wheelchair jerked backwards violently, causing Orison to cry out when she realised what was happening. Pushing herself out of the wheelchair, she dragged herself towards the library—until she was grabbed from behind and picked up with a scream. She gasped when she came face to face with Edmund.

"Put me down, I need to save the library," she pleaded, trying to scramble away, but he took her hand. Orison looked at him.

"It's too dangerous to be here," he said.

Another set of hands picked her up. "I'll take it from here," Taviar said.

"The books!" Orison screamed, struggling in his grasp.

Ignoring her, Taviar took off running down to the South Wing towards the infirmary. Orison's body swayed with his movements as the flaming library grew smaller in the distance and she struggled harder against him.

"Orison, please stay calm. I'm getting you to safety." Taviar's deep voice vibrated through his body.

She struggled against him, but his hands on her hips tightened. "But the books!" Orison sobbed, her emotions taking over. "They're my only escape."

"I'll get you more, Sweets. We just need you away from the flames." Taviar rounded the corner to the infirmary, with Kinsley hurrying after them; she was three shades paler from shock.

Taviar broke out into a hurried walk as they returned to the infirmary. Nurses gave him a wide-eyed stare as he sat Orison on the bed that she had been using for four days. He crouched in front of her and smoothed out her hair. He checked her for any injuries aside from the after-effects of the poison, concern painted over his face. He breathed a sigh of relief when he realised Orison was fine. With a tap on her knee, he stood up and turned to leave.

"Father, I…" He froze and turned around. Orison's eyes widened at what she just said, covering her mouth at the careless mistake. "Sorry."

He approached her, crouching down to her level and took her hand. "No need to apologise, I don't mind." Taviar smiled and pushed her hair behind her shoulder. "What is it you wanted to say?"

"I… I tried to save as much as I could," Orison admitted.

Taviar stood up, guiding Orison to lie back down, tucking the blanket around her. "I know you did, Sweets." He kissed her forehead. "You need to rest to get better, okay?" Orison watched him turn to Kinsley. "You'll keep her company, won't you, Kins?"

"Of course, Father."

Taviar hurried off, back towards the burning inferno of the library. The creak of a chair made Orison look at Kinsley as she sat beside her bed. Through the arched windows they could see the orange glow of flames; the smell of burning was strong. Orison didn't need anybody to tell her that her only escape was in ruins.

Ten

The guards wheeled Orison into the throne room later in the night—special orders from Sila. Her hands trembled in her lap as they opened the double doors. She saw the familiar throne room she had been in countless times.

Her breathing hitched when she saw Yil and Zade kneeling at the foot of the dais in front of Sila. The king sat there, sprawled out, looking smug with a goblet of wine that he sipped. Orison kept looking at the twins; they were just children. What did the king want with them? The guard pushing her wheelchair stopped just before the twins and put the brake on.

"Princess Orison, are you feeling better?" Sila drawled with a smirk.

She glared at him. "Go fuck yourself."

Sila slammed the goblet down, red wine spilling out of the sides. He waved his hand to slam her with magic. The metallic scent filled the room; but instead of hitting its target, it bounced off a shield and slammed into the king. His body convulsed on impact. "What is the meaning of this?"

"I don't know, Father."

Out of the corner of her eye, Orison saw movement from the window. Purple eyes stared back at her in the night sky—Kiltar. She felt somewhat safer knowing he was around. Exhaling a breath, she put her shoulders back and looked at Sila. He was glaring at her.

"The Luxart children have admitted to starting the fire..."

"No, we didn't!" Zade shouted. "You just assumed and dragged us out of the playground!"

Yil growled. "We don't want to go into your smelly library!"

Stifling a gasp, Orison's heart rate sped up. It took everything not to pull the boys away from the king; to cradle them and protect them by any means necessary. She knew they could defend themselves, but they were just ten years old. Glancing around the throne room, Orison couldn't see either Taviar or Riddle.

Ignoring the twins, Sila sat up. "Seeing as I am kind and generous, I won't punish the children. But somebody has to be punished for their actions." He clicked his fingers and guards dragged in Taviar. She gasped loudly and covered her mouth. "Twenty lashes should be sufficient."

Orison looked at the Nyxite hiding in the shadows. *Protect the Luxart family, please.*

Kiltar winked at her. *All of them?*

Yes.

Clicking her fingers, the boys climbed onto her lap, where they cried into her chest. Orison held them close and kissed their heads. She hushed them as she covered their eyes. She winced when the guards ripped Taviar's shirt off. Orison looked at the sky as she prayed Kiltar would come out of the shadows and stop this brutality. They didn't do anything wrong; the twins wouldn't set fire to the library. Orison hushed the twins when they pleaded with Sila not to hurt their father, with tears streaming down their cheeks. She tried not to let her voice waver as a guard brought out a red whip with a frayed end. She jumped and squeezed her eyes shut at the whip cracking before it whooshed through the air.

Holding the boys tighter, she awaited Taviar's screams of pain and squeezed her eyes shut. Instead, the ground shook with a clap of thunder. Orison heard a sickening crack after a terror-filled scream. Slowly opening her eyes, Taviar was still kneeling at the foot of the dais, but the guards around them were unconscious on the floor.

The columns of the throne room had cracks splintering through them like lightning; some of the stone was scorched like it had been burned with fire. Feeling the boys shift, Orison let them go. They sprinted to their father, who had a bewildered look on his face as he held his sons close, giving them a kiss; a single tear ran down his face.

Sila growled, grabbed the whip and pushed himself out of the throne. "I'll finish the job myself!"

It was evident Sila didn't care about the fact that Taviar was holding his children as he marched down the steps of the throne. With a crack of the whip, it caught on fire. He growled as the whip flew through the air, causing Orison to scream loudly. She reached out to try and block the attack, but it just resulted in her falling out of the wheelchair. Hitting the stone floor with a thud, she reached out once again; only for the ground to shake with a crack of thunder as Sila was thrown backwards. The king smashed into a pillar and collapsed to the ground, next to the guards; the whip's fire diminished nearby.

I've taken the shield down, Mist to the Luxart's home, Kiltar said in her mind.

Taviar extended his hand out. "Orison, take my hand!"

With a groan, she was relieved to be able to move one leg, dragging herself closer to him. His hand grasped hers. He grimaced as he pulled her closer and soon a flurry of green smoke engulfed them all. Vines and trees encased them as they were transported away from the throne room to somewhere safer.

Dust rained down on Riddle with a heavy thud as he organised the cashier's desk in Riddle Me This Antiquities;

he looked up to his home above the shop. Grabbing the knife underneath the desk, he made his way up the stairs, treading lightly on each step. He tensed when he heard muffled voices. The grip on his knife tightened as he neared the top. Looking through the baluster, he was relieved to see his husband; but he knew something was wrong. His husband had a purple aura around him, indicating he was charmed—so were their children. Looking at Orison, she had the usual pink aura of the traquelle, but it was tinged with purple.

"We can't go to another country. They won't let us in if they see us in Fallasingha dress," Taviar whispered to Orison. The twins ran off to their bedrooms. "We'll just have to face the consequences."

Riddle got to the top of the stairs. "Honey, why are you shirtless?" He tried to stop his shaking hand by touching the baluster. "And why do you all have Desigles on you?"

"What's a Desigle?" Orison asked.

He looked down at his trembling hand and tightened his grip on the baluster. The ground shook, indicating that the king was angry. "A Desigle is an enchantment where you're bound to its creator as a form of protection. Those who pose a threat to you cannot go near you without bouncing off a shield. If the situation becomes dire, then it automatically Mists the creator to your location," Riddle explained in a hurried tone, stuttering over some words in the process. "Who put it on both of you and our children?"

"I don't know, all I know is that Sila is convinced that the twins set fire to the library." Taviar approached Riddle, taking his hand and looking into his eyes. "I was supposed to receive twenty lashes for their actions, but this Desigle must have prevented it."

Riddle's gaze roamed over the smattering of battle scars on his arms and torso—with a tattoo of their children's initials over his heart. He looked like a warrior, even as he was trying to comfort his husband in a time of need.

The twins ran out of their rooms and held onto Riddle tightly. "Papa!" they cried in unison. He took his hand away from his husband's and wiped the tears rolling down Zade's cheek; then Yil's.

Crouching down to his sons' eye levels, he looked at their purple auras of the Desigle's mark. "All I know is that the Desigle's magic is very powerful and dark. I don't know who put it there, but the wielder is enchanted themselves."

A loud gasp made Riddle look at Orison sitting on the floor. "Kiltar!"

Eleven

Riddle and Taviar stood in stunned silence as Orison explained what she had asked Kiltar to do. All she had thought about was protecting the Luxart family—she didn't know the implications. Orison wasn't aware that Kiltar had been enchanted with something. Besides, who would put an enchantment on a baby dragon in the first place? Another question that went unanswered was how a baby dragon could wield a spell as powerful as a Desigle.

A thud made Riddle look at Orison. She was trying to stand, but kept falling back down. He had to do something to get the last dregs of the poison out of her system. Shifting closer to her, Riddle paused when the ground shook again. His stomach lurched.

Orison looked at everybody. "What is that?"

"Honey, get the kids to the basement," Riddle commanded.

"Kids, basement!" Taviar shouted as he ran over to Orison and picked her up.

Everybody made their way down to the shop floor. The floorboards creaked at the sudden shift in weight at such brief intervals. Once they entered the shop floor, the ground shook more violently; the surrounding antiques rattled from the impact. Riddle ushered his husband to the broom closet with stairs leading down to the basement.

Riddle made him pause. "Give her Shingalt tea before sleeping."

With a quick kiss, he watched his family and Orison disappear into the basement—just in time for the front door of the shop to fly off its hinges. Splinters of wood shattered against a support beam, before clattering onto the wooden floor.

Riddle adjusted his stance as Sila appeared; his eyes glowing like a flame on a match. "We're closed for the night, Your Highness," he said with as much calmness as he could muster.

"Your nephews have committed treason," Sila snarled. A ball of fire appeared in his hand.

Unable to contain his anger any longer, a ball of lightning appeared in Riddle's hand. "My *sons* have done nothing wrong!"

He split the ball of lightning in two and let them fly towards Sila. A loud crack of thunder rattled the store, the impact so loud that some displays shattered around them. Sila's hair whipped around his face as the impact forced him back. He was thrown through the front door and into

Merchant's Row—but Riddle wasn't done, as he followed him outside.

A storm rose once they were in Merchant's Row. Wind tore at Sila's hair as he staggered to his feet with a fireball, fizzing and spluttering in his hand. With a roar like a bear, he hurtled the fireball towards Riddle. If the Desigle wasn't present, Riddle would have feared the king, but he had an indestructible shield. The fire shot towards Riddle, until it came within mere inches away from him and spun; a firenado now ravaged the sky, tearing through Merchant's Row.

Riddle let out a war cry and slammed his foot down. A large gust of wind tore at the firenado, making it dissipate before it could destroy any homes. The wind was so strong that cobblestones were torn out of the ground; sending them flying towards the king, along with multiple bolts of lightning. Sila dodged with a snarl of rage, like a rabid dog eyeing up its prey.

A barrel of purple flame tore through the street, setting homes and businesses on fire in its wake. A roar shook the ground—the only warning both of them had that Kiltar had arrived. Kiltar landed behind Riddle, his purple eyes flaring. Sila was thrown back with another barrage of purple flame. He landed in a heap of debris.

Take shelter, Kiltar said to Riddle's mind.

"Riddle!" Taviar shouted, extending his hand out as he reached from the shop door.

Wind whipped Taviar's black hair around his head as an actual tornado formed. Rain gushed down with lightning and thunder—Fallagh wasn't happy. Riddle didn't hesitate as he ran over to his husband, taking his hand which always made him feel grounded, before disappearing into his antiques shop.

Fighting in his Nyxite form wasn't something Kiltar had done since the curse was placed on him. Yet, instincts took over and rage clouded his judgement. He stared Sila down, purple eyes flaring in anger as he stomped his paws on the ground. The wind from the tornado tore through his fur as Sila staggered up and faced him directly. Sila paled when seeing what he was up against.

Rearing back, Kiltar sent another shot of purple flame through Merchant's Row. The shield that Sila had placed around himself was useless; it fizzled and died when the flames struck him. The king flew through the air like a hand of death had yanked him by the collar, throwing him around like a rag doll as he screamed.

With a beat of his wings, Kiltar took flight and hovered above the street. He sent more flames raining down on Sila who cowered and shielded his head. The tornado gained in intensity. Wind lashed out against roof shingles and signs. Sila regained his footing—blood rained down his face and torn clothes; he looked up at Kiltar with a glare. Tucking his wings in tight, Kiltar swooped down and used his talons to tear into Sila. The king cried out as the claws sank into his flesh, before collapsing to the ground with heavy breaths.

Rising above the street once again, Kiltar rained more flames down on Sila. Something slammed into Kiltar's side, causing him to roar loudly as pain erupted through his body. It burned like somebody had set his left side on fire. From the many battles he had fought and won for Sila, he knew this pain like an old friend—the pain of a Fallasingha arrow tearing into his flesh. Kiltar roared again as a second Fallasingha arrow pierced his side. The pain increased tenfold, causing him to lose the ability to remain airborne.

His wings tucked into his back. He wanted to move them, but the pain was too great. Blood poured down his side and he knew he couldn't remove the arrows until dawn; another limitation of the Nighthex. Kiltar felt cold as he began the frenzy of free-falling further towards the ground. He roared one last time before slamming into the cobblestone street.

Waking up with a cough, Orison propped herself on her elbow. She saw that everything in the storage room under the shop was covered in a thick layer of dust, including herself. A weight rested on her waist. Looking down, Zade had cuddled up to her in his sleep. She gently took his hand and rested it on the pillow; causing him to stir, before settling back down. Orison looked over at Riddle and Taviar wrapped in each other's arms—sound asleep. Another cough racked through Orison's body as dust tickled the back of her throat.

Sitting up, she was relieved that she had regained the feeling in her legs, as she moved them out of the bed. Slowly standing up, she used the bed as support, then a wall as she made her way out of the basement.

After seeing to her needs, Orison hurried through the shop towards the entrance, ignoring the enchanted objects that pleaded to be set free from their iron cage. Unlocking the door, she stifled a gasp to see Merchant's Row blanketed in a thick repulsive-scented fog. The fog smelled like burnt hair and metal, making Orison gag if she breathed too deeply. People mulled about in a daze as they looked upon their fallen homes and businesses; children cried as they picked out their toys from piles of rubble. She sucked in a shuddering breath to see Merchant's Row was completely unrecognisable.

Orison yelped and took a step back when a hand grabbed her ankle. Looking down, Kiltar lay in the bushes outside of Riddle Me This. His face was grimaced in pain. His hand was shaking while trying to hold a wound in his side—blood pouring between his fingers and onto the soil. His skin was almost white as a sheet and his rasping breathing indicated he needed help immediately.

That's when she realised the inevitable—Kiltar, the guard was the Nyxite she had befriended.

With a scream, Orison fell to the floor and put pressure on the wound. Warm blood soaked her trembling hands as Kiltar cried out. She kept reassuring him it would be fine, but the amount of blood didn't make it seem likely. Orison moved his hair from his clammy face; his purple eyes were dull, even in the sunlight.

"Help me!" Orison screamed. Her vision blurred with tears as she held him to her chest. She kept pressure on the wound. "Somebody!" Footsteps approached her and Orison followed the sound. Aeson quickly ran to them. As a groundskeeper, he had his work cut out, with so much damage around. "Help."

Aeson paled to see Kiltar in such a state. "I need to get Eloise."

"But what about Kinsley? She needs you too," Orison pointed out.

He swore under his breath, heavily contemplating who to go to. Orison knew both his girlfriends needed his support and he couldn't be in two places at once.

"Ori, you've got to let go so we can carry him inside," Riddle said. She was in so much shock she didn't even see him come out of the shop. "I've sent Eloise a message. Aeson, go see to Kins."

After a moment's hesitation, she took pressure off the wound. Her bloodied hands trembled violently as she held them up. Kinsley came out of the shop, crouched next to her and wiped Orison's bloodied hands with a wet rag. They watched Aeson help Riddle carry Kiltar upstairs. Orison noticed that he fell into unconsciousness from the injuries he had sustained. Upon hearing that the injuries resulted from a Fallasingha arrow, Orison's blood ran cold; only Sila could have wounded him with such a weapon.

Helping Orison stand, Kinsley let her lean heavily on her for support. Within the past few hours, Orison's escape from the castle was destroyed, a Desigle was placed on her, and she found out more about the mysterious guard—he was the Nyxite. Once inside the shop, both of them paused when they heard screams from upstairs.

"What happens if he dies?" Orison's voice trembled.

"I don't know." She guided Orison up the stairs. "You should get cleaned up."

"No, I need to make sure he'll be okay," Orison insisted.

In the kitchen, Kiltar laid on his stomach across the dining table. Yil raced around collecting supplies for his fathers, who were trying to stem the bleeding until the healer got there. Orison made to step towards Kiltar but was half-dragged into the bathroom by Kinsley.

"Come on, we can get cleaned up before Eloise arrives. You can borrow one of my dresses," Kinsley said.

Orison watched her roll up the sleeves of her white nightgown. The tap screeched as she turned it, water sputtered out into the tub; Kinsley ran her hand under the stream until it reached an adequate temperature. The bathrooms in the homes of Merchant's Row weren't like the bathing chambers in the actual castle, where water flowed soundlessly and was instantly hot. The people of Merchant's Row were seen as a lower class by the king's standard. Turning Orison around, Kinsley helped unbutton her dress from the night before. Feeling the fabric loosen, she held it to her chest, so it didn't fall down. Putting vanilla scented bubbles into the bath, Kinsley faked a smile before leaving Orison alone.

Orison's leg tapped anxiously as she watched Eloise run her glowing hands over Kiltar's bare torso. She looked like an angel in her all-white nurse's outfit. The second healer—Carpathia entered the room with a bucket of water which sloshed onto the floor; her white dress was coated in mud around the hem.

"Sorry I took so long, the king is also injured," Carpathia muttered to Eloise as they worked alongside each other. Orison noticed Taviar looked at the healers with wide eyes. "The Nyxite attack last night nearly took his arm off."

How did you know he was the Nyxite? Orison asked Taviar through his mind.

Riddle told me, he responded.

Do the healers know? she questioned.

Taviar paused. *No, they think he got shot with a Fallasingha blade by accident.*

Biting the side of her nail, all Orison could do was watch. Her heart raced and her stomach twisted into a knot. She exhaled a heavy breath to see Kiltar grimace when Carpathia placed a wet rag on his wound. Orison played nervously with the string on Kinsley's corset belt that she borrowed, which held together the brown peasant dress.

A cup with steam rising out of it hovered in front of Orison's face. "Drink," Kinsley ordered. Cupping it in her hands, Orison took a sip and sank back in the chair as coffee warmed her insides. With a click of Kinsley's fingers, a bowl appeared on a tray in her hands. "Breakfast."

Orison cringed as she took the tray from her. "Porridge with bacon and eggs?"

"It's good. You should try it."

Feeling her stomach growl, she grabbed the cutlery and loaded up the spoon. Placing the mixture in her mouth, it was surprisingly good. Sweet, but the saltiness of the bacon complimented it well. As the healers continued to work, Orison relaxed slightly to see Kiltar's complexion return to a healthy shade of pink; he was going to live.

Riddle whispered something into Taviar's ear, which made his eyes widen. Disbelief painted his features as he looked at Kiltar then back at his husband. While Orison ate, she frowned, wondering what it was about. Before she could ask them, Kinsley started giggling.

"What are you giggling at?" Orison asked.

She cleared her throat. "Aeson just sent me a good morning message." Orison looked over at Eloise, who was trying to stifle a laugh. "Clearly he sent it to both of us."

"Your boyfriend is gross sometimes," Orison said with a small smile. "Having to please two women must be double the fun."

Kinsley nudged her. "Who's being gross now?" When Carpathia placed a wet rag on Kiltar's forehead, Orison's smile faltered and she started to tap her foot anxiously. "He'll be okay. You know the Fae heal quickly."

"But your fathers mentioned something about a Fallasingha blade. Taviar told me what those things do," Orison stated. Lowering her head, she looked at her bowl. "Also, something is wrong. He turns into a dragon. What if that screws up the healing process?"

"It won't," Kinsley assured.

Watching Eloise and Carpathia work in unison to close Kiltar's wound made Orison relax significantly. The bleeding had also stopped once they treated him. Orison wasn't upset that he lied to her all these weeks. Her only concern was his safety.

Twelve

Rain fell around Riddle as he walked up the path towards Saskia's cottage the next day. He hated himself for deceiving Orison; he promised he wouldn't take Kiltar home until he fully recovered. However, the first night wasn't a pleasant experience trying to navigate around his home with an unconscious Nyxite the size of an average horse.

Before Riddle even knocked—the door flung open and Saskia stepped out. Her face paled to see Kiltar.

"What happened?"

"The king shot him with a Fallasingha arrow," Riddle explained.

Saskia ushered Riddle inside. He carried Kiltar through the door, being mindful not to hit his head. Once inside, warmth filled his rain-soaked clothes. He looked to Saskia for advice on where to put him; she pointed to an open door to the left of the stairs. His boots thudded against the hardwood floors. Riddle paused at the door of the allocated room. An orange aura blanketed the cream-coloured walls, the timber frames and the furniture—repair enchantments.

"Just set him on the bed," she instructed.

"Is this his bedroom?" Riddle asked as he followed the instructions. "You have repair enchantments all over it."

Saskia nodded as she clutched the skirts of her rain-splattered dress. Muttering under her breath, she hurried out of the room. Riddle furrowed his brow as he heard the clanking of metal pots and crockery. Finding a wooden chair in the corner, Riddle sat on it, watching Kiltar's shallow breathing and the purple haze of his Nighthex curse shimmering. He'd been unconscious since they closed his wound, yet the curse still wore on.

"Why didn't you tell me this is what he's become?" Riddle asked calmly.

Saskia returned to the room with a wet towel in her hands. She placed it on Kiltar's forehead and smoothed out his black hair. "You can see through the curse?"

"I'm a Charmseer, of course I can see through the curse. When you arrived at the tavern, I saw through it."

"We're still trying to figure the Nighthex out. I didn't know Charmseers can see through it." She smoothed out Kiltar's hair. "I can't believe how different he looks now. How is Orison?"

"She's distraught, understandably. Kiltar's become one of her best friends. Orison didn't want me to bring him home, but if Sila saw that the Nyxite was still on the grounds—he'd be dead!" Riddle replied. "She's going to hate me for deceiving her."

Once again, Saskia disappeared out of the room when the sound of squealing filled the air. A few moments later, Saskia returned with a steaming bowl of porridge, along with a cup of liquid of an unnatural shade of yellow. Saskia sat on the end of the bed, moved her blonde hair away from the food, and carefully spoon-fed Kiltar.

"Thank you for saving him," Saskia said quietly.

Riddle stood up. "Sila burned down the castle library and framed my sons. I have to go into town to pick up some books for Orison. Send me word when he wakes up."

"Of course," Saskia reassured.

He moved through Saskia's home and stepped out into the rain. The shield over his head protected him from becoming wet as he made the walk into Cardenk's town centre. Riddle and Taviar had known Kiltar for years—before the Nighthex took hold and he went missing under mysterious circumstances. It was like seeing a ghost when he came into Grandma Jo's Restaurant. He wanted to reminisce and go drinking in a bar like they used to; before Riddle took on the role of Papa, ten years ago. The Nighthex curse wouldn't allow such a night, anyway.

Rain droplets raced down the window pane. One droplet was in the lead until the race was ceased by a gust of wind. Going back to the starting line, Orison traced her finger down the winning droplet. Her eyes glistened in wonder at how it could be so fast. She had made a place for herself, curled up on a window ledge on the West Wing. She found that watching the rain was the best thing to do since Sila reinstated the shield.

A gust of wind with the scent of water played with Orison's hair. She turned her head to see Aeson leaning against a nearby wall, covered in mud from grounds-keeping. He watched her looking at the rain. His auburn hair covered one of his eyes, which he pushed back; he had one hand in his pocket.

"I think there's a much better place than this cold corridor," Aeson spoke softly, looking at the rain on the glass. Orison scoffed as her gaze fell on him. "Like fresh air and to actually feel the rain on your skin."

Orison let out a sarcastic chuckle. "Says the one who is free." She opened the window and her hand immediately bounced off the shield, though she could feel the wind. "I can't leave this castle. The only place where I can go outside is my balcony."

"Come with me, I think I have a new escape for you."

Without waiting for a response, he walked to the golden compass on the ground where the throne room pointed North. Orison stayed, before climbing down from the ledge and hurrying after him. She tried to ignore the guards who were coming out of the South Wing with charred pieces of the library. Orison ran to the East Wing as they carried books and added them to the discard pile.

Orison and Aeson ventured deeper into the East Wing. She had only been down there when Sila punished her. She was unsure if she could trust Aeson not to send her to another one of Sila's punishments. Instead of the stairs to his chambers, they entered a corridor that Orison had never seen.

It wasn't that she didn't want to explore the castle—she did, but Sila had shields around so many rooms she was afraid to venture into any of them. One time, she tried to enter rooms in the North Wing, before the shields went up. Sila had used her as target practice as punishment with newly recruited guards; it wasn't an experience she wanted to repeat. So, she stayed in her safe locations—her chambers, the room she created, the library or the throne room; and now, the art gallery.

They stopped at a door with ivy growing around it like a chain. She raised an eyebrow and looked at Aeson as she folded her arms over her chest; convinced there was a shield around it, whatever it was. Yet, Aeson chuckled before pushing it open.

Her first encounter of the new space was the fact there was no shield around it. It led to a courtyard with an open glass roof; the surrounding air was crisp. She breathed in deeply as she closed her eyes. The foliage was dense with plants of every size and shape. She blinked in disbelief that she could feel rain on her skin. Aeson ushered her deeper into the new garden, through a curtain of vines, and ventured deeper into the courtyard. Orison gasped to see this wasn't a courtyard at all, but the largest botanical garden she had ever encountered.

A statue of a female, made entirely of plants, had her arm extended; water flowed from the palm of her hands and through her fingers, raining down into a pond. There were various corridors of plants where butterflies and pixies flew around. The insects landed on plants to suck nectar from flowers. Orison gasped to hear birdsong and saw birds singing away while perched on trees with bird feeders. She couldn't believe the beauty.

"How am I allowed in here?" Orison gasped as she spun around, staring at the grey sky over her head. "This is incredible."

Aeson looked up at the sky with her. "I thought you knew about this place until Kinsley and Eloise corrected me." He took in the surrounding site. "I take care of this."

Orison stared at him wide eyed. "You maintain this?" He nodded. "You're so talented."

"Thank you."

He watched her spin around, taking it all in; the rustle of trees made her turn towards the sound. Kinsley appeared with a calm smile, flanked by her fathers. In her hands was a large red box adorned with a pink bow.

"What's this?" Orison hurried over.

"Let's sit in the gazebo. It's heavy and I don't want the contents to get wet," Kinsley instructed.

Everybody followed Kinsley. Pixies were flying around, waltzing to music while another pixie played an instrument from the handrail. Other pixies were watering the plants or singing a cheerful tune while they worked. When they saw they had visitors, the dancers dispersed and lit candles nailed into the support beams; creating a warm ambience in the gazebo. The five of them sat on a bench. Orison smiled as Taviar placed the box on Orison's lap; Kinsley was correct. It was heavy.

"You can open it now," Taviar said.

She made quick work of pulling the ribbon; it fell away, leaving the box for her to open. Orison hesitated to lift the lid. This was the Luxart family, who loved her like one of their own; they would not harm her. They had protected her on enough occasions. Lifting the lid, she gasped loudly to see the box full of books. Taviar had kept his promise of buying her some new ones. Reaching inside, she pulled handfuls of books out, all of her favourites that were lost in the fire.

"Sorry, I went into your head while you were asleep to see what books you liked," Taviar said with a smile. "I don't usually do that."

"I don't care." Orison whirled around and threw her arms around Taviar. He held her close with a kiss on her cheek while rubbing her back. "They're perfect, all of them." She already knew where to hide the books, so Sila couldn't destroy them. "How is Kiltar?"

"Still sleeping," Riddle announced. "We sent him back to Saskia."

Orison accepted it, going back to inspecting her books. She picked one up and ran her finger over the golden lettering. What started as a bad day had become good; a rare occasion in the castle.

Kinsley picked up a book and flipped through the pages. Her gaze fell on Aeson as he looked through some of the books with a smile. Standing up, Orison threw an arm around Riddle. She relaxed when he slowly embraced her, rubbing her back in a comforting gesture.

They stayed in the botanical garden for hours, dancing in the rain and watching the pixies fly around. Orison had a lot of fun for the first time in a long while. She savoured every hour until Taviar got called to Sila's office. That's when reality came back in full force.

The cottage groaned loudly at sunset. A bright light shot through the crack under the door, causing Saskia to wince and cover her eyes. She glanced at Kiltar's room as she put an apple pie in the oven, adding more logs into the wood oven to increase the temperature. Placing her hands on her hips, her full attention turned to his room before wiping her hands on her apron. Her concern over Kiltar was growing exponentially—he still hadn't woken up.

Leaving the pie to cook, Saskia crossed the threshold of her home and tried to open the door. It was jammed by the Nyxite curled up in the entrance. Kiltar must have moved during the change. She cursed under her breath, yet she was relieved that the room was enchanted to repair itself from damage. Any furniture inside would repair itself like the Nyxite was never there.

Closing the door, Saskia moved to the front of the house. She grabbed her cloak, securing it over her shoulders and pulled the hood up. She opened the front door and stepped out into the rain. Using the wall of her house as support, she made her way around to the back. Saskia had to get into that bedroom somehow. Looking through the window, she checked on the oven briefly as it cooked her pie; it would be a treat when Kiltar woke up. Saskia kept telling herself he would wake up; it would be like the dreadful Fallasingha arrows hadn't pierced his skin.

Her concern wasn't just for Kiltar, it was for Orison as well. If the king harmed Orison, causing the Desigle to Mist

Kiltar to her location—while he was still unconscious—he could not protect her. With that thought in mind, her heart skipped a beat as anxiety coursed through her veins. Saskia ran a hand down her face and wondered what she could do while waiting for him to wake up.

The room was dark by the time she got to the window. Clicking her fingers, a candle flickered to life. Saskia witnessed the Nyxite curled up asleep at the doorway, as she suspected. His snoring vibrated the windowpane as she lifted the window and climbed through. Dropping with a thud, she smoothed out her dress, pushing the hood back to observe Kiltar. She reached a hand out to stroke his fur; it was warm under her fingertips.

When she pulled her hand away, she was relieved to see Kiltar's eyes staring back at her.

Thirteen

As soon as Orison got word that the library was safe to enter, she didn't hesitate to venture inside. It still smelled of charred wood, but she pushed it aside. She'd gone too long without trying to find Prince Xabian; he was still missing and there was no new evidence. Orison walked behind Kinsley and Eloise; they looked around the library in shock at its devastation—the burnt sections were closed off with visible purple shields that fizzled whenever somebody neared them.

Once again, they ventured through the labyrinth of shelves, going from the newest section of gold-plated walls to cold, hard stone. The trio passed the gate to *Alsaphus Family Archives*, where candles on the wall lit of their own accord, greeting visitors with a warm glow. Memories of Hogrite burning through her veins made Orison wince, but for Prince Xabian she would push aside her fear to find him. She ran her fingers over Xabian's tellages and picked out the one from the week before. Something was telling her to try, because the final tellage only left her with questions.

"Why don't we look at Neasha's tellage?" Eloise asked, disappearing into the M-N section.

Orison struggled to carry the tellage she picked out, still weak from the Hogrite. "Why would he have anything to do with it?"

"You know about Prince Neasha?" Kinsley asked.

"I saw his portrait in the art gallery." Orison placed Xabian's tellage onto a table.

Kinsley turned to her girlfriend. "Are you sure there would be answers there? He passed away twenty years ago."

Eloise re-emerged into the corridor. "You're right, it might be a dead end, but we could still check. When's your birthday, Ori?"

She cleared her throat. "October sixteenth."

Disappearing into the aisles, Eloise went to check Neasha's tellage while Orison flicked through the pages of Xabian's tellage. The week before her arrival was anticlimactic. It all appeared to be fairly normal—performing royal duties and arguments with Sila. Everything after was more about the bargain placed on her. However, one entry in particular made Orison stifle a gasp—she saw her parents' cottage in the mortal lands with Xabian watching her from the shadows. What was he doing there?

"Strange, the last few books are missing," Eloise announced from her section of the archives, ripping Orison from her thoughts. "Dust outlines where they were at some point, so they were there. Are you okay, Ori?"

Forcing a smile, she nodded. "I'm fine, just shocked about the tellages that are missing," she partially lied.

Something bigger was going on. It was clear that Sila had been in here at some point, to remove the page and entire tellage books. Orison's gaze was fixated on Sila's own tellages that sat in the centre of a stone wall. It was guarded by a green shield that kept crackling like a fire. Another shield that she would have to possibly tear down to find the answers she desired. She needed justice for Xabian; she needed justice for herself.

"We must gain access to that one," she said, keeping her eyes on Sila's tellage. "I also require access to his office."

"Where are we going to find a Tearager?" Kinsley muttered under her breath, running her hands through her hair.

Orison turned to her friend. "I just happen to know one."

All of them paused at the sound of approaching footsteps. Aiken emerged from the shadows with her hands clasped. She gave each of them a low curtsy before she straightened up with a soft smile.

"King Sila has requested an audience in his chambers, Princess." Her attention turned to Kinsley and Eloise. "He has also requested Lady Luxart and Lady Aragh."

Using their magic, Eloise and Orison put back the tellages and stepped forward. Kinsley stayed until Aiken beckoned her to comply. With a dip of her chin, Aiken turned; expecting everybody to follow her back through the labyrinth of bookshelves. They headed towards the entrance where servants cleared away ash from the fire. Picking up her skirts, Orison hurried forward, so she was walking in line with Aiken. The assistant glanced at her but still kept up her quick pace.

"Do you know what he is enquiring about?" Orison dared to ask.

Aiken glanced behind her shoulder. "I think you already know that answer."

She did. Othereal above, she did. He saw them looking at Prince Xabian's and Prince Neasha's tellages through her traquelle. Orison kicked herself; she should have waited until Kiltar made an appearance. He could blind her traquelle long enough to thoroughly research. This meeting was going to be about Sila giving her another punishment, maybe more poisoning. As they rounded the corner, her fear reached its peak. Maybe prying into the castle's secrets would be the end of her existence.

When the doors opened, the noise echoed around Sila's meeting room. Aiken stepped inside, followed by Kinsley, Eloise and Orison. The sound of trickling water could be heard from Sila's reflection pools, sending ripples of water down the walls. A harp was playing to accompany the trickling water, giving a foreboding place a sense of tranquillity.

Each of them walked through the threshold of the meeting room, then through a large marble doorway that led to a stone platform jutting out from the castle. Clouds blanketed the surrounding area like snow, making it impossible to see the trees or mountains; Orison had grown accustomed to seeing out the window. Under normal circumstances, Orison was prohibited from this platform.

Orison's breathing hitched to see Sila sprawled out on his chair. He smirked as he nursed his usual goblet of wine while basking in the sun. A table was between him and Taviar who sat on an adjacent chair. On top of the table was a golden hand-mirror; it didn't have a reflection—it was the traquelle mirror.

"Princess Orison, Lady Aragh, and Lady Luxart, Your Majesty," Aiken announced with a curtsy before moving away.

Looking at her feet, Orison didn't want to look at Sila. She clutched her hands together in front of her, trying to keep her breathing steady. From the corner of her eye, she saw Kinsley and Eloise curtsy with a dip of their chins before standing straight. Out of spite and the fact that Sila didn't deserve any respect for poisoning her, Orison remained standing.

"Curtsy," Sila demanded. Orison finally met his gaze with a glare, watching his yellow eyes flare. Nothing happened when the metallic scent of magic stung her nose; the Desigle prevented it from working. He rolled his eyes. "Do you know why I summoned you three?" They all nodded; there was no point in lying when the traquelle mirror was right there. Sila picked up the mirror, holding it in his hand. "I'm glad you didn't lie for once in your pathetic lives. Orison, I'm glad to see the poison has knocked some sense into you."

"Let me guess, tellages are forbidden now like everything else in the Fallasingha Empire for little old Princess Orison Alsaphus," Orison spat. He glared at her. "You can go and fuck yourself for poisoning me!"

She turned to leave, shying away when Sila appeared in front of her. He snarled. "You have everything in this entire castle, *Princess*," he gritted out through his teeth. "Tellages are not forbidden, but those regarding Prince Xabian and Prince Neasha are! Do I make myself clear?"

Orison looked up at him. "Why?" she challenged. "Is it because they show how you killed them out of sheer spite?"

It was the wrong question to ask on a platform with no handrail. Sila shot out his hand, sending his magic barrelling straight towards Orison. She yelped when it bounced off the Desigle's shield; causing her to fly through the air and slam down onto the cold stone of the platform. She tumbled for a few moments before falling off the edge.

Orison cried out when she managed to break her fall with a rock that she clung to. She grimaced as she tried to pull her way back up to the platform where Sila waited; although she was still too weak from the poison. Taviar appeared and reached a hand out to her.

"Take my hand!" he shouted.

With all the strength that she could muster, she tried to reach out to him, but guards grabbed him from behind. Orison gasped with a whimper of fear as Sila towered over her. His eyes flared as he sneered at her. He slammed his foot down and the platform shook violently. The rock that she was clinging onto for dear life came loose. Orison screamed loudly as she started to plummet down the Visyan mountain range, where death awaited her at the bottom.

Air tore through Orison's dress and hair. She heard Kinsley scream out in terror—her silhouette came into view while she peered over the edge, before guards dragged her away. While she tumbled through the air, the castle gave way to the mountainous rock in which it was built on. Orison tried one last time to reach her arms out for someone to help her. Air pressed down on her too much to scream and tears rained down her cheeks. She wanted somebody to save her. Anybody.

Arms enveloping her in a safe embrace broke her fall. She gasped out a sigh of relief when warmth cocooned her. A flurry of purple night, lightning and thunder blocked out the mountains. Reality hit her that she was going to be safe as she drifted out of consciousness.

Fourteen

Orison awoke with a gasp; her eyes stung and her heart raced. Looking around, she didn't recognise the strange room; white plaster walls lined with timber frames surrounded her. A chest of drawers was next to a closed window. It reminded her of being back in the mortal lands; home with her mother and father. She laid on her side in a strange bed, wrapped up in a knitted baby-blue blanket.

When the door opened, she sat up, pressing her back to the headboard. A person with blonde hair approached the bed. Crockery clicked together on a full tray. When they made eye contact, Orison recognised the person from Grandma Jo's Restaurant; when she had lunch with the Luxarts—- *Grandma Saskia*.

"Good morning, Poppet," Saskia said and set the tray down on Orison's lap with a smile.

A laugh escaped Orison to see that Saskia had made her bacon, eggs and sausages; that she had designed to look like a smiley face. She didn't want to ruin it, but her stomach growled loudly. How long had she been asleep? Looking down, she realised somebody had changed her out of the blue empire dress that she had worn during Sila's rage. Orison furrowed her brow.

Grabbing the cutlery, Orison didn't know where to begin. "Where... where am I?"

Saskia sat in the wooden chair next to her bed. "You're safe in Cardenk. If you remember back to Grandma Jo's, my name is Saskia."

The cutlery screeched when Orison cut into some of the bacon; she winced. "Sorry." Orison was used to getting shouted at if she made her cutlery screech.

"It happens," Saskia said with a wave of her hand and a smile.

"How am I in Cardenk? There was a shield around the castle."

Saskia leaned back in the chair. "Kiltar is a Tearager and the Desigle needed to get you out."

Picking up a luminous yellow drink, Orison sniffed it. Her eyes widened from the sting that it caused. She shuddered and blinked a couple of times. Taking a sip, her face scrunched up at the overpowering sickly-sweet taste. It tasted like somebody had created a drink from a gallon of sugar, mixed with syrup, honey and mango. She started coughing, smacking her chest that burned from it. Her teeth sang out in pain.

"Curpacot nectar does that the first time you try it," Saskia said with a laugh.

Orison dared another sip, having the same reaction. "Curpacot nectar?" she choked.

"From the Curpacot tree. It has healing properties and regains your strength. You've only been out for the night, but your strength has diminished from the Hogrite," Saskia explained.

Orison's eyes widened. "I've never been away from the castle that long."

"I've blinded your traquelle so the king doesn't know you're here." When the door creaked open, Saskia glanced at it as Kiltar stepped into the room. "Morning."

Kiltar gave Orison a smile as she ate a loaded forkful of her breakfast. "How are you feeling?"

She glanced up from her plate. "Confused."

"Aside from confused."

Orison loaded her fork again; Saskia knew how to cook. Another thing that reminded her of home—it was like a mother had cooked her child something. Although the cooks in the castle were experts in their jobs, they didn't make the food with love in their minds.

"I'm feeling okay. Thank you for saving me." She sipped more Curpacot nectar and winced, coughing from the taste. "Apologies, please may I have just some coffee instead? I feel sick."

The chair creaked as Saskia stood up and took the cup. "Of course, Poppet."

Her shoes thudded onto the floor, along with the swish of her floral dress. Kiltar sat at the end of the bed, looking at Orison. She continued to eat the rest of her breakfast. The eggs were cooked to perfection and ideal for dipping. Orison had awoken feeling like she hadn't eaten in a year. She was ravenous and couldn't get enough food.

"Why does Saskia keep calling me Poppet?" Orison asked while wiping her chin with the back of her hand.

Kiltar smiled. "She calls everybody Poppet."

She nodded. "Are the other guards looking for me? Sila is going to be so pissed."

"They are. It's quite amusing watching them search the castle and surrounding areas to find nobody." Kiltar looked at his hands. "The king had no right to do that."

"What happened during the fight?" Orison asked before a big mouthful. Egg yolk dribbled down her chin and she wiped it off.

He looked up at the ceiling. "I Misted you here during your fall. You're here now so I can protect you. You're not safe in the castle."

"Not that." Orison finished up the last of her breakfast, licking the knife clean. "I'm talking about the Fallasingha arrow injury."

Kiltar looked at his hand. "I was blind-sided, they shot me from behind."

Her face fell. Just as she was about to ask more questions, the smell of coffee drifted into the room as Saskia returned;

handing it to Orison with a smile. She sipped it and savoured the taste of caffeine in the morning. If she was here in Cardenk, the possibilities were endless; she could explore something other than the castle. Not only did Kiltar protect her from the fall, but he also gave Orison one of her true desires since arriving in the Othereal—freedom.

Orison managed to get out of bed and explore the cottage alone, while Kiltar bought her some more clothes. Saskia busied herself with cleaning. Orison started with the room she was in, her fingers traced over the dresser. She observed her pale face in the mirror, pushing her gaunt cheeks so they looked full—like before the Hogrite ravaged her figure. She noticed that her purple eyes glowed more brightly than they had since the poison. Orison put it down to the Curpacot nectar working its magic to restore the damage. Behind her shoulder, she saw a wooden chest at the foot of the bed.

Her curiosity peaked as she knelt in front of it, removing the latch; the lid flipped open, with the clank of chains. Inside was a bunch of white fabric. Growing even more curious, she sifted through the soft material until her fingers brushed against something cold, solid and detailed. Pulling out her find, she pouted to see a painting of a handsome man in the king's guard uniform in an ornate frame. The man looked familiar—he had blue eyes like Saskia, but he had brown hair. He looked proud with his hand over his heart, the other on the pommel of his sword. Orison's eyes widened at the realisation that she was looking at Saskia from another time.

"What are you doing?" Saskia snapped. Orison jumped and whirled around, the picture still in hand. Saskia snatched it back and approached her. "I let you into my home and you fucking snoop through my things?"

Orison crawled backwards. "I'm... I'm sorry. I was just curious." She watched as Saskia threw the picture in the chest and dragged it out of the room. "I didn't mean..."

"*This* chest is highly personal, got it?" Saskia interrupted. Orison nodded. "The contents of this chest should be for me to divulge to you in time, not for you to discover. Do I make myself clear?"

"Yes... yes ma'am," Orison said, pressing her back to the bed, hugging her knees to her chest to stop Saskia from seeing her trembling. "I didn't mean to; I was just curious and thought some of your dresses would be in there."

"Well, you thought wrong!" Saskia shouted.

From the corner of her eye, she watched Saskia drag the chest through the living room. Orison squeezed her eyes shut at the dull thuds of it being dragged up the stairs. She didn't mean to pry into Saskia's personal things. Forcing herself to stand on shaking legs, Orison ventured into the living room, pausing to see how similar it was to her home in the mortal lands; the kitchen was to her left, as well as the large living room. However, instead of her father's wood-working table on the far wall, there was a collection of dresses. The place smelled like freshly baked apple pie.

The stairs creaked as Saskia returned. "I'm sorry, Poppet, that's a sore subject. Please don't go through my things again." Orison glanced at her with a nod. "The contents of that chest are the equivalent of looking through somebody's underwear drawer. Highly embarrassing."

Orison gave another nod. "I understand why you got mad."

Tension was thick in the air as Orison delved deeper into the home, running her finger over the brown sofa as she approached the collection of dresses. She stopped at a blue ball gown with golden embellishments. She picked up one of the long sleeves which had ruffled wrist cuffs. Turning to the full-length mirror, she understood why pieces of paper were shoved into its seams. The images showed tutorials on how to apply make-up or pull off certain hairstyles. Orison looked at herself; she still found it strange that she was a Fae now. Behind her, she noticed Saskia watching while standing at the stairs, her hands on her hips.

"Which is your favourite dress in your collection?" Orison asked, turning away from the mirror. "Mine's probably the gold floral one."

Saskia clasped her hands in front of her as she approached the collection, pointing to a green ball gown with a corset type bodice and wide hips. "I feel like a princess in that one."

"I bet you look like a princess too," Orison said with a smile.

Saskia's stern facade melted like ice in Spring. She playfully smacked Orison with the dish rag that hung off her shoulder, a smile on her face. "Oh, stop it, you!" She then descended into giggles. "But... yes, I do. I need to wear it to a ball one time."

Pressing a hand to her stomach, the two of them laughed together until the door opened. Kiltar had returned with a box. He smiled at the women, who were in fits of laughter. Orison didn't know why she was laughing anymore.

Kiltar laughed. "What's funny?"

"We're talking ball gowns which lure men into the beds of very beautiful women," Orison announced and leaned against Saskia.

He raised an eyebrow. "Alright." Kiltar cleared his throat and extended the box out to her. "Here are some clothes, there are horses outside so we can go on an adventure."

Orison paused, but still a laugh escaped her. "Where to?"

"Lake Braloak, I think you'll love it," Kiltar announced.

Her eyes widened. She didn't know where that was, but she knew that sirens resided there. Orison didn't know what a siren looked like in person; she'd only seen them in paintings. Taking the box, she gave Kiltar a smile and hurried back into her room.

Fifteen

Kiltar and Orison had been riding through Loak Forest for the past two hours. He was silent next to her, scanning the forest for any threats with his hand on the pommel of his sword. Orison was just taking in the sights, mesmerised by unicorns drinking from nearby streams and pixies flying around with butterflies. The smile was a permanent feature on her face.

"Explain the Nyxite thing to me," Orison asked, glancing at her waterfall braid over her shoulder; Saskia insisted she practise on a real subject.

He sucked in a breath. "By day, I'm this. By sunset, I'm the Nyxite. I can understand if you're angry that I didn't tell you."

"I'm not angry, just curious. So, it's a curse?" He made a noise of agreement. "Why?"

"The king and I had a difference of opinions," Kiltar divulged.

She watched a feather land on her russet-pink tunic. A smile came to her face as she picked it up from amongst the gold details on the cloth. Orison returned to their conversation. "Are all Nyxites cursed?"

"Unfortunately." Kiltar looked down at the reins in his hands. "And I have no idea how to remove the curse. It's really vague. I need to find an act of eternal love."

Orison threw her head back with a laugh. "Why is it always true love's first kiss that breaks the curse in faerie tale lands?" She caught Kiltar looking at her. "What?"

"I don't need to find true love's first kiss, just an act of eternal love. There's nothing else to specify what needs to be done."

"That makes absolutely no sense."

Kiltar pulled his lips into a straight line. "Tell me something I don't know. Anyway, look, we're near the lake!"

Orison turned her attention to the forest in front of her. At first it was the labyrinth of trees along their path, the skittering of animals and unicorns; and the sound of twigs breaking under horses' hooves. She marvelled at the sound of the most beautiful singing she'd heard in her entire life. It came from behind a curtain of willow trees.

The willow trees tickled her arms as they passed through to the most enchanting picture that Orison had ever laid her eyes on. Crystal blue waters greeted her. Rocks jutted out of the water, like perfect platforms to sunbathe for hours. Snow-capped mountains framed the lake—spanning for miles. As they stood on the beach, the singing intensified. Walking her horse over the bank, Orison took in her surroundings. A group of women on another set of rocks were singing while they brushed their hair. Her breath caught in her throat when she saw they had fish's tails instead of legs.

She jumped at the sound of a large thud. When Orison glanced behind her shoulder, she realised Kiltar had dismounted his horse. He extended his arms out to her; she fell into them as he helped her dismount her own horse. Orison smiled as he set her down on her feet, the boots he bought her sunk into the coarse sand. Kiltar took the horses by their reins and tethered them to a nearby tree. The beautiful view before her was something that Orison wouldn't forget. A tear rolled down her cheeks at the fact that this was real, not a picture.

"Are you well?" Kiltar asked, returning and slinging a bag over his shoulder.

Orison tore her gaze from the view. "Just, Sila was hiding this from me," she replied. "Where are the water nymphs?"

"They live in rock pools inside the mountains, not on the beach like the sirens," he explained.

Orison wrapped her arm through Kiltar's arm when he extended it out to her. They walked around the water's edge; the coarse sand made it difficult to walk. Occasionally, they slid close to the water, which Kiltar was adamant that she shouldn't go near. She kept taking in views in a mesmerised state. Hearing the splash of water, Orison's attention fixated on the most handsome male that she had ever seen, swimming towards her. It made her pause. He had sun-kissed skin, piercing blue eyes and long blonde hair. Her stomach did somersaults.

"Hello beautiful, do you want to go for a swim?" he asked.

Orison made to step towards the water, but Kiltar pulled her back. "He's a triton, ignore him."

"What would happen if I went with him?" Orison glanced behind her shoulder as they resumed their walk. Three other tritons were in the water watching them. One had brown hair with a braid, another had white hair and the third triton had black hair.

"Death," Kiltar answered.

Orison's eyes widened, as she pressed herself against Kiltar for safety. As they left, the tritons watched them, the pair approached the sirens on the rock—who were continuing to brush their hair. Some tritons sat amongst the sirens, showering them with affection. That's when it struck her. This wasn't a place of tranquillity; it was a trap to lure unsuspecting people to their doom. It was the perfect environment for sirens, tritons and water nymphs to do their bidding.

One of the sirens approached the pair. Her tail was like a sunset—yellows blended into oranges, into reds, into pinks and ending in purples. Her eyes were the same piercing blue and she had black hair that pooled around her like ink.

"Enchantments grow like the vines of the great ivy," she said with a smile of razor-sharp teeth; her voice was like a song. Orison crouched in front of the siren. "Curse-breaker, give me your hand and we can free the enchanted one."

Her eyes narrowed. "What does she mean? I'm not a curse-breaker."

"Nothing, it's siren talk," Kiltar said and resumed walking.

Orison looked at the siren who smirked at her. "Do you know the whereabouts of Prince Xabian?"

"Ignore her," Kiltar said sternly, from far away.

"Once lost, all can be found within the Village of Warriors," the siren said. Her webbed hand came up onto the lakebed and she snarled. "Shields can be broken with the assistance of lost souls."

Feeling hands underneath her arms, Kiltar steered Orison away from the siren as she swiped her hand; narrowly missing Orison's ankle. The siren hissed as she disappeared back into the dark depths of Lake Braloak. The only sign of her being there were the bubbles on the surface.

Giving up the fight, Orison walked alongside Kiltar when he let her go. She glanced behind her shoulder when the singing subsided and she heard the splashing of water. More sirens watched them; it unnerved her to see that their eyes had now turned red. The riddle confused Orison. She remembered Taviar explaining that Cardenk was the Village of Warriors because of its proximity to the castle. However, she was staying in that village and hadn't seen Xabian.

A tree branch hit Orison's face, pulling her out of her thoughts. She pushed it away with a laugh as they entered a clearing near the water's edge. It had a perfect view of the lake without the risk of being taken by the sirens, who were still staring at them with red eyes. A few moments later, the singing returned; and the glaring sirens had all but disappeared. The singing enticed Orison towards the water, but she refused to give in to their wishes.

Kiltar sat on the ground and rifled through the bag; he pulled out two brown parcels. Kneeling on the ground, Orison watched him as he extended one of the parcels to her. Whatever was inside was heavy.

"What's in here?" She lifted it up and down.

Kiltar pulled at the string. The paper fell away to reveal a sandwich. Pulling back the bread, it revealed turkey with cranberry sauce and gravy. Her stomach growled in response as she sat on the ground properly. She looked out at the water as she took a bite, the singing still telling her to take a dive into the water. From this vantage point, she could see the sirens jumping and leaping through the water; it appeared as though everything had returned to normal. Her thoughts kept wandering to the siren who tried to pull her into the water.

"How is your first day of freedom?" Kiltar asked, sucking gravy off his thumb.

Orison turned to him after a glance at the water. "Incredible. I've never seen anything so beautiful before."

She looked at her sandwich. "Apart from angering the sirens, that was scary."

Upon her next glance at the water, she gasped to see a pink dolphin leap out of the water with a siren on its back. Orison hadn't seen a dolphin in real life. She had only ever heard about them from the books that her mother read to her, while her father carved wood. She took another bite of her sandwich, savouring the tranquil environment. Her eyes widened to see an elk behind Kiltar's shoulder. It bowed its head to Orison before running off.

"You know, I have to return to the castle at some point. I don't want to put that kind of pressure on your magic."

"I'm fine," he bit out. A heavy silence settled over the pair as they ate. Orison drank from the canteen of water and glanced at Kiltar who stared into space. He lowered his head. "What did that siren say to you about Prince Xabian?"

After taking her last bite and wiping the crumbs off her trousers, she said, "A whole lot of nothing. She talked in riddles." She cocked her head to the side. "If I remember rightly, Taviar said Cardenk was the Village of Warriors. That's where she said I'd find Prince Xabian. But I've been to Cardenk and never seen him. I'd surely recognise him and others would as well."

Kiltar sucked in a sharp breath, resulting in him choking on his food. He coughed and spluttered so much that Orison had to smack his back. "I'm fine." He said, wincing. "You would definitely recognise Prince Xabian if he was in Cardenk. You're correct there. So, where could he be?" Orison shrugged. "Sunset is a good few hours away. Do you want to take another walk around the lake?"

"This Prince Xabian thing is so confusing. Every lead is a dead end," Orison grumbled.

"Like I said, if King Sila doesn't want you to find him, you won't." He packed up their picnic, then helped her to stand up. Kiltar walked back to the water with Orison by his side. "If he is somewhere in Cardenk, then he's well hidden."

Falling silent, they strolled around the lake. They went beyond where the sirens and tritons called home; where they hissed as the pair walked past.

Kiltar and Orison wandered for hours; stumbling upon wild unicorns, griffons and trolls—who were tending to flower patches. Before coming to Othereal, Orison thought that trolls were large, grotesque things who lived under bridges. They were indeed grotesque, but they were tiny things that looked like potatoes plucked straight from the ground.

As the hours ticked by, they stumbled upon the water nymphs in the rock pools. Orison knew they were running out of time, judging by how anxious Kiltar was with the approaching sunset. They made their way back to their horses and re-entered the dark depths of Loak Forest.

Kiltar was tense beside Orison, his attention focussed on the sky, his eyes wide in horror. The sky above them had turned an orange colour with bursts of pink, yellow and purple. Sunset. His stomach did somersaults and the lunch they shared suddenly wasn't sitting right. He moved in the saddle as his heart started racing. Kiltar tried to stay calm; he'd never shifted in front of anyone. It was always in the comfort of his own room or in the woods behind Saskia's home. There was too much shame from having the curse and for him to change in front of people, especially Orison. It was a gruelling process he had to live with until he figured out how to break it.

"Saskia's home reminds me of my home in the mortal lands," Orison admitted, in an attempt at distraction from the inevitable. "I've been expecting Father to come down the stairs any moment and hold me. Of course it never happens."

"Really?" Already, his eyes began to glow like somebody had shone an Othereal light into them. When he closed his eyes, the light emanated through the skin of his eyelids. "That must be difficult for you."

He had run out of time. Orison was going to see him change whether he liked it or not. All he needed was a few more moments to be back in Saskia's cottage, where he could change with privacy. Fate had other plans.

"Kind of. Sila forbids me to speak of my parents, so this conversation is quite liberating." Orison's eyes widened when she saw the fur growing on the back of his hands. His breathing was coming out heavy, like he had run for miles.

Kiltar winced as he stopped his horse. "We've run out of time." Orison stopped her horse, taking in the fur sprouting out of his cheeks. Pain erupted through his body like a wildfire. He dismounted the horse stiffly, as the pain slithered up his spine; he bit back a howl as he felt the change happen. "Run!"

Orison's horse stirred and stomped its hooves. "I'm not leaving you."

"Just run! Don't stop until you get back to Saskia," he gasped, as he leaned against a tree. Kiltar's forehead was slick with sweat. He screamed as his leg twisted back at an unnatural angle, snapping like a twig being stepped on.

With a nod, she turned her back on him. "I'll get help."

"Don't!" he began, only to holler when his arms snapped along with his other leg.

Giving him one last look. "I'll get help," Orison repeated with determination.

She gave the horse a kick; it whinnied and began thundering through Loak Forest. Leaving Kiltar alone to suffer the change of the Nyxite, she glanced behind her shoulder when she heard a blood-curdling scream. His spine had snapped in multiple places as wings tore through his shoulder blades. Kiltar gripped the ground underneath him. His horse bolted from what was happening, when horns sprouted from his head. Then, Loak Forest exploded in a blinding white light.

Sixteen

Her horse didn't stop until it arrived at Saskia's little cottage by the river. Orison swung herself from the saddle. Her boots thudded on the compact earth, as she vaulted over the white picket fence and ran to the front door. She opened it with a thud against the wall, causing Saskia to gasp and look up from her knitting.

"Kiltar's in trouble!" Orison shouted and pointed to the forest, east of the property. Breathing hurt and her legs shook. Saskia slowly stood up. "Please, we've got to help him, he was screaming…"

"Oh, Poppet, you got yourself in a right state," Saskia crooned as she hurried over to Orison. She cupped Orison's face in her hands. "Come on, let's get you some tea."

"No! He turned! He's in trouble and hurt," Orison spat out as quickly as possible, struggling as Saskia tugged her over to the sofa. "Thank you, but I don't need tea." She pulled at the vice-like grip around her hand. "Please, help him!"

Giving up the fight, Saskia whirled around. "Everything you saw is normal. That's what happens when he changes into the Nyxite. I'm not helping because there is nothing to be done *to* help."

It stunned Orison into silence. She let Saskia pull her to the sofa and lower her onto the plush cushion, in a daze. The sound of Kiltar's agonised screams bounced around in her head, replaying on a loop. Orison buried her head in her hands. A tut made her sit up. She placed her hands on her thighs and looked, as Saskia came over with a steaming mug of tea.

Taking it from her, Orison looked at her. "Are you sure he's going to be okay?" She took a sip of tea, wincing at her tongue being burnt from not blowing on it beforehand. "He... he was screaming. I watched his bones..."

"More than sure, he's been enduring it for two months at this point." Saskia returned to her rocking chair, picking up her knitting. "I know it's scary watching the change. It terrified me the first time, but now I'm just used to it. Kiltar will come home after he's adjusted."

Orison took another sip. "He'll be fine, Kiltar will be fine," she muttered to herself. Tapping her foot on the floor, she put the mug on the coffee table and clasped her hands together. "How could the king curse somebody with something that barbaric? He was in agony."

The clicking of the knitting needles paused as Saskia gave Orison a knowing look. Yes, Orison did already know the answer to her question, but it didn't make the Nighthex any less barbaric. Orison sat at the edge of her seat; the tea too hot to drink for the time being. It wasn't calming her nerves in the slightest.

"Oh, we need something stronger than tea to calm your mind," Saskia noted with a tut, once again, discarding her knitting. "I don't have any alcohol in the house. We can go to a pub in Cardenk at dark. How about it, Poppet?"

Orison forced a smile. "That would be nice."

"Aside from the change, did you enjoy yourself?" The rocking chair creaked as she rocked in it, watching Orison.

Looking at her hands, she sucked in a breath. "I tried finding Prince Xabian. I asked a siren for assistance, but they just gave me riddles to decipher." Orison turned to Saskia when she clicked her tongue. "But other than that, it was incredible. I saw my first dolphin. I didn't know they could be found in lakes or rivers, before today."

A smile spread across Saskia's face as she rocked. "There is a species of dolphin that live in lakes and rivers. You shouldn't be asking the sirens for assistance, though, Poppet," she advised. "After your tea, we'll venture into Cardenk."

Orison took a sip of tea; it had cooled enough that she could drink it comfortably. Saskia had returned to her knitting, where the needles clicked together in quick succession. She was right, Cardenk would take Orison's mind off Kiltar and whether he was okay. If she didn't go, then she'd stay up all night wondering if he was safe. Orison should be having fun during her chance at freedom. It's what Kiltar would want.

Grandma Jo's Restaurant took on a different life at night. Many varieties of creatures danced on the dance floor. People sitting on the side lines stomped their feet to replicate the sound of drums; as others played fiddles, pan flutes and lutes. Some revellers sat on people's knees, holding mugs of beer in the air while shouting. It was a different celebration than what Orison was familiar with in Alsaphus Castle.

Seated at a table, Orison and Saskia shared a bacon and chili cheese pizza. Fanning her mouth from the heat, Orison grabbed her beer and smiled to see Saskia struggle with the cheese. She set her drink down as she looked at the crowd.

"They always do the best pizza here," Saskia said as she grabbed a napkin.

Orison was about to reply when somebody approached the table. The person standing before them was a curvy woman with her breasts almost spilling out of her red dress, she had bright orange hair in curls.

"Care for a dance, my lady?" she asked.

"Thank you, but I'm trying to eat my dinner," Orison said, pointing to the half-eaten pizza.

The female waved her hand. "It'll be there when you get back."

Casting Saskia a look, she waved Orison along. Wiping her mouth and hands of the grease, Orison stood up and let the woman guide her to the dance floor. It was an overwhelming spectacle in the crowd of people. She was used to the slow ballroom dances, not this sort of high-impact dancing, where people created art with their fluent movements. There was no structure; it was all for fun. People skipped around each other; bowed low; and passed from partner to partner. Some women did river dances or pirouetted, showing their skills to worthy suitors.

Orison squealed as the woman grabbed her hand and spun her around. She gasped when the person grabbed her by the waist. She came face to face with Aeson. "Where the fuck have you been?" he whispered, taking her hand and swaying.

"I've been at Saskia's home." Orison looked around. "Where's the woman gone?"

"It was me all along. I'm a shifter, remember." He spun her around. "The king's furious at not knowing your whereabouts. If we didn't find you today, I'd have to change into you."

Orison paused and looked up at him. "You can do that?"

Another twirl around, Orison stumbled into the arms of somebody who looked like herself, before the curvy woman returned; she was speechless. Somebody else scooped her up, denying her the chance to react, and she was face to face with Kinsley.

Orison smiled. "Hello."

"My fathers are going to kill me if they find out I used a discovaker to get your location," Kinsley hissed. "I was worried sick."

Orison looked at Saskia. "I've been staying here, in a cottage on the outskirts of the city. Kiltar took me to a safe house after Misting me away from the castle." Aeson took her hand and they skipped in a circle. "Why are Riddle and Taviar going to kill you for using a discovaker?"

Kinsley skipped along. "A discovaker is witchcraft. I had to use your hair and some other stuff to find your location..."

"My hair?" Orison interrupted in horror, her jaw fell open. "How the fuck did you get my hair?"

"Your hairbrush, dufflepud." Orison baulked at the Fallasingha insult. "Anyway, whatever is happening with your traquelle isn't normal and the king is furious. He's destroyed some rooms in the castle."

Orison shook her head and rolled her eyes. When the music stopped, she returned to her table for a drink and another slice of pizza; Kinsley and Aeson right on her heels. When she sat down, she noticed a bag at Saskia's feet; the two of them must have come prepared for a long search.

"Are you okay, Poppet?" Saskia asked Orison as she sat down.

"I'm fine." Orison drank her beer; she scowled to find that it had become warm.

Kinsley turned to Orison. "I'm going to assume you don't want to go back to the castle." Orison shook her head. "Alright, Saskia, can we stay with you? We'll bring Eloise along after she's finished her duties in the infirmary."

"Of course, Poppet."

Orison watched Kinsley and Aeson return to the dance floor as she finished her dinner. Her mind kept drifting to her search for Prince Xabian. She rubbed the back of her neck as she tried to figure out her next steps. Orison had to be out of the castle for this to work. The search had become an obsession; it was the only thing to keep her mind busy while trapped in the castle. Now that she was out, that search could continue and she had to bring their prince back to Fallasingha. Although she didn't know how much time she had before Sila caught up to her; she would continue her search outside of the castle, until that dreadful time came. She had to do it for the Empire.

Their shoes clicked against the cobblestone path illuminated by Othereal streetlights. Kinsley leaned against Aeson, singing drunkenly the songs from Grandma Jo's

Restaurant. Saskia glanced behind her, laughing. Orison hugged herself as a gust of cold air from the river chilled her to the bone. It comforted her to see Saskia's cottage; it felt like coming home. The exterior reminded Orison of her home in the mortal lands—with its white plaster exterior and thatched roof; even if it was in the wrong location and not surrounded by the trees of the Nalan Forest.

A thud broke her train of thought as Kinsley tumbled to the ground after tripping on a rock. She sat on the ground looking sorry for herself with a grin on her face. Aeson scoffed out a laugh as he helped her regain her footing. He checked her over for injuries, but there weren't any that her Fae healing couldn't fix, so they resumed their walk.

Once they got to the white picket fence, Saskia took the lead in unlatching the gate to her home. Everybody followed behind her as she walked up the cobblestone path to the front door; except Orison. She was at the back of the group and paused when she heard rustling from Saskia's vegetable garden; notoriously the cabbage patch.

Orison walked towards the noise. She used the warm glow of the Othereal light that was illuminating the front door to find her way. She narrowed her eyes. There was a shadow moving in the blanket of darkness. She jumped back when the sound of planters crashing to the ground echoed around the void. Once Orison regained composure, she was more determined to figure out what it was. The smell of soil was strong in the air. Her foot rolled on a carrot with its roots still attached.

"Who's there?" Orison called out to the shadow. It paused; her stomach did somersaults from nerves. "I command you to come out!"

The shadow began moving; she reeled back in horror at the fact that it was approaching her. Produce squelched as the void swallowed up the food; consuming everything in its path like a malicious entity. Only then did it come into the light.

"Kiltar, look at what you've done to my vegetables!" Saskia reprimanded. Orison looked over her shoulder to see her standing on the doorstep with her hands on her hips. "You're paying for new seeds."

Orison turned back to Kiltar; relief flooded her to realise he was actually safe. She extended her hand out. He pushed his head against it and Orison ran her fingers through his soft fur with a smile as he purred. His Nyxite form was much, much larger than the last time she saw him; he was about the size of a large moose, with wings. She had to look up to see those purple eyes with a million galaxies swirling around in them.

"It's good to see that Kiltar has fully healed after the battle," Kinsley said with a smile.

Saskia smiled. "That's the Curpacot fruit working its magic."

"Do you use Curpacot fruit to heal everything?" Orison asked.

Saskia waved her hand and smiled. "Minor ailments. Say if you're sick, in shock, or unconscious—it heals them. Anything like cuts or scrapes, it cannot. Come, let's go inside."

She opened the cottage's front door and held it open for Orison and Kinsley to enter. When they were inside, they found Aeson already sitting on the sofa by the fire, waiting for everybody else. Kinsley soon joined him. Orison sat at the edge of the armchair, clutching her hands together.

"Today I went to Lake Braloak with Kiltar, and I think I may have a lead in finding Xabian," Orison announced, glancing at Saskia as she disappeared upstairs.

Aeson held Kinsley's hand as he looked at Orison. "What is the lead?"

"I asked a siren for assistance with finding him, and she said he's in the Village of Warriors, which is here. But nobody has seen him, so where could he be?"

"You seriously asked a siren for assistance in finding Prince Xabian?" Aeson exclaimed, shock written all over his face.

"Aside from that, if he was here, then everybody would know. He's just missing, poof, gone," Kinsley said, as she leaned against Aeson.

Orison rubbed her hands together. "She also said lost souls can tear down shields, before she tried to drag me into the lake." Moving her hair over her shoulder, she played with the end of her braid. "I know they are just riddles and siren talk, but maybe this is the clue that we needed to figure out the mystery."

"He must be behind a shield then, if that's what she predicted," Aeson said, huffing out a breath as he rubbed Kinsley's shoulder. He was silent for a few moments. "Should we go to Parndore tonight? There might be clues with a seer."

"You've got to be joking! Orison can't Mist that distance yet, and it's a two-week ride on horseback," Kinsley gasped. "But we never got to do it the other day."

The stairs creaked as Saskia returned. "I don't think it's safe to go to Parndore tonight, Poppets," she warned.

Aeson stood up. "But we have dragons, we have the power of flight." Orison and Kinsley exchanged a speculative glance. "We have Kiltar who is a Nyxite, he can fly. I can turn into a Wyvern; we'll easily get to Parndore Castle in an hour."

All of them jumped when the door burst open. Kiltar watched from the door; his eyes flared and he looked around. Before anybody could say otherwise, Aeson hurried outside and changed into his Wyvern form. The red dragon towered over Kiltar with the beat of his wings. It made Orison freeze.

"Dufflepuds," Saskia muttered under her breath. "Fine, you can go to Parndore, but please send word every day to tell me the king hasn't captured you."

In unison, Kinsley and Orison stood up, making their way out of the front door towards the two dragons. Her heart raced as she looked up at Kiltar. She ran her hand through his fur and tried to stifle her nerves; she had never ridden a dragon before. Kinsley was perfectly at ease as she mounted Aeson, her hands on his neck. Orison squealed when Kiltar picked her up by the back of the collar and sat her on his back. Following Kinsley's lead, she placed her hands on his neck. A scream tore out of Orison as he shot off into the night.

Seventeen

Warm air brushed across Orison's face as she dared to sit back, still holding a tight grip on Kiltar's fur. She looked across at Kinsley. Her black hair billowed behind her—like flying a dragon was as easy as riding a horse. Below them were the twinkling lights of towns and cities that Orison was yet to explore. She let her mind wander about what people were doing down there. Were parents tucking their children into bed? Were they having dinner or partying in the taverns?

An earthy smell lingered in the air. Orison was in awe of Kiltar's strength, as he beat his giant wings to stay airborne. Despite not having anything to stop her plummeting from his back, she felt a sense of safety and solace. Now she was onto the next adventure to Parndore, some place that she had only heard about in Taviar's stories.

"We're almost there," Kinsley announced.

The stars of towns and cities blinked out into dark oblivion. Orison's heart rate picked up at having to trust Kinsley's judgement. She gripped onto him for dear life. She bit back a scream when he banked in unison with Aeson, tucking his wings in as they dived at high speed. Orison squeezed her eyes shut; the feeling of free-falling carved a pit in her stomach. All the wind was stolen from her lungs when he extended his wings for a soft landing.

A thud made Orison's teeth knock together; her body jolted. Orison was breathless, like she had just run through the entire gardens at Alsaphus Castle. Slowly, she opened her eyes to see that they were on a stone walkway illuminated by nothing but moonlight. Kinsley dismounted Aeson and once she was a safe distance away, he turned back into his Fae form. Dismounting Kiltar, Orison ran her hand through his fur and petted him. Kinsley clicked her fingers and an apple appeared in her hand, which Kiltar gobbled down immediately.

"I think we could give him something else," Orison managed to say, still trying to catch her breath from the landing.

A smile spread across Kinsley's face. "Do you want fish?" she said in a high-pitched voice, like she was speaking to a baby. The Nyxite glared back.

"Don't talk to him like that," Orison reprimanded.

Kinsley finally noted the glare. "I'm sorry, it was just too funny not to." With a click of her fingers, a raw fish appeared in her hand; Kiltar gobbled it down. "There you go."

"How do you do that?" Orison asked, clicking her fingers, but nothing appeared. "Is it like an invisible pocket that you have access to?"

Aeson wrapped his arm around Kinsley's waist. "If it was an invisible pocket, it'd smell awful. What you do is think of something you want and your magic takes it from somewhere nearby. Changelings consider it stealing, but it's very useful for survival in certain circumstances."

Taking in their surroundings, Orison gaped at the castle turret towering over them. Entire sections of the castle were reduced to only a handful of bricks. Nature had overtaken the ruins with ivy and moss. Trees grew through the windows that were missing glass. At the end of the walkway, a wooden door hanging off its hinges led into the castle. The rest of the property—from what Orison could see, was in total ruins.

She noticed Kinsley and Aeson approaching the door; she hurried after them with a quick glance at Kiltar over her shoulder.

"What about Kiltar?" Orison called out.

Aeson paused at the door, taking in the Nyxite. "In that form, the castle's too unstable for him to go inside; it'll alert the king, otherwise. He'll have to wait out here until dawn."

Placing her hand on the door, Orison turned to Kiltar. "Will you be okay out here?" He merely stared at her. The once large purple eyes from when the Nyxite was a baby, had shrunk with his growth. Kiltar huffed out a breath. "I know, but if you go inside, you'll alert Sila of my location and I can't have that. I need this." With a blast of wind, Kiltar took off into the star-filled sky. Orison felt bad for him, but it was for the best. If he was truly her protector, he would understand.

"Come on, I know a place where we can spend the night," Kinsley said, disappearing into the stairwell.

As Orison stepped through, sheer darkness greeted her—until Kinsley clicked her fingers. Sconces on the wall illuminated, casting the dusty stairwell with a warm glow. She looked one last time at where Kiltar once stood, before descending into the crumbling remains of Parndore Castle.

Down they went, into what was left of the belly of the castle. Open doors led to sheer drops or to buckled flooring that was unsafe to walk on. Windows showed nothing but the dark abyss of night outside. Cracks lined the walls and stairs as they descended further. The only sound was the echo of their footsteps and their heavy breaths.

At the bottom, they stumbled into a large room. Another click of Kinsley's fingers and the candles ignited. Orison knew this room had once been the kitchen, despite having no furniture to indicate its purpose. Given the giant fireplace, the lingering smell of bread, and the fact that it was the basement—there was no denying it.

Kinsley and Aeson continued past the fireplace and opened a rotted wooden door. Following behind them, Orison peeked into the medium-sized room that was illuminated by moonlight. Inside the room was a double bed and a single bed—a servants' room. Aeson clicked his fingers and a candle on the nightstand lit the room. Despite the disrepair, this room felt comfortable.

"What is this place?" Orison finally asked.

Kinsley sat on the double bed with a heavy sigh. "My secret hideout. Usually, I come here to be alone and think. Other times, I take Aeson and Eloise here so my family can't listen in." The sound of Aeson's gasp brought a smile to her face. She winked at him, noting the way his cheeks had turned pink. "It's mine, when I need to be by myself without responsibilities, and it's relatively safe."

Taking up the empty bed opposite Kinsley, Orison began to relax. "Are these beds even safe to sit on?"

Kinsley ran her hand over the blanket. "Yes, these weren't here originally. I found them while exploring Parndore one day, and they were a perfect replacement for the furniture before the beds."

"Now *that* furniture was unsafe to sit on," Aeson interjected.

She stared at the flickering candle, allowing Aeson to kiss her. "I used to come here as a girl when mother and father were arguing, my biological father and mother, I mean."

Orison frowned. "Taviar was married to your mother before Riddle?"

Her eyes widened. "What? No. Taviar was my uncle." It gave Orison an explanation for Sila's insistence on calling the Luxart children Taviar's niece and nephews. "Mother was his sister. But she used to argue with my biological father a lot.

She passed away while birthing my brothers, and my father couldn't cope with the loss. Her dying wish was for Taviar and Riddle to raise us as their own if we become orphaned, which they've more than fulfilled."

"I'm sorry," Orison said and laid down on the bed that groaned in protest.

"Don't feel bad. Though it's sad, I wouldn't have it any other way. Fathers gave me such a happy childhood, and I have no idea where my brothers would be if they didn't step up," Kinsley said with a smile. Aeson laid next to her with his arms around her waist. "But now that I'm twenty, I would like to spread my wings, so to speak, so I come here for freedom."

"You could move out," Orison suggested, staring at the cracked stone ceiling.

After a few moments, Kinsley made a noise. "Let's get to sleep. I don't think Eloise is getting out of Alsaphus Castle until tomorrow morning. Do you, honey?"

"No, I'll send her a message and tell her to meet us in the morning," Aeson replied.

With a wave of her hand, a blast of cold air snuffed out the candle, plunging them into darkness. Another click of Kinsley's fingers and a blanket settled around Orison. "Thank you," Orison whispered.

The room fell silent. Orison admired the struggles that Kinsley had faced in her brief lifetime and how this was her escape. It made her feel less alone about being trapped in one place. However, unlike Kinsley, who was free and could do whatever she desired; Orison was on the run from her captor.

The next morning, Kiltar sat at a veranda table outside a small cafe with Kinsley, Aeson and Orison. Parndore Castle towered above them on a steep hill. The morning sun shone through glassless castle windows and cast a spotlight over the townspeople who were waking up. The true extent of its decay could be seen from the café; only two turrets remained standing, with the rest in a pile of bricks or half-rectified walls.

He sipped on his coffee while they waited for their food to be brought out. Kiltar fixed his attention on Orison. She was scribbling down something in a diary, using a metal stylus that she had purchased from a souvenir shop, before coming to the cafe. She was scribbling little drawings of flowers or birds along the margins, but her hand covered what she was writing. Kiltar was impressed at her skill for drawing, from what he could see. Closing the diary, Orison started tapping the leather binding with the stylus, her brow furrowed in deep thought.

Movement out of the corner of his eye made him turn his attention, thinking it was a server but it was Eloise. Her brown hair fell in soft waves against a grey dress with puffy sleeves. She kissed both Aeson and Kinsley before sitting on the last remaining seat; thanking the server who handed her a menu with a soft smile.

"We suspect Prince Xabian is somewhere in Cardenk," Orison stated in a hushed voice. "Where would you look in the city if you were looking for a prince?"

Eloise looked up from her menu, watching as a server delivered their food to the table. "There's catacombs underneath Cardenk," she stated, allowing room for the server to pour drinks. "He could be there."

Orison cringed. "That's sick."

"El has a point. If Xabian's disappearance is linked to Sila, then I'd imprison him in the catacombs because those are highly illegal to enter," Kinsley explained, as she cut into her chocolate pancakes and took a bite.

"Fuck, do we have to go down there?" Orison shuddered.

Eloise shook her head. "You are a royal, so you can legally go down there with Kiltar." She leaned back in her seat. "But if the rest of us tried, instant execution."

While eating, Kiltar pointed his fork at Eloise in agreement. She couldn't do it. If she did, the king would be alerted to Orison's location in a heartbeat. Then Orison would be locked in Alsaphus Castle with more shields than she could count. It was out of the question and another dead end to the prince's whereabouts; it was getting tedious and annoying.

"Or, we could ask the people living on the viaduct. They may have the answers to your burning questions and a way to enter the catacombs illegally," Kinsley suggested.

"Or we could just relax." Aeson ate his breakfast and sat back. "I'd rather relax."

"After we visit a seer, then we relax," Orison promised.

Kiltar tried to eat his breakfast, but his mind raced. "The cataphiles would have reported if Xabian was in the catacombs, they practically live there. Let's just relax after the seer and make the most of Orison's freedom."

Everybody around the table made noises of agreement. Despite being two months since the prince went missing, they were clutching onto frayed ropes with leads to his whereabouts. Maybe it was too late to save him and that's why there were no more tellages from his name.

Orison sat back while she ate a piece of ham. "Seer, then we can relax," she repeated.

"We're going to have so much fun," Kinsley said with a squeal. "There's so much to see and do here, we can have a repeat of Cardenk."

The three women at the table broke out into laughter; Kiltar and Aeson exchanged glances with a smile. Everybody tucked into their food and coffees were passed around the table; except for Kinsley, who opted for a hot chocolate. During breakfast, they solidified their plan to reach out to a seer to assist them on the quest, still holding onto the hope for more leads to the prince's whereabouts.

The bell rang as Orison stepped into the seer's grotto. The smell of incense instantly assaulted her senses, along with another earthy scent that she wasn't familiar with. Shelves lined the outer walls, all full of jars with unknown substances inside; other than that, the entrance appeared to be empty, aside from a plush red curtain concealing another room. Despite the loudness of Parndore beyond, once that door closed behind her, the seer's grotto was deathly silent—to the point that somebody could hear a pin drop. It was an eerie feeling, so much so that Orison had to look over her shoulder to ensure that her friends were waiting outside.

Mustering up her courage, she approached the red curtain. She pulled it back slowly and stepped into the room, where a woman was sitting at a large round table with a crystal ball in the centre. Orison stifled a gasp to see the woman's eyelids sewn shut. Despite appearing as though she was in her early twenties, the woman's pure white hair suggested she was much older. Trying not to make any noise, Orison bit her lip to silence her breathing and turned around to leave.

"Princess Orison Durham," the seer drawled. Orison paused and turned back around. "You have questions I may be able to answer. Please take a seat."

A seat appeared out of nowhere in front of the woman. Orison hesitated, but tentatively took her seat. The wooden chair groaned as it adjusted to her weight; she clasped her hands in her lap and looked down. Instinct told her she wasn't supposed to be there.

"I have quite a few questions, actually," Orison began and shifted. "First, I would like..."

Without warning, the seer reached over the table and grabbed Orison's hands. She winced as the seer's ice-cold skin met her own. The seer's hands glowed in a pale white hue and the icy sensation intensified. Orison watched in horror as the seer's youthful face morphed into a frail old woman with deep-set wrinkles that clung to her bones and turned grey. The seer's jaw opened, letting out a haunting scream as she began to convulse because of whatever image she was seeing. Out of nowhere, a howling wind whipped around the room, conjuring up pieces of paper and stinging Orison's face with her hair; furniture shattered as it smashed into walls.

It felt like it lasted for an eternity, then the seer collapsed in her chair. "Stop searching for the prince." She rasped. Her face still mottled and grey; her once luscious hair was reduced to two strands on her bald head. She rasped. "Out."

"But I didn't..."

"Get out!" the seer screamed.

Stumbling over her own feet, Orison fell out of the chair and raced through the shop. Her boots banged against the old wooden floorboards; her heart racing at what she had just experienced. She didn't get any answers about what had just occurred or where to find the prince. The bell chimed as she stepped back into the street and ran down the road towards a fountain. Her face was deathly pale and her breathing heavy, as she dipped her face in the fountain.

Orison screamed when a hand pressed on her back; she fell to the cobblestone floor. "Are you okay?" Kinsley asked, crouching down to her level. "You look like you just saw a Rokuba."

"I don't know what the fuck just happened, but I'm not going back there." She looked at the seer's grotto. "Please, can we just relax today?"

Kinsley helped her up and they joined the rest of their group. Despite the seer's warning, she couldn't allow herself to stop searching. The prince needed to come home. She had to take her mind off the experience with the seer; she didn't want to be reminded of it.

Eighteen

To take Orison's mind off the recent horrendous encounter, Kinsley and Eloise dragged her into various shops to try on clothes or hair accessories. They bought what they could afford. Sometimes the shopkeepers recognised Orison and gave her clothes for free—she guessed it was a privilege of being a princess. Aeson and Kiltar hung back, keeping a close eye on them; in case there were any threats or if the king was alerted that the princess was there. When the women were satisfied with their shopping, they ventured off to explore the local historical sites to further educate Orison on Fallasingha history.

With all the fun they were having, time passed quickly; it felt like only an hour had passed before sunset came. They headed back to Parndore Castle, before Kiltar would change in front of thousands of witnesses. But as the sky grew more orange and fire-red, Kiltar realised they had run out of time. He decided to cut his losses and Misted there instead, to prevent a catastrophe.

Throughout their walk, a large crowd of people caught Orison's attention, along with the sound of drums. She paused to look at what was happening, standing on her tiptoes to get a better vantage point; however, she couldn't see anything. Glancing over her shoulder, Orison saw that Kinsley, Eloise and Aeson gave permission to follow the sound. A smile spread across her face as her friends ushered for her to go. She wasn't used to being granted permission so easily in the Othereal—not without a fight.

She ran over to the crowd and pushed through until she was at the front where a fire barrier prevented anybody from going into the performance area. She was grateful for the spectacle before her own eyes. Occasionally, Fire Singers on Merchant's Row would provide people with the gift of a fire dance. This was no different, except for the fact it was on a much larger scale.

Two shirtless men spun chains of fire in dizzying circles around themselves, creating rings of fire that hummed through the air to the beat of the drums. Behind the men were a handful of other people in the shadows, beating drums and tapping their feet as they got lost in rhythm. A chorus of gasps pulled Orison's attention to a third male who leapt through the air and into a front flip where he landed on one knee as he breathed fire. The people with a front-row seat parted ways to make room for the performance.

Emerging from the shadows were five beautiful women dressed in ornate dresses. On their hands and wrists were bands of fire. They danced along to the beat, clapping and shaking to the drums, making the fire on their bodies dance in perfect harmony. The two men with chains had changed their entertainment, this time juggling with flaming pins. Orison's eyes lit up in amazement. As the women spun around the men, it looked like their feet were nothing but flames—a giant tiger made purely of fire leapt towards the crowd before dissipating into fireworks.

"This is beautiful," Orison gasped.

One of the women took the hand of a child, gently pulling them into the performance area. Soon there was a chain of people, all coming together in a giant dance of fire. Men, women and children laughed as they skipped along to the beat of the drums. Orison, Eloise, Aeson and Kinsley were swept up into the chain. The laughter of the participants was contagious. It took Orison a while to find the correct footing, but nobody cared, as long as she was having fun.

Each link of the chain eventually broke off into different groups. Orison was spun around in dizzying circles as they passed her from one stranger to the next. She could have stayed in Parndore's main square forever; dancing with fire until her feet hurt, laughing or smiling until her cheeks ached—forgetting everything that was weighing her down. She was free.

After two hours of dancing, some of the performers passed around drinks and free food. The hospitality in Parndore was something Orison hadn't experienced anywhere outside of Merchant's Row. Taviar had warned her that the hospitality in the city was infectious; he was correct. Orison wished she could stay in the city for much longer than a day, but she knew she had to move on before the king found her.

Stumbling through the crowd just after midnight, Orison's head was spinning from the copious amounts of alcohol that she had consumed. She searched for Kinsley; they both needed to be sober enough for their journey tomorrow. Where that journey led, she didn't know.

The search didn't take long; she found Kinsley on the edge of a fountain making out with Eloise and Aeson simultaneously. Scratching the back of her neck, Orison knew she was capable of Misting herself back to Parndore Castle. She didn't have to rely on Kinsley, despite being drunk and untrained.

I'll meet you at the castle, Orison told her through her mind.

Kinsley stared at Orison as Aeson kissed her neck. *Meet you in the morning.*

She dipped her chin and Misted herself back to the castle in a flurry of purple night and stars.

A scraping sound made Orison jolt up in bed. Sunlight streamed in through the single window and a dark figure stood in the doorway. Despite the pounding in her head, she tried to focus on the dark figure. It was Kinsley, who had a dreamy look on her face; she crawled onto the double bed and laid down, staring at the ceiling with a grin. She was wearing the green dress from the night before, but now it didn't sit correctly on her body—the sleeve hanging off her shoulder and the corset belt being off-centre. Orison did a double-take when she noticed Kinsley wasn't wearing any shoes.

"Somebody had a great night," Orison commented, lying back down and tugging the blanket up to her neck.

Another grin spread across Kinsley's face as she laughed. "You don't want to know the details. All I can say is, I'm very satisfied in more ways than one."

They both laughed. Orison stretched with a yawn. "Where are we going today, hungover and all?"

"I was thinking of exploring Cleravoralis," Kinsley said with a smile, still staring at the ceiling. Orison's heart leapt with excitement. "I've always wanted to see it. Aeson is meeting us this afternoon to go there."

"Well, let's get cleaned up and head out there," Orison told her with an excited smile.

Kinsley nodded. "I didn't get any sleep, so I'll get a few hours before we go."

Orison couldn't fault that. She saw to her needs in a bucket that Kinsley had assigned, then Misted to the main town to use a bathhouse, getting cleaned up while Kinsley slept. Orison grabbed breakfast and some lunch that they could take to Cleravoralis. She was ready for a new adventure.

The flight to Cleravoralis took an hour on Aeson's back. He landed in a large clearing within a dense forest. Birds chirped in the trees, pixies flew around; trolls ran and hid, once they saw the Fae had landed in their territory. Around them, the forest smelled like fresh pine wood and the earthy scent of rain. Kinsley was the first to climb off Aeson's back, then helped Orison dismount. Back on solid ground, Orison inhaled the crisp air as she looked around. In the blink of an eye, Aeson shifted back into his Fae form and stretched, shaking out his body like a dog when it got wet.

"Does it hurt when you change?" Orison asked him. She knew how much pain Kiltar experienced when he made the change and didn't want that for Aeson.

He shook his head. "No, it feels as normal as using your powers."

Orison had yet to experience the normality of using her powers. It still felt unnatural and awkward in this early stage of being Fae, but she could understand why. She turned to look around the forest, pausing at a corridor of trees that gave way to a large open field; but it wasn't an open field at all—mounds of ivy were growing into the shape of buildings.

"I knew nature had taken hold, but not like this," Kinsley muttered under her breath as she adjusted her satchel, tugging down Aeson's shirt that she was wearing. "Let's go."

They turned towards the mounds of ivy. Kinsley's feet crunched over leaves and other foliage as she approached. Orison looked down when soft ground became moss-covered cobblestone. Both women looked at each other when they realised that this was all that remained of Cleravoralis. It was upsetting to see that in twenty years the town had become ivy and moss infested stone, instead of a city.

Orison looped her arm through Kinsley's as they walked into the city. "It's kind of sad," she admitted. "Somebody cursed to be a Nyxite caused all this destruction."

"Some people say this place is cursed, but it's just hearsay," Kinsley said, looking around.

Kinsley rolled up the sleeves of Aeson's shirt, that hung over her black trousers. She savoured the cool nature of the surrounding forest, her curls bounced with each step. With a tug on her arm, Kinsley followed Orison into a building that had a visible opening.

The door was a curtain of ivy that they pushed aside; the floor was buckled, making it hard to hold their footing. They had to crouch down where sections of the roof had caved in. From what they could see, it looked like the occupants had just left for the day; the table still held four placements. The rocking chair that was caged off by fallen roof timbers still had a blanket on it. Every other room was overtaken by nature and any semblance of the occupants permanently destroyed.

Orison emerged out of the wrecked home. Her foot crunched over charred pieces of roof tiles. All of them jumped when they heard something collapse within one of the buildings—probably a roof caving in under the weight of the ivy.

Shortly thereafter, Orison watched Kinsley emerge onto the street, brushing dust off her trousers. Kinsley looked at Aeson who leaned against a broken street light. "It's all plants, with some furniture," she said, wiping her hands together and taking in their surroundings.

Ultimately, there was nothing left of Cleravoralis, even when the three of them ventured deeper into the ivy-covered city. Orison had assumed that at least one resident would have stuck around to maintain the town. If all Nyxites were cursed, as Kiltar had claimed, then this particular Nyxite was enraged. There was a motive behind this attack.

They found themselves on the main street, which was evident by the fallen shop signs on the cobblestones—now overtaken by moss. Kinsley looked up at the lone clock tower in the middle of a forgotten fountain. Vines poured out of the spout like the water that used to flow through its inner mechanisms, pooling at the bottom with thorns. The air was silent, apart from the birds that took up residence in the missing clock face, singing an afternoon song. It was beauty in the face of chaos, a true testament that time was the real warrior in this war.

A bad feeling washed over Orison; it was like a heavy weight on her shoulders, telling her something was watching them. She paused, letting the rest of the group walk ahead as she observed the situation. Nothing appeared out of place; Orison suspected it was an animal at first. Shaking off the bad feeling, she took all but two steps before the metallic scent of King Sila's magic stung her nose and a cyclone of leaves spun around her. She didn't need to turn around to know who had appeared—she saw the fear in Kinsley's eyes as soon as she turned around to check on her.

"Game over," Sila sneered.

Kinsley cried out as guards surrounded Aeson, forcing his hands behind his back. He wasn't blessed with Desigles protection—like Kinsley and Orison. Struggling against their grip, he tried to change into a bird to fly away, but the manacles of fire seared his wrist and nullified his powers.

"Run!" Aeson screamed, before guards blew a powder into his face that knocked him unconscious.

The guards stepped toward Kinsley. "I love you; I'll rescue you, I promise," she said to Aeson.

Orison fled, grabbing Kinsley's hand as she tried to navigate through the vine-riddled town. Every so often, they had to leap over a branch or a piece of debris, but all exits leading out of the main square of Cleravoralis were blocked by the king's men. Orison gasped when she glanced over her shoulder to see the guards close behind her. Sila walked at a leisurely pace with a smirk on his face. Pushing herself harder, Orison slowed down as she struggled to breathe. *Run*, Kinsley said to her mind, *run like Fallagh, my future queen.*

Throwing her magic blindly at the guards was no use; they wore something that protected them against it. Orison grimaced as cramp became a vice around her calf; regardless, she continued to run. Remembering the Desigle, Orison realised the king couldn't change the location of where she Misted to; she needed freedom, even if it was just for one more day.

Orison thought of Cardenk and soon a flurry of purple night and stars enveloped the pair of them. She glanced at Kinsley when she gripped her hand tighter. The purple night and stars were replaced with green smoke and vines, as they

Misted to a different location entirely. A place of sanctuary away from the prying eyes of a heinous, power-hungry king.

Nineteen

Seagulls cawed around the place where they Misted to, their calls enhanced by the acoustics of a bridge. As Orison turned to face a possible exit, she could see a rolling coastal town built into tiers against a cliff side. The seafront was heaving with people, either enjoying the stifling heat of the environment or selling goods to visitors. It was a far cry from the forest areas that she was used to. The sweltering air made the smell of locally caught fish overpowering, making Kinsley retch.

"Where are we?" Orison asked.

Kinsley pushed her hair away from her face, her forehead already gleamed with sweat. "Tsunamal." Wind roared through the bridge and from purple smoke, Kiltar appeared. "Well, it's about time you showed up! Did the Desigle only just notify you of the literal shit we were in?" She let out an exasperated breath. "You should have come with us to Cleravoralis."

"Some of us have other duties aside from trying to keep you both alive," Kiltar snapped. "And yes, it only just Misted me here. This place stinks! Let's just talk about this at a hotel."

Walking along the footpath, they helped each other onto a dock where a set of stone steps led to the bustling seafront. Fishermen haggled their daily catch; others were selling handcrafted goods from little stalls. It was very different from the sleepy villages they had visited prior to Tsunamal. Kiltar approached a fisherman, bartered for a large cod and a turkey; and handed over his coin. Then the friends continued throughout the city.

Finding a set of stairs, Kiltar allowed Orison and Kinsley to go first, watching their movements from behind as they began their ascent higher into the city. The steep incline was gruelling to climb; the streets were narrow and winding. By the time they made it to Siren Bed & Breakfast, the group was soaked in sweat. Being up this high gave them the perfect view of the sea, where boats bobbed along on their journey to distant shores. Orison wished she was on one of those boats, no matter the destination. Seagulls hovered in warm air pockets or dived where they found food sources.

As Kiltar opened the gate, he led them both into a beautiful courtyard. Flowers were in full bloom around a flowing fountain, where ornamental fish spat water into a large basin. Orison looked around with a smile on her face, clasping her hands in front of her as she took in the beautiful sight around her.

"Orison," Kiltar's voice cut through her reverie. He gestured to the inn's entrance and she hurried after him. "Is this your first time in a coastal city?"

"No, I've been lots of times," she lied.

"Liar." Kiltar smirked. She gave him a glare. "Nobody gawps like a fish when they're used to being in a coastal city."

She playfully smacked his arm. He flinched with a laugh as he held the door open for them. Kinsley and Orison stepped into the brightly lit entrance; the door closed when Kiltar joined them. In the centre of the foyer was a table with an enormous bouquet of flowers placed on top. Along the white panelled walls were oil paintings of unique landscapes that made Orison smile.

"Welcome," a female behind the desk said to them. She had pale blue skin; Orison could have sworn that she saw gills on the woman's neck.

Kiltar stepped forward, putting a bag of coins on the desk. "Three rooms please."

The woman sucked in a breath. "We only have two rooms left, I'm afraid. The Honeymoon Suite and a double."

"We'll take it," Kiltar chuckled. "Don't want to climb any more stairs." The clerk laughed. When he glanced over his shoulder, Orison baulked at the fact that they had the Honeymoon Suite, of all rooms. "Kinsley, you can share the suite with Orison. I'll take the double."

Kinsley smiled. "Sure. I'll make a call to Eloise and tell her the situation."

Stepping up to Kiltar, Orison watched him exchange the money for the keys. She took the Honeymoon Suite key while Kinsley was outside talking to her girlfriend; Kiltar pocketed the other one. Orison was thankful that she wasn't sharing a room with Kiltar; it would have been awkward with him being a guard on duty. Regardless, Orison didn't want to stray too far from Kiltar, especially after what happened in Cleravoralis.

On the second floor, the only differences from the foyer were the paintings on the walls. There were nautical themes with various aquatic creatures, in golden frames. It was comforting to see that Kiltar's room was on the entrance to the corridor. When he opened the door, Orison saw a double bed and a door leading to a balcony that overlooked the ocean. Leaving him to wash up, Orison made her way to the Honeymoon Suite. A giggle from behind her made her turn around. Kinsley was hurrying to her; more like skipping. With a shake of her head, Orison placed the key into the lock.

"Out of all the rooms—the Honeymoon Suite," muttered Orison as she turned the key.

Kinsley laughed as she pushed the door open. "Are you coming in, Wifey?"

"I thought it was tradition to carry me over the threshold, Wifey," Orison replied as she twirled into the room with a curtsy. "I suppose walking through has to be acceptable."

Both women fell into fits of giggles. Orison's laughter ceased when she saw the ocean view that stretched on for miles. It was like she was on a boat, despite knowing she was in the heavens above a bustling city. Tearing her gaze from the stunning view, she turned to the bed and groaned when she saw rose petals raining down in the perfect formation of a love heart. She stifled a laugh to see chocolate roses bloom out of nothing.

"Of course, the Honeymoon Suite has to be enchanted," Kinsley said with a slight giggle. She scratched the back of her neck at the awkwardness of the situation. "We're just friends, Room." Hearing a metallic clink from a metal tin, she turned her head. "But thank you for the chocolate-coated strawberries, anyway."

Running her fingers over the soft quilt, Orison tilted her head to the side. "Are we sharing a bed or is somebody taking the sofa?" Her gaze fell on the white sofa near the bed. "I don't mind either way."

Eating a chocolate-coated strawberry, Kinsley looked around. "Eloise said we can share the bed, so I suppose it's alright." She pushed the rose petals to one side and laid down. "It's an extremely comfortable one."

"You asked your girlfriend for permission?" Orison asked, tugging her boots off.

"I didn't have to, but it puts my mind at ease," Kinsley said, staring at the ceiling.

Orison laid beside her, looking at herself in the mirrors hanging above the bed. "The mirrors are kind of creepy."

"But you can watch your performance," Kinsley said, laughing.

Orison propped up on her elbows, looking at her friend. "Ew, Kins!" Kinsley giggled, tears streaming down her cheeks. "Othereal above."

Aside from the mirrors above the bed, Kinsley was correct that it was the most comfortable bed she had ever rested on. Pushing herself off the bed, Orison went exploring.

Another room near the front door was a bathing chamber. All of the walls were made of black rock; a hot spring bath lay in the centre. A cool ocean breeze flowed through the open gap where a window should be. Water from the tub trickled over the edge and down the cliff face that the inn was built upon. Turning back to Kinsley, Orison found she had fallen asleep where she lay. Orison returned to the bathing chamber and stepped inside. She locked the door to enjoy the warm Tsunamal air and relax in the comfort of a hot bath.

The sound of a fist pounding on the door stirred Orison from her slumber. "Ori, are you in there?" Kinsley shouted.

With a groan, she rubbed her eyes and looked around the bath she was in. "I'm going to come in there if you don't answer me. Three..."

"I'm... I'm fine. Just fell asleep, don't come in," Orison called back.

"Othereal above!" Kinsley gasped. Water splashed as Orison neared the side of the tub. She looked around for a towel. "Kiltar made lunch, it's ready when you are."

Grabbing a towel nearby, Orison lifted herself out of the tub as she wrapped it around her body. Water splattered onto the stone floor. Still groggy from sleep, she looked around for her clothes. She was sure that she had left them on the floor—only to find they were missing. Orison groaned as she approached the door.

"Ori, are you okay?"

Unlocking the door, Orison opened it slightly, using the door as a shield against her body. "Room has taken my clothes," she admitted, feeling heat go to her cheeks. Kinsley pointed to the footstool at the end of the bed. Her clothes sat cleaned and neatly folded. "I suppose it's for the best, I had been wearing them for three days. Still, why did Room do that?"

"I actually don't have a clue. It's kind of perverted."

Hearing the ruffle of fabric, Orison looked over her shoulder to see a pale pink dress landing on a hook next to a fluffy white robe. She rolled her eyes. "Thanks, Room."

Orison disappeared back into the bathing chambers, getting dressed in the outfit that Room had picked out. The pink fabric hugged her figure perfectly, providing a sheer train that trailed behind her. Returning to the room, Orison made a beeline to the balcony; the smell of grilled meat as her guide to a fully prepared lunch. She hadn't eaten since breakfast, and at this point, the picnic that she picked up from Cleravoralis would be inedible. Turning the corner, she found Kiltar and Kinsley sitting around a fire pit. He did a double-take when she made an appearance.

"You look beautiful!" Kiltar exclaimed.

Orison sat down with a smile. "Thank you."

Taking a plate of grilled fish and turkey from Kiltar, Kinsley set it on her lap. "It is a possibility that Prince Xabian probably sought passage to another land from here," she stated as she picked at the fish.

"But the sirens said he's in Cardenk," Orison corrected.

"Maybe they lied," Kiltar said, eating some turkey.

Kinsley looked down at her plate. "Will you tell us what happened at the seer's grotto?" She gave her friend an apprehensive look. "Come on, Ori, it may give us clues. You looked terrified, didn't she Kiltar?"

Taking her plate from Kiltar, Orison sighed and told them everything. How the seer grabbed her by the hand, knowing she wasn't a princess to the Alsaphus line; and how she turned into a frail old woman as she sought Orison's future. Even talking about the visit to the seer made Orison feel paranoid and uneasy; like the seer was inside her soul and wreaking havoc on it.

Kiltar poked at the meat sizzling in a pan above the fire pit. "I don't even have to ask if you're going to follow the seer's warning. I know you're still going to search."

"Of course, I'm going to keep searching. If the king didn't stick his dick in everything and actually looked for his family, then I wouldn't be stepping up to the plate," Orison snapped, earning a chuckle from Kinsley. "I need to know he's safe. It's been two months and nobody seems to care about him. What if he's injured, or... or the king killed him and he's dead in a ditch somewhere?"

They both looked at Kiltar when he let out a hearty laugh. "Do you even know the king?"

Orison rolled her eyes. She already knew that the king could murder people and make it look like the person never existed. Why not add his brother to the mix of those victims? She'd seen it plenty of times. She sat back as she ate her lunch, looking out to the sea. Maybe he did go off to distant shores without anyone realising.

There was an awkward silence, with only the crash of waves against the rocks and the clattering of their utensils on their plates. In the end, they talked about other topics, such as how Orison felt in Parndore and Cardenk. She reminisced about Lake Braloak, excluding the riddles the sirens provided—they didn't need to talk about Prince Xabian now.

At sunset, when Kiltar had gone somewhere to make the change in private, Room provided them with wine. Once she was tipsy, Orison talked about her life in the mortal lands and how Saskia's home reminded her of it. Also, how her mother used to brush her hair while her father told her faerie tales. Orison was under the impression they were nothing more than stories. Her father was an excellent storyteller. He was a strong man from his job as a woodworker, so he could put up a good fight if provoked. Her heart ached at the fact that she would never see them again.

When she woke up, her view was of Kiltar staring down at her. With the halo of sunlight around his head, he looked like an angel; the stars in his eyes danced as he took in Orison's features. He was smiling as he gently ran his hand up her arm, making her shudder. The air around them felt like a magnet, there was a tug towards him that she hadn't felt before.

"Can I kiss you?" he asked.

Orison nodded as he played with her hair. He brought his mouth to hers; the kiss was sensuous. Kiltar pulled her closer as his hands wandered over her body. She sank into the pillows of the bed; Orison ran her hands up his back as he deepened the kiss and a moan escaped her lips. His hand travelled up her thigh. As if snapping out of the spell, Orison soon realised what was happening.

"Stop," Orison said quickly, pushing him away. "What are you doing here?"

Kiltar sat up, snapping out of the spell. His eyes widened. "Holy shit!" he shouted. "I'm... I'm sorry. I don't know what came over me."

Propping herself up on her elbows, Orison looked around. She was definitely still in the Honeymoon Suite. No windows or doors were open; it was just how she left it when she and Kinsley went to bed. Even though they had drank alcohol the night before, neither of them were drunk enough to black out, nor switch rooms.

"Othereal above," she gasped, tugging down her nightgown that had risen up from Kiltar's wandering hands. Orison touched her mouth and looked at Kiltar. Realisation set in on what had made their morning kisses occur. "Room!"

Kiltar raised an eyebrow as he pulled a pillow onto his lap. "What about the room?"

"It's enchanted to encourage lovemaking," Orison groaned as she collapsed back against the pillows. She looked at herself in the mirror above her bed, turning to Kiltar when he started chuckling with a shake of his head. "Stop laughing."

He held his hand up with a smile. "Well, it's funny that it almost succeeded. Almost." The comment earned him a glare. "You aren't a bad kisser, in case you wanted to know."

Orison rolled her eyes as she brought up the blanket to hide her cleavage. Room had given her a skimpy red nightgown that she kept tugging down so it didn't show off any more of her body. Both of them jumped when the door burst open and Kinsley stepped into the room.

"How in the Othereal did I end up in Kiltar's bed?" Kinsley spat, throwing his shirt to him. He quickly put it on and looked at the two women.

"I suspect the room has figured out I'm not attracted to women and switched our rooms, knowing we're in a group together," Orison explained and climbed out of the bed. "I'm going to change into something that doesn't make me look like a whore." Orison's cheeks still felt like they were on fire, her lips tingled from the kiss. She gave Kiltar one last look as she left the room and slipped into the bathing chamber.

When in the bathing chamber, Orison saw to her needs. She partially forgave Room when it provided her a midnight-purple wrap dress with dainty slippers after she had taken a bath. The dress was perfect for a day at the beach. Plucking it from the hanger, she put it on and used her magic to fix her hair. Orison was ready to face Tsunamal. A drastic plan came to mind; she just hoped she could pull it off without being caught.

Twenty

Tsunamal was heaving with people on the seafront who were exploring the beach. Orison, Kiltar and Kinsley navigated their way through the crowd to the docks; where visitors sought passage to faraway lands that Orison could only dream of.

The noise surrounding them was almost deafening. Men barked orders as their boots pounded on the wooden pier; they unloaded the imported goods brought into Fallasingha from other realms. Ships bobbed on the ocean waves. Away from the docks, people relaxed on the sand and children played in the water. Seagulls hovered in the air and cawed as they swooped through the cloudless sky.

A lowly man sat at a desk offering destinations to places that made Orison's heart skip a beat in excitement. Her need for travel was like a need for water in a vast desert. The list was endless—Marona, Valhaevn, Karshakroh. She didn't need to look at the prices; Kiltar had stolen a handful of gold coins from Sila's vault so they could sail to safety. Orison coughed as smoke from the man's pipe hit her airways. He looked at her with brown, vacant eyes; his beard unruly.

"Three passages to Karshakroh," she said as confidently as she could.

He grumbled something. "Twelve bronze." She put down a gold coin. The dealer's eyes widened in wonder. It was more than enough for a stateroom on the ship. Bronze meant sleeping in the galley, pressed against strangers in cramped quarters riddled with diseases and rats. "You want the staterooms?"

"Yes, I require them with my lady in wait. My husband is over there," she pointed out Kiltar who leaned against a pillar nearby. "Three staterooms."

He scooped up the coin while puffing on his pipe. The man pushed three golden sheets of parchment with Karshakroh stamped in the centre. Orison thanked him while putting the tickets into her bag, then headed back into the throng of people. She smiled at Kinsley and Kiltar as she got closer to them. Kinsley's smile disappeared, turning to an expression of horror; Orison's heart skipped a beat. Kinsley shouted something inaudible, making the hairs on the back of Orison's neck stand on end.

"Orison," a voice crooned.

She turned around, only to face a mysterious grey powder—it was instant. One minute she was awake, the next collapsed on the pier with a thud. Before Kiltar or Kinsley could come to her aid, the powder allowed her assailant to reach through the Desigle's shield and Mist her back to Alsaphus Castle.

When Orison regained consciousness, she immediately knew where she was from the grey brick ceiling above her. Her heart raced when she realised she was back in Alsaphus Castle. The sound of slurping made her roll onto her stomach. Lifting her head, she forced herself to face Sila slouched on the throne, sipping from his usual goblet. He glared at her.

"It's nice to see you've bothered to wake up." She reeled back, hitting the nearest pillar. Taking in her surroundings, guards were stationed everywhere. *No!* She fumbled for her bag, but it had been taken from her. "Are you looking for this?" Sila held her bag up and pulled out the tickets she purchased. "Thinking you can seek passage to Karshakroh, of all places? You're nothing more than a pathetic brat!"

Orison cried out when he set fire to her tickets. She covered her mouth to stifle the noise. She should be on a boat escaping him; not in the throne room being interrogated by the brutish man who kidnapped her from the mortal realm. Where were Kinsley and Kiltar? Were they captured? Orison's mind reeled with the possibilities of their fate.

The doors of the throne room echoed against the stone walls as they were flung open. It took all of her effort not to turn around. She squeezed her eyes shut, not wanting to see who they had rounded up, yet the loud thud deceived her. Orison yelped to see Aeson on his knees, tendrils of greasy auburn hair in his face. His skin was mottled with bruises and he had a split lip; manacles of fire prevented him from moving.

"Let him go, he's done nothing wrong!" Orison shouted.

"Nothing wrong?" Sila roared with laughter—a rarity to hear. "Nothing wrong!" She jumped when he threw his goblet of wine, which shattered on the stone floor as he approached her. "He helped you deceive me and make me look like a laughing stock, you fucking wench!" Orison trembled and looked at the floor. "Look at me!"

She raised her head, glaring at Sila. Her nails dug into the stone floor as her blood boiled. She wanted to see Sila's blood spilled for hurting Aeson and for what he did to her. Aeson turned his head to look at her. One of his eyes was swollen shut and dried blood painted his face, which made her even more angry.

"I am the one that defied you, not Aeson. Let him go!"

Sila glared. "He's sentenced to an execution because of your defiance. His death is your punishment for running away from me!"

The sting of tears made her blink her eyes. She wouldn't let Sila see her cry anymore—he enjoyed it too much. She pushed her emotions down into a dark crevice where she felt no emotion. Sila was a monster that she hated with a passion. If she didn't have the Desigle, she would claw his face off. In actuality, she didn't know the true implications of the Desigle. Her trembling hands shook for a different reason—rage.

"You're a monster." Orison snorted and spat in his face.

Sila wiped the ball of saliva from his face and glared at Orison. "Take him back to the dungeon."

The guards grabbed Aeson roughly, dragging him away. He allowed it to happen as though he had given up what little fight he had left in him. He stared at the floor; no life left in his eyes. Orison wondered if Eloise had been to try and heal him. The throne room doors opened and once the procession of people passed the threshold, they closed.

"Who helped you survive this past week without me?" Sila's question made Orison jump. She turned to him. He played with his cufflinks as he watched. "Who helped you defy me and make me look weak?"

Orison remained silent, staring at the floor, hoping he'd go away. She knew he couldn't touch her, nor the guards who meant her harm; but the way Sila stared at her felt like a heavy weight had slammed down on her. Orison wouldn't show him weakness, even if he was her worst nightmare incarnate.

Standing up, Sila strolled down the dais and crouched to her level, sneering at her defiance.

The ground shook as Sila tried to grab her face and make her look at him; but flames seared his hand, causing him to cry out as his skin blistered. Orison heard him call her a wench again as he held his hand to his chest, fire-red hair falling into his face as his breathing increased. She bit back a smirk; for once she felt powerful, not weak like Sila wanted. Now he was the weak one for trying to force her into something.

Orison finally lifted her head. "My personal guard Misted me to a safe location when he saw you push me from the tower," she explained.

Sila raised an eyebrow. "What personal guard?" He glared at her. "You're too pathetic to have a personal guard, so why would I provide you with one?"

The guards around the throne room seemed to step closer to listen; the surrounding air grew heavy. She needed Kiltar or Kinsley, wherever they may be. Looking at her hands, Orison wrung them together on her lap.

"Well, he said you hired him to be under my jurisdiction as princess," Orison said boldly, looking at the king.

He sat back on his throne with a scoff. "Do you think you're so special to have a guard, after your behaviour?" Orison glared at him. "You're nothing without me. Now give me the name of this so-called guard so I can execute him accordingly for being a spy."

She said the first name that came to her head; the name of the bartender she knew in the mortal realm. "Darius Hardin."

A guard stepped forward. "Princess Orison is lying, Your Highness."

Orison screamed, shielding her head as he threw another goblet of wine at her. She bit her lip as she sobbed out of fear. She heard the clatter of the goblet on the stone floor as it bounced off her Desigle, landing somewhere else.

"Tell me!" Sila screamed so loud that her bones vibrated.

"Kiltar Sarling!" Orison screamed back, out of terror. Her hands shook violently on her shoulders as she held herself. "His name is Kiltar!"

Sila laughed. "There are no guards in this castle by that name and never will be."

Twenty-One

Leaves rustled along the stone pathway in Saskia's garden. With a flurry of purple night, Kiltar staggered towards the stone wall. He grimaced as he tried to catch his breath; Kinsley Misted next to him shortly after. Orison was gone. The king had succeeded in his quest to return Orison to the castle; Kiltar had failed to stop him.

Saskia stood up from her cabbage patch. Her oversized sun hat covered her eyes, but he could tell that she was concerned. It was written all over her face. Pulling off her muddy gardening gloves, she approached Kiltar and put a hand on his arm. He turned and pulled her into a tight embrace like she'd go missing too, needing the comfort after failing Orison.

"Is everything okay, Poppet?" She rubbed Kiltar's back.

"Orison's gone. The king succeeded in returning her to the castle," Kiltar gasped. He squeezed his eyes shut. "I failed."

She swayed from side to side. "Oh, Poppet. You didn't fail, it was going to happen eventually." She kissed his cheek and patted his back, looking at Kinsley over his shoulder. "She has her Desigle. Kinsley will be her watchful eyes too, so will Eloise and Aeson. You did all you could in the time you had."

Kiltar held Saskia close to him as he tried to relax. Watching an undercover guard Misting Orison away in a flurry of blue smoke had made him scream. The entire dock had looked at him in bewilderment. There were so many people, no one noticed someone being knocked unconscious and Misted away. Kiltar, Kinsley and Orison were never destined to travel to brighter horizons.

"I need to go back to the castle," Kiltar announced as he pulled away and turned to Kinsley. She had been in too much shock to say anything since the incident. "I have to see if she's okay."

Saskia baulked and placed her hands on her hips. "No, you don't. Not while you both look like you just peered into the Mirror of Zaneth. You need to calm down before either of you go, or people will be suspicious." He groaned with a roll of his eyes, but she pointed to the front door. "Go."

Teetering on his feet, Kiltar led Kinsley to the entrance of the cottage, leaving Saskia to return to her duties in the garden. He hoped that Orison was okay in the castle and wasn't subjected to too many horrors.

There are no guards in this castle by that name. Sila's words kept ringing through Orison's head ever since they had passed his lips. Now, Orison didn't know who Kiltar was. She couldn't believe she fell for the inkling that she could trust him. That trust had been taken away until she got her answers.

She had slept most of the day, exhausted from the side effects of the strange powder blown into her face. By the time she had peeled herself out of bed, the sun was setting behind the mountains, casting her chambers into a soft iridescent glow. Orison opened her bedroom door and made her way over to the window seat behind her dining table. With a heavy sigh, she sat down on the plush cushions and looked out at the forest of trees through her window. She should be down there—exploring cities and towns, dancing with Fire Singers or pixies, or on the boat to Karshakroh. She should have been on that ship.

Memories of the past week slammed into Orison. It took her away from Alsaphus Castle as she pictured the fire dancers, Parndore Castle and Cleravoralis. She remembered the sirens and water nymphs in Lake Braloak, and Tsunamal. Orison was so lost in her head that she didn't feel the phantom wind filling her chambers, or Kiltar standing right behind her until he cleared his throat. She jumped and grabbed the window ledge to look at her intruder. Her eyes widened when she saw him; he looked relieved to see she was okay, but Orison was furious.

"Guards! Spy in the castle!" Orison shouted without taking her eyes off of him. "Guards!"

"Orison don't..." Kiltar started. She grabbed a nearby vase and with one swift movement it flew through the air. He dodged out of the way, causing glass and flowers to shatter across the floor; water pooled at his feet. "What the fuck has he done to you?"

Grabbing a cup from her dining table, Orison threw it at him. It bounced off his shoulder before shattering on the floor. "How fucking dare you lie to me about being a guard!" she shouted. "I believed you because I don't know any better in this shitty realm, only to find out you're a spy!"

Kiltar laughed at that. "No, Ori, spying is..."

"You don't get to call me Ori until you explain yourself!"

"Apologies, Orison, spying is an unnecessary task for me. I already know enough of the castle's secrets, so it's pointless." She glared at him and blinked a couple of times when his eyes started glowing. Sunset, of course. "I used to be a guard before the curse. I'm no spy."

"He said there has never been a guard called Kiltar and never will be," she snapped. The glowing had increased. They were running out of time to talk this out. "You're changing, you need to leave before Sila kills you."

A burst of light erupted out of Kiltar and he screamed in agony. Orison stumbled backwards onto a curtain holdback; she winced as pain enveloped her. The surrounding room shook violently, plates on the dining table rattled until they shattered to the ground. His screaming intensified to the point that Orison cupped her hands over her ears. Out of fear, she screamed as well, until the light had dissipated and Kiltar's Nyxite form crouched in front of her.

With rapid breaths, she pushed herself away from the bench and approached Kiltar. Glass crunched underneath her slippers; she knelt in front of him. "If you're here to help me, you must assist me with getting Aeson out of the dungeons." She ran her hand through his fur. "Tonight."

Before Orison could say another word to him, Kiltar ran out of the dining room and disappeared into the night via her bedroom. Orison collapsed on the cold stone floor, wincing as glass cut into her hand from the vase she had smashed. Placing her hand over her heart, she tried to wrap her head around the information. Today had been long and gruelling, challenging her in more ways than one. Her hand trembled violently as she took in the surrounding destruction. When the door to her chamber opened, Orison looked up to see Aiken.

"Othereal above, what happened, Princess?" she exclaimed. She hurried over to Orison, her feet crunched over glass and porcelain. Aiken plucked her off the floor and Orison collapsed against the servant.

"Lost control of my balance and my magic, I'm fine," Orison lied. She was not fine—she should be halfway across the Falshak Sea by now; and her friend was in the dungeons. Eyam Misted into the room with a dustpan and brush.

"Aiken, could you assist me with getting ready for dinner?" Orison pleaded.

With a nod, Aiken pressed a hand to the small of Orison's back and guided her into the bedroom. She appreciated Aiken not saying anything about her trembling hands or the rapid beating of her heart. While getting ready, Orison told Aiken everything she had experienced over the past week in an excited rush—only to be filled with misery at the probability she may never experience such things again.

The guard uniform was heavier than Orison imagined; no wonder the guards were muscular. Regardless, she would adorn this disguise to save her friend and free him from execution. She brushed her hair into a ponytail. Kiltar waited on the balcony for her to finish getting ready. Her stomach was a war of butterflies as she practised a deep voice. She had to do this for Aeson, Kinsley and Eloise; but most importantly, for herself.

Misting to the servants' stairwell, Orison descended into the belly of the castle, to where the servants' dormitories and the dungeons were. The stairs were more worn out than on the higher levels. Each dizzying step made her apprehensive as she descended. She steadied herself to prevent tripping from wearing boots a few sizes too big. Her only relief was that no servants were around so early in the morning.

Orison had been prohibited this far down, due to a shield that Sila erected. After this experience, she didn't particularly want to again. She swore when she slipped on a slick section of stone. Voices filtering out of a corridor at the base of the stairs made her tense. She gripped the pommel of the sword at her hip, which she barely knew how to use. Orison was a guard now, so she had to pretend that she knew the power that this weapon possessed. Steeling her nerves, she stepped into the corridor and turned towards the dungeons.

Orison bit back her need to swear when she saw who was guarding the dungeon entrance—Alioth. It was guaranteed that he'd recognise her. The entire plan was about to fail. The butterflies in her belly returned with a vengeance, no matter how much she tried to stay calm. A crack at the bottom of the dungeon door was void of light, kept in an artificial night, just like it was during the day. It was a drab place where people went in but rarely came out. After clearing her throat, she lifted her chin and approached the guards, regardless of whether or not they recognised her.

"Evening, gentlemen," Orison said in the deep voice she had been practising for hours. "The king needs assistance in his chambers. I've come to take your posts."

Alioth gave her a speculative look. "You look familiar." Her heart beat wildly in her chest, not knowing if she was already caught out on her lie. "Are you one of the new recruits?"

She dipped her chin. "Yes, I am." Names ran through her head. "The name's Luke, Sir."

The guards exchanged a suspicious look. Indeed, her cover was blown. She silently kicked herself for it; Luke was the most mortal name she could have used. "Are you sure about that, Prin..."

A loud boom came from the cell room. It shook the room that Orison and the guards were standing in, raining dust down on Orison until it ceased. Through the crack in the door, a glow of purple flame danced in the shadows as the prisoners made a successful escape. The guards whirled around with their swords drawn. Orison took small steps back as Alioth plucked a key from the hook and slid it into the lock. The metallic click echoed around the stone walls; the door swung open, immediately revealing a gaping hole in the castle dungeons.

"Help!" One guard shouted. "The prisoners have escaped! Help!"

Before the second guard could whirl around and grab Orison, she Misted out of the dungeons—just in time for long horns to alert the other guards and the king of Aeson's escape.

Misting into the throne room on shaking legs, Orison hid behind Sila's throne. She covered her mouth to stifle her heavy breathing as she pressed her back to the cold stone. The guard uniform was going to be a bitch to get off; she'd get caught with the noise it made. Forcing herself to prevent poking her head around the stone at the sound of thundering boots, she stayed staring at darkness to the sounds of guards bellowing instructions.

"Psst... Ori."

Turning her head, she saw Zade in the shadows peeking out from behind a pillar. He clicked his fingers with a smirk. Orison looked down in awe as the guard uniform peeled off her body and transformed into her pale pink nightgown. She covered her body out of instinct, not necessity. She knew Zade was a powerful type of Fae, just not that powerful.

Like a cat, Zade ran stealthily towards her. Grabbing her arm, they Misted in a flurry of green smoke back to her bedroom. Zade lit a single candle with nothing more than a look as he pushed her towards the bed. She tried to resist, but he was laying her down.

"Zade, stop for a minute," Orison exclaimed, holding his hands. "What are you doing awake? Don't you have school in the morning?" She jumped when the meeting room door burst open and shook the room. Orison didn't hesitate to slip under the covers.

"Pretend to be asleep," Zade whispered before climbing under the bed.

Orison rolled onto her stomach, pulled the blankets to her chin and closed her eyes to pretend she was in a deep slumber. The sound of voices carried from her meeting room. She tried not to react to a familiar voice that made her heart race—Sila. Her bedroom door opened; heavy boots echoed as they surrounded her bed.

"Just as I suspected, Orison is asleep in her bed. As her traquelle said, she has been there since midnight," Sila drawled. "As far as I'm concerned, dragging me in here was a ruse to help the prisoners escape. I should be down in those dungeons right now on the hunt, but no! Instead, you're wasting my time!"

Her eyes remained closed, keeping the impression that she was asleep. Little did any of them know, Zade was hiding underneath her bed.

"There was something wearing the princess's face. I swear it," a guard hissed.

"Execution for all of you!" Sila ordered. "Guards!"

Cries of protest filled the halls, followed by chains clinking together. Orison opened her eyes, pretending to be bleary from sleep as she took in the room; watching the guards drag their fellow men into the meeting room. She mumbled something inaudible as she rubbed fake sleep from her eyes. Orison should have felt remorse. Instead, she felt satisfied that Sila had no idea where she had been in the early hours or what she had looked like. She was also glad Zade had changed her outfit when he did.

Orison sat up on her elbow, yawning and stretching dramatically as she tried to see past Sila. "What's going on?" she asked. "Is there an assassin?"

"Go back to sleep, we'll talk in the morning," he said with a calmness that unnerved her immensely. He never spoke like that to her.

Sila gently closed her bedroom door. She waited for the sound of her meeting room door to close before she relaxed. Zade rolled out from under the bed and brushed dust off his blue tunic, fixing his hair with a smile. He had saved her tonight, in more ways than one. If either of his fathers discovered where he'd been, which she was certain they already did, their reaction would be dreadful.

"Now tell me what you're doing out of bed," she ordered.

Zade looked at the floor. "We went to see you. When you were discussing Aeson's escape with Kiltar, we overheard everything and decided to help." He extended his arms out. "Tada!"

She sat up quickly. "Yil is helping too?"

"He's the one who helped Mist Aeson to Grandma Saskia's."

Orison scoffed, shocked that they had thought of this. "Go home. Your fathers are going to be worried sick, and you're going to be too tired for school." She cringed at how much she sounded like her mother.

She didn't have to say it twice. One moment he was there, then he disappeared in a flurry of green smoke that smelled of freshly baked apple pie. Collapsing on the bed, Orison tried to calm her racing heart. It took a long while for sleep to present itself.

Twenty-Two

King Sila's office was a literal depiction of his ego. Like Orison's chambers, the wood-panelled walls had oil paintings of war or photos of Sila himself—like the one above his fireplace. Gold-framed windows looked out over the forest of trees, like a guardian angel always watching in case something happened. In the centre of the office lay Sila's large oak desk with stacks of paperwork on top. The desk rattled as he propped his feet up while signing paperwork; a trembling Orison before him.

"Did you enjoy your little adventure in the dungeons last night?" Sila asked as he licked his index finger to turn the page. "I didn't think it was somewhere a princess wanted to explore."

The leather chair creaked as Orison shifted. "I was asleep all night," she lied. "May I enquire what happened?"

Sila tapped his papers. "Really?" He looked her up and down. "Two guards insisted they saw you when your little friend and a few other prisoners escaped. Funnily enough, there are reports that a guard uniform is missing from the barracks. Somebody must have distracted the guards long enough to allow the prisoners to escape."

With a click of his fingers, the office doors opened and two guards flanked Taviar as they escorted him into the room. Despite the Desigle's protection, it still made Orison gasp with surprise. The king could only smirk at seeing the situation unfold; he reached over to pluck a sugar-glazed orange from a bowl.

"What are my orders, Your Majesty?" Taviar asked.

"I want you to check if the princess is lying about her whereabouts last night. We may need to get her a new traquelle, if I find she's been in forbidden parts of the castle." Sila plucked out another glazed fruit, popping it in his mouth with a smile.

With an exhalation of breath, Taviar placed both hands at the side of Orison's head. She felt him brush against the shield she had created; it was a fatherly touch that told her to trust him. Lowering the shield, Orison jolted as she felt him enter her mind like it was a door.

The only time she had allowed Taviar to do this was when he taught her how to protect her mind from other Mindelates. She had made a shield so impenetrable that even Zade couldn't pass through it. Orison watched as Taviar's eyes rolled to the back of his head while he explored her mind like it was a library. Then his fatherly hand retreated, leaving Orison feeling strange, just as it had the first time.

"She is telling the truth, Your Majesty," Taviar lied. He knew the king couldn't tell if he was lying—he didn't have Mindelate abilities. "And, if I remember correctly, the princess cannot even access the dungeons. There's a shield preventing her from entering the lower levels. Even if she wanted to go down there, it's impossible."

"I forgot about that," Sila drawled. Orison bit back a laugh at his pointless interrogation. "There is also a shield to the barracks." Tapping his fingers on the desk, he stared into space. "Your boys are mischievous. What about them?"

"Not possible, neither of them are Projeers or Tearagers," Taviar pointed out. The king gave him a look. "Zade is a Fire Singer and Yil is an Animunicate; along with the Mindelate ability."

"The girl?"

"Kinsley's just a Mindelate, Your Majesty," Taviar stated.

Sila huffed out a breath. "The guards who lied to me shall be executed accordingly. Leave, both of you."

He waved a dismissive hand as he stared into space. Orison didn't hesitate to follow Taviar out of the office. The king was acting too strange for her liking—being too nice when he was normally a brute. He had to have something up his sleeve. She needed to enter his office when he wasn't there and find the logbook, along with the missing tellages. She required Kiltar.

Floorboards creaked as Saskia hurried to the dining table where Aeson lay on his stomach. Pain-filled groans escaped him and he was wheezing. He clutched Kinsley's trembling hands as Eloise worked on healing his injuries. Saskia patted Kinsley on the shoulder as she passed a warm bucket of water to Eloise. The nurse gave an exasperated thanks as she took it.

Saskia walked back to the stove, filling a bowl with porridge laced with Curpacot nectar and returned to Kinsley, giving her the spoon. "Make sure he eats this, all of it."

Peeling her hands away from Aeson, Kinsley helped him sit up. She took the bowl and loaded up the spoon. Aeson guzzled the porridge greedily, wincing when the spoon caught on his split bottom lip. He stared at his girlfriend with his unswollen eye, love radiating through his yellow irises as she gave him a reassuring smile. Kinsley replaced the porridge with a glass of water that he drank through a wooden straw. He grimaced while drinking generously, before Kinsley resumed feeding him.

"The king put a shield around the dungeons so I couldn't go in there after each torture," Eloise said quietly, fixing a hole in his side. "I kept trying to go in there, but I couldn't. I just had to listen to him screaming."

She broke down crying, causing Saskia to hurry over and hold her close. Rubbing her back, Eloise sobbed on her shoulder; it wasn't her fault he was in such a state—it was the king's. Saskia vowed to herself she would protect Aeson as best as she could, get him a new home away from the castle. He could never go back there, nor return to his job as a groundskeeper.

When Aeson finished eating, he returned to a light sleep. Saskia approached the sink and washed the dishes, Eloise and Kinsley took a nap in the room that Orison had occupied. Saskia looked out the window at the birds, listening to their song with a soft smile on her face. A phantom wind picked up and Taviar's arrival startled her. He gave her a small wave.

"Good morning," she said softly.

Taviar looked over her shoulder at Aeson sleeping on her dining table. He sighed with relief. "How is he?"

"Fine, Eloise healed most of his injuries. She's taking a nap." Saskia rubbed the sponge around the bowl until it squeaked with cleanliness. She gestured to the door. "You can let yourself in."

Saskia watched Taviar disappear behind the wall as he made his way to the door. He looked around the cottage, then his eyes settled on Aeson on the dining room table.

Saskia dried her hands as she approached Taviar, who was looking for something.

"Where's Kins?"

Saskia guided him to the bedroom and opened the door. She watched him approach Kinsley and gently run his hand through her hair. Kinsley stirred with a groan and her eyes fluttered open. She flinched when she saw her father standing above her, causing Eloise to stir.

"No, I'm not going home. I need to stay," she mumbled before settling back down.

Taviar crouched beside the bed. "I'm not here to bring you back home. Just checking you three are okay. Go back to sleep, Kins. I love you."

Kinsley muttered. "I love you too," before settling back down. Taviar stood up and tucked the blanket tighter around the couple, planting a kiss on Kinsley's forehead. He exited the room and sat in the chair beside the table that Aeson was lying on. Moving Aeson's hair from his face as he checked on him, he observed the injuries that Eloise couldn't fix.

"It's such a shame, isn't it?" Saskia said, as she approached him.

"I kept trying to get the guards to spare him the beatings, but they wouldn't listen. Glad Orison got him out," Taviar admitted. "She almost got caught. I need to scold her at some point."

Saskia made a noise as she watched Taviar check Aeson over, consequently causing Aeson to stir. Taviar shushed him back to sleep before leaning back in his chair. Sadness grew across Taviar's face at what the guards had done to his daughter's boyfriend. It made Saskia admire the father even more; how accepting he was of his daughter's relationship, despite how other people viewed it.

"He's eating, thankfully. I fed him Chimera Broth when he first arrived, and Kinsley fed him Curpacot Porridge this morning," Saskia said with a smile.

Taviar looked at her. "I can pay you for food expenses."

She waved her hand. "I don't require payment for basic decency."

"Both girls were inconsolable when they discovered he was sentenced to execution," Taviar said solemnly. "They were so relieved when they discovered that Orison got him out."

Approaching Taviar, she noticed dark circles under his eyes from lack of sleep during this trying time. Taviar was worried for Aeson—he was part of their family. Saskia rubbed his shoulder in a comforting gesture. They both looked at the wounded groundskeeper on the table. Kinsley did not have a job, apart from occasionally helping Riddle with the shop, now Aeson was also out of work.

Rain beat down on Merchant's Row where a crowd had gathered outside of Riddle Me This Antiquities. People were witnessing a fallen soldier who was trapped in the stocks, to be whipped. For twenty minutes, there was nothing more than agonised grunts. Then the whip whistled through the air and the soldier screamed with pain. The crowd roared with joy, like it was a game instead of some insidious behaviour conjured up by Sila.

Unlike the rest of the crowd, Riddle didn't need a front-row seat. He stood in the doorway of his antiques shop with his arms folded over his chest and watched as the rain painted the pristine cobblestones red. He winced and closed his eyes as another scream erupted from the soldier.

"Papa, why is that man being punished?" Yil asked as he approached his father.

He sucked in a breath as another scream tore through the air. "I don't know," Riddle lied. "Go inside and do your chores with your brother."

After he ensured that Yil had gone to help Zade, Riddle closed and locked every window shutter on the upper floor with a flick of his wrist. He hated that his children were numb to these occurrences because they happened so often. There was no point putting a sound barrier around the shop and desensitising them to something they'd been experiencing since they were new-borns.

The king's insatiable anger was cruel. No child should be exposed to the agonised screams or the sound of someone's last words of pleading for forgiveness. All Riddle could do was attempt to avoid his children from watching—listening was bad enough.

Once Taviar had told Riddle that their children had helped in freeing Aeson and a few prisoners; he had been in a state of disbelief all day. If Sila discovered that either of the twins were involved, the entire family would most likely end up like the fallen soldier—if they didn't have their Desigles for protection. His sons would never be on that platform; Riddle would kill the entire squadron before that happened.

The soldier was silent again. Maybe he passed out from the pain, maybe he died. It couldn't have been a more heinous punishment for a Fae to endure. Although they had their super healing abilities, it was no use against a whip. As soon as the wounds healed, more lashes would score their back and it would be repeated until their beheading. Riddle hoped the beheading part was soon, to put the poor soul out of his misery.

Feeling his stomach roll, Riddle hurried back into the shop and rushed to the upstairs bathroom. Clutching the toilet, he threw up his breakfast; he retched and barfed again. Small hands rubbed his back and patted his shoulders. He placed his hand over his son's hand as he stood up from the toilet, then collapsed on the floor. Riddle looked at Zade, then his gaze fell on Yil in the doorway, both looking worried.

"Are you okay, Papa?" Zade asked.

"I'm just not feeling well," he lied and stood up, guiding his sons into the living room. "Have I told you the story of the town of Tontemgoref?"

The twins giggled. "Yes," Yil answered with a smile.

"I would like to tell you boys again."

Seating the twins on the sofa, both curled up on either side of their father as he began telling them about the town of Tontemgoref—where there was no misery or suffering and everybody lived a life of eternal bliss. It was as if the town was enchanted with something that made it that way.

The story drowned out the distant cries of the soldier as the whip cut into his flesh. It also kept Riddle's nausea at bay. For once, he didn't have to lie to his children to make everything seem okay; like most parents had to do when something was seriously wrong. The children forgot about their chores and the room they were in was their own Tontemgoref. They didn't have to think about the real world—they had each other.

Twenty-Three

From the window ledge on the South Wing of the castle, Orison watched the unconscious Alioth being dragged through Merchant's Row. His back was ravaged from his two-hour whipping. Like a slug, he left a trail of blood in his wake, leading to the spot of his execution. Some would call Orison selfish for framing him, but her friend's safety was more important than that. She hugged her knees to her chest as she continued to watch; a large crowd followed behind him like it was a party.

"I wouldn't feel too guilty. He deserved it," Kiltar said, appearing next to her out of nowhere.

Her gaze drifted to him. "This might sound sick, but I don't feel guilty."

"It's a good thing. I say Avachal has finally caught up with him." Kiltar stared at the courtyard, as Orison raised an eyebrow. "What you changelings would know as karma."

"What did he do?"

"He was a wife beater in his downtime. Also fucked anything that moved, whether or not they wanted it." Kiltar shook his head, a darkness in his eyes.

Orison shuddered. "Well, now I'm feeling even less guilty about framing him. What an Eryma."

Kiltar began laughing and sat on the window ledge next to her. "Fallasingha is rubbing off on you." She grinned. "Describing somebody as a pig that grows Venus Fly Traps on its spine."

After stretching her arms, Orison hugged them and rested her head on the stone wall, watching the crowd as they danced in Alioth's blood. She should feel disgusted at herself, but she felt nothing. Now that Kiltar had told her how Aloith spent his time, the punishment was more than deserved; see how he liked it. They both fell into a mutual silence that provided them the comfort they needed.

The guards dragged Alioth up a hill. He would be guillotined at sunset for his crimes after a long, gruelling series of trials. Orison hadn't realised how difficult it was to kill a Fae until that moment.

"I need access to Sila's office," Orison announced. Kiltar didn't seem fazed by it, as he stared down at the courtyard. "I need to find the logbook of the bargains and the missing tellages."

Finally, his gaze slowly left the courtyard and landed on Orison. She pleaded with him silently; she didn't know or care about the consequences, she just needed answers that Kiltar could provide.

"I'm not going to allow you to do that, it's suicide," Kiltar told Orison. She glared at him. "But I will look for it on your behalf and send it to your chambers."

"Thank you!"

He tensed when she threw her arms around him, both of them teetering on the window ledge. He reluctantly wrapped his arms around Orison. Memories of their amorous exchange in the Honeymoon Suite while in Tsunamal made him push her away. She looked up at him with a bewildered look.

"Let's get this over with then," Kiltar exclaimed with more enthusiasm than he should have.

Swinging his legs off the window ledge, he outstretched his hand in silent order. Orison took it as she hopped off. Both walked hand in hand through the South Wing, passing rooms and through the library. They were under a protective shield to conceal their whereabouts from prying eyes and King Sila. Kiltar and Orison stopped at the large compass in the centre of the crosswalk. Butterflies fluttered in Orison's stomach; sucking in a shuddering breath, she turned to Kiltar. He looked determined to get the answers she needed—all she had to do was let go of Kiltar's hand and he'd go to the East Wing searching for the books.

He kissed the back of her hand. "I'll be back with the answers you seek."

"Thank you, again," she said.

She stood frozen to the spot as she watched him walk away; through the archway and up the winding staircase to the king's office. Her hand tingled where his lips had been, the same way her lips did when they kissed in Tsunamal. That morning had changed a lot in their friendship—it was like a magnetic pull towards him. There were many lingering memories of that morning. She had to admit she was growing feelings towards him, but finding out he was hiding his true identity terrified her.

A heavy feeling overwhelmed Kiltar as he reached the final step to Sila's office. While standing there, hesitant to go inside; he could see the orange light of the shield that blocked his path. It took a wave of his hand for the shield to dissolve. The wooden doors to the office finally welcomed him without alerting the king.

Opening the doors, he slipped into the office without a sound. The room was shrouded in darkness, due to the rain clouds; despite the large windows that usually let in ample light during the day. It took a moment for Kiltar's eyes to adjust to the dim light. He couldn't put on the overhead lights—that would raise suspicion and give away his location.

He approached the large stack of paperwork, sifting through each one to search for the missing tellage books and the logbook of contracts. It puzzled Kiltar as to why Sila didn't just put a shield around the family archives. That would have been easier than stealing entire tellages and tearing out pages. None of what he was looking for was in the stack. It was full of tithes to other countries or allegiances the king refused to uphold.

"*Prince Xabian Alsaphus, Prince Neasha Alsaphus, Prince Xabian Alsaphus...*" an eerie voice chanted to him.

Kiltar paused, looking around the office for where the voice was coming from. Checking behind the obnoxiously large painting of Sila only showed him a wooden wall. Running his hand over each panel, the voice grew louder as he searched. His hand brushed against a built-in dresser where the voice was practically screaming at him. He didn't remember the dresser being there the last time he ventured into the office—before banishment from the castle.

He opened the top drawer; it was unusually empty, even by Sila's standards. As Kiltar ran his hand through, it snagged on a lip; his eyes widened to realise it had a false bottom. Lifting it up, all was revealed. In two neat rows were the tellage books, along with Prince Xabian's final entry. Carefully, he picked them both up; and with a click of his fingers, they disappeared into oblivion.

Kiltar flicked through the logbook which was in alphabetical order, finding section 'D'. He found *'Durham'* written in the Fae tongue. Kiltar had never seen the log before. Taking out the page, he got goosebumps having it in his hand. Pocketing the log, he put all the drawers back as he found them and quickly left the office.

Pacing in her meeting room, Orison nervously chewed on her thumbnail. It kept running through her mind of the various ways Sila could catch Kiltar. She didn't want that to happen; he could easily end up like Alioth for her selfish actions.

When the wind picked up in her chambers, she whirled around in anticipation for Kiltar to be back with the answers she requested. Relief overwhelmed her when her instinct was correct. Kiltar stood before her with a sheet of paper.

"I couldn't find the tellage books," he said. "This is the logbook page I managed to find."

She swore under her breath as she took the page. Turning it over, Orison's thumb brushed over the royal crest embossed on the top left. She saw her real last name in the Fae alphabet, thanking the Luxarts for teaching her how to read the language. The page felt cold to the touch, like it once thrummed with magic.

"Have my parents seen this?" She looked at both sides of the page.

"Of course not."

Kiltar guided her to the sofa. The pair sat so close that Orison's leg pressed against his thigh. With trembling hands Orison gasped and covered her mouth at the information she read.

Markus and Georgea Durham, hereby agree to surrender their first born to King Sila Alsaphus of the Fallasingha Empire at the age of adulthood in exchange for financial stability.

Tears stung Orison's eyes. She quickly pushed them away from her cheeks, yet she couldn't stop reading it over and over again. She tensed when Kiltar held her hand; it was a gesture of comfort that she needed. It resulted in her dropping the page entirely as she let her emotions take over. He pulled her to him and Orison cried in anguish on his shoulder, struggling to breathe as she pounded his chest. She felt her heart breaking; it was the worst pain she had ever felt.

"Why?" she asked through shuddering breaths. "Why did they bargain my life?"

Kiltar rocked her gently. "That's what Faerie bargains are like."

In his tight embrace, Orison pressed her face into his chest and screamed. Despite the scream being muffled, he shushed her gently. She felt him run his hand through her hair as he rested his chin on her head.

She pulled away; her hands trembled violently as she pushed away her tears. "There has to be more," Orison said sternly, looking around.

"Orison ..."

"No!" She held her hand up to silence him, wiping her nose with the back of her hand. She took a shuddering breath. "When I looked through Prince Xabian's tellage, he... he mentioned that my parents paid a tithe to nullify the contract. Where is the rest of it?"

He picked up the log. "The king clearly tricked your parents. Once a Faerie bargain is proposed, it can't be nullified. There was never any tithe to be paid in order to void this."

Orison buried her head in her hands. "Mother fucker!" she screamed.

Kiltar shifted to the edge of the sofa and they both sat in silence. He laid a hand gently on her back, placing the log page on the ground beside them. It made him feel sick that the king had created a tithe, keeping Orison's parents under the impression he would revoke the contract. How much money had they given up under false pretences? Orison didn't need this. She had hope, but it had been shredded into pieces of confetti because of the king's deception.

When Orison finally relaxed, Kiltar prevented her from falling forward; he pulled her into his chest and realised she had fallen asleep sitting up. Carefully, he picked her up bridal style and carried her through her meeting rooms, then laid her on her bed. Kiltar tugged the blanket over her so she wouldn't be cold. Moving back into the meeting room, he picked up the discarded log and read over it again. He was livid.

Sila didn't deserve his title for doing this to an innocent mortal family. They never had a good relationship with the mortals, but this was below the belt.

Kiltar needed a drink after this discovery, before sundown. He wanted to drown his sorrows and hide this contract from the king's prying eyes. He was unsure where to hide it, so he made the only sensible decision and returned it to where he found it. Kiltar hoped Sila didn't notice the tear in the bindings or the subtle change in the book's placement.

Orison awoke to the sound of birds chirping through her window. She was so upset; she didn't remember falling asleep or even getting into bed. Sitting up, she pulled back her blankets and stood up, using one of the bedposts to subside the dizziness. Orison crossed her bedroom to enter her meeting room—looking for somebody to talk to, but Kiltar had gone.

Her stomach growled from hunger. She placed her hand on her stomach to quieten it down as she looked at the time; it was way past dinner and Aiken had yet to retrieve her. Furrowing her brow, Orison approached the bedroom door. She opened it and made to step into the hallway, only to bounce off a shield. Orison's eyes widened at the reality of the situation.

"No." Orison touched the shield, her heart rate sped up; panic setting in. She would cry if she hadn't cried so much beforehand. "No!"

Banging her fists against the shield, she collapsed as her breathing came out in heavy pants. Her body was electrified by the shield that kept her inside. Orison ran her hands through her hair and screamed to the ceiling; it had come closer while she was asleep. He had trapped her in her bedroom.

Sila gave no inclination that he knew about her antics in recent days. The strange behaviour was finally explained, this—her bedroom, was her prison cell.

"Oh, stop all that racket, it's not that bad," Sila drawled. Orison used the shield to help her stand as she glared at him. He started to set the table. "Dinner."

"Why?" she was panting as she stared him down. He ignored her. She grabbed her lamp and threw it at the king with all her might. "Answer me!"

Sila whirled around, using his magic to stop the lamp from hitting him. He threw it back at her. Orison yelped and jumped out of the way, as it shattered on the ground in a mound of porcelain and glass. Her heart raced as she peeled herself off the wall and faced her captor, her hands balling into fists.

He rolled up the sleeves on his shirt. "You really thought I wouldn't notice you going into my office and finding those tellage books?" Sila flexed his hands, glancing at Aiken as she swept up the broken porcelain. "And look at what you've done to my lamp with your pathetic, childish behaviour."

"I don't know what you're fucking talk about, your office is shielded! If I was a Tearager, I wouldn't be trapped in this bastard castle. I would have ran like hell the minute you turned me into a Fae!" she shouted.

The king turned to her. "You're forbidden from mating with that guard you keep seeing, unless he wants to be executed alongside his family." He pointed to the table. "Eat."

Orison gasped. "Fuck you!"

"I said eat, now!" he hollered, slamming down a cup so hard that it shattered.

She grabbed her plate and sat at the furthest placement away from Sila. A chicken pot pie, with potatoes and carrots appeared on her plate. The king's exasperated huff told Orison that he was fuming. Taking her fork, Orison stabbed at the pie; ignoring his burning gaze, she clutched the knife in the other hand. It was taking everything for Orison not to throw it at Sila; her downfall was her lack of training.

"When will this bullshit stop?" she spat.

Sila folded his arms over his chest. "When you can be trusted to act like an adult."

"So, never. Beautiful!" She ate a forkful of food and massaged her temple where a headache was forming.

He rubbed his hands together. "You should be thankful I gave you this room! I could have easily thrown you in the stable as a mortal, where you belong. You forget this room is mine, so is the entire castle. I don't appreciate having my things tampered with ..."

Orison drowned out Sila's voice as she ate. While he ranted about how great he was and how much he owned compared to her, she kept thinking of all the ways to make his life a living hell. She'd start out small, giving him a life of minor inconveniences, then work up to the big stuff. She knew at one point, she'd start administering small amounts of poison hidden in his food and slowly increase it until his death.

The shield trapping her in her bedroom and the banishment from seeing Edmund was the final straw; something had snapped within Orison. She was going to regain her freedom one way or another and it had to begin with the king's death. Once she had achieved that, she'd take the throne and make Fallasingha anew. Then a real search party would begin to find Prince Xabian.

Her gaze fell on Sila when she realised he was waiting for a reply. She had been staring into space for the entire rant and hadn't even touched her food. Clearing her throat, she shifted in her seat.

"Sorry?"

"You are useless," he snapped. "Don't go into my office again, do you understand?"

"Not like I can go anyway," Orison retaliated. She discreetly swapped the sugar with salt by using her magic—a trick the Luxart twins taught her.

Sila tilted his head to the side. "Do you know a Tearager? Is that how you got into my office?"

"No," she lied.

Sila sat back and put three teaspoons of salt in his tea; it took all of Orison's will to not laugh while she ate. He put his feet up on her dining table, regarding her with a smug expression, then he took a sip. Sila started coughing and spluttering, glaring in disdain as he used a napkin to wipe his tongue.

"That's it, the servants are getting disciplined for this."

Orison looked up. "What for?"

"Putting salt in a container that looks like sugar. How much of a dufflepud do you have to be!" He grabbed the containers as he stood up. "These are going to be banned from Alsaphus Castle immediately."

Sila Misted out of the room with the metallic scent of his magic stinging Orison's nose; he was the only Fae she knew of to have magic smelling so putrid. As she sipped her wine and continued to eat, she noticed something on the chair that Sila occupied—a note. Clicking her fingers, the note flew into her hand. Turning it over several times, it was the same as all the other notes before this one. She instantly knew what it was as she opened it: '*No amount of kisses can turn a frog into a king, especially when he's already a toad. Call my name.*'

Orison groaned loudly, burying her head in her hands out of frustration. She wanted to scream the sender's name until her voice was hoarse. She wished the sender would set the shield on fire and rescue her from that damn room. Alas, like every other note, she had no name to scream. Instead, she felt empty and powerless at the fact she couldn't control her fate.

Twenty-Four

A dull thud filled the infirmary as Eloise mixed herbs in a medicine bowl. The mixture was a green sludge resembling frogspawn. She was so familiar with making mixtures like these that she no longer became nauseated. The alchemical table that Eloise was working on was full of books and vials. A cauldron was on the table to create medication for families who lived within the castle—most importantly, the king.

In her opinion, the infirmary was the least dreary part of the castle. The room had white plaster walls, with beds a few yards apart from each other. The open arched windows let in the morning breeze. There was a calmness in this space that allowed Eloise to think.

Hurried footsteps pulled her out of her reverie. She turned towards the noise and saw her fellow Healengales running into the infirmary with Sila yowling in pain and shouting insults. Eloise gasped when she saw his arm caught in a Nyxite trap. Behind her co-workers, several guards followed with hands on the pommel of their swords. Sila cried out as they set him on a nearby bed. Discarding the medicine bowl, she grabbed some herbs and a piece of wood wrapped in cloth. She ran over to the king's bed.

Eloise set herbs on the table and handed the king the piece of wood. "May I enquire what happened?"

"Bastard children, that's what. I'm going to fucking kill them!" Sila shouted.

Her mouth fell open until Carpathia spoke. "The king fell down the stairs outside of his chambers and he landed in a Nyxite trap." She took hold of the trap, checking what damage it had done. "I require assistance, Lady Aragh."

Pushing aside her need to laugh at the king's predicament, Eloise moved over to where Carpathia stood. "Bite down on the wood, Your Majesty, we're going to remove the trap," she instructed.

The king's back arched, letting out a muffled scream as Eloise pressed down on the release lever. With a metallic thud, the trap was released from its grip on his arm. Carpathia held her hands over the wound. Blood seeped through her fingers and onto the stone floor, like she turned a tap on. Eloise discarded the trap into the corner, before returning to the king's side. Her hands glowed as she worked with Carpathia to stem the bleeding.

"There was a step missing, I swear it," the king spat through gritted teeth. "It was gone!"

"Upon inspection, all the stairs are intact, Your Majesty," a guard replied.

"*Don't* lie to me. If the step was there, I wouldn't have fallen!" Sila remarked.

Leaving Carpathia to wrap a bandage around the wound, Eloise checked Sila for other injuries as he argued with the guard. Aside from minor bruising, which was already healing, he was fine. She had known the king since she was fourteen; she was now twenty-one. Eloise knew that he would happily throw himself down the stairs for his own gain. This, on the other hand, didn't appear deliberate. He grimaced and flexed his hand.

"You should rest today, Your Majesty, while you're healing," Eloise advised.

He glared at her. "Do I look like I have time to rest?"

"No, Your Majesty, but the Nyxite trap is made of Fallasingha ore. It will take a few hours to heal, despite us stopping the bleeding." Eloise explained calmly.

His eyes rolled as he sat up and looked at his arm, where several indentations were already scabbing. Sila flexed his hand again as he inspected how he fared. Eloise supported him as he stood up and made sure he wouldn't fall. He stormed out of the infirmary. The king regularly dismissed her advice; she wasn't surprised he was going to work, regardless. She watched the door for several moments before returning to her medicine bowl at the alchemy table.

Kiltar walked beside Saskia as they navigated their way through the Cardenk market. Vendors and patrons haggled; the sounds of people calling out special produce echoed around the compact buildings. It was chaotic, like every market day in Cardenk and Saskia's basket was heavy with goods. "Have you heard about Orison's shield coming closer?" Saskia asked, stopping at a jewellery vendor. She ran her finger over some jewellery. "She must be distraught."

He swore under his breath. "No, I haven't heard. I should go over there."

"Not yet, Poppet. You should get her something to take her mind off it," Saskia suggested, placing her hand on his. "Like some earrings."

Kiltar shook his head; he knew she didn't care for jewellery. With the shield coming closer, she needed something more. They made their way through the market, he kept searching for something to take Orison's pain away. Over the last few months of protecting her, Kiltar had found out a lot about her—the way she liked the smell of flowers, travelling, reading, and learning about Fallasingha. He needed to apologise for leaving her alone while Sila brought the shield closer. He should never have left her alone.

He followed Saskia through various corridors, until she stopped at an antiques vendor. She was picking up little golden trinkets of animals or flowers, showing them to him for approval of what Orison liked. Kiltar kept shaking his head; though they were pretty, they weren't for Orison. From the corner of his eye, he did a double-take to see a Faunetta's Atlas on top of a jewellery box. The small golden globe of the Othereal was perfect.

The Faunetta's Atlas worked like a tellage. The owner could pick it up and be transported to any place in the Othereal without leaving their home. Kiltar picked it up and placed his finger on Tsunamal. It instantly transported him to the sandy beaches. It was rare to find an atlas in such pristine condition.

"How much is the Faunetta's Atlas?" Kiltar asked the vendor.

The old man behind the table flashed a smile. "Five gold for the atlas. You know your antiques, Sir." Kiltar smiled and looked at Saskia. She stared at the globe in his hand with a wide-eyed stare. "It's a rare specimen that one, I usually wouldn't charge so much."

"I know, and it's perfect."

Kiltar fished out five gold marks from his pocket, placing them in the vendor's awaiting hand. The vendor smiled as he took the Faunetta's Atlas to gift wrap it. Kiltar had won the jackpot. Five gold marks were nothing when it came to seeing Orison's smile. She could escape from that room if she had this gift.

In her chambers, Orison kept the balcony door and all her windows open, needing to feel the outside air on her face; air that Sila banished her from. Sitting by the balcony, she stared longingly at the forest, hugging her knees to her chest. She wondered what people were doing in Cardenk right now. She wished she was in Tsunamal, feeling the warm air on her face, or in Parndore dancing with the Fire Singers. Orison closed her eyes when a gust of wind played with her hair; she savoured the feeling of it on her face. When she opened her eyes, it surprised her to see Kiltar. Pushing on the shield, she tried to go to him.

"Kiltar!" she called out, waving him ahead. "Come here!"

He didn't hesitate to make his way over; Orison used the door to help her stand. She had her entire plan to divulge to him, without King Sila prying and eavesdropping. Seeing Kiltar was like taking a deep breath after nearly drowning. When he was in her bedroom, she tugged him into the meeting room of the chambers.

"What's the urgency?" he asked as she sat him down. She put her hand on his thigh.

"I'm getting revenge on Sila," Orison announced with a smile. He nodded and narrowed his eyes in silent response. "I know you're thinking how, but the Luxart twins have agreed to help me implement the pranks I have set up."

Kiltar started laughing. "The Luxarts will not be happy when they find out."

"They've told me they're hunting for something called a Carchaol. I don't know what it is but if it hurts Sila, I don't care," Orison said.

"A Carchaol? No, Orison, you must call that off," he instructed. Orison frowned. "In the mortal realm, you know what snails look like, don't you?" She nodded. "Well, it's a snail with eight appendages that sucks its victims into its body; their venom is highly toxic. Fortunately, they don't like eating Fae, but they're blind so it will eat him anyway and spit him out."

Orison covered her mouth as she laughed. Kiltar was reluctant at first, but before long, he broke out into laughter as well. She waved her hand in the air, then began coughing as she tried to regain composure. The twins' plan to unleash the Carchaol onto Sila was perfect—more than perfect.

Standing up, Kiltar explored her room. Orison pushed herself off the sofa and followed him. He looked at the wood-panelled walls of her meeting room, pouting at the pictures of war; like he was in an art gallery and he was an art critic. Orison didn't want to look at pictures of war—especially the ones where somebody had their skin flayed off. He ventured into her bedroom with Orison close behind, inspecting the pictures there, too. Kiltar stopped at the foot of the bed to look at the picture that she had turned towards the wall.

"Why is that picture turned around?" he asked as he rested his finger on it.

Orison folded her arms over her chest with a puff of breath. "Check for yourself."

He pulled the picture away from the wall so he could inspect it. His eyes widened in horror as he saw an oil painting of a snarling chimera in the middle of a hunt. Its muzzle was covered in blood that dribbled on its paws where the carcass of a deer lay; its neck snapped at an unusual angle. Kiltar whistled as he backed away with a shudder. After seeing that, he understood why Orison had turned the picture around.

Turning to the balcony doors, Kiltar created a seam down the middle of a shield, so it acted like a curtain leading to the balcony. He pressed a finger to his lips in a hushing motion before taking her hand and guiding her onto the stone platform. The feeling of the sun on her skin after so long felt amazing. She stretched her arms out to bask in it and to feel the air through her fingers. A smile sprang to her face; Kiltar chuckled as he sat on the handrail, watching her in awe.

"Don't open that other door. If you do, Sila will see the seam. There's a shield around the balcony, so don't try running off," Kiltar instructed with a smile.

Orison approached him and leaned against the stone. "As long as I have access to something outside, I'll take it." She looked at the birds below them. "Kiltar, I have a favour to ask."

He looked at her with those purple eyes, the stars in them shooting across on a silent wish of protection and salvation from Sila's grasp. "What do you require?"

"Poison the king for me." His eyes widened. "A book said Braloak root will provide what I desire for his punishment."

Kiltar shifted, hair falling into his face. "That is a very dangerous poison, Princess."

"And I'm not playing," Orison retorted.

"He has his meals tasted before he eats," Kiltar reminded her.

"Use your invisibility to slip the extract in after that's happened," she looked at him; he sucked on his teeth and stared into space. "Start off small and slowly increase the dose. A small dose gives him headaches, half a vial causes stomach distress. I want him to suffer slowly."

Orison raised an eyebrow when Kiltar began laughing from shock. He looked at her in disbelief until he saw how serious she was. Before him was the potential queen, if Sila bothered to teach her—she was terrifyingly persuasive. He exhaled a shuddering breath and nodded.

"Fine, I'll do this. I'll go into Cardenk and acquire the poison before sunset." Guilt was eating away at him, even though he wanted revenge just as much. "When shall we start?"

She tapped her chin. "After the twins have been successful with the Carchaol, he'll think the sickness is a side effect of being eaten by one. I'll give word to them."

Scratching the back of his neck, Kiltar clicked his fingers; the box containing the Faunetta's Atlas appeared in his hand. Orison's eyes widened. "I got something for you," he said with a smile.

She leaned forward as he opened the box, presenting to her the tiny golden globe. It mesmerised Orison, she wasn't used to this map of the world. She could see Fallasingha's stag-like outline and the Elf Kingdom's Akornsonia. Across the sea, there was Karshakroh and other islands she didn't know the names of. She kept turning it with her mouth agape.

"It's called a Faunetta's Atlas, it's like a tellage; put your finger on any destination and it'll transport you there without leaving this room."

She placed her finger on where she thought Cardenk might be and the world around her faded away. *In Cardenk's main town square, it was bustling with people going about their business—people exchanging goods for cash. Orison saw revellers at the pubs. She could smell freshly baked pastries and apple pies that she craved from the restaurant where they had eaten. Children played hopscotch or jump rope in the street, even though they were supposed to be at school.*

Tearing her finger away, a single tear rolled down her cheek. "Othereal above, it's perfect." She pulled Kiltar towards her and kissed him. As Orison went to pull away, he pulled her back in as he deepened the kiss. She pulled away and looked at his lips. "We're not under any spell this time. Do you want to carry on where we left off in Tsunamal?"

Kiltar gasped and passionately looked her up and down. "Okay."

Taking his hand, Orison guided him back into the bedroom with a smile on her face.

Neither knew how long they laid in each other's arms; their breathing had returned to a steady pace. He ran his hand through Orison's hair, staring at the ceiling in euphoric bliss. The exchange was something that made them both forget about their predicaments—his curse and her royal prison. They could have stayed in that bed all day, making passionate love; but they knew the servants wouldn't approve. Kiltar would get caught and she didn't want to face those consequences.

"We've ruined our friendship, haven't we?" he asked, lazily drawing circles on Orison's arm.

She rolled over to face him, her finger circling on his chest. "Not unless you make it weird. You were helping a friend out." She ran her fingers through his hair. "Especially now that Sila won't allow me near Edmund."

Kiltar nodded, smiling at her; the smile that she returned didn't match her eyes. Clicking her fingers, her pink robe appeared in her hand. She tugged it around her naked body as she sat up, moving her blonde hair over her shoulders. He picked up his guard uniform from the floor, pulling the white shirt over his head. A deep satisfaction had settled in his body after the boundary they crossed; he didn't regret it.

"Thank you," Orison said.

He scoffed as he tugged on the black trousers. "Never had a woman say that to me after bedding her."

Orison laughed as she looked at him. "I needed to escape for a while."

Picking up his jacket, Kiltar looked down with a nod. He knew sex was a small evasion for Orison; the freedom she felt from it didn't last. She needed to flee forever, break her ties to King Sila and run for the hills. Stepping around the bed, he pulled Orison into his embrace and rubbed her back, feeling the silk texture under his fingers.

"We'll find a way for you to escape for good."

Orison nodded, pulling away as she stood up. She held the robe close to her as she made her way to the bathroom door. "I'm going to call the servants to run me a bath. We can meet later if I'm not doing anything before sunset."

"I would like that." Kiltar smiled as he turned towards the balcony door. He pointed to the Faunetta's Atlas. "If you ever get bored or upset, you can travel now."

Disregarding the call of the servants, she picked up the Faunetta's Atlas, smiling at it. "I had a meeting with the Elf King about Akornsonia. He told me something about a city called Irodore. I might travel there while enjoying the bath."

"Irodore is beautiful. Maybe when you get freedom, we can go together."

Orison nodded, holding up her pinkie finger. "Pinkie swear—for freedom."

With a laugh, Kiltar looped his pinkie around Orison's. That was the end goal for her revenge—freedom. Now they both knew that she had friends on her side to execute the plan, it was brilliant. As the saying goes; revenge is a dish best served cold. But in Orison's case, she wanted that dish to be piping hot and the ability to burn Sila with it.

Twenty-Five

Eloise wrapped her nurse's veil around her brown hair. She grabbed the apron from her dresser and tied it around her waist. Her room in the castle wasn't anything to write home about; the drab grey stone walls in the lower section felt more like a dungeon than a home. Over her shoulder, Eloise looked at Kinsley who was laying on her stomach in her bed; fast asleep beside Aeson. She smiled to herself as she continued to get ready for work.

While fixing her leather belt which was filled with pouches of medicinal powders, around her waist; she jumped when her bedroom door banged open. Eloise whirled around; Kinsley sat up holding the blanket to her bare chest with Aeson opening one eye. In the doorway, Matron Victoria stood with her hands on her hips; her gaze scanned over the triad. Her face was chiselled in a stern expression and her olive-coloured eyes glowed. She never knocked when she required her Healengales. She had the highest position, after all.

"You are needed upstairs, Healer Aragh."

Checking the clock in the corner of her room, illuminated by the morning sun, it read seven o'clock. Eloise slipped her feet into her shoes and smoothed out her dress. "Is there a guard injured during training, Matron?"

"No, the king has sustained another injury," the matron said, glancing at Kinsley and Aeson.

Kinsley gathered her own clothes from the floor along with Aeson's. "What kind?"

"You aren't entitled to such information, peasant," the matron snapped before disappearing down the corridor.

"I'll tell you everything later," Eloise said as she checked her uniform one last time.

Giving Kinsley and Aeson goodbye kisses, she hurried from her chambers. In the corridor, bleary-eyed nurses were emerging from their chambers; some weren't as alert as Eloise. She walked hurriedly to the steps. Running up the stairs, she paused in the doorway at the scene before her.

The king was on the same bed as the day before, only this time, large pustules covered him. Eloise's stomach rolled to see them. She made her way over to where Carpathia and another Healengale called Rihannah were working to ease his suffering. When she looked at the king's face, he was green and covered in sweat.

Eloise ran through the symptoms: pustules, pallid skin and sweat. This could only be Carchaol poisoning. All the other Healengales stood by the beds, preparing their magic; but spells would be useless for this ailment. Looking around them, all the beds were filled with guards presenting the same welts all over their bodies.

Eloise ran through the room to her work table. She grabbed a bucket with some bandages, a couple of knives and several vials of Carchaol antidote. While she ran back to the king, she handed a vial to each healer attending to the guards. The king was barely conscious when she returned to him; he laid in the bed, groaning.

"The king and the guards are poisoned with Carchaol venom. We need to drain the welts before administering the antidote!" Eloise called out to everyone; her voice surprisingly calm as she handed a knife to Carpathia. She gave the antidote to Rihannah. "Heat up the antidote under your armpits while we get to work."

A chorus of pained groans filled the infirmary; Eloise glanced over her shoulder to see even more guards coming in with welts over their body. She swore under her breath. Who let a Carchaol into the castle? Every single Healengale had their work cut out for them. She would work on the king and if any others needed her help, she could try to fit them in.

"Is there anything I can help with?" Kinsley asked, holding the door open as more guards came in. Eloise didn't see her emerge from the nurse's chambers.

Eloise swallowed the lump in her throat. "Find Yil, get him to assist the guards in getting the Carchaol out of the castle. Immediately."

With a nod, her girlfriend disappeared down the stairs. Turning to the king, he let out a low groan and squeezed his eyes shut. His breathing was becoming delayed as the poison worked deeper into his veins. Adjusting her grip on the knife, she raised it above her head and brought it down on the king.

Out of sheer boredom, Orison had pushed all her furniture into the bay window of her meeting room. After Kiltar had left the day before, she had been testing the Faunetta's Atlas—discovering that it had more abilities than just showing her places she desired to visit. It could also play music from those lands. She set the atlas to play the drumbeats from her travels to Parndore with the Fire Singers. It didn't take long for her to get engrossed in the music and recreate the fire dance. Closing her eyes, Orison skipped around her chambers and spun into a pirouette. Her chambers dissipated and she was blissfully back in Parndore with the Fire Singers.

She had created her own world. The suffocating circumstances of her chambers quickly dissipated. This large plateau was her place of solace. Orison was a Fire Singer—spinning tendrils of flames around her feet and hands as she swayed to the music. A smile spread across her face. Her brief reprieve was torn away when the music stopped abruptly, like a smothered candle. Blinking a few times to become accustomed to her chambers again, Orison was confronted by Taviar and Riddle. Both men had stern expressions and their arms were crossed.

"We need to talk to you," Riddle said calmly with a hint of strictness; the Faunetta's Atlas in his hand. "We know what you've been doing."

Orison pouted, running her foot over the cold stone of her chambers. "I don't know what you're talking about."

Taviar approached her, staring into her eyes. She backed away when she felt him brush against the shield in her mind. "Please don't lie, we are all Mindelates." She looked at the floor. "We know you've been making Yil and Zade instigate the king's recent ailments."

"You're an adult. You should know better, Ori," Riddle pointed out, putting his hand on his hip. She knew he meant business because his sleeves were rolled up.

She looked at him. "I'm sorry, I'm just so irate."

"We understand you're mad, we do. Nobody wants this." Riddle gestured to her chambers. "But we don't want our sons growing up thinking this is okay, or that it's how we deal with situations. They'll end up in the dungeons, Orison, if they're caught. Please stop this, leave it for the adults to deal with, they're just children." He gave her a pleading look. She loathed how much she had broken their trust, with her hunger for vengeance. "Will you?"

"Okay, today was the last one."

Riddle held his arms out and smiled. She allowed him to embrace her. "We love you, sweets. Just don't want to see any of us get hurt." Gripping his shirt tighter, Orison savoured his comforting embrace. He pulled away slightly to hand the atlas back to her. "At least you have this for an escape. That's something, right?"

She beamed as she held the atlas to her chest. He pushed her hair behind her ear and kissed the top of her head. Orison looked down at the globe in her hand, while forming a plan that didn't involve the twins. She looked at Taviar who tapped his foot on the floor.

"Today, you injured sixteen guards with the Carchaol incident," Taviar stated. She gasped and cupped a hand over her mouth; Riddle's hold tightened. "That's why we needed to talk to you, so it doesn't happen again."

"I'm sorry, I didn't mean for anybody else to get hurt." Orison stared at the ground.

Taking the Faunetta's Atlas again, Riddle resumed the music she was so immersed in when they first arrived, then it changed. This time it was a dance she hadn't heard of—one from Karshakroh. "Let's have a dance, Princess."

Orison let out a nervous laugh as Taviar took her hand and walked her through the steps. She learned quickly and confidently. Soon they were twirling around her chambers; once again, getting lost in reality—like she did when she devoured books. In that moment, she had created a safe haven for herself.

The sunset filtered through the windows of Aeson's new home; casting a warm peach haze onto the floral wallpaper in his kitchen and turning it into a cosy colour. Eloise hummed cheerfully as she set the table. Kinsley smiled, glancing over her shoulder while she finished cooking dinner. The aroma of roasted meats and vegetables filled the kitchen. Aeson stepped into the room with a bottle of wine and Saskia by his side. He popped the cork, making Eloise squeal and jump. Everyone roared with laughter.

Aeson poured the wine into four teacups. "To new beginnings!"

"To new beginnings!" the girls exclaimed in unison.

Eloise held out the chair for Saskia, who thanked her as she settled in the seat. When Aeson pulled out a chair for Eloise, she sat down grinning after he kissed her.

Bringing the pots on a cart, Kinsley kissed Aeson quickly and set the food in the centre of the table. Aeson assisted her so she didn't burn her hands, then pulled out a chair for her. When he was seated, he used his magic to lift the lids. He noticed his favourite honey-glazed parsnips and Boar Wellington.

His mouth salivated to see the perfectly cooked pastry with boar inside. "Othereal above, I fucking love both of you." Aeson looked at Saskia. "And you, as a friend, for getting me this apartment."

Aeson didn't know how he got so lucky to have two women who knew him so well; this meal was the perfect house-warming dinner. When Kinsley initially proposed the idea of including Eloise in their relationship, Aeson was nervous; but after so long, he couldn't imagine it any other way. He smiled as he looked at them as they shared jokes and laughed. Saskia gave an approving smile as she watched them.

Using his magic, he filled everybody's plates before grabbing his cutlery. Aeson's attention snagged onto Eloise, who looked exhausted, with dark circles under her eyes. He wondered what happened at work today; was it something bad and something he could comfort her with? He would wait for her to decide, knowing that with big decisions, she liked space to think it through.

"How is the king and the others?" Kinsley asked Eloise, beating him to it.

Aeson straightened up as he tucked into his boar. "What happened?"

"The king has been experiencing some ailments recently. He's been in and out of the infirmary since he brought

Orison's shield closer," Eloise replied with a tired sigh. "This morning, he ran into a Carchaol—along with a group of guards."

"Serves him right." Saskia laughed, causing everybody to look at her.

Tearing his gaze away from Saskia, Aeson exclaimed. "Othereal above!"

"Well, Fathers looked into it; turns out Orison has been getting my brothers to pull pranks on the king. They led the Carchaol into the castle." Kinsley shifted in her seat. "Fathers are livid and have grounded my brothers for a week"

"About time she put him in his place," Eloise grumbled as she piled up her fork and ate.

Aeson's focus stayed on Eloise. All these pranks must have been why she was so tired. But he had more pressing matters to discuss with both his girlfriends; the reason he invited them today—and Saskia, as a witness. He shifted nervously in his seat.

"Are you okay, Ae?" Eloise asked, reaching over and holding his hand.

"Yeah." He cleared his throat. "Actually, I wanted to ask something." The girls exchanged glances before looking back at him. Saskia lifted her head to hear what was being discussed. "I was wondering if both of you would like to move in with me."

The clatter of a fork against porcelain made him jump. Saskia sat there with her jaw open, looking at the triad in awe. Aeson had already spoken to Kinsley's fathers about this. He knew she had wanted to move out of home since her twentieth birthday. They fully supported the decision; now it was just up to Kinsley to give her answer. However, Kinsley sat there frozen, like this was the biggest decision of her life.

"If I was to move in here, I'd have to speak to Matron," Eloise said and looked at her plate of half-eaten food. "But I won't be upset if Kinsley agrees."

Kinsley cleared her throat. "I'd... I'd love to. Just have to speak to my Fathers."

"I spoke to them and they granted me permission to ask you. I will support you if you want to further discuss it with them," Aeson explained with a smile. Kinsley returned it as she drank her wine. "I'm not expecting an answer right this minute, but think about it."

"This is so exciting to witness," Saskia said with a beaming smile.

Aeson could already envision what it would be like. The home was big enough for the three of them. He would have a custom-made bed built for the three of them and other pieces of furniture weren't an issue to obtain. Whether one or both moved in, it would be better than living alone and unable to see either of them; because of the king's tyranny. It would also give Orison another safe house in Cardenk, if she ever escaped.

Twenty-Six

It had been two days since King Sila Alsaphus had been discharged from the infirmary; two days since Kiltar had started to administer drops of Braloak root into the king's food. He could already see Sila's deterioration—dark circles under his eyes, slurred speech and complaints of headaches. Kiltar knew he should feel guilty, but it was satisfying to diminish the man who implanted the Nighthex on him.

After watching the taster eat some of Sila's breakfast, Kiltar stepped behind the king. Reaching over his shoulder, he placed two drops of the root into the fried egg on Sila's plate and into his tea. Kiltar was thankful he could hide using the invisibility guise; he was also thankful Braloak root was a clear liquid. Stepping back into the shadows, Kiltar watched as the king stirred the tea before taking a drink.

"Why is Orison not here?" the king snapped to Taviar, shrinking back in his seat. "Incompetent whore."

Taviar's grip on his cutlery tightened, his jaw tensed. "Your Majesty, you put a shield around Orison's chambers; she can't leave her rooms."

"Did I?" Sila slurred out. He nodded in response and looked at the guards, who exchanged glances with each other. "Oh. Bring her here, now."

"You need to drop the shield if you want her to join," Taviar pointed out.

The king hiccupped and dribbled on himself—something was wrong. He clicked his fingers multiple times and Aiken appeared next to him with her hands clasped in front of her. She curtsied low before Sila, awaiting her next instruction.

"How may I be of service, Your Majesty?"

The king hiccupped again, a sheen of sweat on his brow. "Bring Orison here."

"Is she in trouble, Your Majesty?"

His head lolled back; more dribble spilled out of his lips. Sila's eyes widened as he straightened up. "Why would she be in trouble? It's breakfast, she eats it here. Now bring her."

"Yes, Your Majesty. I'll retrieve her right away."

Kiltar's face hardened in concern. This wasn't normal. He stifled a gasp to realise his mistake; he put the extract in the eggs—Braloak root's potency increased in eggs. Yet the king's breakfast was untouched; something more was going on.

From the shadows, he watched Aiken Mist back with Orison beside her. She looked at Sila immediately. Her eyes darted around the room until they settled on where she could see Kiltar. He dipped his chin, a gesture which she copied.

"Sit, now," Sila ordered, tapping a spot next to him as he hiccupped and dribbled.

Orison obliged. "Thank you for allowing me to eat here today. Are you well?"

Sila waved his trembling hand with a dazed smile. "Just some side effects of an incident with a Carchaol, I'm fine..."

The room filled with gasps when Sila took a staggering intake of breath before collapsing face-first into his untouched breakfast. Guards scrambled to assist the king; the first person to sit him up was Taviar. Sila was out cold and his head lolled back. Kiltar was confused—it was the same dosage as yesterday, but the reaction was never this great.

He watched one of the guards call for the Healengales. They filed into the room in single formation with a stretcher between them. They placed Sila on the platform before lifting him up and walking him out of the dining area; his breakfast discarded.

My chambers, after breakfast, Orison said into Kiltar's head.

There was no denying her request; he had to tell her of his innocence. This wasn't the Braloak root in his tea, it was something more potent. A scream came from the servants' staircase. Kiltar whirled around as a nurse ran out in tears.

"Leopold is dead. He's been poisoned!"

As he suspected, something more potent than Braloak root was administered before his involvement if one of the royal tasters was dead. Braloak root wasn't lethal in the small quantities that he was administering.

Wooden swords clashed together as Zade and Yil practiced sword fighting in Orison's chambers; while she and Kiltar tried to solve what happened in the dining room. Despite being incapacitated, Sila had reinstated the shield as soon as she returned to her chambers. Though the twins were forbidden to play pranks on the king anymore, they were able to retrieve books from the library. Orison was still figuring out how to do it herself, using her magic. Her meeting room gave the twins suitable space to sword practice under adult supervision.

Orison glanced up from her books when the twins made war cries as Zade went in for an attack and Yil fended him off. She cringed when Yil slammed Zade to the ground with a zap of his magic. Zade recovered quickly, trapping his brother in a headlock and rubbing his knuckles against his temple; Yil squealed and tried to free himself.

"Oi! Stop that, play nice," Kiltar reprimanded.

Zade paused. "But…"

A single look from Kiltar made the twins push each other away and return to sword fighting like nothing had happened. Orison's shoulders shook as she laughed silently at their antics. Kiltar smiled at her radiating beauty. When the door slammed, it pulled him out of his reverie. Everyone jumped with fright.

"Did you make my brothers poison the king with Mortelock?" Kinsley shouted upon entry, placing her hands on her hips. She did a double-take when she saw her brothers. "Or they can tell me themselves, did Orison give you the poison?"

Zade pushed out his chest. "I require five gold and nothing less to reveal the secret."

"No," Orison said. With a roll of her eyes, she turned to Zade. "You can be quiet." He returned to sparring with his brother. "The twins had nothing to do with it this time. I listened to your fathers. They just helped me retrieve some books about poison."

Orison jolted with a gasp as Kinsley jumped into her mind—her fault for not having her shield up. Yil ran over and held Kinsley's hand as her eyes rolled to the back of her head. Orison could feel Kinsley going through the lies that Orison had spun; and what had occurred since the shield came closer. When she retreated, Kinsley was gasping for breath. She allowed her brother to sit her on the floor.

"Sorry for shouting at you and jumping into your head," Kinsley gasped when she came back around. "I thought my brothers had gotten into mischief again."

"It's okay, I understand," Orison said, returning to her books.

Kiltar laid his book down. "If the king was poisoned with Mortelock, it's a miracle he's still alive. Who would do something like that in broad daylight?" He shifted. "I thought Braloak root was bad enough, but Mortelock!" He whistled at how lethal it could be.

"You're the one who's been poisoning him with Braloak root?" Kinsley asked, leaning on Yil to help her stand up. "Dufflepud, it is a miracle he is alive with two poisons in his system."

The room fell silent as the severity of the situation settled on all of them; like a heavy blanket. Even the twins stopped to listen to the discussion. Orison's stomach churned. She had read about Mortelock—a slow working, odourless poison; it took ten minutes for results to show and an hour to be lethal. The Healengales had time to administer the antidote. Groaning, Orison buried her head in her hands.

"Leopold died because he fell down the stairs when the Mortelock rendered him unconscious," Orison stated. She heard this information from the twins who eavesdropped on the guards talking. "Would he poison himself?"

Kiltar shrugged. "I doubt it. He didn't seem remorseful, unless he was planning on suicide."

"The servants said as soon as the symptoms started to present themselves, Leopold tried to alert the king—but that's when he fell," Zade interjected.

"So, somebody else poisoned the king," Orison said matter-of-factly.

She grabbed the nearest book on poison, flicking it to a page about Mortelock. Orison's brow furrowed as she read the information about the side effects and reactions to the poison. Swearing under her breath, Orison ran a hand down her face.

Riddle put one of his antiques into a velvet pouch and carefully placed it in a leather box; he slid it underneath the desk. In the logbook, he wrote down the details of its recipient and who would come later to retrieve the artefact.

Leaving Yil to attend the cashier's desk, Riddle grabbed a feather duster and dusted the shelves. He glanced briefly at the antiques in the iron box, beckoning Riddle to set them free; but for the safety of Fallasingha, he couldn't. Once he finished dusting, he grabbed the broom from the storage closet and swept away dust bunnies. He smiled when he heard Yil humming a song while reading through the inventory.

It was a considerably slow day in Merchant's Row. On days like these, Riddle savoured the time with his children; to keep himself occupied and not face relentless boredom.

When the bell above the entrance door rang through the shop, Riddle straightened up as he ceased sweeping.

"Welcome to Riddle Me This Antiquities!" Yil called out with a smile. It quickly faded and his face paled when he saw who their customer was. Even Riddle tensed to see the king standing in the middle of the shop.

Riddle was at the cashier's desk in a flash, clutching its sides as he protected Yil, who cowered behind him. A dull thud came from the walking stick that Sila was using to help him walk. Riddle sucked in a breath when seeing how gaunt the king looked—hollowed cheeks and dark circles under his eyes.

"Search the place," was Sila's only command.

Guards filtered into the antiques shop, making Riddle gasp as they searched every nook and cranny. He stopped some antiques from shattering to the ground, as guards rattled the shelves for any hidden compartments or drawers—there were none. Sila silently supervised, tapping his thumb against the handle of his stick. His limbs shook as he stood. Riddle offered him a chair, but the king profusely refused.

Riddle could tell something was extremely wrong with the king and he knew it wasn't something his children had done. He let them search, despite being wary of the priceless antiques he had acquired over the years. He had nothing to hide, and searches were a regular occurrence in Merchant's Row—especially when there was something the king didn't approve of. The guards approached the iron chest with the enchanted artefacts. Riddle's throat went dry to see the chest's yellow glow turn red.

"What's in the chest?" a guard asked, failing to open it.

Riddle tapped his finger on the desk. "Enchanted artefacts. For the safety of the Empire, the chest should never be opened."

"Open it," Sila growled. "It's the perfect place to hide Mortelock if he's in possession."

Riddle looked at the guards with disdain. "Your Majesty, this is an antiques shop, not an apothecary. We don't stock such a thing as Mortelock," he explained. The king glared at him. "I don't even know where to purchase such a thing."

"That's what somebody trying to hide Mortelock would say," Sila snarled. "Get the keys!"

"Your Majesty, remember the Desigle," one of the guards said.

The king turned to Riddle with a glare. Nodding, Riddle closed his eyes as he unhooked the keys from his belt loop. He slowly walked over to the crate; guards stared icily at him as he approached. Riddle's hands trembled as he pulled out the key in the shape of a skull and knelt in front of the crate. Goosebumps covered his arms when he heard the enchantment singing songs of praise at getting their one true desire.

Three objects were inside the crate: a necklace with an emerald green pendant, the Mirror of Fears and the Clock of Reverence. If the Ouse escaped from the necklace it was trapped in, it would feast on the elf population for its collection of faces. The Yurei in the mirror would be free to suck the life out of any living creature; leaving a mummified corpse in its wake. The worst to escape would be Zenocho from its clock prison—the ghoul with no face but could eat anything in its path, even a three-storey house if necessary.

Riddle felt nauseous when the lock clicked. The padlock fell to the floor with a heavy thud. Hearing a loud gasp, he looked towards his home above the shop and saw Kinsley and Zade in the stairwell; watching the procedure. During normal checks, they wouldn't bat an eyelash at the crate, but this was different. If anything went wrong with this search, he found comfort in knowing that two of the strongest Fae in the house could assist. The lid of the crate creaked and slammed to the floor, making the crate rattle. The guards searched through the three enchanted items in there.

"You can hide something in a clock, you know, like a vial of Mortelock," a guard said.

He turned around while holding the cuckoo clock containing Zenocho. The ghoul had an intricate prison. Carved into the wood were skeletons holding weighing scales; alongside angels and demons. It not only told the time—it also had a calendar, different phases of the moon, and weather conditions. Time slowed down when the guard started to unscrew the back.

"Don't!" Kinsley cried out.

It was too late. The guard had opened the back, regardless. A black hand of death shot out and latched onto his face. The guard seized, letting go of the clock as his hands slackened, causing the clock to fall. Zade Misted into action, catching the clock before it shattered on the ground. He groaned with the weight of Zenocho as the ghoul feasted on the guard; Yil Misted to his brother for assistance.

Sila's eyes widened at what he was witnessing; he staggered back at Zenocho's antics. The great king, who rarely let his fear show, had slightly cracked by the ghoul in the clock. Especially in his fragile state, his guard wasn't up. With a cry of pain from the guard, Zenocho devoured him into its lair.

"Kins, the crate!" Riddle shouted, watching the twins return the backing onto the clock.

The clock rocked violently in Zade's and Yil's hands as they returned it into the crate. Kinsley Misted to her father's side and with all their strength, they closed the crate with a metal thud. She sat on it, yelping when the lid jostled about with a loud roar emanating from its depths.

"Papa, lock it!" Kinsley cried.

She winced at using her entire strength against a 2,000-year-old beast. Securing the padlock back where it belonged, Riddle collapsed against the iron chest that kept rattling. The ghouls inside returned to chanting their need for freedom. The sound of the other guards stepping far away from the chest echoed through the shop, horror written on their faces.

"I warned you not to open that," Riddle gasped.

"That guard was disposable," Sila snarled, moving towards the door with a limp. "May I enquire if you know who would poison me?"

Riddle shook his head. "No, and I don't know how they'd succeed with so many guards at your disposal, Your Majesty."

"Good point. Leave him and the children, we'll search the next shop," the king drawled.

All the remaining guards followed a heavily limping Sila out of the shop and into the deathly silent street. Once they were all in the clear, Riddle collapsed to the ground in relief that it wasn't just his shop they were checking. He laid down to stare at the ceiling, his breathing heavy.

"Papa, are you okay?" Kinsley asked as she climbed off the chest.

He nodded as he stared at the timber-framed ceiling. "I'm okay, just in shock."

"That was a close call."

He couldn't agree more. Riddle had an inkling that if someone had indeed poisoned the king with Mortelock, it explained his gaunt and sickly appearance. They could only sell such dangerous poisons on the black market; none of his children knew about this. Riddle had no clues about who would poison the king with such a lethal ingredient.

Picking himself up off the floor, Riddle inspected his shop. Almost everything was in ruins; shelving units were on a slant. Guards had removed antiques from their correct position, some were even in the wrong section. The Luxart children wasted no time in helping Riddle clean up the mess and revamp the shop. Riddle paused briefly while moving a heavy shelving unit, when a scream tore through the air from Sila destroying a neighbouring shop. Then he came to a revelation—Orison.

"Kins," Riddle said in a hushed voice. "Has Orison been poisoning the king?"

She gave a smile in response. "Maybe."

"How?"

"The guard known as Kiltar has been putting Braloak root in the king's food." She adjusted the position of a porcelain ballerina. "But they don't know who put Mortelock in there today."

Riddle scoffed out a laugh. Of course, Orison had more than just the twins to do her dirty work. He wasn't worried about the Braloak root, that caused enough illness in small quantities; he was certain Orison knew of this. But Mortelock was not as readily available and she clearly wanted the king to have a prolonged suffering. He knew he should turn Orison in, but the king deserved it—and an insidious part of him wanted to see how it played out.

Twenty-Seven

Wind tore at Orison's hair as she stood on the platform outside of Sila's chambers. She only had the moon to guide her to his bedchambers. Steeling her nerves, she crossed the balcony towards the doors. With painful slowness, she lowered the handle on the king's balcony door; it opened silently to the darkened reflection room. Before stepping inside, she glanced over her shoulder to see Kiltar perched on a nearby gargoyle licking his paw. Orison was thankful he had lowered the shield around her rooms for this mission.

Her bare feet met the cold marble floor as she tiptoed across the reflection room. The numbness in her feet gradually increased, yet Orison pushed forward to make her plan succeed. The sound of snoring grew louder as she got closer to the bedchambers. Her hand slowly wrapped around the door handle as she pushed it down, grimacing when it made a slight squeal. The only hint that the king had heard was a slight change in his snore, before settling back down.

Orison slipped into Sila's room. Propped up in a seated position, Sila's hands were on his belly. The walking stick leaning against his bedside table made Orison attentive. A glass of water lay on the table, along with her target—the traquelle mirror. It was a simple gold-plated mirror with swirly designs on the back. Crossing the room on her tiptoes, she reached for the mirror, only for her foot to bump against the walking stick. She fumbled to catch it, but she was too late; it clattered to the floor.

She froze on the spot and her eyes widened in fear as the king stirred; he couldn't catch her like this. Orison watched as his eyes opened. Before he could turn his head to look at her, she dived underneath his bed—her heart pounding. He was so delirious from the poisons; he couldn't have seen her. Covering her mouth to stop her rapid breaths, she listened as the bed groaned when he moved. She stifled a gasp as a candle was lit. Orison watched Sila's shadow as he reached out for his stick. So focused on watching his shadow, she didn't see him staring directly at her.

"How did you get out of the shield?" Sila snarled. Orison froze and slowly turned to look at him. His yellow eyes flared as he tracked her movements—like an animal. She crawled out from under the bed, speechless from fear as she faced him. He snarled at her. "Answer me!"

Orison grabbed his cane and held it out defensively, trying to stop fear from making her arms or legs shake. "We all have our secrets. How did you find where I was hiding?"

"I saw your foot, *Princess*." With eyes flaring, the king grabbed his duvet, flinging it away from his legs. Before he could get out of bed, Orison's grip on his walking stick tightened and she jammed the handle under his chin, with as much strength as she could muster. The king jolted, his head snapped back painfully as he fell into unconsciousness, collapsing back on the pillow.

Swearing under her breath, Orison approached the bed tentatively; the king was out cold. She propped the walking stick back against the bedside table; then groaned as she pulled the king back into the position he was in before she disturbed him. All she could hear was her own heartbeat. With a brief glance at the traquelle mirror, she reached out and grabbed it, holding it against her chest.

"I'll wipe his memory." Orison froze as she turned to face Aiken, who stepped out of the shadows. "It's about time you whacked him. Go, I'll take it from here."

Orison backed into his bedchamber door, fumbling with the door handle. When it opened, she bowed her head to the servant and ran out of the room. Her bare feet thudded on the marble floor of the reflection room; she didn't know how much time she had before the king woke up. Fumbling with the balcony door, Orison finally got it open. She frantically glanced around the balcony for Kiltar, who was hovering at the end of the platform. Mustering up her courage, she ran faster, wincing at the cramp in her shin from exertion.

When she ran out of platform, Orison took a leap of faith into oblivion.

They soared through the Visyan Mountains, avoiding the large rock formations that threatened to stab unsuspecting intruders entering their territory. Orison steadied herself on Kiltar's back, stretching her arms out. She let out a loud cheer of joy to feel the wind through her hair and the power of Kiltar's muscles beneath her, as he flapped his wings. She punched the air with an enormous grin at her accomplishment.

Destroy the traquelle mirror, Kiltar's voice said in her mind.

Orison held onto Kiltar and looked into the face of the traquelle mirror for the first time since taking it. She was never allowed to look into a traquelle. Orison was surprised to see herself in bed asleep, part of Kiltar's magic to trick Sila into believing she was there. Gripping the handle tighter, she threw the mirror as far as she could, into the labyrinth of rocks below. It disappeared from view as Kiltar banked sharply to the left and beat his wings.

She didn't know where he was going, but she trusted he wouldn't take her back to the castle. The mountains soon disappeared, replaced by dense clouds; giving Orison a sinking feeling because her visibility decreased. Orison gripped tightly onto Kiltar's fur. When he lurched and dived, she felt herself slipping and held onto his horns instead. The clouds gave way to reveal land that was getting closer with each passing moment. Bracing for impact, she squeezed her eyes shut and shuddered.

Landing with a thud, Orison slowly let go of Kiltar, daring to open her eyes. They were on a sandy beach where a lake reflected the moon; like a mirror framed by mountains. She gasped loudly when seeing it. Orison could tell this wasn't Lake Braloak; the area was too calm and mountainous—this was a tranquil hideaway from life, an oasis. Sliding off Kiltar's back, Orison buried her toes in the sand; savouring the feel of the coarseness, with a smile.

"Where are we?" Orison asked, looking over her shoulder.

Lake Horusk, he said in her mind.

Orison turned around, approaching Kiltar. "This place is beautiful."

Go. Enjoy yourself, Ori.

She looked delighted as she walked backwards, his eyes watching her intently as she picked up the skirts on her purple nightgown and ran towards the water. Dipping her toe in, she squealed out of excitement. She never thought she'd feel it again—the only water she had felt these days was her bath water. She dared another step until the water was ankle deep.

Don't go too far, Kiltar warned.

His eyes seemed older than his years; and underneath it all, he looked sad. Kiltar was miserable for being in this form—he was unable to join Orison, incapable of saying anything out loud and he was trapped until sunrise.

Orison came back from her time in the water and hugged him. He wrapped his giant wings around her body, despite him dwarfing her tenfold—the Nyxite had grown exponentially. Now he was about the size of a house.

Pulling away, Orison ran her fingers through his obsidian black fur. "Playtime is over," she said with a smile. "You have to return the princess to her tower."

Play in the water a little longer.

"It's cold," Orison said with a giggle. She sat down, savouring his warmth against the frigid cold air. "Thank you for bringing me here."

You need the fresh air.

Orison stretched with a groan. "We still have to look for the prince. But we've run out of options; everything leads to a dead end," she stated as she looked at the water. "I don't know how I can look for him when I'm trapped in my room. I always have to ask you and Kinsley."

She closed her eyes as Kiltar pressed his nose against her, savouring his comfort. Orison leaned into the affection as she looked at the beach. The air felt crisp and she felt free, even if she was only here for the night. Laying down in the sand,

Orison looked up at the galaxy over them with constellations of a stag, a bear and a scythe.

The stag is for Fallasingha, the bear is for strength, and the scythe is for prosperity, Kiltar explained as he looked up at the night sky with her.

"It's beautiful," Orison said. She shifted slightly as Kiltar curled up near her.

Despite knowing that she had to return to the castle at some point; she wanted to stay in this moment and wished she could stop time, so she could spend hours here. A sudden bout of tiredness weighed down on her. Orison's eyelids grew heavier by the moment; she yawned, trying to keep herself awake. Sleep won in the end. Orison drifted off on the beach with only Kiltar to watch over her and bring her back safely.

When the sun rose over the Visyan Mountains, the earth shook Cardenk to its very core. Potted plants fell from window ledges, crashing to the ground in piles of clay and soil. Window panels cracked in their frames and buildings groaned. Large cracks appeared in the cobblestone path; some parts creating large crevices into the catacombs below.

Cardenk fell silent when the earth settled; until bewildered citizens stumbled out of their homes in nothing but their sleepwear. They all converged in the village's main square to look up at the castle. There was no secret that if the ground shook, the king was furious about something; with this much destruction, it was safe to say he was livid. Amongst the citizens, Kinsley was wrapped up in Aeson's arms. She rested her head on his shoulder and took a deep breath. There was only one reason the king would be so furious—Orison.

Somebody tugged at her wrist, making Kinsley turn her head. Her gaze fell on Kiltar. "Is Orison safe?" Kinsley asked. She glanced at the castle. "Please tell me."

He nodded. "Out of harm's way. We need to get to Saskia's cottage. It's not safe in the centre of the village."

"Do you think another tremor is coming?" Aeson asked.

"I don't *think* another one is coming, I know it," Kiltar said sternly.

As if on cue, the ground began shaking violently once again. Taking Kinsley's hand, Aeson ran with Kiltar by his side, dodging market stalls that started to collapse. All three of them looked over their shoulders as people screamed, scrambling towards safety as the clock tower crumbled. It rang one last time over Cardenk as it fell to the ground, taking people down in its wake.

Terrified people fled the village as it descended into chaos; they slammed into the group like a tidal wave. "We need to get out of here," Kinsley exclaimed, letting Aeson pull her through the crowd with Kiltar pushing on her back at random intervals. He and Aeson were protecting Kinsley from getting trampled on or crushed.

Kinsley heard children crying and screaming in fear as their parents carried them through the destruction. They turned away from the main streets where buildings were close together.

Escaping the suffocating area, the trio ran to the water's edge where Saskia's little cottage sat on the outskirts of Cardenk. A figure emerged from the building; Kinsley gasped when she realised it was Saskia, who was running towards them. As they ran to cross the bridge, they skidded to a halt—the bridge had collapsed. The river's current swept up pieces of stone; only the stairs leading to its precipice were still standing.

Saskia caught up to them on the opposite side of the river. She gasped when she saw the route into the village had been cut off. Taking Kinsley's hand, Aeson Misted both of them to the other side of the river, Kiltar following suit soon afterwards. When they looked at Cardenk's main square, smoke rose into the air from an apparent fire.

Under normal circumstances, when the king was in a rage, Cardenk fared well. But today was not normal; the king was the most furious he had ever been. His people were suffering because his magic was not his to own and he couldn't keep it in check—like the normal Fae.

Leaves crunched beneath their feet as they made their way over to the cottage. Kinsley was thankful that the only thing damaged was the stone path to the front door. The house was still standing to provide them safety.

Twenty-Eight

Sila had destroyed his chambers. He broke the bed in half; two of the four posters were destroyed beyond repair. His pillows and bedding were strewn about—the stuffing scattered all over the floor. The king had flipped over the side table; glass mixed with the feathers on the floor. He had shredded entire paintings and split sofas into two—like they were made for a doll's house. Around the chambers, servants searched tirelessly for the missing traquelle mirror. Riddle and Taviar had joined as well. Even the Luxart twins searched; their small statures allowed them into places the adults couldn't venture into. It took four Mindelates to convince the king that the twins hadn't stolen the missing traquelle mirror. Guards also searched while the king sat on one of his sofas, his face buried in his hands.

Riddle looked for its purple haze, but it wasn't anywhere in the king's chambers. He knew the king kept it on his person at all hours of the day. He frowned, wondering where a magic mirror could have disappeared to. A thief couldn't get past the increased security Sila had hired since the Carchaol incident. Everyone knew it was impossible to climb up to the balcony to his chambers and it was a death wish to fly on a dragon.

The air shifted from warm to ice-cold. A dark figure materialised in front of Riddle; he baulked at the hooded figure before him. Despite his fear, he bowed. The figure returned with a curtsy before moving past him and approaching the king.

"You called, Your Majesty," the enchantress said by way of greeting. Their voice sounded ancient, like it came from the time of Fallasingha's creation. To unbeknownst people, they might have sounded foreign.

Sila sat forward. "Did you take away my traquelle mirror?" he questioned. "That wasn't the agreement we came to when you placed the traquelle on my daughter."

"Your Majesty, I do not take back what I have given to assist a father's woes." The enchantress pulled out a scroll, unravelling its golden spool. "As per the contract we established, you need to pay me for the damage of my property and for misplacing the mirror in the first place. My clients only get one mirror per traquelle."

"I did not damage your property, nor did I misplace it," Sila snapped. "It was stolen!"

"Ten thousand gold marks tell me that it is shattered at the bottom of the Visyan Mountains, whether it fell or not. You damaged my property and must pay."

The king glared at the enchantress. The arm of his chair creaked as the wood splintered when he gripped hold of it. His nostrils flared as his anger increased.

"How the fuck did it get at the bottom of the Visyan Mountains?" Sila shouted. "It was on my bedside table; you are a liar!"

Riddle took a step towards the door, in anticipation of things getting increasingly ugly for everybody in the room; especially for the enchantress who was only doing their job. Taking Taviar's hand, he pulled him into his embrace, waiting to see what else the enchantress had to say. As soon as the twins came near, the parents held them close.

"I never lie, Your Majesty. Asking how is irrelevant now; you still got my property destroyed because of your incompetence," the enchantress said with lethal sternness.

Sila collapsed against the sofa. "What does this mean for my daughter's traquelle?"

"It ceases to exist. That's the price you pay for being careless."

Thrusting his hand out, a bolt of fire slammed into the enchantress. Their body seized as they let out a cry of agony before turning into dust. Their cloak was the only evidence that they were there to begin with. Riddle looked away as his stomach churned.

"Bring in Orison," Sila snapped.

A guard shifted. "But Your High…"

"Bring her in!" he screamed. The guard bowed and rushed out of the room.

Riddle watched the door as he rubbed Yil's shoulder. He got down on one knee, holding both sons at arm's length, looking into their green eyes. "School is starting soon. I want you to go home and get yourselves ready, okay?" The twins nodded in unison; he kissed both boys on their cheeks before he stood up. "Go on then, we'll see you after school, be on your best behaviour. I love you."

The twins Misted off to Merchant's Row in a flurry of green smoke. When Riddle turned, he froze to see the king watching him with a stern facial expression. He knew nobody else in the room could leave; but Taviar and Riddle had to ensure Orison's safety. Riddle was hopeful that Orison hadn't done something she'd regret, though he knew the probability of removing her own traquelle was high.

Lake Horusk had to have been a dream; it was too perfect, too right. Orison had woken in her bed with the sun on her face. She was squeaky clean and well rested—as though she didn't get sand between her toes or feel the cool water around her ankles. She felt deflated because there was no evidence of her journey last night. However, her nerves overwrote that emotion by wondering what the consequences of destroying the traquelle mirror would be. Judging by the way the castle kept shaking, it wasn't anything appealing.

Orison looked at herself in the mirror as Aiken brushed her hair, humming softly. It surprised Orison to see she didn't have dark circles under her eyes. It matched how she was feeling—refreshed. It was the first time since arriving in the Othereal that her eyes had a glow to them which they didn't have before. Maybe it was because of Kiltar giving her a trip to Lake Horusk, allowing Orison to witness something new which made her smile. Or, more ominously, it was the traquelle that was draining her. When Guards filed into her room, she turned to look at them.

"The king wishes to have an audience with the princess," the head guard announced.

Aiken lowered the hairbrush. "The princess is occupied with her morning duties. Whatever it is, it can wait until she is adequately dressed." Running her hands through Orison's hair, she parted it into three sections. "It is rude to watch a lady get dressed."

"This is a matter of great importance; the king cannot wait."

Orison stopped Aiken's hand and turned to the guards. "I'll go, if the shield is down."

"It is, Your Highness."

She turned to Aiken. "Please return when I call you and we can finish our morning." Orison received a curtsy from Aiken as she stepped back.

Taking the guard's hand, she Misted to the king's chambers. Orison stumbled when she saw the destroyed mess it had become in a matter of hours. Lifting her skirts, she was careful where she stepped, not wanting to step on glass or broken pieces of wood. The smell of charred hair turned her stomach. A pile of smouldering ash before the king was where it smelt the strongest. As she stood before the king, Orison curtsied low and straightened up.

Orison looked at everybody around the room, waving at Taviar and Riddle. They gave her a small wave back. "May I enquire what this is about? Or is it an invitation to breakfast?"

"No, you may not know, and this isn't an invitation to breakfast," Sila snapped. He clicked his fingers at Taviar, waving him to step forward, which he obliged. "Emissary Luxart, I doubt she had anything to do with it; nevertheless, check."

When she felt Taviar brush against the shield she had created in her mind, she lowered it and prayed he didn't tell the truth of her antics last night. Orison was almost certain he wouldn't—he had lied about all the others. It was something she needed to do. In normal circumstances, she wouldn't stick up for herself, but that time had gone. Her gaze fixated on Taviar's eyes that glowed as he checked. She felt him retreat and watched him crouch down to whisper something into Sila's ears.

I told him about a staff member who has been stealing things, Taviar said into her mind.

Why am I here? she questioned.

Orison jumped when the king clapped. He rubbed his hands together with a wicked smirk on his face. He sat up, looking at everybody with a new sense of energy he hadn't had since the Braloak Root was put in his food. She took a step back and her feet crunched on some discarded wood.

"Perfect, now we have the little shit that's been poisoning me and the one who has put Orison in danger!" Sila exclaimed. Orison sucked in a breath, wondering who he had in mind for such activities. She looked at the Luxarts who shrugged. "We can rejoice and have a party! With the execution on the balcony, the castle will be safe once again."

Clearing her throat, Orison looked around. "I didn't know you were being poisoned, Father," she said with as much fierceness in her voice as she could muster. "Who was it?"

"Jeffrey Havisham," Sila said with a clap of his hands.

Orison baulked. "Your second taster?"

"Who else has access to my food? And all the cooks were checked," Sila exclaimed. "Plus, he's the little shit that's been stealing."

A bout of dizziness made Orison stumble into the wall to prop herself up. She felt like she couldn't breathe. The knowledge this person was about to die at her hands made her feel sick, but the need to weaken the king was greater than her remorse. He couldn't keep treating people like shit off the bottom of his shoe. Orison was glad it wasn't Kiltar.

"I'll get to work sending the invitations," Taviar said with a bow.

When the Luxarts departed hand in hand, Orison's fear spiked when she was alone with Sila. He smirked at her as he sank back on his sofa, a hand above his head. She turned to leave, thinking Sila was done with her like the rest of the staff.

"Orison," he called out. She paused before turning to face him. "I will extend your shield to the gardens today for this joyous occasion."

A smile spread across her face and she curtsied. "Thank you, Father, for your kindness."

He waved his hand, dismissing her. Orison hurried from his bedchambers and into the reflection room. Her heart was racing now that Sila had extended the shield. She didn't know what to do with herself given that he had granted her a bit of freedom. Exhaling a breath, Orison headed to the double doors of the East Wing, where she could enjoy the castle as she pleased.

Kiltar waited in the shadows until Orison emerged from the king's chambers. She looked puzzled, rubbing her hands together like she was lost and had big plans for the day. When she took a step towards the stairs, she retreated to the doorway of Sila's chambers while muttering under her breath. In her distracted state, he strayed from his hiding spot and pulled her into his chest; she whirled around, staring at him wide-eyed before relaxing.

"Are you okay?"

She cleared her throat, looking at the stairs before Kiltar. "Yeah, erm." Orison shifted on her feet with a smile. "Sila's letting me have the day out of my room—a celebratory gesture for catching the criminal who poisoned him with Mortelock. I can even go outside if I wanted to. There's so many possibilities."

"Come with me," Kiltar said, taking her hand.

He led her down a passageway she hadn't considered going down before. It was no wonder why, when an obsidian shadow covered the entrance. Orison held her breath as Kiltar walked her through it. They came out on the other side into a corridor with golden walls. Several doors lined the walls, but he led her to the large double doors made of solid iron at the end of the corridor. They had a brass lion's head door knocker. Kiltar didn't knock as he turned the handle and strolled in casually.

Stepping inside, Orison gasped to see a four-poster bed with sun streaming through the floor to ceiling windows. A writing desk sat next to the large cast iron fireplace. Like the corridor, the room had gold-plated walls with red undertones. From the thick blanket of dust and musty smell in the air, Orison sensed its occupant had been away for a long time.

Orison freed her hand from Kiltar's, folding her arms over her chest. "If this is a ploy to try to bed me again, I'm not interested. And you seriously need to clean up." She stepped further into the room where a chuckle escaped her.

He snorted out a laugh. "Actually, these are Prince Xabian's chambers. Maybe we could get clues on his whereabouts here." Kiltar took in the chambers, then cringed. He smacked the bed, creating a thick dust cloud. "I don't think it's very arousing to be choking on dust."

She giggled and covered her mouth. Orison took in their surroundings. At Kiltar's announcement of who occupied this room, her jaw fell open at the reality of what she was witnessing. The fact it was Prince Xabian's chambers explained why there was so much dust; plus the mysterious dark shadow preventing her from exploring this section of the castle. Kiltar watched Orison walk around the room, touching the trinkets and weapons, flicking through his books.

Everything was the same since Kiltar was last here, but time wasn't kind to things that went neglected—like cleaning. He crossed the room; the bed creaked when he sat on it and he coughed from a cloud of dust. The soft red velvet comforter felt fuzzy under his touch, yet there was some semblance of the soft material remaining. Casting his gaze out of the window, he looked at the early morning sun low on the horizon; it made him exhale a breath. A creak made him look at Orison who had found a chest at the foot of the bed.

Pushing himself off the bed, he went to help her investigate its contents. Before him were piles of books that Orison had picked up. She ran her hands over the leather binding; with a furrowed brow, she picked up a small owl figurine sitting on a branch.

"This... this is my father's work," she muttered more to herself than anything, turning the owl over to see a signature and nodding. "Yeah, it's his." Her eyes glazed over as she flicked open the books. She gasped loudly, almost collapsing; Kiltar caught her before she could fall to the floor. "These are my mother's books. She... she used to read these to me before bed."

"Maybe they gifted these to him after finding out he's trying to prevent the bargain," Kiltar proposed.

Orison shook her head. "What if the prince is in the mortal realm?" She used Kiltar as support to pick herself up. "That... that's the only explanation why Xabian could have my family's things and why nobody has seen him." She let out a hysterical laugh. "That's it, we can't find him because he's in the mortal realm!"

Kiltar looked around. "You sound ridiculous."

"Maybe, but this is the biggest breakthrough we've had in finding him," Orison exclaimed. She gathered up her family's belongings in both hands, with a smile on her face. "We need to get a portal there."

Kiltar tensed. "Orison, we can't get a portal to the mortal lands; that's suicide!"

"So, you're suggesting the prince is dead?"

"No, just..."

Orison cut him off with another hysterical laugh; he blinked a couple of times—she wasn't listening to him. She groaned as she held her head, eyes wide in revelation; her grin so big that he could see her teeth. He knew she was level-headed, but when she set her mind to something, she was determined to follow it through. However, magic didn't work in the mortal realm the way it did in the Othereal; it was suppressed—like a paralysed limb. The fact she was formulating this plan terrified Kiltar.

"That's why Sila won't let me out of the castle. He's been hiding the portal to home and hiding the way to Prince Xabian," she exclaimed with a smile. "I've figured it out!"

"No," Kiltar said quickly.

"What do you mean, no?" Orison snapped. "There's a portal in Cardenk, Xabian is there. I could go home and see my fa..."

Kiltar pushed her against the wall. Before she had a chance to say another word, he pressed his mouth to hers in a powerful kiss.

Twenty-Nine

Orison tensed before relaxing into the kiss. When he tried to pull away, she pulled him back in. His hand on the small of her back tightened; she held onto his wrist. The kiss deepened and her heart ricocheted around her ribs when she realised what they were doing. Orison pushed against his chest and he pulled away. She panted. Then her eyes widened at the realisation of what had occurred.

"What was that for?" she asked.

He pressed his head against hers. "Promise me you won't do anything reckless."

"Why?"

"I... I just need to hear it," Kiltar said, stepping away. "Only enchantresses can conjure portals to the mortal realm. That realm is a harsh environment for the Fae."

She sighed, folding her arms over her chest as she took in his behaviour. "I promise I won't do anything reckless."

Moving to sit on the bed, Kiltar lowered his head. Orison saw he was fighting something in his thoughts. She didn't know why he was reluctant to consult an enchantress to create a portal; if it was to find Xabian, they had to do it. The man in front of her was breaking before her very eyes; what was it that made him look so defeated? Orison wanted to plead with him to tell her.

"What's going on?" she finally asked.

Kiltar came to the realisation that he had to say it. "We can't create a portal realm because Prince Xabian isn't there."

Orison tilted her head. "What do you mean?" She held her family's belongings close to her. "He has to be there, there is no other explanation. We need to give the prince justice here."

"What I mean is that..." He exhaled a breath and closed his eyes. "I mean, I'm Prince Xabian. Next in line to the throne, cursed with the Nighthex put on me by the king," Xabian said, pacing the room. "That is why we cannot open a portal to the mortal realm, because I'm right here." He stood up.

Xabian took a step towards her, but she stepped back, eyes glazed over with tears. "Get out," she commanded, her voice shaking. When he didn't move, she shoved him. "I said get out!"

The sound of her sobbing cut him like a knife. Xabian wanted to explain everything. Taking one last look at her, he Misted out of the room back to Saskia's home—like a coward. The confession had destroyed everything they had built over the past few months. Xabian hoped he could reconcile what they had eventually.

Saskia's rocking chair creaked as she sat knitting herself a new cardigan. She hummed while working, with her glasses on the tip of her nose. She paused when noticing Xabian had entered the room and looked directly at him. Xabian placed his hands on his hips as he regarded her, looking flustered as he collapsed on the sofa. His magic smelled different, indicating something was wrong—his magic didn't usually smell like fire.

She resumed rocking as her needles clicked together; a smile on her face at the solace it gave her while waiting for Xabian to say what was on his mind. He was silent for so long that it made Saskia look up, concerned that he may have disappeared. She found him staring into space like nobody was around.

"I hurt Orison today," Xabian admitted, looking at his hands. "I told her who I am."

Saskia dropped her knitting needles onto the floor. She used her magic to pick them up. "Oh, Xabian. Why would you do that?"

"She was talking about creating a portal to the mortal realm to retrieve me. What else was I supposed to do? Let her do it?" Xabian spat. "I couldn't. It's suicide for a changeling who has no proper training..."

The rocking chair creaked when Saskia rested against it. She laid her hands on her stomach, tilting her head down. The thing that stood out to her was the portal to the mortal realm. Though Orison could afford the enchantress to create one and then some more, Xabian was right—her magic was still too untrained to make the passage.

"She was going to find out eventually," Saskia grumbled. "You're a dufflepud for not being honest when she proposed the plan to look for you."

Xabian looked longingly at the clock on Saskia's mantle—watching the minutes ticking by. Another minute closer to sunset, when he could disappear for the night and go somewhere far away. Saskia put her knitting back in the basket and shifted in her chair.

"I vowed to protect her but ended up hurting her. She cried because of my deception. I should have been honest from the start and I shouldn't have made her look for me," Xabian admitted, tearing his gaze away from the clock.

Saskia clicked her tongue. "She'll forgive you in time."

She watched him lie down on the sofa as he stared at the ceiling. "In a matter of minutes, I betrayed Orison's trust. I know I've destroyed her. Is this what the king wanted when he cursed me? Probably."

"Stop moping. This is Orison we're dealing with. She forgives easily when it's somebody she trusts, she gives the benefit of the doubt." Saskia resumed rocking in her chair. "Your brother deserves no forgiveness."

"Fuck, I still have to poison him tonight at dinner."

He didn't know if Orison still wanted him to poison the king, but he made a promise and would fulfil it. Only this time, he'd be invisible to her too and disappear without a trace. Orison probably thought the Alsaphus family were all manipulative people and unable to acknowledge the emotions of others. Xabian wasn't like that; he pretended to be Kiltar because he was a coward. If Orison turned him in, Sila would execute him; one final death sentence.

Xabian's throat bobbed as he swallowed. His initial thought was that without him there to protect Orison, the king could do anything. This wasn't correct—he still had the Desigle protecting her. If Sila tried to harm Orison, it would Mist him to her, regardless. She'd hate him for still protecting her diligently, but that was his job.

"You're right, I am a dufflepud for not being honest," Xabian said after a bout of silence.

Saskia stood up, approaching her stove. "It's natural instinct. How about some tea, Poppet?" She grabbed her kettle and filled it.

Whilst Orison was getting ready to watch an execution, hating Xabian's guts. He was at Saskia's moping around about the truth he had to reveal to protect her. Talking to Saskia helped a bit, but there was still nagging in his head, a deep-set guilt on his shoulders he couldn't lift; his heart ached.

The next morning, a long line of creatures from around the Othereal snaked its way out of the throne room to the castle beyond. Each had a gift in hand—a tithe for today's execution. It wasn't every day that Orison was allowed to sit on a throne beside the king with a crown on her head. However, it was a treat for Sila to catch the criminal that wanted to do them harm.

Sitting with her back straightened, Orison had her hands clasped in her lap, feeling the soft material of her navy-blue dress. The colour matched Sila's suit and made her eyes wide-open. She felt sickened that it made them look like family, especially after what she had discovered today. While waiting for the tithes, she thought about Xabian more than she would like to admit.

A smile spread across Orison's face when she recognised King Idralis with Emissary Nazareth by his side. She hadn't seen them since that morning when Sila ridiculed them at the breakfast table. Either Sila had banished them from Fallasingha or they weren't bothered with his attitude—she didn't know, but it was good to see them again. Both looked regal; and Nazareth's prosthetic leg was proudly displayed to show that Sila's previous comments didn't worry her.

Idralis carefully presented a plant at King Sila's feet. Orison sat forward to inspect the beautiful pink lotus flower; it had an iridescent golden hue. "My tithe, for the execution."

Sila scoffed. "A measly plant, King Idralis? Pathetic." He looked at the plant with scorn. Orison kept looking at the plant, mesmerised by it. "I have many plants on my lands; this will just get eaten by the worms."

"Ah, but it's not just any plant, King Sila," Nazareth spoke up, her gaze falling on Orison. She gave her a warm smile. "The plant is a rarity of Akornsonia. The trees have requested it be a gift for the princess; it plays the most beautiful song. She will find great use for it."

King Idralis waved his hand and Orison gasped that Nazareth was indeed correct. It was the most beautiful song she had ever heard, more beautiful than the sirens singing in Lake Braloak. She scooped up the plant with a smile, gently rubbing the petals, making it sing more. Orison glanced at Sila, who shook his head in disapproval.

"Emissary Nazareth, I wouldn't enable the princess' desire to travel to Akornsonia," Sila stated.

"Thank you for your tithe, it's beautiful." Orison looked at the plant in her arms.

With a click of his fingers, an intricately carved wooden bow appeared in King Idralis' hand with a matching quiver of arrows; Nazareth produced a large vase with a cork in it. In unison, they set the gifts down at Sila's feet. The Arkonsonian elves bowed and took a step back with warm smiles. Sila sat forward and looked at it.

"That's a much worthier tithe; enjoy the execution," the king spat.

Orison watched Idralis and Nazareth turn and leave the throne room. She tensed when Idralis lingered at the door, staring directly at her for a few moments before leaving. She didn't know why Sila had to be so unjust over a musical plant. Orison clicked her fingers and Aiken appeared by her side.

"Please take this plant to my chambers and make sure it's watered," Orison instructed, running her fingers one more time over the waxy petals. "Be careful with it."

With a curtsy, Aiken Misted away with the plant, leaving Orison alone with the Fae king. Sila clicked his fingers and the next person stepped forward, leaving a basket of apples. Orison heard his grumble of disapproval, but he accepted the tithe, regardless. She didn't know what more he could want, he had everything.

The next person to step up to the dais was a male dressed in rags—a shirt reduced to nothing more than a single piece of thread around his neck and trousers torn at the thigh. It was apparent that he was mortal; he had a dazed look in his eyes. Beside him was a locked box with a rotating handle on the side. Orison glanced at the king, who huffed out a breath with a roll of his eyes. He glanced impatiently at the clock in the back corner of the room.

"I present to thee, entertainment!" the mortal exclaimed with a giggle.

Orison waved her hand. "Let's see."

The mortal unlocked the box with delirious giggles. Orison gasped loudly when she saw a dozen gingerbread people biscuits hanging from strings around their necks. She turned to Sila when she heard him laugh. She didn't know what was more disturbing—Sila laughing or seeing people biscuits being hung. As the mortal moved the handle, metallic music emanated out of the box. It sounded like he had stolen the music from another device, as it warbled off-key with loud clanking noises. The mortal furrowed his brow; the music died abruptly and he smacked the box's roof.

"Dance!" he shouted at the cookies. They swayed from the vibration before coming to a stop. He smacked the box again. "Why aren't you dancing?"

Sila clicked his fingers. A hooded figure emerged out of the shadows. "Executioner, put the Awakened in for the execution. We'll have a double celebration."

"What's the Awakened?" Orison whispered, watching guards carry the mortal away.

He glanced at her. "Something I should have done with you." Sila smiled sweetly as the next patron approached the dais. Despite being confused, Orison smiled sweetly at the next creature. "What is your tithe?"

Before them was a blue pixie who she recognised from Grandma Jo's Restaurant. Orison zoned out of the conversation when the mortal finally realised where he was being dragged to and started to shriek out his protest. He was still swearing that the gingerbread people cookies could dance and sing, like sugar plum fairies. If this was what an Awakened was, she didn't ever want it to be her fate.

Collecting tithes took up most of the day; Orison received more things than were necessary. By the time they finished, night had fallen outside the castle. The guards began lighting the torches, signalling it was almost time.

THIRTY

Othereal creatures swayed in slow movements to the tune of a phantom orchestra playing a slow beat. Most wore porcelain masks with intricate designs on them; the masks made it so that the creatures appeared as one and the same. Some stood on the side lines eating food, drinking wine or awaiting fitting suitors. Leaning against a pillar, Orison ate a skewer of meat, tensing when a flower presented itself in front of her. Turning her head, King Idralis smiled at her with Nazareth by his side; her chewing slowed as she took in his features—he was even more handsome up close.

"The trees tell secrets like they pass on a wildfire, Princess," Idralis began, looking her up and down with a grin. "Are you well?"

Putting down her skewer, Orison dabbed at her mouth with a napkin. "I'm quite well, thank you for your concern." She looked at him and Nazareth. "I don't know what secrets the trees tell."

Idralis leaned against one of the stone pillars. "I've sent you several notes offering you rescue, but you ignored all of them. I've been waiting for your call; do you not want to be saved?" He clicked his fingers and a strawberry appeared in his hand.

"You were the note sender?" Orison asked, her mouth agape. Idralis popped the strawberry in his mouth and chewed, clicking his fingers for another. "I've been wanting to scream your name but it's very difficult when you don't leave one in your notes."

Nazareth turned to her king. "I told you we needed to leave your name on the notes, but you didn't listen. Honestly, you weed."

"As Nazareth points out, that was my mistake. I apologise," Idralis admitted. "We wish to take you from Alsaphus Castle and give you refuge in Akornsonia. You will be free from the Fae King until your time on the throne comes."

"I don't make elf bargains," Orison pointed out. Taviar and Riddle had both warned her not to make elf bargains, as these were even more dangerous than making bargains with the Fae. It solidified her fear of leaving this glorified prison and going to another.

Nazareth turned to Orison as Idralis ate another strawberry. "We're not making a bargain, Princess. The trees have told us you need rescuing immediately, so we're here as a helping hand to appease the woes of the trees."

"Like I said, princesses don't deserve to be locked in towers," Idralis said.

Orison went to reply, but Kinsley bumped into her. Kinsley baulked and curtsied low. "King Idralis and Emissary Nazareth, pleasure to be in your company."

Idralis and Nazareth bowed. "Lady Luxart, how is your family?" Idralis asked.

"My family is well, thank you," Kinsley replied, looping her arm through Orison's.

"Just let us know, Princess," Idralis said before disappearing into the throng of people with Nazareth on his arm.

With a gentle tug, Orison let Kinsley pull her towards the nearest window ledge. Orison's head was still reeling that the Elf King and his emissary were there to collect her; and that Sila had treated Idralis like utter crap. Only Sila would have the audacity to do something like that. If she declined this offer, Orison was scared that King Idralis may give up on her, then she would never be free. Her stomach twisted into a sickening knot. She had to get free.

Sitting down, Kinsley had a beaming smile on her face. "I'm moving in with Aeson."

"Congratulations!" Orison squealed, throwing her free arm around her shoulders. "I'm proud of you, you're going to make so many memories." Moving away, she picked up the half-eaten skewer and ate a piece. "Wish I could help you with packing."

Kinsley waved her hand and smiled. "It's okay. I'm just happy my fathers gave us consent." She looked at Idralis who was staring at them while talking to Nazareth. "What did Idralis want?"

"He and Nazareth have offered me a way to escape." Orison put the bare skewer on the plate. "Actually, he's offered me a way out three times. This would be the fourth. I'm just worried it's an elf bargain."

Looking at the dancers, Kinsley tapped her fingers against the window ledge. A clink made both of them look at the space between them. Two slices of cake had appeared, both with cherries on top. Orison looked at the cake strictly intended for only the king's consumption; two slabs had been taken out, which made her smile. A note lay next to hers. She picked it up; *'You can trust us.'*

"King Idralis wouldn't do that to a friend of mine," Kinsley said. Orison looked up at her as she ate some cake. "We used to see each other."

Orison nodded. "Would you trust that this offer is in earnest, then?" She set down her fork and looked out the window, seeing her own reflection. "Where would I even go?"

"Most likely somewhere in Akornsonia." Kinsley ate some cake and looked around. "The king has no jurisdiction there unless he calls for war. You'll be safe."

The ringing of a large bell cut their conversation short. All music died down in the ballroom and the procession of dancers ceased. The rustling of fabric echoed as they turned to an awaiting guard at the entrance to the throne room.

"King Sila is ready for you to accompany him to his chambers for the execution," the guard bellowed. "If you all follow me."

He stamped his feet before marching away; a line of guests following him. Orison stood up, wiped cake crumbs off her dress and looked around for Idralis or Nazareth; neither of them were anywhere to be seen. As the last of the guests filtered out, Orison left the throne room with Kinsley close behind, both ready to watch men be punished—one for a legitimate crime, the other for losing his mind.

Bodies crammed together to get the best view of the execution; however, the best view was reserved for King Sila and Princess Orison. She looked at the guillotine that sat on the edge of the balcony awaiting bloodshed. The noise from all the guests echoed around the mountain.

Orison glanced at the man who had kept her prisoner. He cackled loudly at a beautiful pixie with glowing green skin; her wings fluttered with each of her giggles. He swirled his wine around, drinking generously with a smile. Orison knew how the night would end for them and it made her shudder. She looked around the balcony for Idralis and Nazareth. Not finding either of them in the crowd, her stomach churned at what she was contemplating.

"How are you feeling?" Eloise asked, appearing next to her. "You look a little flustered."

"Just a little hot, is all," Orison partially lied with a smile. She was uneasy because she had a chance to get away from her captor, but she couldn't say that in Sila's presence.

A goblet appeared in Eloise's glowing hand; Orison's eyes widened to see ice crystals appear around the golden embellishments. She handed it to Orison. "This should cool you off."

"You can control ice?" Orison shuddered at the burning cold of the goblet.

"Only for medicinal purposes, like what you need." She looked at the guillotine. "It's a shame, but somebody has to pay for treason, don't they?" Taking a sip of the iced water, Orison nodded. Eloise waved at Kinsley who was nearby. "I'm sure you've heard the good news," she asked.

Another nod. "I have, congratulations. Are you moving in as well?" Orison enquired.

"I am, Matron gave me permission as long as I come back when called." Eloise had a beaming smile when Kinsley came over, giving her a kiss. "The show is about to start."

Three bell tolls rang around the Visyan Mountains. Orison shifted to the edge of her seat. The balcony thundered with heavy footfalls, making the ground shake as a large ogre entered, dragging three prisoners by their necks.

Orison recognised Jeffrey, he clawed at the bindings with tears in his eyes. The other two prisoners were the mortal who accepted his fate and somebody else who she didn't recognise at all.

"I advise you watch for when you rule these lands," Sila snapped. She ignored him. She couldn't do anything but watch. "This is the only way for people to know you're in charge."

Orison rolled her eyes; there were better ways to get people to know you were in charge. Fear wasn't one of them—the king clearly didn't acknowledge that. She watched the ogre shove the mortal onto the chopping block. Orison was unnerved by how they appeared in a daze, accepting their fate like it was nothing. The ogre pulled a lever and the blade went down. With a thud, the head of the mortal separated from his body; blood sprayed out like a popped bottle of champagne. At first the crowd was silent, before erupting into cheers. It was disturbing to see the guests dancing in the blood; Orison's stomach churned to see vampires lapping it up like dogs.

She sank back in her seat, looking at the sky with a heavy heart. Her stomach was rolling like a storm out at sea; threatening to expel the cake, meat and water that she had consumed. Orison's body was getting hot—despite the coolness of sweat on her skin, and her hands trembled slightly. From her previous experience at being poisoned, this felt different. She was inadvertently panicking about being too late to reach out for Idralis' help; but if she found him, she'd be on her way to Akornsonia.

Jeffrey was shoved onto the chopping block, despite his best protests. He glared at the king. Sila was unfazed as he fed grapes to the pixie who he had become over-friendly with. Sila had a smile on his face, like this was the best performance he had ever witnessed. He loved bloodshed, whereas Orison actively avoided it.

"I curse thee king, you shall die on the next full moon at the hands of somebody you trusted. Bless Fallasingha for a new tomorrow," Jeffrey spat, shaking with rage. At the threat, Sila stopped eating and sat forward with a glare.

Jeffrey muttered some final words under his breath as the ogre pulled the lever. There was another heavy thud when the blade dropped and his head fell into the bucket below him; his blood sprayed the mortals who still danced in the blood. The crowd roared with applause; the king did not cheer this time, but sat back in his chair, shaking his head. He huffed out a breath, rubbing the thigh of the pixie.

"Nothing comes of a liar. I'll be fine on the next full moon," Sila spat and tapped the arm of Orison's throne.

She moved away from Sila, crossing her ankles as the third person came up after they dragged Jeffrey away. Orison stiffened to see a band of thorns on Jeffrey's wrist—from her teachings with Riddle, the band of thorns was a very dark practice of witchcraft. At the next full moon, the king would not be fine at all, for the curse was solidified.

The heavy thud of the third head pulled her back to reality. She blinked a couple of times, finding her throne suddenly uncomfortable, despite the cushioned seat. At her feet was a red sea. She looked to the sky as a clap of thunder rattled around them and the heavens opened. Orison gasped at the icy feeling of rain seeping into her dress; she blinked the rain out of her eyes. The guests didn't care; they danced in it regardless, with wide grins on their faces. Sila stood up and walked the pixie to the dance area with a smile on his face.

It was then that she made up her mind about the Elf King's offer, she needed to get out. It was now or never.

Pushing herself from the dais, she picked up her skirts to stop them being ruined and headed into the crowd. Side stepping past creature after creature, she checked every face for Idralis or Nazareth—to no avail. Orison hadn't seen either of them since they made the fourth offer; she hoped she wasn't too late. Near the doors into Sila's reflection room, she saw Idralis walking away. Running up to him, she grabbed him by the wrist; he turned around with a wide-eyed stare.

"Take me to Akornsonia, save me from the king."

THIRTY-ONE

As Sila had promised, the shield was reinstated first thing in the morning after the execution. Orison didn't care about this for the following two weeks, knowing that behind the scenes, King Idralis was planning her escape to get to safety in Akornsonia; where the elves lived. She had been using the Faunetta's Atlas to get acquainted with the country. It made her giddy with excitement that she could see something new, even if the elves were thought to be dangerous.

Throughout the week, her mind kept wandering to Xabian. She hadn't seen him since his confession. Before she left, Orison wanted to confront him. However, that wouldn't to forgiving him so easily. If he ever showed up again, she wanted him to tell her the truth. Orison had been too angry to allow him to explain during the confession.

King Idralis had clarified that the escape wasn't an elf bargain. He didn't want her to swear herself to him; it was just one royal protecting another. He would allow her refuge in his lands and she could do as she desired until she took the throne. Idralis promised there would be an alliance between Fallasingha and Akornsonia when her reign began.

As she finished eating her breakfast on the agreed date, a note arrived next to her tea. Picking it up, she unfolded the page and read, '*Wait for the quake and head to the East Wall.*'

Though she didn't understand the quakes meaning, she created a flame and set fire to the note, using wind to discard the ash. The plan was in full swing. Her stomach became a lead weight with nerves. A floral scent filled her nose and she had a sudden urge to check her rooms. Pushing herself out of her chair, she made her way into her bedroom.

Everything seemed in order as she checked the four-poster bed—until she wandered into her dressing room. Most of her clothes had disappeared except for a green tunic and a pair of wool-lined trousers; leather boots sat beneath them. The servants were definitely going to know something was up if all her clothes weren't there. Orison spied another note attached to the hanger; '*Your maids have been dismissed for the day. The rest of your clothes and belongings are in Torwarin.*'

Reality was sinking in. She was glad she had destroyed the traquelle mirror; the escape was impossible otherwise. She laughed, then began crying with relief.

Orison tapped her feet in time with the clock on her mantle, counting down the minutes until she got the signal. She had dressed herself, finding the tunic and trousers to be the perfect fit, even down to the boots; it must have been elf ingenuity to know her size. By her door she found a cloak which she had adorned to conceal herself when she fled from the castle.

When the ground shook, Orison gripped the sides of her sofa and listened to the chandelier clinking together like a wind chime; the vase on her side table rattled against the wood. Orison instantly knew that was her cue to move.

Mustering up her courage, Orison tried Misting to the East Gardens, hoping she didn't smash into the shield. When Orison landed, her boots crunched on the grass. She felt the crisp air on her face and smelt its aroma, which overwhelmed her senses. Though her instincts told her to stay and savour the moment, she didn't have that luxury. She had to keep moving and fled towards the East Wall like Idralis had requested.

Orison ran as fast as she could and found the enormous stone wall that Idralis talked about in his note. She saw nobody around. Looking up, she realised she may have to climb over to get to the meeting point. Orison was too scared to call out for her rescuer without alerting the patrol guards. Rubbing her hands together, she gripped hold of a piece of the stone; finding her foothold, she groaned as she lifted herself up the wall. Orison began her ascent until she missed her next step and fell to the ground with a heavy thud. She grimaced and moaned, rubbing her stinging spine. Orison tensed when she heard a warm laugh. Fearing the worst, she slowly turned around, only to see Nazareth standing behind her.

"I think the door would be better than climbing," she said and extended her hand. "Pleasure to meet you again, Princess Orison, and an even greater pleasure to be at your service."

Orison took Nazareth's hand, brushing off pieces of tree bark from her clothes once she stood up. She noticed there was a wooden door built into the wall that wasn't there before. She frowned, tilting her head out of confusion.

Walking with confidence, Nazareth walked through the door, Orison followed close behind. Nazareth had tied up her hair with leather; Orison realised it had feathers on strings sewn into the bands. Today, she was wearing a deer hide over a grey tunic. She had a heavy splattering of freckles across her nose, complimenting her forest-green eyes.

Nazareth took Orison to four horses; there were two buckskins, one appaloosa and one black. All of them were grazing on grass. Orison immediately walked over to a buckskin as it reminded her of the horse that Bara, her teacher, had back in the mortal lands. It lifted its head, huffing warm air into her face. Orison laughed as she petted its muzzle.

"Hello," she said with her eyes glowing.

"That's my horse," a man said, his voice thick like honey. Black hair fell to his shoulders with deep green eyes. "Nice to meet you, Princess Orison, I'm Guard Captain Khardell of Akornsonia." He petted his horse. "Her name is Crystal, she's a beauty."

Orison pushed her hair behind her ear. "I'm sorry, she just reminded me of a horse in the mortal lands."

"No need to apologise. She loves attention," Khardell said. He pointed to a guard with white hair in a braid, mounted on a piebald horse. "That guy is Balvyre and his horse is Badger." Orison laughed. "You can laugh, everyone does." He pointed to another guard with brown hair mounted on another piebald. "That one is Echo, the horse is named Spot."

"And I'm Feud!" A guard with red hair came out of the tree line. He took the black horse with a smile. "This is Nightmare."

Nazareth pointed to the other buckskin. "That is Maelstrom, you can take that one." She stepped up to the appaloosa. "I'm taking Snow."

With a click of Nazareth's fingers, mounting blocks made from roots appeared beside each horse. She climbed up and mounted Snow. Climbing up her own block, Orison mounted Maelstrom, using her magic to unhook the reins from the trees. In true guard captain fashion, Khardell put his men into formation once Feud was on his horse, creating a circle around Orison. King Idralis meant business if he sent so many of his guards to guide her to Akornsonia.

Orison cocked her head to the side. "Should we Mist to the forest?"

"Torwarin Forest is warded to prevent the Fae Misting in, and elves can't Mist unless a Fae guides them. So, I'm afraid it's a two-week horse ride," Nazareth announced, patting her horse's neck; it whinnied in protest as it tried eating more grass.

Rubbing her horse's mane, Orison smiled to herself at the fact she was being rescued. Khardell took the front position, Balvyre at the back, with Echo and Feud on either side. With a click of Nazareth's fingers, the horses trotted beside each other before they broke into a gallop towards the North of the Fallasingha Empire. The trees went by in a blur of greenery, leaving the glorified prison behind. Orison hoped Sila didn't notice she had gone until she was far away from his grasp.

The first to notice Orison's disappearance was Riddle and Taviar. They Misted into Cardenk as quickly as they could, before the king woke up from a strange unconsciousness that had befallen him. Walking hand in hand, they looked for

Orison, checking every face that passed them; but nobody was her, not even in disguise. They turned down the street where their daughter now lived, hoping she was safe there.

Cardenk was the only place they thought could guarantee finding Orison's location. However, she was gifted a Faunetta's Atlas; she could Mist to any known location in the empire—if she wasn't so untrained in the practice. The worst scenarios kept running through Taviar's head; he didn't want to take her back to the castle, he only wanted her safe.

Finding the home in the centre of the street, Riddle knocked on the door quickly. He kept checking around in case Orison ran out the back. He knew Kinsley would be home, and usually wherever Kinsley was, Orison was around as well. They were like sisters since they first met.

Aeson opened the door with a puzzled expression while he dried his hands with a dishrag.

"Is Orison here?" Taviar asked before Aeson could greet him.

Aeson shook his head as he threw the dishrag over his shoulder. He gave a slight laugh. "Of course not. She can't leave her room. You both know..."

"The entire shield has gone and Orison is missing," Riddle interrupted.

"Othereal above, do you want to come in?"

"No time, we need to find her," Riddle said with urgency in his voice.

Aeson turned to the stairs leading to his home. "Kinsley, your fathers need you now!"

A voice came from the depths of the home. The stairs creaked as Kinsley dashed down, using the wall for support. She appeared next to her boyfriend; holding his arm, she smiled at her fathers and looked around the street for the reason behind their unexpected visit.

"Do you know where Orison is?" Taviar asked. His daughter stayed silent and bit her lip before looking down. "Kinsley Brooke Luxart, tell me if you know of her whereabouts."

She sighed. "Orison has sought refuge in Akornsonia with King Idralis. He made arrangements and she should be two hours from the castle by now."

Taviar's eyes flared with rage. "You better tell me Kiltar is with her."

"I don't know. And Kiltar is a ruse, it's Prince Xabian," Kinsley admitted.

Tearing his hand away from his husband, Riddle stormed down the main street of Cardenk and Misted to Saskia's home. He knew that Xabian was meant to protect Orison, hence the Desigle, but he'd allowed her to go off with the elf folk. In Riddle's opinion, they were dangerous. The entire situation was easily preventable if Xabian had done his job and now more people than just Orison were in danger. Riddle needed to know why Xabian would let this happen.

He was shaking with worry as he fumbled to open Saskia's gate. Riddle walked up the footpath and knocked loudly on the door. Saskia cracked the door open and peered through the gap with a smile.

Riddle looked at her. "I need to speak to Xabian."

"Of course, he's moved bedrooms. His new room is upstairs, second door to the left."

The door creaked as she opened it wider. Riddle stepped in, bypassing Saskia as he made his way to the stairs. Using the wall for support, he jogged up the stairs, finding the second door to the left. He knocked and entered, without waiting to be invited inside. Xabian straightened up from his work at a writing desk. His eyes widened and he turned quizzically at Riddle's furious expression.

Riddle had always been capable of seeing Xabian's true self before the curse took hold. For Orison's protection, Riddle had always downplayed how he saw Xabian when they were all in the same room together. It was like seeing a ghost when Xabian arrived at Grandma Jo's Restaurant when Riddle celebrated with his children.

Thrusting his finger towards the castle, Riddle shouted. "Why the fuck are you not out there with Orison?"

"Is she injured?" Xabian asked, clutching his chair. "What happened?"

"She made a deal with King Idralis and is on her way to fucking Torwarin—that's what's happened!" Riddle yelled, breathing heavily. "You are meant to be protecting her!"

Xabian stood up with enough force to topple his chair over. "She's done what?" he cried. "Fuck!" He ran a hand down his face and shook his head. "I didn't know she would do that. How?"

"Yeah, good question, how?" Riddle exclaimed sarcastically. "You are supposed to be watching her! Fallagh knows what she's being subjected to now. Torwarin is not the Fae jurisdiction, they could torture her."

"Well, the Desigle is still in place, and I've not been Misted to her, so she is safe for now," Xabian stated; more to reassure himself than Riddle. "At sunset I'll find her immediately."

Riddle watched Xabian pick up his chair and sit back down, burying his head in his hands as he shook his head in disbelief. He didn't care about how Xabian felt; he needed Orison to be safe and not subjected to the elves mistreating her. Placing his hands on his hips, Riddle stared at the prince in the chair; he looked grief-stricken.

"Why haven't you been watching her, Xabian?"

Xabian looked at Riddle. "I told her who I really was. Now she hates me and doesn't want me anywhere near her."

"I'm not surprised with you lying to her this whole time."

He looked away, squeezing his eyes shut. Riddle stood there, taking in the reaction of how his words hit something deep in Xabian. He was remorseful about it and it was eating him up inside; he could tell Xabian was fighting with the demons in his head.

"Just, please be patient until I make this up to her," Xabian said quietly.

Riddle stepped closer to him and crouched down. "When you find Orison, please tell her everything."

Avoiding eye contact, Xabian stared off into the distance. There was a part of Riddle who was glad to see Xabian suffering from Orison's hatred. He had led her across Fallasingha to find a prince who was by her side the entire time.

Standing up, Riddle left Xabian to his own devices. Taking the stairs slower than on his arrival, he thanked Saskia for allowing him into her home and swiftly departed. Outside, he staggered to the nearest wall and tried to calm his nerves. An immense weight was lifted off his shoulders by confronting Xabian, only for another weight to be added—this time for Orison's safety.

THIRTY-TWO

Fire crackled as the group settled down for the first night of their journey. The tired horses snoozed near a tree to the sound of elf guards sharing stories. Orison hugged her knees to her chest, smiling about the stories being passed around. She took the canteen of alcohol Khardell offered her, taking a sip.

"Did I tell you about the time I climbed through a castle toilet?" Nazareth began, massaging her leg stump as she looked around the group. The men roared with disgust at the reminder of the story and shook their heads. "Hey! Stop judging, it's a good story!"

Orison straightened up. "I want to hear it, please tell."

The camp fell quiet, turning to look at Orison with mixtures of shock, confusion and distaste. Nazareth laughed as she looked at her friends. The story wasn't told because a metallic thud echoed off the trees. Nazareth grabbed her hunting knife and aimed it at the darkness. A moment passed, then two, until Feud appeared through the dense canopy of trees with a hamper filled with food from the nearest town of Old Liatnogard.

"Put your knife away, it's just me," Feud reprimanded.

Doing as she was told, Nazareth inched closer to the fire, rubbing her hands together as the smell of freshly baked bread filled the camp; Orison's stomach growled. Feud handed out bread bowls to people with metal pots of something else, until he got to her. She looked down with a puzzled expression.

"Veal soup. It'll do us good on the road. Proper warrior's broth," Khardell explained, pouring the soup into the bread. "You put the soup into the bread, fucking delicious."

"At least taste the food before you have an orgasm, Othereal above," Echo exclaimed, causing the campers to erupt into laughter. "Are you comfortable, Orison?"

Her laughter dwindled. "Very! Thank you."

Murmurs filled the campground; everyone was too busy eating. Orison set her bread bowl down on her sleep mat and poured the soup inside. She realised she didn't have utensils and saw that other campers were drinking from their bowls. After a moment's hesitation, Orison cupped the bowl in her hands and brought it to her mouth. She drank the hearty soup, which was perfectly spiced and made her feel at home. A laugh made her set the bowl down; Feud extended a spoon to her. She looked at the other campers, confused.

"I thought we didn't have utensils," Orison said, feeling her cheeks heat as she took the spoon.

Feud waved his hand as he slurped from his own spoon. "Them lot are animals; you can ignore them, being a princess and all."

Overhearing Feud, Nazareth howled like a wolf; the others copied, followed by a symphony of other wolf calls from deep in the forest. Orison looked around, mesmerised. She smiled when she saw Nazareth had soup running down her chin; who didn't seem to mind as long as she ate something. Continuing to eat, the campers had fallen into a unified silence as they filled their bellies.

Conversations returned when the soup was devoured, laughter began and alcohol flowed freely. Echo and Khardell danced like they were an old married couple, their singing slurred with grins on their faces. Nazareth watched from her sleeping mat, urging Feud to dance with Orison. He quickly obliged, scooping Orison from her sleeping mat and swaying her from side to side in a traditional elf dance. It always surprised her how different parts of the Othereal had individual customs for dancing. Despite her many dance lessons, she stepped on Feud's foot; her eyes widened in horror.

"Sorry." Orison flinched, thinking he would be angry at her.

Feud roared with laughter. "Drink to a princess who's bad at dancing!"

They all raised their canteens of beer and drank. Orison laughed out of confusion; she wasn't used to having such a relaxed atmosphere around her. A mistake like that would have had her humiliated in front of the staff in Alsaphus Castle. She noticed Echo whisper something in Khardell's ear and they disappeared into the canopy of trees.

The camp fell silent once again—an awkward silence as everybody knew what the two were doing. Feud scratched the back of his neck and looked at Nazareth as she laid down on the saddle bag she was using as a pillow.

"I think we should get some sleep," Feud instructed. "I'll take the first watch."

Orison coughed and nodded. "Definitely; we need sleep."

Settling down on her sleep mat, Orison tucked the blanket around her and closed her eyes, willing sleep to come. Feeling something watching her made Orison open her eyes. Feud was studying her like she was an unsolved puzzle; it made her shudder. When he looked away, Orison felt safe enough to fall asleep.

Flying all night was draining, especially when there was no reward. The forest was a labyrinth to an oubliette—one wrong turn and an unsuspecting creature might get lured into a trap; or become so lost, they could never come out alive. Orison's floral scent was weak against the scent of pollinated flowers and mildew. Xabian's sense of smell was stronger in his Nyxite form. At sunrise, when he crashed to the earth to turn back from Nyxite, the scent was dull on the trail he was on, until he took a route North.

Stumbling through the brush, Xabian came to a clearing and collapsed to his knees when he saw charred ground from a recent campfire. Orison's scent was the strongest it had been since he embarked on his mission. He had arrived too late. The birdsong from nearby trees angered him; it was a joyous song for a non-joyous occasion. Xabian felt powerless that he couldn't do much in his Fae form when he didn't know where she was—he couldn't even borrow a horse with the Nighthex pressing down on him.

Looking up to the heavens, Xabian sucked in a breath and let out a scream of desperation. He hated the cards that were handed to him, hated the king for what he had done. He collapsed to the ground, exhausted, his belly growling from dire hunger.

He had let his guard down and had become complacent in thinking Orison would stay put in her room until Sila thought of bringing the shield down. Of course she would conspire with King Idralis when he offered her a way out. Xabian had always known she was desperate, but hadn't realised how desperate. He deserved this suffering for underestimating her.

Blindly making his way through the forest and overwhelmed by his emotions, he managed to find his way to Old Liatnogard. As he walked through the high street, confused shoppers stopped in their paths to watch the strange man pass through their town; like he was in a trance. In actuality, he was too deep in his thoughts to notice his surroundings.

Eventually, Xabian found his way to the nearest pub. The patrons fell silent when he entered. Men at surrounding tables who were playing cards regarded him with suspicion. The only people not paying him any mind were the alcoholics at the bar. Xabian sat on one of the last available seats as he carried on staring at nothing—once again he had failed.

Rubbing his tired eyes, Xabian huffed out a breath. He shouldn't be moping; he should be looking for Orison, but he had to wait until sunset. An overflowing mug of beer appeared in front of Xabian. His attention landed on the bartender, who had a very stained shirt and was busy cleaning a glass.

"It's on the house, you look like you need it."

"Thank you." Xabian looked at the menu. "Can I get the eggs and sausages please?"

The bartender disappeared behind a door. Xabian heard him shouting to the cook in the back room before he returned to tend the bar. Xabian kept his head down, drinking his sorrows away; not caring how early in the morning it was. He needed a distraction. Maybe he'd go to a brothel while in Liatnogard, but he felt like he couldn't do that to Orison. Not that she cared. Xabian tugged on his hair and groaned; why couldn't he get her out of his head?

"You look like a beaten-up man without displaying the bruises. Want to talk about it?" the bartender asked, while polishing a cup.

Xabian tapped his fingers on his mug. He unloaded the entire mess of the situation, leaving out the fact he was Prince Xabian and she was Princess Orison. He gave them both false identities. That's what he liked about pubs in Fallasingha—they were like therapy places, with bartenders who genuinely listened.

Orison sat on the riverbank as she watched the elves strip down to nothing. They dived into a pool at the bottom of a waterfall to bathe. She hugged her knees to her chest, not daring to strip down that much and expose herself. The men were waist deep in the water; Orison's body heated at the sight of their sculpted chests from days of training as warriors. She had to look away when the Elven men entered more shallow waters to collect mud. They scrubbed themselves with it and spoke about what they'd do when they got home, like it was a normal afternoon. She noticed Nazareth was amongst them, standing stark naked, holding onto Echo for support as she rubbed river mud along her bare chest.

"Princess, we can't have you smelling like an ogre's arse crack. Come in, the water's lovely!" Khardell called over. She shook her head and waved them to carry on.

Only at this moment did she realise she had grown accustomed to the cushy lifestyle of being a royal. Before Othereal, she would have done the same as the elves—dived in stark naked for anybody to see. Now it terrified her and made her stomach tighten. Plus, she didn't have a change of clothes. She would wait to see if they had running water in Torwarin.

The movement of water caught her attention. Khardell was coming up to her. Orison caught herself staring when the water was only up to his knees. She quickly tore her gaze away and tried to focus on his face; he smirked.

"Othereal above," she muttered under her breath, feeling heat go to her cheeks.

Khardell stood there with his arms folded. "I usually take a lady's word, but you do need to bathe, Princess. We don't know when we'll see another opportunity and if Idralis sees you coming to our lands dirty, he'll have our necks for not taking care of you."

Though the water looked inviting, she couldn't. "I don't have a change of clothes," Orison whispered, looking at the others who were now observing them.

With a click of his fingers, a fresh pair of brown trousers and a white tunic appeared. Khardell turned around and disappeared back into waist-high water. Orison stood up and untied her boots—kicking them to one side. Shrugging off her dirty tunic and trousers, she made her way to the water's edge, squealing at the frigid temperature before sinking in. Orison swam up to the group of elves who handed her slabs of mud to use on her arms.

Nazareth nudged Orison. "Did you like what you saw?"

"I guess Khardell's fine." She rubbed the cooling mud on her arms and shoulders.

Echo snorted. "He's a nice ride."

"Oh, you are disgusting! Sit under that waterfall and think about what you just said," Nazareth spat, pointing to the gushing water.

He laughed. "Then what would you hold onto for support? You left your crutches at home."

"Touché." Nazareth turned to Orison. "I've been leading this lot for a hundred years and they still surprise me."

Nazareth waved Orison along. Both of them swam up to the waterfall as the men switched places with the girls. As they passed through, the force of the water on Orison's head made her teeth knock together painfully. She tolerated it. They made their way to an underwater ledge where Nazareth hauled herself up, using her magic to clean the mud off her arms.

Running her fingers through her hair, Orison shook out the twigs and other dirt that had accumulated from the journey and from sleeping on the ground. She was starting to feel better, not as weighed down. She began to relax under the waterfall. If they didn't have a journey to embark on, she could stay here for hours.

After the group bathed, they all used magic to dry themselves off and got they dressed into clean clothes. Khardell was tying his hair back as Orison stroked Maelstrom's muzzle. She fed it an apple from a nearby tree; it huffed out a warm breath on her hand. She tensed when something whizzed past her head. Orison turned to see an arrow embedded into a tree rocking with a hum from being recently shot. Another was shot at her soon after, then a barrage of them hurtled through the air towards the group.

"Ambush!" Khardell cried out. "Get on your horses!"

Feeling strong hands lift her up from behind, Orison kicked her legs, struggling to get out of their grasp as panic set in. "It's just me," Echo assured, sitting her on top of Maelstrom.

She heard him say something in a language she didn't understand. She barely had enough time to react as Maelstrom bolted into the dense growth of the forest. Orison scrambled to grip the reins, letting the horse take her to its destination; no matter how much she tried to get it to slow down, it wouldn't.

The thunder of hooves made Orison look over her shoulder to see Khardell protecting her from behind. He had an arrow nocked to a bow, turning on their assailants. He loosed the arrows in quick-fire succession. Beside him, Nazareth and Feud were holding shields and their swords were drawn.

"By the order of King Alsaphus, you must stop and hand over the princess!" a guard shouted. Orison recognised the voice instantly—Edmund.

"Never!" Khardell shouted back.

Digging his heels into the sides of his horse, it trotted faster until he was side by side with Orison. She needed to think and to figure out a plan. There were six of them in the group. She had never Misted more than herself before, but to protect them, she was willing to try. Orison didn't even know if there was a limit to the amount of people that a Fae could Mist at once.

"Under Fallasingha Law, we command you to halt!" Edmund shouted.

"Let me into your mind," she said breathlessly, turning to Khardell.

He glanced at her as more arrows barraged past them. The thunder of hooves from the horses of the king's guards grew louder as they caught up. Khardell nodded his consent and she dived into his head. She searched for somewhere to anchor herself, somewhere she could Mist to. She looked at Khardell's memories of when the Elven group journeyed to Alsaphus Castle. There was a Fallasingha town near Akornsonia—Navawich.

The king's guards appeared out of the underbrush, encircling them; they were running out of time to flee. In one last-ditch effort, Echo fired arrows at them, with Nazareth and Feud swinging their swords in long sweeping arches. More arrows narrowly missed Khardell and Orison—her unbound hair flying behind her. Maelstrom slowed when Orison pulled on the reins until she was near her comrades.

"Everybody, join hands!" Orison shouted, reaching her hand out.

All struggled to join hands on top of moving horses, but after a few moments, they all managed to succeed at keeping the formation. She had no idea if this would work, but to protect her rescuers, she had to try. Orison thought of Navawich with its wheat fields swaying and windmills on the horizon. Purple night and stars engulfed everyone as Orison carried them all to safety—not realising arrows were travelling with them.

Thirty-Three

Crash landing in the middle of the wheat field, Orison got on all fours and threw up violently. Her eyes stung as an ice-cold feeling settled over her. She was shaking violently and she retched again as she dug her nails into the soft soil. Orison instantly knew she had used up her entire reserve of magic; it was only a small amount from being so untrained. Now she understood why Taviar told her to be careful. In this instance, she didn't care, her rescuers were safe. A hand on her back made her tense and turn her head—Feud moved her hair from her face as he tried to soothe her.

"Is everybody okay?" Orison asked. Looking around, she couldn't see anybody else through the towers of wheat around them.

She tried to stand up, only to scream in agony as a searing pain made her collapse back to the ground. Bringing her leg to the front, a pain-filled noise escaped her when seeing an arrow protruding out of her thigh. Blood flowed over her trembling hands and to the soil below.

"Can I take the arrow out?" Feud asked, concern darkening his already dark eyes.

Orison nodded, wiping the tears away from her cheeks and smearing blood all over her face. She'd never been shot with an arrow before; it had to be the worst pain she had ever experienced. It burned and made her leg tingle. Feud waved his hand and her leg quickly became numb. She watched him grip the arrow, wincing at the strange tugging sensation on her wound. He placed his hands over the wound. They glowed with magic; and when they lifted, she had four stitches made out of vines.

A loud, elongated wail made both of them tense. They turned towards the sound when it happened again, followed by screaming words in the Elven language. Orison couldn't see anything through the wheat and she couldn't stand up either. Feud staggered up to see over the towering masses. He took a step towards the chaos in a blind stupor of horror; he snapped out of it when he remembered Orison was helpless on the ground.

"Get on my back," Feud instructed.

Standing up on shaking limbs, her injured leg still numb from his magic, Orison limped towards him as another wail filled the field. Holding onto his shoulders, she jumped on his back. Feud grasped her non-injured thigh and held her hand on his shoulder before making his way through the wheat field where the wailing increased. Feud was so tall,

Orison felt like a child again—back when she was small enough for her father to carry her on his shoulders.

They didn't have to walk far. At first, all Orison saw was Nazareth and Echo on the ground; Feud's grip on Orison slackened. With a stumble, she lowered herself down, gasping at the sight before her. Khardell lay on the ground with an arrow protruding out of his chest, his eyes lifeless as they stared at the blue skies over them; there was no bringing him back.

Nazareth was the one wailing. Tears streamed down her face as she held her hands to her chest, staring down at Khardell's lifeless body. Pulling her into an embrace, Echo held Nazareth close as heavy sobs wracked through her body. Feud sank to his knees out of despair for their fallen captain. Guilt punched Orison in the gut.

"I'm sorry," Orison gasped, covering her mouth with a trembling hand. "I'm sorry, this is my fault, I caused this."

"No, don't blame yourself," Echo reprimanded. She looked at him with tear-filled eyes. "This is King Sila's doing. We knew this was something we risked when getting you to safety."

Orison pressed a hand to her chest, her face in abject horror. "This was a suicide mission?"

"For some," Feud said quietly, looking at Khardell with an empty look in his eyes. "The king will pay for this. King Idralis will not accept the murder of his guard captain."

Echo stood, taking Nazareth's hands and helping her up. She stumbled a little before looking at her trembling fingers covered in blood. He shushed her as they disappeared into the wheat, more than likely to wash her hands. The sound of wheat moving behind them made Orison turn around. Xabian appeared out of the towering mass; his clothes were a mess and so was his hair.

"Stay back!" Feud shouted, unsheathing his sword, fury in his eyes.

Holding her hands out, Orison looked between Xabian and Feud. "Stop! He's here because of the Desigle he placed on me. This is Prince Xabian Alsaphus."

Feud's jaw dropped. "I threatened the missing Prince of Fallasingha with my sword?" She nodded with a roll of her eyes. "Sorry, Prince Xabian."

"Whether or not he can be trusted is another question entirely," Orison grumbled.

Xabian lowered himself down to his knees, inspecting her for injuries; pausing at the hole in her trousers and stitches in her leg. "The king's guards shot me with an arrow; Feud helped sew it up. I'm fine, just numb."

She tensed when he held her close. "I thought I lost you, thank Othereal you're safe."

"You drained your magic for us. I don't call that fine," Feud retorted. It earned him a glare from Orison.

"Why would you do that?" the prince demanded.

"To protect my rescuers," Orison spat. She noticed a lipstick stain on his neck. "It didn't take you long to jump into bed with another person."

Feud stood up. "Personal shit aside, if you want us to trust you, then you better help us with this mess." He gestured to Khardell.

Moving away from Orison, it was the first time Xabian saw Khardell's lifeless body. He nodded, taking a small switchblade out of his pocket, easing out the arrow and setting it on fire. With Feud's help, he sat Khardell up and eased off his blood-soaked white tunic before gently laying him back down—just as Nazareth and Echo returned with supplies. Each had assigned themselves jobs to prepare the body for travel.

The wheels of the cart squealed as it travelled North through the forest that led to Torwarin. Nazareth steered the single chestnut horse they had managed to borrow; only time would tell the fate of the other horses which they had begun the journey with.

Orison winced as the magic numbing her leg started to wear off, a deep throbbing pain seized her leg. She was careful to avoid Khardell's body as she shifted to get comfortable.

As she was jostled from side to side, she looked over at Echo who was sound asleep. Orison didn't know how she could sleep with her leg in this condition; she needed a medic to do something.

She looked up as their cart was cast into shadow by a large gateway made of roots. Bells began to chime followed by the sound of long horns that bounded from tree to tree. Orison could have sworn she saw dark shadows moving between the branches. A pit formed in her stomach at the possibility that it might be Sila's men as the cart rolled to a stop. Xabian tried to place his hand on Orison's arm for reassurance, but she shrugged it off; moving away from him with a huff of breath. Nazareth stood up from the bench and climbed down.

"My King, we have been blessed with an early return, but we come back with bad news," Nazareth said with a bow.

King Idralis stepped out of the shadows wearing a crown of thorns. He nodded with a grim facial expression. "Yes, the trees said as such." His gaze caught on Xabian for a moment. "Josiah, please can you take Orison to the infirmary while we make burial plans for Captain Khardell."

It was all a blur from there, people came and went. Xabian tried to help Orison down from the cart, but she pushed him away. In the end, Josiah carried her through a labyrinth of wooden cabins. Children laughed as they played in the street, only to stop when they spied two Faeries amongst them—enemies being treated with honour. Josiah took Orison to a cabin down a narrow street; pushing the door open, several elves stopped conversing and stared at the two newcomers.

"Why are the Fae in my infirmary?" a woman with flowing black hair demanded.

Josiah sat Orison down on the bed. "This is Princess Orison Durham, a guest of the king. The trees tell him she was shot with an arrow. She needs assistance and her companion Prince Xabian Alsaphus needs something to prevent his Nighthex from taking hold."

When Xabian tried comforting Orison again, she shoved him away. She was still fuelled with rage at the memories they shared; how he had strung her along for months for nothing but trouble. She struggled to breathe as she tried to wrap her head around what she was going to say to him. They needed to clear the air. If her leg didn't hurt so much, she would have punched him for lying to her. For being aware of her search and worry for his wellbeing. Also, the Desigle binding them that never asked for; she wanted the bond severed.

"I need to speak to the prince immediately, in private," Orison said, tears in her eyes.

All the elves turned to her. "But you need assistance, Princess."

"Please," she pleaded.

The elves bowed and ascended the stairs to the second floor. Orison's glare was lethal; Xabian averted his gaze like it hurt him terribly. She was so angry that she was shaking;

usually her magic would spark under her skin, but she had nothing left to give.

"Let the nurses look..."

"Why?" she asked quietly. "Why not be honest with me from the start?"

"Shame and embarrassment."

"You were there when I was searching for days. Even when I tried to open a portal to the mortal realm; only to discover that you've been with me this entire time posing as a guard!" Orison shouted and threw her hands in the air. "Did you enjoy seeing me make a fool of myself from whatever ditch you came out of?"

"You have the audacity to talk, when you've made an elf bargain!" Xabian shouted.

Orison scoffed loudly. "Do not turn this back on me because you aren't man enough to give me answers. Your bullshit has been going on for weeks!" She threw her hands in the air. "We even slept together! Was it just a ruse to warm my bed, then laugh about me?"

"I hated not telling you. It is embarrassing to be overpowered by your own brother," Xabian spat, sitting on the bed next to hers. "I only did this to protect you from that fucking malicious piece of shit that shares my blood. But the more time I spent with you, the more I hated myself, Orison. But I know that you no longer want to be my friend because I didn't man up and tell you."

He stood up and approached the door; Orison watched him fling it open and disappear onto the street. She jumped when he slammed the door using his powers. She didn't have the opportunity or energy to tell him that she truly wanted to stay friends.

Thirty-Four

The sunlight through the sheer curtains woke Orison up from her slumber. Her bed felt like she was lying on a cloud, a patchwork quilt over her. Rubbing her eye with the heel of her hand, she stretched her arms, feeling like she had the best night's sleep in her life. Looking around, she was in a room made of wood. Two large windows showed a twinkling lake that reflected the golden sun like a mirror; a door led out to the water. Easing her way into a sitting position, her hair fell over one shoulder as she looked outside in awe.

On the lake, Orison watched men standing on logs submerged on the water. They wore nothing but loose-fitting trousers and hit each other in long sweeping arcs; someone was calling orders that echoed across the lake. She was yearning to run to the water's edge, to see the men up close, but at the same time she was scared—was Idralis truthful in telling her that she had freedom in Torwarin?

After getting ready for the day, Orison stepped out onto the wooden balcony of her cabin. The wooden floor creaked and was warm under her bare feet as she made her way to the stairs. Her eyes glued to the men on the lake, she wondered what they were doing. She paused at the top of the stairs, unable to go any further. Did she have to ask permission to leave the cabin? Would a guard stop her at the bottom? Instead, she sat on the top step watching the men from there, mesmerised by their fluent movements. At Alsaphus Castle, she was forbidden to watch the guards training.

The sound of long horns made her tense. Was that an alarm alerting the guards that Orison had left her room when she was forbidden? She gripped the handrail, scrambling to stand up quickly before guards could put manacles of fire on her. Orison knew it would be just another glorified prison. All she wanted to do was watch the guards, but now they were going to lock her up. That's how it was in the Othereal.

"Are you well, Princess?" Feud asked as he approached her with a tray of food and drink.

Orison tensed and turned to him, taking the tray. "Sorry, I know I overstepped where I shouldn't be. I will deal with whatever punishment King Idralis proposes."

He scoffed. "Your only punishment is ignoring your growling belly. Come on, there's a bench and table on the lakefront."

Making her way down the stairs, she realised there was no shield. "But the horns."

"Ignore those. They informed King Idralis that you're awake and to get you some food. You must be starving after two days," Feud said as he walked Orison to the lakefront.

She hurried after him. "Two days?"

Feud nodded. "Out like a light for two days." Pausing as they came upon rocky terrain, he looked at Orison's bare feet. "Where are your shoes?" She shrugged and hugged her arms. He clicked his fingers and pink slippers appeared in front of her; Orison didn't hesitate to put them on. "Much better."

He led her through a small canopy of willow trees that gave a cool breeze in the warmth. As Feud had said, there was a table with a bench. He set the tray down, using his magic to clean the log of tree sap, then handed Orison some wooden utensils. Lifting the lid on a full fry-up breakfast, he removed another lid to reveal black coffee.

"I shall leave you be," Feud said with a bow.

As he turned, Orison grabbed the cuff of his guard uniform. "Will you stay?"

He hesitated at first, then sat opposite her. Orison tucked into her breakfast, cutting her sausages; eating as she watched the guards on the lake training with women. A lead guard called orders to change positions; a loud splash sounded as they tackled someone into the water with a war cry.

"After you've eaten, I have to return to my duties. You can explore Akornsonia to your heart's content," Feud explained, fiddling with his arm cuff. "Guards will be in the trees but will leave you alone, unless a threat presents itself."

Orison slowed her chewing as she looked at him. It was a strange concept to be allowed outside the confinements of her own bedroom—it was even stranger to be allowed to explore the entirety of Akornsonia and be left alone. Though guards would follow her, it would be like they weren't there.

"Is Prince Xabian still here? He needs assistance."

Feud smiled at her. "Yeah, Xabian's still here. He's getting the assistance he needs."

Orison breathed a sigh of relief; though she hated him right now, she still cared. Knowing he was safe made her feel better, but she needed to talk to him when she found him. Looking around her, Orison watched people building cabins, women tending to small chicken farms and children playing. It would take a while to re-adjust to a free way of life, away from the prying eyes of a brutal king.

Xabian grimaced at the mug of brown sludge in his hand. It bubbled like a swamp and even smelled like one. His stomach churned. He didn't want to drink it, but the infirmary nurses insisted he did, under the order of King Idralis. Everything was screaming at him to pour the drink down the drain and forget he ever laid eyes on it. But an infirmary nurse was watching his every move.

"Drink," a nurse instructed.

"May I enquire what will happen if I do?"

The grey-haired nurse pointed a finger at him. "It will prevent the curse for three days, no more, no less, and when time is up, you shall return."

"And then I take another dose?"

His heart sank when she shook her head. "No, Prince Xabian, this is your one and only chance at getting a break." The words were a heavy weight on his shoulders. "This potion is a gift from the Keres Waters. If you indulge in its gifts again, you will meet your demise."

Looking down at the bubbling brown sludge, he had to do it. Pinching his nose, he dipped his head back and drank. The taste was rancid, like he was drinking warm vomit. He retched but forced it down; the liquid burned Xabian's tongue. Once it was down to the dregs, he was relieved it was over. When he hiccupped, it brought up the vile liquid, but he forced himself to swallow it back down. The stomach cramping was immediate.

The nurse gave Xabian some mint leaves to chew on. He groaned loudly as another cramp made him keel over; hiccupping again made him feel dizzy. He was grateful for the minty taste of the leaves; it replaced the taste of stomach bile. Xabian allowed himself to relax when the leaves made the stomach cramps subside. He returned to feeling the way he did before drinking the Keres Waters.

"Is the princess awake?"

The nurse glanced at Xabian as she wrote in a notebook. "You know she is resting, as should you." She checked his forehead with the back of her hand, shaking her head. "You need to stay here."

"But I need to see her." He tried to stand, but the nurse pushed him down.

"And if you vomit this potion up, drinking the Keres Waters would have been pointless. It's your turn to rest," the nurse snapped.

Reluctantly, Xabian sank back down on the bed, twiddling his thumbs. He winced as he moved, clutching his stomach as it cramped again with a pain-filled groan. Were the waters supposed to give him a stomach ache? The nurse walked out of the room and up a flight of stairs, leaving Xabian to deal with this himself. His hairline was coated with sweat. Nothing good ever tasted sweet; this was definitely the case with the Keres Waters. It was flushing the curse out of his system for a couple of days.

To take his mind off the pain, Xabian thought about Orison. The trees had advised Idralis to place him far away from her. However, it never stopped him from visiting Orison while she slept in her bed and ensuring she wasn't dehydrated. Was she still asleep? It had been hours since his last visit. He hoped she was okay and getting the necessary care from the nurses while she recovered from using her entire resource of magic.

Xabian retched, his body trying to make him throw up the Keres Waters, but he wouldn't allow that to happen. He curled into a ball as another stomach cramp made him grunt in pain; his whole body shook as it tried to battle this strange substance. Letting out a cry of pain, his breathing increased as he clutched his stomach. Then the world went dark.

Night had fallen over Torwarin by the time Xabian awoke. He recognised his own cabin around him with only the moonlight to highlight the wooden walls. Somebody had moved him while he was unconscious. If it was night, that meant he had damaged some of King Idralis' furniture when the Nighthex took hold—he would have to apologise. Xabian didn't want to move, out of fear of damaging more property. The only inkling something was different was the fact he felt weightless—how he did during daylight hours.

He slowly sat up; looking down, he saw his legs. His eyes widened in awe. Waving his hand in the air, the Othereal lights flicked on in their sconces. Xabian inspected his furless hands, turning them over and over like it was the first time seeing them. His head shot up; he needed a mirror.

Throwing the duvet off his body, he ran into the bathroom and looked in the mirror. His eyes widened to see a man staring back at him; the same man before the Nighthex was placed on him. He ran his fingers through his fire-red hair, inspected his teeth and counted the freckles on his face. The only evidence that the curse was still there were the purple stars in his eyes.

Xabian could admit he doubted the Keres Water's power. It did more than he expected and he was here at night in his Fae form! He whirled around and hurried out of the door. He had to find Orison and show her, if she would even face him.

Checking the library or bakery proved pointless. She wasn't in either of those places, despite Xabian knowing she loved both. He checked the many shops around town—to no avail; even asking the elves proved pointless. She wasn't in her cabin like some of them suggested, nor on the lakefront. The possibility of her running away was highly unlikely. He saw the horse paddock on top of a hill and remembered that Orison loved horses; it was the only place he hadn't looked, so he made his way over.

At the paddock fence, he found her riding a purple unicorn with black colouring on its ankles, like little socks. The unicorn turned around before breaking into a full gallop; Orison cried out, attempting to get the creature to stop. The unicorn was trying to throw her and Xabian could only watch as she came off the saddle and landed in the soft dirt.

"Shit," he exclaimed, climbing over the fence and running up to her.

The unicorn leapt over a jump before slowing into a trot. It was making a noise that sounded like a laugh—if that was even possible. Xabian eased Orison into a sitting position; she flicked her hair out of her face.

"Rhosasia, you promised you wouldn't do that again!" she shouted. The unicorn shook its head, causing its black mane to glisten in the moonlight. "Mother fucker."

"Are you okay?" Xabian asked.

Orison turned to him and screamed, covering her mouth. "Othereal above, Xabian, is that you?"

"Yeah, it's me."

"But it's night! Is the curse broken? What is happening?" She looked shaken as she took in Xabian's features. Orison went to touch him, but quickly put her hands down.

"The elves made me a potion that puts the curse to sleep for three days. If I drink the potion again, it's lethal." Rhosasia nuzzled his arm and huffed out a breath. Xabian petted her. "Are you coming to apologise to the princess?"

The unicorn made a quick movement of its head before trotting off, glancing back at them before it galloped far away. Clearly, the apology wouldn't be happening. Xabian took Orison's hand as he helped her stand up and brush mulch off her white tunic. Orison cast a glare at Rhosasia who was more bothered about eating grass. Without warning, she slapped Xabian across the face. He staggered back, holding his cheek and looking at her in shock. She didn't look remorseful; she looked furious.

"That's for lying," Orison spat. He winced when she punched his chest. "And that."

Rubbing the spot on his chest where she punched him, he groaned. "I deserve both of those; holy shit, you're really strong."

Orison rolled her eyes before she moved towards Rhosasia. The unicorn trotted away upon seeing her approach like it was some kind of game—something that would continue for a few more moments. Unfortunately for the creature, it wasn't used to dealing with Fae having the ability to Mist. It took Orison a few attempts to Mist in front of the unicorn, her magic still recovering from being depleted. When she materialised in Rhosasia's path, the unicorn skidded to a halt and reared with a whinny. With a determined smirk, Orison grabbed the reins.

"I got you now," Orison said with a laugh. Rhosasia tried to bite her. "No, no biting!"

"You had to choose the baby," a deep voice said with a chuckle. Orison turned to see King Idralis at the paddock fence. "She's a handful."

Orison stepped back quickly. "Sorry, I should have asked for permission."

Back in Alsaphus Castle, the king had forbidden her from taking the unicorns out—he strictly confined them to their stables. However, he allowed the guards to take them out once a week. Despite asking Sila on multiple occasions to ride a unicorn, he always rejected Orison's pleas. When she found Rhosasia in the stables, Orison wanted to make that dream a reality. Now that she thought about it, she should have asked Idralis' permission.

She waited for him to reprimand her and put up a shield around her cabin. Instead, he simply said, "You're alright, she needed a ride anyway, thank you," Idralis said with a smile.

"You're not angry with me?" Orison questioned with a puzzled expression.

King Idralis shrugged. "She's been cooped up in those stables for three days. She needed to be out. You saved my people some work."

Xabian stepped up beside Orison. "Do you require assistance with anything, King Idralis?"

"We need a plan of retaliation for killing Captain Khardell. Meet me in my cabin at your earliest convenience, preferably tonight," Idralis requested. "If it's tomorrow, we can work with that too."

Both of the Fae bowed when Idralis walked away, then Xabian got to work getting Rhosasia back into the stables. Being as young as she was, the unicorn resisted all the way until he gave her an apple to follow. After making sure Rhosasia was back in her stable with adequate food and water, Xabian checked that the other horses and unicorns had enough as well.

Xabian had to show Orison the way to King Idralis' cabin because she didn't have the grand tour of Torwarin. On the main street, Xabian pointed to a restaurant and one of

Torwarin's many bakeries—it was the one bakery that she had already discovered. Xabian made a detour and showed Orison the library. He would have gone inside the small wooden structure if they didn't have to attend the meeting.

Navigating Torwarin's dark alleyways which were occasionally lit by small shops or taverns, Xabian realised that Orison was no longer following him. Backtracking his steps, he eventually found her outside of the bookstore. He smiled when she ran her hand through a trolley of books. She picked up each book, stroking the spine and flicking through pages.

"We have a meeting to go to," he explained. "Come on."

"Couple more minutes," Orison grumbled, reading the first page of a red leather-bound book. By the swirling design of the letters, she recognised the language. "This one is written in Fae."

Xabian shook his head and rested on the wall by the door that led to the bookstore's interior. Before he could protest, Orison walked past him and into the bookstore. Xabian tensed when he heard a loud audible gasp; he was quickly beside her. Nothing was wrong—a miniature train track mesmerised her. It was above their heads and the toy train was weaving its way around the store, puffing smoke.

"Orison," he warned as she made her way deeper into the labyrinth of shelves.

She glanced over her shoulder. "It'll be fine, Idralis will understand." Her fingers brushed against leather-bound spines written in Fae and Elf. She paused and frowned at the books written in the common tongue. "By the way, I haven't made an Elf bargain."

"Why else are you here?" Xabian asked, hands in his pockets as he leaned on a bookcase.

Orison picked up a book. "Idralis knew what Sila was doing." She read through the first page and put it back. "He was the note sender."

He followed her deeper into the bookstore, looking at the entrance, knowing they really shouldn't keep King Idralis waiting. Orison disappeared down another corridor, Xabian followed and found her picking up two books.

"We'll go soon. I don't have any books in my cabin," Orison said.

"I'm sorry for lying to you," Xabian said. He handed her a green-bound book with gold foiling. "You should get this one, I think you'll love it."

Orison put her two books on a shelf to look through the one he suggested. "I suppose I forgive you. As long as you don't lie to me again."

Xabian nodded, watching her read the synopsis, then the first page. "Why do you do that?"

"The synopsis can sound good, but you need to see if it's as gripping as it makes out," Orison explained without looking at him. "I think you are right; I will like this."

A note appeared in Xabian's hand. He knew immediately what it would say, but he still read it. *Where are you both? The meeting is starting.*

Xabian handed Orison the note. "You're explaining why we're late."

She laughed as she hugged the green book to her chest, making her way to the counter. Xabian chuckled when she picked up the two books that she was originally interested in. He sent a mental note to Idralis that Orison had found the local bookstore. He watched her place all the books down on the counter.

"Good choices," the cashier grumbled. Orison got her money out. "No charge for royalty."

Xabian picked up the bag and made to walk out of the store, only to see she wasn't following. "Ori," he snapped.

With a flap of her hands, she ran after him. They were already late; Xabian didn't want to be delayed any longer. Planning a battle was more important.

Thirty-Five

The sound of the knitting needles clicking together accompanied the creaks of the rocking chair. Saskia looked down with a proud smile at the blanket she had been working on. A thudding sound from upstairs made her look up at the ceiling. A heavy feeling settled into the room; it should only be her in the cottage, nobody else. Grabbing a fire poker, Saskia stood up and made her way up the stairs, her guard training had kicked into high-gear.

Hiding in the shadows, she kept her footsteps light as she inched up to the second floor. She kept her breathing steady to avoid alerting her intruder. Moving to the bedroom that Xabian used, she pushed the door open; it was empty. She shifted slightly to her bedroom, using the fire poker to open her door—empty. Inching along the wall to the last bedroom, she used the fire poker again and opened that door—empty as well.

Saskia exhaled a breath, deciding it was nothing more than paranoia. It was probably Xabian coming home after finding the princess. Turning, she made her way down the corridor, swinging her fire poker like it was an umbrella. She jogged down the stairs, humming a song to herself; she could go back to her knitting. When she reached the bottom step, a heavy feeling settled on her shoulders—the feeling of being watched.

She whirled around with the fire poker extended, ready to poke somebody's eye out if they dared to come near her. Out of the darkness, somebody all dressed in black approached Saskia from behind and smashed a rock over her head. She fell to the floor with a heavy thud.

When Saskia came around, her head pounded like a drum. She groaned and touched her head; her hand was red with blood. Her eyes widened. As she looked around, Saskia cried out when she realised that she was in Alsaphus Castle; more specifically in Sila's chambers, locked in an iron cage. Her heart thundered in her chest when she turned her head and saw Sila smirking at her. She shouldn't be here—he had banned her from entering the castle.

"You're finally awake," Sila drawled, pulling up a chair and sitting in it. "I would hope you have intel on the whereabouts of Princess Orison."

"I've not spoken to her recently," Saskia responded truthfully. "Not since you brought her back to the castle after her last escape."

"Interesting," Sila said. "What about Prince Xabian? I know he's been living with you. If I use you as blackmail, would he hand Orison over?"

Saskia closed her eyes and pressed her head to the bars of the cage. She knew Xabian wouldn't hand over Orison for anything. It still wouldn't stop King Sila from trying—he was cruel like that. He huffed out a breath as he stood up. With a click of his fingers, a cup appeared in his hand, which he pushed through the bars. She took it and sipped on the contents, thankful for some water.

"I thought you banished me from the castle," Saskia pointed out.

Sila smirked. "I need to get Orison back somehow. You're the perfect person to use because Xabian will want to protect you." He clicked his fingers and his infamous goblet of wine appeared. He took a sip. "I will get her back."

"There is no doubt you will," Saskia grumbled.

In actual fact, Saskia doubted he would get her back; wherever Orison or Xabian were. Riddle had placed a sound barrier around the room when he spoke to Xabian in private. She knew they were more than likely heavily protected somewhere. Sila wouldn't get her back without a fight. Of course, the king wouldn't listen to reason; he would be in his own little fantasy until he realised that for himself.

"Seer Aislin says that she's in Torwarin," Sila said as he sipped wine. "It's easy to get to. Maybe I can try to reason with King Idralis."

That revelation made Saskia tense. Had Riddle been so furious with Xabian because she made a bargain with the elves? No, Orison wouldn't be so foolish. In the short time she had known Orison personally, not through the words of her spies, Saskia had come to realise that she was a clever person who made calculated decisions.

"Why would she be in Torwarin? That's Elf territory," Saskia pointed out. The king shrugged with a pout, tapping his foot. "You have no jurisdiction in the Elf territory if she's there."

"We can come to an agreement in some capacity; I will get her back, mark my words," he spat as he drank. "Apparently, she's not under an Elf bargain. I doubt that though, she's a foolish person."

Saskia laid down in the cage with a heavy sigh. She knew she would eventually face repercussions from housing Xabian, but not this. She kept thinking of her home that she had built and her dresses that she had made; amongst other things. Did Sila make the guards who dragged her here bring her some clothes? It made her shift with anxiousness. Her mind was racing with possibilities she didn't want to think about. Then there was the matter of escaping—how would she get away? She didn't realise she was falling asleep until Sila spoke again.

"Seer Aislin says she's in Akornsonia." He scoffed out a laugh. "The Elf Kingdom is not a safe place; they pillage villages. How do you think they created Akornsonia? That was my land before he got his hands on it."

Saskia turned her head to face him. Akornsonia was never part of Fallasingha—another delusion Sila had made for himself. He wanted to have everything and give nothing in return. When she was the guard general, Akornsonia regularly wanted to form alliances and Sila refused every time. Maybe keeping Orison safe would be that push to an alliance.

"I doubt she is safe too," Saskia lied as she stared at the cage's ceiling. "You know what Idralis is like; we both do."

The lies she was feeding to keep Sila happy would buy Saskia some time; she wouldn't go down without a fight. She would escape the Fae King's capture soon—he was the one who taught her all the ways to escape, after all. In his eyes, she had become an entirely different person when she transitioned, but she hadn't changed at all. Sila had made a grave mistake bringing her here, and she would get revenge for herself, Xabian and Orison.

Underneath King Idralis' home was the war room. There was a map of the Othereal erected on the stone wall, along with pieces of information about strengths and weaknesses of each country. An oak table sat in the centre, surrounded by armchairs.

One of the king's servants hummed as they set down a selection of drinks, cakes and sandwiches. The servant was silent as they poured tea into Orison's and Xabian's cups, then finally Idralis' cup. It surprised Orison to hear Idralis thank the servant—something Sila never did. Putting sugar in her tea, Orison took a sip; pausing when she saw Idralis pour amber-coloured alcohol into his tea.

Creaking on the stairs was the sign that Nazareth had arrived. She walked across the room, cradling pieces of parchment in her arms as she sat next to the king. He assisted her in picking out key pieces of information that could be handy to retaliate against King Sila. Nazareth poured herself a drink, dismissing the servant from doing it. Orison had an inkling this meeting would be gruelling and difficult.

"I apologise in advance. I'm unsure how these meetings work," Orison said as she drank some tea, shifting in her seat.

King Idralis waved a dismissive hand. "You can learn." He tapped his mug. "First matter of business, Princess Orison; how was your first actual day in Torwarin?"

"It's been incredible—different, but incredible! One of the bakers let me use their ovens today when I asked. I helped them sell their stock because one of their staff members didn't turn up. Then I rode Rhosasia."

"That sounds wonderful. I'm glad you've enjoyed yourself," Idralis said with an enormous smile. "Now, even though I don't want to impose any limitations on you, Orison, I do advise that you don't go back into Fae territory. This is just a precautionary measure to prevent King Sila from taking you back to Alsaphus Castle." Orison looked at him, then looked down at her hands.

"Will you put up a shield to keep me in Akornsonia?" she asked.

"Though I can create shields, I really can't be bothered. They're so tedious. You're an adult, so it's your choice to heed the advice or not."

Breathing a sigh of relief, Orison looked at King Idralis. "You're... you're giving me a choice?" He nodded. "Thank you, King Idralis."

Everybody jumped when he clapped his hands. "Alright, retaliation efforts for the fall of Captain Khardell, Nazareth." She pushed some parchment toward Idralis who looked at the information, then at a map of the castle. "In private, we've discussed the possibility of setting fire to the castle. What would you say about this plan?"

"It's too dangerous," Xabian pointed out. He reached out and circled the spot of Merchant's Row with his finger. "There are families and vulnerable people in this area. We can't misplace or injure them; fire would do that. We need a new plan."

Nazareth tilted her head. "I had no idea there were families living in the castle." She rested her chin on her hands. "Your Majesty, do you have any other ideas?"

"Illusions," Orison muttered under her breath. Everybody turned to look at her. "Do you have anybody who can cast illusions? I can, but not for very long."

"Mindelates can't cast illusions, you can just put ideas in people's heads and make them think they're seeing things that aren't actually there," Xabian explained as he drank his tea. "We do need an Illusage."

The elves exchanged a look before the king spoke. "We have that ability. What do you propose, Princess?"

"Sila fears Nyxites. We could cast an illusion of a Nyxite threatening the king; and while doing so, infiltrate the castle while the guards are preoccupied," Orison explained.

Everybody at the table had fallen silent, looking at Orison in surprise. To Orison, it wasn't even a good plan; she had no idea if it would work—it was just something roaming around in her head. Creaking of the stairs broke the silence; somebody appeared on the step. They leaned over the banister, looking breathless.

"A message for King Idralis is at the gate," they announced before disappearing back upstairs.

Each of them exchanged glances, silently guessing what the message could entail. Without hesitation, they pushed the armchairs away from the table. They cleared away the maps and parchment before ascending the stairs and stepping out into the night.

The air was heavy around Torwarin, as a dreaded silence settled on the village. The king's men had gathered around the main gate of Akornsonia with crossbows aimed at the messenger; guards flanked King Idralis, Emissary Nazareth, Xabian and Orison. They were led by the newly appointed Guard Captain Echo. While they walked shoulder to shoulder, Orison looked down when Xabian took her hand; whether it was for his comfort or hers, she couldn't tell.

When Idralis got near the gates of Akornsonia, guards got down on one knee as a sign of respect, their heads lowered as he passed each individual until he arrived at the gate. This was a type of respect that was earned, not demanded.

Orison gasped when she saw Taviar standing at the other side of the gate; he had a scroll in his hands. He shifted when his gaze met Orison's; they waved to each other. Taviar paled to see Xabian like he once was; there was no denying the missing prince had well and truly been found.

"Welcome, Emissary Taviar. How may I assist you today?" King Idralis asked.

Taviar handed over the scroll. "I apologise in advance. King Sila is distraught and won't listen to reason as of late."

"Apologies accepted," Idralis drawled as he opened the scroll.

"How are you, sweets?" Taviar asked Orison. "You look happier."

Orison wrapped her arm around Xabian's with a nod. "I'm great, thank you. How are you?"

The sound of King Idralis snorting cut their conversation short. With a shake of his head, he rolled up the scroll and handed it to Nazareth, who pocketed it. Looking at her king in silent question; he didn't answer her. He moved closer to Xabian, weighing up the information in his head.

"You can tell the king that no amount of money can buy Princess Orison back. The prince and myself have come to an agreement that I will protect her from King Sila until she takes the throne. I plan to uphold that agreement," Idralis snapped. Taviar's eyes widened as he looked at Orison. "I suppose there is no other option but for me and Sila to go to battle. I hope the king receives this message loud and clear."

"Message received, and I shall deliver. Thank you." Taviar responded with confidence. He bowed to the king. "Please continue keeping Princess Orison safe; I have great confidence that you will."

King Idralis bowed, then he watched Taviar walk away and Mist in a flurry of green fog. Turning to the two Faeries who he was keeping safe, King Idralis gestured for them to return to Torwarin. As they all began walking back to town, Orison kept glancing over her shoulder to where Emissary Taviar had stood. When she looked at Xabian, she noticed he looked troubled over King Sila's order.

"Is a battle actually going to happen?" Orison questioned.

"Unfortunately," Xabian replied. "Not a war, but a battle nonetheless."

When they entered town, the heaviness of the messenger still lingered around the citizens. Orison noticed people peering through small gaps in their curtains, as they tried to see if they led the messenger into Akornsonia. They retreated when they realised it was only Idralis. The only other people on the street were those going to the pubs or buying last-minute things from the shops that were still open.

"The trees tell me Emissary Taviar isn't faithful to the king," Idralis said as he walked beside Orison and Xabian, hands behind his back. "What are your thoughts?"

"To be honest, he's never been faithful to the king. He only took the position because he needs the money to raise his children. He has been stuck with it since," Xabian explained, a glum expression crossed his face. "Don't know how he can tolerate being belittled every day. The king refuses to acknowledge Taviar as a father; it would infuriate me."

"Both Taviar and his husband are fathers; the Fae King is behind in his ways!" King Idralis spat with a shake of his head. "I can't be bothered going back to the meeting; we can conclude it in the morning. Do you want to come to the pub with Nazareth and me?"

"That'll be great," Orison piped up with a smile, looking at Nazareth walking behind them.

The group meandered through the labyrinth of buildings built close to each other. They followed the sound of drunk revellers singing and stumbling out of the pub, yelling from the top of their lungs. It made Orison giggle, remembering her night in Cardenk; and when she turned eighteen in the mortal lands and had her first night out with her friends.

The pub was a small building; most people drank outside in the spring air. As soon as King Idralis arrived, some patrons inside cleared a table for him and his companions—without him having to say a word. Despite his many protests, they insisted. Orison noticed it wasn't because they were scared, but because he was so highly respected. People saw him as a deity.

Idralis ordered a pitcher of ale and a plate of chicken wings for their table. He gave Orison some suggestions on places she could visit in Akornsonia and the best places to get clothes in Torwarin. It felt like they were drinking with a friend instead of a king. It must have shaken Idralis when he got the message from King Sila. Orison truly appreciated that he stuck to the agreement. She didn't want to think about what would have happened if he had taken the money.

Thirty-Six

Irodore was a city like no other. Wood or stone bridges zigzagged from various treetop islands, all offering something different to discover. Creatures from across the Othereal roamed around each island, exploring the various attractions or businesses. The largest spectacle that Irodore had on offer was the Temple of Lioress. Built into a cliff face, the entrance had stone carvings of the deities—Lioress and Fallagh, holding stone flowers in the palm of their cupped hands. Legend had it that they worked together to create the Othereal, separating the mortal lands from the magic realm. Deep in the cliff's belly was the tomb of Lioress; her final resting place.

Moving between large groups of tourists, Xabian held a bouquet of flowers to his chest. He glanced over his shoulder when he felt Orison hold his hand. She forced a smile but he could tell she was uncomfortable. He pulled her into him for protection from the surge of people pressing into her; she glanced around and shrunk into Xabian. When the leader of one large group realised who was amongst them, he started shouting in a foreign language; the message spread like wildfire and the path cleared for Orison and Xabian. There were some benefits to being the most highly talked about prince and princess—this being one of them.

Xabian looked up at the entrance to the stone temple. He let Orison out of his embrace as he came to a stop. He blew a kiss to the two deities and bowed deeply; smiling when Orison did the same.

They walked in unison to the opened temple doors, stopping at where a bowl of Fallagh water sat for visitors to cleanse themselves. Xabian dipped his hand into the bowl, smearing a line of water across his face; closing his eyes, he sent a silent prayer to Lioress and Fallagh. He was proud when Orison copied him. No other surrounding visitors knew this was the correct protocol when visiting Lioress. Watching a handful of people run down the stairs to her tomb without a blink at the bowl, Xabian knew it was disrespectful.

"Why do we have to do this?" Orison whispered, gesturing to the bowl and entrance.

Xabian turned to her. "It's a sign of great respect and honour for the deities who created these lands. Some visitors know this is correct protocol, other visitors don't know or care; as long as they see the tomb."

As they stepped through the doorway, Orison's jaw fell open in awe. Sconces on the wall illuminated their descent in golden hues. Taking her hand, Xabian guided her down the stairs. He watched as Orison inspected some of the writing on the gold walls. There were prayers of life in the times of war written in the Fae tongue, other pieces that neither of them could read and some drawings. Visitors leaving the temple inched away from the Fae prince and princess approaching them. The pair ignored every visitor on the stairs that had several turns before they got to Lioress' tomb.

The tomb was made of pure gold and engravings of prayer to the afterlife were written in Fae and Elf tongue. Some carvings wished Lioress a good eternal rest; offerings were scattered about on the floor along the walkway. Xabian clutched the flowers in his hand tighter as he approached the gold sarcophagus where Lioress lay; he placed the bouquet on top before he got down on one knee.

"Dear Lioress, we are humbled to visit you today," he spoke. He kissed the ground where her sarcophagus met the earth before straightening up.

Orison knelt down on the floor. "We are humbled to visit you today, Lioress." She kissed the ground and stood.

Most visitors to the temple just wanted to see if the stories were true—that she lay there in eternal slumber. The gold sarcophagus wasn't open, but it had a painting of a sleeping woman to signify who was in there. A royal like Xabian had to show the utmost respect. Knowing the castle had accepted Orison as royalty, he had to teach her the correct protocols; she was progressing amazingly.

"We shall do nothing more than look around, Lioress," Xabian stated with a bow.

He watched Orison bow before joining him at his side. She copied when he walked about with his hands behind his back to avoid touching anything—unlike what some visitors did.

Lioress had everything, including bowls of water and food; as well as golden jewellery boxes, rocking horses and other goods to keep her spirit entertained. There were so many jewels and pieces of armour that Xabian lost count after a while. When visiting either Fallagh or Lioress, he always brought flowers. He knew their spirit may get bored of being showered with riches galore—from bearers wishing for something that could not be granted.

They tensed at the sound of stone moving. Slowly, Xabian turned around to the source of the noise; he staggered back when he saw that the sarcophagus had opened. A beautiful woman with brown curly hair and luscious red lips sat up like she had just awoken from a nap. She looked around the crypt before her eyes landed on Xabian and Orison.

"Sorry for waking you, Your Majesty," Orison said with a low curtsy.

Lioress looked down at Orison. "Please rise." She did immediately and held her hands in front of her with her head bowed. "Princess Durham of Earth and Prince Xabian of Fallasingha, you need to return to Torwarin and assist with the injured when the moon rises."

"What do you mean, Your Majesty?" Xabian asked.

"Return to Torwarin and assist your saviours."

Instead of answering his question, she laid back down and the sarcophagus closed, rattling the surrounding crypt. The pair stayed where they were, too scared to move in case she woke up again and told them to go back immediately.

"Do you think we should return?" Orison asked in a hushed voice.

Xabian turned to the door. "It's still early in the morning. We can probably explore Irodore and head back in the afternoon."

Taking Orison's hand, Xabian guided her back to the entrance. It intrigued him about Lioress' prophecy; what was happening in Torwarin tonight? Xabian was thankful that he had time to show Orison the wonders of Irodore—it had always been his favourite city.

Ascending the stairs, their footfalls echoed around the stone walls. As they returned to sunlight, a heavy weight pressed on Xabian's shoulders—a sense of foreboding about what tonight held. He was confident they'd arrive back to Torwarin by nightfall. As they stepped outside, he guided Orison to the nearest stationery shop across the bridge to buy some parchment. Xabian had to warn Idralis of the threat to his people.

Vines creaked on tree branches while supporting the people who swung from the trees. Screams and laughter echoed across the dense canopy as the visitors let go of the vines and descended into the black abyss covering the forest floor. The screams could be heard across Irodore, coaxing the most daring individuals to take part. The elf who was patrolling the swing laughed as she let one screaming visitor leap off the platform. She grabbed hold of another vine for the next participant. When she turned, she baulked and curtsied low.

"Princess Orison and Prince Xabian," she said, keeping her head down.

Orison glanced over her shoulder when the whispers of other visitors increased in volume; she wasn't used to the attention. She also worried for Prince Xabian—walking around Akornsonia after being missing for three months would spread like wildfire. Nobody knew the truth of what he had to endure because of King Sila. People had always been fascinated by Orison in particular, the illegitimate princess; under the claim that she was King Sila's daughter—nobody knew that was a lie.

"You may rise," Prince Xabian said.

The elf rose and handed over the vine with a smile. Orison gripped it. "Put your foot in this foothold here," she instructed, "and let yourself go."

Orison followed the instructions and looked down at the dark abyss below her. It made the world spin as her stomach muscles clenched and her heart raced.

It looked like the forest would swallow everything whole. Increasing her grip on the vine, Orison glanced at Xabian as he held up three fingers; she nodded and he began counting down. Squeezing her eyes shut, at the count of one, she pushed herself off the platform with a yelp.

It felt like she fell forever; it went on for so long she began screaming—her grip on the vine so tight her knuckles went white, her blonde hair flowed behind her. As the vine went taut with a groan, it suddenly yanked her. Opening her eyes, she couldn't describe the rush of the experience. It felt like an entirely different universe than the Othereal.

With a glance at Xabian, it mesmerised Orison by the way his fire-red hair flowed behind him like a flame.

The vine contracted, lifting Orison higher into the forest, making her heart race and her stomach flip. She clutched the vine tighter, too scared to look down at the black void below. With one big shake of the vine, Orison struggled as she lost her grip and tumbled through the air.

It felt like hands were clawing at her tunic and pulling her into the pits of hell as the forest swallowed her up. She reached out for Xabian, hoping he would Mist to her, like the last time she was falling into an unknown abyss; but darkness clouded her vision, making her lose sight of him.

"Xabian!" she screamed.

As panic invaded her thoughts, she let out a blood-curdling scream. She squeezed her eyes shut, letting fate decide if she lived or died; it was in its hands now—nobody was going to save her. Her body flipped as the trees swallowed her and the pull on her clothes increased tenfold. Orison decided this was it; she was meeting the end.

She slammed into a net of leaves that rustled on impact. It jostled her around for a few moments before she came to rest. She struggled to breathe as she blinked her eyes open, wiping the tears away from the corner of her eyes as she laughed. She should have been scared by the ominous darkness that greeted her upon arrival into its lair, but instead, she was exhilarated. With a hand on her forehead, she breathed a sigh of relief.

"Are you well, Princess?"

She tensed at the voice. Turning to the source, two elves stood at the net with a lantern to illuminate the way; smiles on their faces. One of them pulled the edge of the net down, causing Orison to tumble onto the solid ground on shaking limbs. She placed a hand on her chest as she gazed at the great height she had fallen from; all she could see was a speck of blue sky.

Leaves rustled, and Xabian soon appeared with two more elves and another lantern. She ran up to him and wrapped her arms around his waist, burying her head in his chest. After a pause, he wrapped his arms around her.

"What's the matter?" he asked.

Pulling away, Orison looked at him. "Sorry," she said with an awkward laugh, "it was a thank you for encouraging me to do this. I've never done something so exhilarating before. Can we do it again?"

Following a pair of elves through the darkness, Xabian smiled. "You seriously want to do that again?" He pointed to the vines. Orison nodded with a smile so bright that it could have replaced the light from the lantern. Xabian scoffed. "You're wild."

They entered a hoist made of tree branches. An elf closed the gate behind them and turned the crank that would take them back to Irodore. The shift of the hoist made Orison stumble into Xabian. She allowed him to hold her steady as they ascended to the treetops; so caught up in the moment she only just remembered Lioress' warning.

Hooves thundered through the forest, stirring up dirt as they galloped through the soft soil. Night had fallen, causing the forest to take on an ominous mask. Orison and Xabian were riding at a full speed gallop, both anxious in anticipation of finding out if the prophecy was true—if Torwarin was really under threat. Neither of them knew the forest like the elves did and had to trust the horses' instincts. As they got closer to the town, the sun was rising on the horizon—or so Orison thought. She looked at Xabian for reassurance that they had been riding for four hours and not an entire night.

A burning smell stung her nose; the temperature was rising from a chilly spring breeze to a warm summer wind. The pair kept riding, needing to investigate—a deity had assigned them a job.

"Do you think they got the message we sent?" Orison asked over the sound of hooves.

Xabian's face was stern. "I sure hope so."

Her stomach churned as the true scale of the fire came into view; it was worse than she imagined. She didn't have faith that everybody made it out safely. Even the trees surrounding Torwarin had caught on fire, their trunks snapping before crashing to the ground. Orison needed to get over there to see if the people had survived.

"We need to Mist to Torwarin," Orison instructed. "It should have been the first thing we did!"

Xabian looked at her, then back at the raging inferno. "We can't. Torwarin is warded, to prevent Fae Misting in, remember? We'll injure ourselves!"

She groaned loudly; she had completely forgotten about the restrictions. They were choking on the smoke and ash blowing through the air that felt like a thousand degrees—yet they rode on, into the pits of hell incarnate, anyway.

On the outskirts of town, flames licked the sky with a forked tongue, eating away at the labyrinth of buildings in Torwarin's town centre. Orison couldn't help but gasp to see the events unfold before her very eyes. She glanced over her shoulder when she heard wolves and other animals crying out from the trees as fire devastated them and their homes. Turning back to Torwarin, she saw the guards for the first time swinging from tree to tree.

The horse that Orison was on reared up as she tried to guide it into the inferno; it immediately threw her and she landed with a heavy thud that knocked the air out of her lungs. She groaned in pain as the horse bolted back into the dark abyss of the forest from where they came.

Crouching down beside her, Xabian placed his hand on her back. "Are you injured?"

"No, I'm fine, just winded," Orison groaned. She tried sitting up; only to be knocked back down with a cry of pain as an agonising burning ripped through her veins. "Why is my magic burning?" Her hands trembled violently as jolts of electricity bounded through her body; sweat beaded on her forehead.

"Your magic is waking up after depletion," Xabian gasped, swearing under his breath. "Why now?"

"What should I do?" Orison questioned in a shrill voice.

Xabian held her arms. "Wield it. I'll guide you to make sure you don't burn out again. Do you understand?" She nodded. "On the count of three, we go together."

Water formed on Orison's trembling hand at the same time Xabian conjured up his own. She stared at Torwarin and thrust her hands towards the nearest burning home. Her magic stopped giving her pain almost immediately, granting her the chance to watch the flames fizzle and die.

Xabian stood up and helped Orison to stand. They worked in unison to douse as many of the flames as they could—Xabian taking the right side and Orison the left; sometimes using ice to save Torwarin. They both worked their way to the main shopping area; although it was a slow process, neither of them cared. Lioress would be proud of them.

People who hadn't found shelter screamed as they ran down alleyways. Buildings cracked as roofs caved in, the fire roaring its satisfaction at what it devoured.

Orison's gaze followed a family running into a basement. She skidded to a halt, tensing when the sound of a child crying chorused the roaring of fire. She looked around frantically for it.

"There's a child," she told Xabian, breathing heavily. "We need to save them."

Xabian didn't hesitate. He looked through burning buildings and down alleyways. Behind a tower of crates, he found the child clutching their knees to their chest, wailing for their mummy. He scooped the child up, rubbing ash from their cheeks and tugging the red cloak tighter around them; it didn't stop the child from wailing.

"Keep moving, we'll look for the parents," Xabian instructed, as he took off running, using his free hand to douse the flames. "What's your name?"

The child looked around, then cried. "I can't find mummy!"

"Okay, we can find her. I'm Prince Xabian and this here is Princess Orison." Xabian checked the child for injuries as he ran beside Orison, trying to keep the tremor out of his voice. He could only see a minor cut in their brown hairline. "When we're somewhere safe, do you want to see King Idralis?"

The child stopped wailing, clutching tightly onto Xabian's shirt as they ran through the cramped streets of Torwarin. With some of the fire under control, they were now looking for any other misplaced children or anybody who needed assistance. As they went deeper into the heart of the city, it was more difficult to breathe and they couldn't see anything; with the smoke becoming thicker. The roar of flames was almost deafening, but water and ice thrown in its direction silenced the noise.

"Orison!" she heard somebody scream.

She whirled around, baulking at who was running up to her while screaming her name. It was somebody she had lost hope of ever seeing again since being forced into the Othereal. She had to hold onto Xabian, so she didn't drop to her knees in shock.

Orison stopped dousing the flames as she tried to work out if this was a trick from somebody's magic. She gazed upon the pot-bellied man in a torn tunic and soot staining his clothes. He had a white receding hairline and covered in sweat—she knew this was no magic.

"Bara, why are you in the Othereal?" Orison gasped as she came face to face with her old boss and teacher during the time when she was nothing more than a mortal.

Thirty-Seven

"There is no time to explain how I'm here. We need to get to a safe house; around here," Bara explained with a smile. He guided Orison, Xabian and the child in the direction he came from.

"But I don't understand," Orison said, jogging up to him.

Following her old boss, Orison glanced at Xabian with the child resting their head on his shoulder, still searching for their parents. She threw ice and water at a few more fires that had ignited before approaching a basement door. The only indication that this was the right place was the sound of chatter and wailing babies. Bara descended the stairs, the trio close behind.

It was evident that the safe house was the basement of a pub, judging by the large barrels of alcohol stored underneath the stairs and in the centre of the room. The people of Torwarin were crammed wall to wall, chatting amongst themselves; soothing seated children or assisting the injured. Orison looked around in a panic. She didn't know where to start with aiding the victims—there were so many.

"Cyra?" a woman's scream ripped through the basement. A woman with salt and pepper hair, wrapped in a white knitted cardigan ran up to the pair, tears streaming down her face as she picked up the child. "I thought I told you to stay close." She kissed her child's head over and over; Cyra started smiling. "Why did you run off?"

Xabian pinched Cyra's cheek. "I told you we'd find Mummy. May I ask your name?"

"Raquelle. Thank you so much, Prince Xabian and Princess Orison. We are forever in your debt."

Orison looked at him as Raquelle walked away. She realised Xabian should be on the throne—not Sila, who would have easily left Cyra in that street terrified. The man before her saved a family's world from being ripped apart.

"Orison!" she gasped loudly to see Yil running up to her with a smile.

Crouching down to his level, she held him by his arms with wide eyes. "What are you doing here?" She checked him for injuries. "No, you need to get back with your…"

Orison's jaw fell open as Taviar approached her. Riddle followed closely behind, carrying Zade; they both gave her a soft smile. She turned to Bara, who sat on the stairs looking around the cramped room. She had to be dreaming; this couldn't be real. Why were there so many people she knew? There were no words to describe how she was feeling. It was an information overload as she tried to make sense of the situation; like a maze, she came to a dead end at each turn.

"I can't do this," Orison gasped, stumbling up the stairs as she needed some air.

Taviar pulled her back as she wrapped her hand over the latch. "It's not safe up there."

She backed away from the door and squeezed her eyes shut. Exhaling a shaky breath, Orison pushed her hair off her face with trembling hands; she willed herself to calm down. Bara made his way up the stairs towards her, sadness in his eyes as he looked over what Sila had done to her—the pointed ears of being a Fae and her blue eyes were now violet.

"Look at what they've done to you," he whispered, disappointment lacing his smile. "You were powerful out there."

Orison pulled him into a tight hug, finally letting the emotions overflow like a river bursting its banks. His rough stubble scratched against her cheek, but she didn't care. As she breathed in his scent of freshly baked bread, it reminded her of home. She had missed Bara, the man who worked beside her when she helped run his bakery. On market days, they would sell out of the freshly baked products. He brought on her love of baking, the man was like a second father to her.

"Will you tell me how and why you are here?" she asked as she pulled away.

Lowering his head, he nodded. "King Sila captured me, like he did with you, except he tortured me for a couple of days. Sila's cronies brought me here, but when King Idralis said you were not in Torwarin, Sila set fire to everything. I fled while he was distracted, hiding in the infirmary with the Luxarts so he couldn't find me."

"I can tell the nurses fixed you up while you were there," she said with a laugh, looking at his now-straight nose—it used to be crooked after breaking it by slipping in the kitchen during a busy day. "I still remember when you broke it."

Bara roared with laughter, tugging her into another hug; she groaned with a smile as she held him. It felt good to have somebody from the mortal lands here, to see somebody who had watched her grow up. Orison had many questions about the bargain, but those could wait until after she had assisted the injured. She pulled back and made her way down the stairs.

"You do realise this is going to start a war, you know, you being here and not as an emissary," Orison told Taviar with her arms folded over her chest.

He walked with her to the injured, watching as Orison crouched down to check on the burns that were already starting to heal. "I'm aware, but I'm ready for a change of leadership. I would like to be your emissary."

Orison paused with strips of cloth in her hand, looking at him. "You... you want to be my emissary when I take the throne?"

"Or Xabian's, whoever takes the throne first."

She crouched down as she dipped the strips of cloth in the water. She looked over at Riddle sitting on the floor and cradling Zade in his arms—Zade was fast asleep. Orison gave Taviar a smile as she stood up. They both checked on the injured and placed pieces of wet cloth on the burns, which the elves had sustained from the fire. Despite the bizarre turn of events, she got lost in the mission, hoping King Idralis got the warning so that he could prevent as many deaths as possible.

Alsaphus Castle was becoming more miserable the longer Orison stayed away. The king was descending into madness from the situation and the daily poisoning of Braloak Root; which was now a dosage of half a vial administered by Eloise. The daily poisoning flamed his newly found wrath, a wrath that made the staff flee the castle at an alarming rate.

Pottery clinked together as Eloise followed Aiken and an undertaker into Sila's chambers. Her hands were clasped in front of her and her shoulders were back, to make herself appear taller. Her gaze shifted to Saskia's cage hanging from the ceiling; she was asleep against the bars—a black veil concealed her face, she looked peaceful under unfortunate circumstances.

Bypassing the reflection pools and the cage, Eloise kept her head down. The doors to his bedchamber opened on a phantom wind, and she walked through the makeshift doormat of blood. As a Healengale, she was used to her uniform being dirty, though it wasn't a pleasant feeling as her shoes stuck to the floor. Aiken picked up her skirts and stepped over the puddle.

Eloise averted her gaze away from the bed. Three courtesans, naked as the day they were born, lay face down with their throats cut. The once-white bedding was painted red by the slaughter of the three innocent women. Eloise stood by the door while Aiken provided the tea laced with Braloak Root to Sila; she watched as the undertaker inspected the bodies. The king himself sat on a chaise at the end of his room wearing nothing but a towel to cover his lower half.

"Healer, come," Sila demanded, smacking his lips together after drinking.

Eloise approached, curtsying before him. "How may I be of assistance, Your Majesty?"

"Can you fix this?" He gestured to the bed. "I lost control and one of them was my favourite courtesan."

She looked at the bed, then returned her attention to Sila. "Your Majesty, I'm only a healer. I can't bring back the dead.

You'd have to consult a Morntomb to bring her back, that is, if Fallagh herself hasn't claimed her soul already."

He sipped more tea and pouted as he looked at the bed. "That's unfortunate."

"Very much so, Your Majesty."

Sila waved his hand to dismiss her; Eloise bowed, but when she turned to leave, she felt him grope her bottom. "Maybe you should replace her."

Everybody tensed at his boldness. Tears stung Eloise's eyes as she walked away, still feeling the king's phantom touch. She exhaled a breath as she returned to the door, trying to keep it together but knew she would become a sobbing mess behind closed doors. Aiken was watching her as she removed the blood-soaked sheets. She glanced at the undertaker.

He's going to need more courtesans, she said to Eloise's mind. *Talk to your boyfriend and girlfriend, then come back to me when the plan is in order.*

She knew what Aiken was implying. Eloise forced a smile as she looked down; indeed, she would have to speak with Aeson about a plan. Carefully, the undertaker used his magic to remove the three bodies from the bed, muttering to himself. When the plan was under way, it would only be a matter of time before the king got his comeuppance.

If Eloise wasn't assigned by King Idralis to be a spy for Akornsonia, she would flee like the rest of her Healengales. For now, she would follow his orders and administer the king his poison until it was time for the battle to commence.

In recent days, the king's chambers were like a never-ending cycle of courtesans. Most only survived a few days before the king slaughtered them in unrestrained rage; this day was no different. After slaughtering three courtesans at the crack of dawn, it only took three hours before the king wanted more brought in—but one courtesan wasn't like the others.

Aeson checked himself out in the mirror. Disguised in his female form, he pushed his breasts up so they half spilled out of the red stay he had borrowed from Kinsley; he smoothed out the matching dress. He still didn't understand why women wore such blasted things; he could barely breathe—even without the weight of a dress on top. Flicking his red hair over his shoulder, he checked his make-up one last time. The make-up was another thing he didn't understand about women and had to get Eloise to help apply it.

"You shifters terrify me," Aiken gasped.

He laughed, but in this form his voice had been altered into a song of seduction. Aeson felt physically nauseous to be touching the king in any sexual manner, despite permission from both his girlfriends to do so. He had to do this for

Eloise's revenge; he would bring down the world to see his girlfriends' smiles. With a glance at himself a second time, he followed Aiken through to the king's chambers, where Sila lay on the sofa in his meeting room.

"Is this courtesan Harriette?" he checked Aeson out, shifting on the seat as his yellow eyes surged in approval, amongst other things.

"Yes, Your Majesty," Aiken said with a curtsy.

"Delectable to meet you, King Sila," Aeson said with a curtsy.

With a predatory gaze, Sila tapped the space next to him. Aeson sat down and ran his hands through the king's hair—the same way he had watched many times in pubs, when the women found a suitor to warm their beds. His other hand was on the king's thigh. He forced himself to look dreamily at the king.

He looked down at the evidence of what this disguise was already doing to the king. It was only a matter of time before he revealed who he really was. Aeson kissed Sila's jawline while rubbing his chest. The king sucked in a breath as he ran his hands up Aeson's thigh, tugging on the ribbon that held the stay together—he heard the fabric tear as the stay fell off his frame.

"You're exquisite," the king drooled as he cupped the courtesan's breast, kissing Aeson roughly.

"And you're a monster," Aeson snarled, and slapped the king's hand away.

The king paled as Aeson revealed his true self. He stood up and wiped his mouth with the back of his hand; Sila gawped like a fish. As he was about to call out for the guards to arrest him, Aeson thrust his hand out; the king gasped for air and clawed at his neck. Approaching the king, Aeson straddled his hips and brought his face close to Sila's.

"If you ever touch my girl again, I will personally do more than choke the life out of you. Do I make myself clear?"

The king let out a whimper as a single tear rolled down his cheek. Watching the king twitch as he lost the air in his lungs filled Aeson with glee. With one big heave, Sila slumped back on his sofa, his head rolled back. Aeson breathed heavily as he took a step back, running a hand down his face as he held the skirts up so they didn't fall down.

"I can clear minds," Aiken announced.

Aeson whirled around, forgetting Aiken was still in the room. She appeared out of the shadows with her hands clasped in front of her. He thought about what he had done to the king; he was already a wanted man to begin with and this added to the evidence. But the king needed to be taught that women weren't just objects to touch or fuck whenever he pleased, especially without consent.

"That would be wise. I am wanted across the empire," Aeson said. "Could you also put some thoughts in there to leave women the fuck alone unless they consent?"

Aiken curtsied with a smile. She stepped up to the king and got to work swindling up a story in Sila's mind of the rights and wrongs. Only the two of them knew the truth, the third being Saskia, who observed everything from her cage.

"Aeson," a tired voice said. He looked around and gasped to see Saskia pressed against the bars of a cage. She looked dishevelled, with a split lip and black eyes. "Get me out, please, I beg of you."

He grabbed a nearby chair; it groaned as Aeson stood on it. He reached for the padlock and cried out in pain as his skin burned and sizzled when he made contact. Aeson should have known it would be enchanted. Holding his blistering hand to his chest, he stepped down from the chair as he backed away to take all of Saskia in.

"I can't. The padlock..." Aeson winced as he looked at his hand. "I'll come back. We'll find a way out together."

She shook her head. "Just go, I'll think of something. Get Kinsley and Eloise to safety. He's going to start a war with Akornsonia."

The destruction in Torwarin was unfathomable. Entire streets had been burned down to pieces of charred wood; a heavy fog hung in the air like a blanket, and the smell of fire coated everything. Regardless, the Torwarin residents were resilient and got to work to rebuild or clean if they weren't injured or drained of their magic.

Water sloshed on the charred ground as Orison ran with a pail of water to the over-crowded infirmary. She handed the nurse the full bucket, only to have an empty one handed to her. It had been a constant cycle of trying to calm the burns. She was exhausted from having no sleep the night before, and she was slowing down.

Orison jogged through the street, Xabian joined her as she made her way to the lake. "Go to your cabin and sleep. I'll take over."

"But Lioress..."

He stopped her before she could dip the bucket into the lake. "I don't care. You've been working all night. I can take over."

Orison admitted defeat, handing him the bucket. Using his shoulder to help her stand, she immediately felt dizzy; thinking she might pass out. Rubbing her eyes and yawning, she definitely needed sleep. She started walking along the water's edge, feeling like she was floating.

Mustering up her magic, she thought of her cabin and the bed calling her name. A flurry of purple night enveloped her, and she felt herself being transported. Orison landed with a heavy thud inside her cabin on unsteady feet. Exhaustion was weighing her down. Crawling along the floor, she pulled herself onto the sofa, feeling too exhausted to get to her bed.

She clicked her fingers and a blanket appeared over her; relieved she had unlocked that ability like Kinsley and Eloise had. Snuggling into the blanket, Orison fell asleep almost immediately. She dreamt of what she had experienced in Irodore, swinging through the treetops and falling through a dark abyss before her world was engulfed in flames.

Despite the nightmare, she was so tired that she couldn't wake from it.

Thirty-Eight

A birds song woke Orison from her slumber. She gasped loudly as she sat up, a hand on her racing heart. It was a torturous sleep, filled with nightmares and only scarce breaks of serenity in between. Rubbing the sleep out of her eye with a groan, Orison tensed when she realised that she was in her bed; somebody had moved her from the sofa. Turning her head, she stifled a gasp to witness Xabian asleep next to her. He was half hanging off the bed like he too had passed out from exhaustion.

Looking at him closely, his fire red hair covered the face that looked so much like Sila's; *if* he was a kinder man. After a moments hesitation, she gently brushed his hair away from his face which made him stir. Orison winced and bit down on a gasp. His purple eyes opened, and Xabian lifted his head; pushing himself up on his elbows.

"Sorry," she whispered.

He groaned. "I should be sorry, I passed out in your bed." Orison looked at him as a sadness darkened his eyes. "I've almost slept away my last day of freedom. Are we well?"

"Much better." She looked at his features again. "We'll figure out how to break the curse." He snorted to indicate he didn't believe her. "We will, stop being pessimistic."

Xabian was about to respond when a heavy knock at the door interrupted the conversation. Making him avert his gaze to the bedroom door. "Who's that?"

Orison crawled to the end of the bed to look into the living room and entrance. Taviar was looking through the glass in the door to see if anybody was inside. He knocked again, which made Orison swear under her breath as she climbed out of bed.

"Are you coming with me?" Orison asked as she grabbed the nightgown hanging on a hook and tugged it on.

Xabian groaned into the pillow with a stretch. "Give me a minute."

She accepted it as she walked through the cabin while fixing her hair, smiling at Taviar as he looked through the window again. Opening the door, she gestured for him to come in. He strolled in with his hands behind his back before finding his way to the sofa. He glanced at her bedroom, where the sound of water hitting the basin echoed through the walls.

"King Idralis wishes for an audience with you and Xabian," Taviar said as he looked around the cabin.

Orison sat on a chair next to him. "Alright, we'll be over when Xabian is ready." She held her growling stomach; she hadn't eaten all day. "How are you doing?"

"It's taking some getting used to, but it's a more relaxed environment than the castle," Taviar said with a sad smile. "The twins seem happy being here."

"You'll be able to return when the king is gone. We'll do repairs if he's destroyed Merchant's Row in his rage," Orison reassured.

The floorboards creaked as Xabian entered the living room; he wore nothing more than black trousers. He sat next to Orison with fire-red hair that dripped water onto his chest and ran down like rain on a window. Shifting on the sofa, Orison cleared her throat. Xabian was silent as Taviar regarded him for a few moments before resuming his conversation.

"Idralis wants an audience with us. We should get ready for it," Orison reiterated.

She watched him make his way up the stairs to the second bedroom to get ready. When the elves discovered his cabin had burned in the fire, they requested he take the spare bedroom in hers; it made Orison feel safer to have somebody around.

After a shower, she would have to find something to wear that didn't make her smell like smoke. She looked down at her dirt encrusted fingers and the soot still smeared on her skin.

"I was so worried when I found out you'd gone to Akornsonia," Taviar commented. "Now I realise I shouldn't have worried at all."

"King Idralis has been extremely kind. I'm glad I took up his offer of rescuing me," Orison replied. "It was my choice, and I wish to remain under his security until I take the throne. The king encourages me to explore his lands. I have freedom that Sila doesn't provide."

"I'm glad to hear that. What happened to Prince Xabian?"

Orison looked at the stairs where Xabian had disappeared to. "The elves gave him a potion to relieve him of the curse for three nights."

With a nod, Taviar stood up. "I'll leave you to get ready."

Once he left, Orison stood up and made her way to her room. Even though Xabian was around, she was sure he had been eavesdropping, but she'd find that out after the meeting.

King Idralis' cabin was unscathed in the fire—the only damage to it was a piece of the roof charred by smouldering ash and tree sap. The stairs creaked as Orison followed Taviar and Xabian inside. The king's cabin was like the rest of Torwarin's population with wooden walls all around. He didn't show off his wealth, except for a gold-encrusted blue sofa in front of the fireplace in his meeting rooms. A painting of him hung proudly above the hearth.

The group passed a few closed off rooms before they got to the one labelled as an office. Taviar knocked on the door and entered when invited inside. They all stepped into the small space, where a chest of drawers had been pulled away, revealing the stairs leading to the war room. Each member of the group made their way down to the basement.

Inside the war room were more maps and pieces of information than the last time Orison or Xabian were in there. The information was strewn about on any free space on the table or hung up on the walls. The smell of fried meat made Orison's stomach growl. Nazareth stirred some tea with a plate of fried chicken beside her; while the king tapped a section of the map as they talked in hushed voices. Hearing the footfalls of the three Fae, Idralis turned and bowed to them all.

All found their places at the table. A servant came over and provided each of them with a plate of fried chicken, sausages and mashed potato; while Idralis regarded the map. Orison picked up a drumstick of chicken. Too famished to wait for permission to eat, she bit into the juicy meat that made spices dance on her tongue. She sat back with a smile and noticed Taviar looking at her in shock. It was only now that she noticed he had dark circles under his eyes to indicate his tiredness; he hadn't had the luxury of sleep. While eating, she went to pour herself some wine only for a servant to do it for her and then fill each of their goblets. She was usually allowed to pour herself a drink, but it gave her more time to devour her food after an exhausting night.

"Xabian, I want to say a huge thank you for pre-warning us of the attack last night. The death toll would have been much worse if you didn't," King Idralis said with a low bow. "And Orison, thank you so much for your efforts last night and for going without sleep to assist people not of your own. Without either of your assistance, more of Torwarin would have been lost to the fire. The trees didn't disappoint me when they predicted you were both good allies."

She smiled as she sipped her wine. "Thank you for your kind words, Your Majesty. If we didn't get warning from the deity Lioress, we wouldn't have known to return."

"She doesn't present herself to just anybody. You must have pleased her greatly. I can see why," King Idralis said with a smile.

Orison noticed Taviar looking puzzled, so she recited her trip to Irodore. He listened intently as she explained how she entered Lioress' crypt and got a message to help Torwarin when the moon rose. By the end of this story, he was looking at her with his mouth wide open. Lioress hadn't appeared for centuries and for her to appear to two Fae who merely wanted to visit her grave, was a miracle.

"Which leads us into discussing retaliation efforts for two reasons," Nazareth said with a smile. "The guards have discovered a war camp south of the gate. Rumour has it, they plan to attack again if we don't give in to King Sila's demands."

The chair creaked as Xabian sat forward. "How much was the bond to buy her back?"

"A thousand gold," Idralis replied, leaning against the table.

"That's pathetic." Xabian sat back, arms folded over his chest. "We could set up a camp outside of the gate and monitor King Sila's proceedings, then what happened last night won't happen again."

"I second that idea," Taviar said.

King Idralis set down a piece of parchment. "It's King Sila—he'll attack Torwarin again regardless, knowing Orison is within the city walls."

Orison ate some more chicken as she leaned her elbows on the table. "What if I'm in the camp you guys set up?"

"We made an agreement that I will protect you. That would put you in danger," Idralis said as he looked down at her. "However, if you feel you can handle it, I won't stop you. Your choice."

"I shall think about it, thank you," Orison replied with a smile.

She noticed Idralis exchange a look with Xabian before nodding their heads. Orison shifted in her seat, clearing her throat as she drank wine and discussed war efforts. When all of them started delegating in Elf tongue, she completely zoned out and asked the servant for a couple more pieces of chicken. She didn't know their language yet, though she wanted to learn. As they talked, she ate her food and tried to act like she was listening, though she had no idea what plan they had finally come up with.

The sun was setting by the time the meeting concluded. Orison walked along the lakefront with her hands clasped in front of her. Grass crunched underneath her boots as she took each step and watched the sun dance along the rippling water. She smiled and crouched down on the water's edge. Birds sang their night call, masking the sounds of construction within Torwarin, that were winding down for the day. A warm breeze flowed through the air as she watched the water. Xabian joined her a few moments later.

"You know, if we didn't get warning last night, I would have rented out a hotel. We would have watched the Irodore lanterns, like you talked about," he admitted abruptly.

Orison turned to him, smiling. "I would have liked that."

"You might have seen them in the Faunetta's Atlas." She nodded. "It's even more beautiful in person. There are food vendors who sell the best honeycomb or chocolate apples." He waved his hand in the water.

"Maybe we can go when this is all over," Orison proposed, looking at him.

He looked at her. "Yeah, next time."

She dipped her hand through the water. "Hopefully, the curse is broken by then."

Xabian straightened up. "I have no idea what to do for my last night of freedom. I spent the day sleeping and planning a fucking war like a…"

Orison stood up, taking Xabian by the hand to help him up. "How do you want to spend your last night of freedom?"

They walked side by side to a fishing platform. Xabian sat her down, kicked off his shoes and dipped his feet in the water; encouraging Orison to do the same. They were silent with only the birdsong to serenade them. He appreciated the sunset radiating orange, purple and pink colours into the sky; he wouldn't be able to watch it tomorrow.

Xabian shrugged. "There's so many things, I couldn't fit them all into one night." He dipped his head back as he looked at the sky. "I always thought my first night away from the curse I would get blackout drunk, maybe waste money in a brothel."

She giggled as she hugged her knees to her chest as she regarded him. "Maybe you could get drunk tonight?"

Xabian scrunched his face up, shaking his head. "I wouldn't want to do that to people who already have a difficult time trusting the Fae. Have you ever seen a Fae male drunk?" She nodded, remembering the night at Grandma Jo's Restaurant. "Well, I have a knack for losing myself when that drunk, and I don't want to scare these people."

"I wouldn't mind sleeping with you again," Orison proposed with a pout, glancing at Xabian. His eyes were wide in shock. He guffawed and scratched the back of his neck. "The first time was nice; and after last night, I need something to calm my nerves."

Looking at the water, Xabian shifted to face her. "Then what?"

"We could go to town and eat pizza."

Xabian stood up and helped her stand. "Okay, I wouldn't mind that. Beats scaring elves."

Orison laughed. "This is so fucking weird." He laughed as he looked around. "Well, let's get this night started!"

She made her way to her cabin; swinging her hips from side to side, she glanced over her shoulder with a smirk. If it wasn't inappropriate with guards watching their every move, he would have taken her right there on the fishing platform.

Following her up the steps to the cabin, his self-control weakened and his instincts took over. Xabian pinned her against the wall, making her let out a gasp, which he swallowed with a rough kiss as his hands travelled up her body.

"You're mine."

Thirty-Nine

Laughter filled Orison's cabin; the ping of something hitting glass rang out. Propped against the sofa, Orison and Xabian were chuckling while holding wooden rings; a pizza lay between them. Xabian tossed a ring and it bounced off the glass bottle that he aimed at; only to land in the fireplace. Orison held her stomach as she laughed even more.

"You're such a bad shot," Orison teased, as she took a bite of pizza. "Were you even trained on how to use weapons?"

Waving his hand, the ring returned; he let out a laugh as he nudged her. "Fuck off." Orison giggled as she tossed her ring; it rattled against the glass. "You know I'm just letting you win at this point."

She shook her head as she summoned the ring to herself. "Keep telling yourself that."

Xabian and Orison took it in turns to toss their rings; she laughed every time Xabian missed, as did he. The reality of this being his last night of freedom was a distant memory. In this moment, it was only the two of them and the cabin was their world. Orison threw her ring towards the bottle;

Xabian smirked as he used his magic to deflect the ring and it went flying into the chandelier above their heads.

"Cheating gets you nowhere," Orison pointed out with a giggle as she retrieved the ring. "For that, you have to go in the lake."

He scoffed loudly as he took in the lake. "You can't be serious." Using the sofa to stand up, Orison picked up a pizza slice and ran through to her bedroom. Xabian followed her, groaning when he saw the back door open. "Ori!"

"Cheaters go in the water!" she shouted to him from the lakefront.

Xabian approached Orison as she ate the slice of pizza. She saw this as entertainment and Xabian knew he deserved it. At the water's edge, Xabian kicked off his shoes and shirt; he squealed loudly as he stepped into the water, the cold seeping into his bones. The feeling of an oncoming winter lay in the water. He turned to Orison and she smiled at him.

"Happy now?"

Finishing her pizza, Orison nodded as she went to return to the cabin. Xabian conjured up a ball of water and threw it at her. She squealed when it soaked into her light pink dress. Turning back around, her eyes narrowed at Xabian as she regarded him. Treading the water, he swam away quickly with a laugh; but not before she created a wave, which dragged him to the deep water. He conjured an air bubble to stay under the water for as long as possible, feeling mischievous and invigorated.

He felt the disruption in the water as she entered. The water rippled around him as she swam closer; Xabian heard splashing, as well. Though he couldn't see her, he knew when she stopped and searched for him. Swimming closer to her, he smirked as he grabbed her ankles. He broke through the surface as she screamed in sheer terror, covering her mouth.

Orison smacked his chest. "Xabian, I was worried sick!"

A loud laugh came out of Xabian as he pushed his hair away from his face, the cold temperature making him shiver. He grew concerned when he saw Orison's lips had turned blue and she was shaking.

"Let's get out of the water," he said as he swam to the water's edge.

Back near the shore, they pulled themselves out of the water. They trembled as they dried themselves off, using their magic. He kept glancing at Orison as she took her hair out of the braid, shaking her arms with a smile and stretching. Xabian couldn't deny that she was up to something; he hoped it didn't involve water again. He went to step towards the cabin so they could continue to ring toss, but Orison tapped his arm with a sly smile.

"Tag, you're it!"

She took off running with a giggle; shaking his head and scoffing, Xabian chased after her. He hadn't seen this side of her before. It was a pleasant change from what he was accustomed to in the castle; she had come alive in Torwarin.

Catching up to her quickly, he grabbed her arm with a laugh; she whirled around with a beaming smile on her face. He prayed she wasn't up to something else.

"I didn't cheat this time."

"Good, or you'd be back in the water."

He scoffed as he looked at the sky. "No. No more water."

Xabian watched as she began to walk back to the cabin with a giggle, looking behind her shoulder to see if he was following. It was their night to strengthen their friendship. A night to forget about the imminent battle on the horizon against their own nation and the curse's return.

Water ran from the tap as Xabian brushed his teeth, occasionally staring at himself in the mirror. The curse had returned while he slept. Within seconds, his hair had gone back to the darkest black and the freckles he had in his old life had disappeared. Though he appreciated what the Keres Waters had given him, it wasn't enough time. He couldn't cherish the freedom, with an impending war.

Orison appeared in the bathroom doorway. She radiated beauty after the previous night; enhanced by the navy-blue nightgown she wore, which highlighted her eyes. She smiled at him, despite the lingering sadness of the curse returning.

The shaking ground made both of them look up at the ceiling. When he next looked at Orison, his eyes were wide with curiosity while holding onto the sink. Both of them waited a few moments until the ground shook again; there was no denying what was happening.

"Sila's in Torwarin," they said in unison.

"What is *he* doing here?" Orison hissed.

Xabian spat toothpaste into the sink. "You know what he's doing here."

"He has no jurisdiction here, so he can't do shit," Orison snapped.

"Do you think he cares?"

Orison clicked her fingers; a navy tunic and some black trousers replaced the nightgown. They both paused when the ground shook again.

"Why does the ground shake when Sila is mad?" Orison asked. They rushed through the bedroom to the back door.

"His magic was given to him," Xabian replied. "He wasn't born powerful like me, hence why he knows so many enchantresses."

They scampered down the stairs to the path that led to the lake. The air had a heavy weight in it, like the Torwarin population was waiting for something to happen again.

Lightning crackled around Xabian's fingertips as the pair hurried across the lakefront towards the Torwarin gate; it was the only logical place to find Sila. Orison was breathless trying to keep up with Xabian's long strides.

"You have stolen my property and I demand it back!" they overheard Sila shout as they approached King Idralis' cabin.

"I have stolen nothing," King Idralis stated calmly. "What property do you propose I have stolen?"

"My emissary and Princess Orison Alsaphus. Do not pretend you're clueless when you are a thief!" Sila shouted back.

"The trees tell me you're not related to Princess Orison. Thus, your claims of her last name are false. She left of her own accord and so did Emissary Luxart, therefore I am no thief," King Idralis replied with an unnerving calmness. "You need to understand you cannot own people."

Dashing from the canopy of trees, Xabian stormed up to Sila; shooting a bolt of lightning out of his hands, which slammed into his brother. The blast sent the Fae King crashing to the ground with a cloud of dirt. Sila rolled onto his hands and knees, lifting his head to reveal blood running from his nose. His eyes widened and his complexion paled as he took in his brother standing before him—Xabian's hands were balled into fists.

"Brother," Sila gasped and tried to inch away.

"Hello, coward."

Sila tried to stand but fell back down with a groan, leaning against a tree for support. He winced as he moved his hair over his shoulder. He wiped his nose, inspecting the smear of blood left behind; evidently his nose was broken from Xabian's attack, but was already healing. Regardless, Xabian stood his ground, staring down at the man who had given him this curse—he couldn't regard him as a brother any longer.

He watched as Sila raised his hands to surrender, but Xabian was too angry to back down. When the Nyxite curse reclaimed him, it ignited a storm of bloodlust in his veins. Xabian now wanted revenge for his ongoing suffering.

"Leave Torwarin. You hold no law here," Idralis snarled.

Sila looked over Xabian's shoulder, fixating on the shadows where Orison hid behind a tree. "There she is. Come out now, Orison," he coaxed. "You can be safe if you come home."

Reluctantly she stepped out of the treeline, standing behind Xabian and holding his arm. "I'm not leaving Akornsonia. You can grovel all you want, but I'm treated with dignity here, something you never provided."

The Fae King staggered up, swaying slightly as he regarded Idralis. "Do you know the trouble you caused me when you stole Orison? I have no staff and people are listening to your word against mine." He laughed erratically. "By keeping her here, you're making me weak."

"You've made yourself weak," Idralis snapped. "If you treated people fairly and with respect, they wouldn't leave."

The wind started blowing; Sila sniffed the air, his yellow eyes landing on Xabian. A growl rattled out of Sila as his eyes flared with rage and his breathing grew heavier. Orison's grip on Xabian's arm tightened briefly; Sila had sensed something that he hadn't before.

"You've fucked her, haven't you?" Sila snarled. "Tainted *my* property with your filthy hands!"

"Orison is nobody's property. Get that into your thick skull!" Xabian shouted. "You're the one who has the filthiest hands of us all. Now leave before I make you leave!"

Holding his hands up, Sila pouted as he started walking backwards—staring at Idralis before looking intensely at Xabian and Orison as he went. Leaves crunched under his feet; another unnerving laugh passed his lips. When it appeared as though he would turn around and leave Torwarin silently, Sila glared at Xabian and pointed a finger; causing lightning to spark once again on Xabian's fingertips.

"We used to be unstoppable, you and I, but you lost yourself," Sila snarled. "What happened to the two brothers who went to war together for our kingdom? We used to be a team! Just know if you stay here, Fallasingha will fall."

"That brother died when you cursed me with the Nighthex!" Xabian shouted back.

"Leave!" Orison screamed.

When she stamped her foot on the ground, a gale force wind threw Sila through the gate. Xabian's lightning cast him even further away. The Fae King slammed into the compact earth with a cry of pain, skidding to a halt far away from the gate to Torwarin. Orison breathed heavily, unfamiliar with standing up to Sila in such a way. She watched as he struggled to stand, kneeling before the gate as he pointed to them.

"This..." Sila snarled, gesturing to them all. "This means war! Prepare for battle."

All of them watched Sila Mist away from Torwarin with a flurry of orange smoke. Xabian held Orison close to him. His gaze turned to Idralis, who gestured for them to enter his home and started walking. Neither of them hesitated to join him.

In the Fallasingha war camp, Saskia listened to the sound of soldiers training and servants talking amongst themselves, while she stared at the tent entrance. The veil Sila was making her wear limited her vision, but she could see enough to know her surroundings. The bindings that kept her tied to a support beam were cutting into her skin—making her wince. She tensed when the camp fell silent. The sound of heavy footsteps made her anxious.

Sila ripped open the entrance flap, Saskia looked up at him in horror. He clicked his fingers and the single lantern hanging from the ceiling illuminated the tent. Sila crouched down beside her, sneering at her. She glared at him, wanting him to know how much she loathed this tyrannical beast; despite knowing he couldn't see her eyes through the veil.

"What is the matter, Your Majesty?" Saskia asked Sila. Noticing that he looked furious, she shifted. "You don't look happy at all."

"You know what's the matter," Sila snarled. She remained silent, resting her head on the beam. "Did you know that Xabian is also in that flea pit Idralis calls a country?"

"No, I did not," she replied truthfully. "I don't see why it matters to you. As long as Orison is freed from your manipulation, and not used as a pawn in a game of lies to boost your ego."

The sound of Sila's slap filled the tent. Saskia's head snapped to the side. "Shut your fucking mouth!" he shouted, jamming a shaky finger towards her face. "We used to have such a good relationship before you threw it all away."

"We could still have that relationship if you didn't have archaic beliefs about women with power." She rested against the beam with a sigh.

Running his hands down his face, Sila scowled at her. She was testing him and he knew it. Saskia had already planned how she would escape. She had tried to implement the plan once before, but the guards found her—the second time she would get away and be free.

"Try me again, Saskia, and I'll sentence you to execution," Sila snarled. "I'll allow you a bath tomorrow, then we'll bargain you for Orison."

She kept her head down as he stood up; she flinched when he spat at her feet. Without his knowledge, she was trying to get out of the bindings. Instead, she was making her skin raw. Through her veil, she watched Sila stomp away as he returned to the war camp; the lantern light diminished with his departure. Closing her eyes, Saskia kept praying to Fallagh for Orison's safety. Tomorrow, she could try her plan again. Tomorrow, she'd go to the safety of Torwarin.

Forty

The elf children of Torwarin laughed as they played. Some children ran around a large oak tree; others were on swings tied to tree branches; or they battled against each other with wooden swords as they copied the soldiers' movements. Zade and Yil had made some great friends; Riddle and Taviar smiled as they watched their sons from a nearby bench.

"They seem to be enjoying themselves," Taviar commented.

Riddle kissed Taviar. "Yes, they're settling in well." He turned to his husband. "I heard Sila has declared battle. Is it true?"

"Unfortunately, he has," Taviar replied quietly, resting his head on his husband's shoulder. "They're planning to move the women and children out of Torwarin, but it's not final yet."

Riddle rubbed his husband's arm as he looked upon his children. Then he considered the rest of the children. They didn't have a care in the world, nor knew of the danger they were in. He had lived long enough to have seen countless battles waged by Sila, for the smallest of inconveniences. One battle was how he met Taviar; when Sila was bored and became fixated on a weaker kingdom.

"We need to protect the children," Riddle whispered back. "They aren't safe in Torwarin if he's waged a battle. You've seen the damage he can cause."

Taviar looked at his hands. "I'll have to speak to Idralis. We can lead the evacuation of the women and children."

"Where would we go?" Riddle asked as he looked at the children before him. "I don't know these lands the way you and Idralis do."

"Wherever King Idralis considers is safe," Taviar simply replied.

Both looked at the children. Zade and Yil had now taken to sword fighting, a mini battle between the Fae and elves—in this instance, it was only for fun. These children before them were the future of Fallasingha and Akornsonia; they needed protecting as much as anybody. All parents had to make sacrifices in some capacity—leaving their homes being one of them.

"If we do this, what about Kinsley?" Riddle asked, turning to his husband. "Orison would have a say in it."

"You know they can hold themselves, they're adults. Kinsley already calls us every day on the Teltroma," Taviar replied with a smile; Riddle let out a laugh.

Over the past few days, the Luxart parents had abandoned their home and business in Alsaphus Castle to provide a safer life for the twins. Now, after getting settled, they were running again to protect the children of Torwarin.

When King Idralis gave them a destination, they would round up each of the families and set out on a journey of the unknown. There were many places in Akornsonia that Taviar had yet to explore. They could go to the coast and seek passage on a ship to a far-off land that Idralis had an alliance with, or they could lie low in a town until they had won the battle. None of these children needed to witness the torment of battle, not at their tender ages. Taviar had been exposed to battle as a child and he could still remember the fear. Taviar's heart skipped a beat at the unknown and the safety of the children.

"Father, Papa, are you well?" Yil asked, Zade appearing next to him.

Taviar looked at his sons and held them close. "We're going to go on an adventure with your friends." He looked at his husband with tear-filled eyes; his hands trembled against both his son's backs. "I have to speak to King Idralis."

"It's going to be a big adventure," Riddle announced with a forced smile.

"Are we going to go to Tontemgoref?" Zade asked.

Taviar shook his head, trying to keep a brave face. "No, we can't go there. You know the stories." His son nodded. "We're going to see lots of new places and give you lots of memories to tell your future children, if you want them."

Yil's eyes lit up as his father laid out the plans. "When are we going?"

"I'm going to speak to King Idralis now, and when we know where we are going, we can leave," Taviar said with a smile as he stood up.

They had to leave straightaway; it was now Taviar's job to protect them. While Taviar negotiated with Idralis, Riddle bade farewell to the people staying behind. As they took their children by the hand, they made their way to King Idralis' cabin for assistance. For the future of Fae and the elves, they would flee.

Flour powdered the baker's kitchen when a ball of dough dropped onto the worktable. Bara grabbed the rolling pin and rolled the dough into a thin sheet. Next to him, Orison kneaded another slab of dough with a determined look on her face. The surrounding kitchen had various worktables and ingredients organised on shelves or window ledges. The stone oven was already roaring as it waited for its next batch of pastries, making the air humid.

"You have an unfair advantage now," Bara laughed as he picked up a cookie cutter in the shape of a person. Orison smiled, flicking water at him, which made Bara gasp. She returned to her own slab of dough, hair falling into her face. "Remember your hair. People want flavour, not to taste hair." She looked at him. "Have you eaten hair? It tastes disgusting!"

With a click of her fingers, her hair was tied up into a messy bun. "I've missed your pep talks when baking." Orison fell silent. "Actually, Sila forbade me from baking."

"King Sila is a bastard, but at least he reunited me with you," Bara replied. "That hair thing is showing off. Could you do it with my hair?"

Orison leaned against the worktable as she threw her head back and laughed. It felt good to bake with her old boss after so much time apart. Moving the dough around her hand, she slapped it down on a floured section of the worktable, using a rolling pin to flatten it out. She grabbed a circular cookie cutter.

"Tell me about what happened," Orison requested quietly as she worked. "Not about you being here, but about the bargain stuff."

Her old boss sucked in a breath as he placed each cookie on his baking tray; she continued to work while he contemplated how he would word things. Even though Orison could force the information out of him with her Mindelate abilities, she trusted this man with her life and would allow him to tell her in his own words.

"Your mother and father always had difficulties with money." Bara placed the tray into the oven, then sat on a nearby chair with his hand on his knee. "When they found out they were expecting you, they didn't want you sleeping in an alleyway cold and hungry in the snow. That's no life for a baby, love."

"One day, your Aunt Claudia visited them during market day. She suggested they speak to the Fae should they come into town; they roamed around on missions or some ridiculous quest. At first your parents declined." He ran a cloth over his bald head. "As the pregnancy wore on, your mother was growing desperate. When summer rolled around, she worried for your safety during winter as a new-born. They followed your aunt's advice, finding King Sila on a mission to collect a debt. He gave them a card to contact him when the time was right."

Looking up from her baking, Orison leaned against the table. "How do you know this?"

"I used to feed them scraps and they told me stories about what they encountered." She nodded, filling her baking tray with circular cookies. "Anyway, they made the bargain in your mother's last month of pregnancy. They got the cottage that you grew up in, almost immediately. When you were born, life was good, though you did always have a shadow."

Placing the tray into the oven, Orison sat adjacent to Bara. "A shadow?"

"That boy there, what's his name? The one you were with."

"Prince Xabian?"

Bara's face lit up. "Yes, Prince Xabian! He warned me of your prophecy; he fixated on stopping it from coming true.

Put a spell on you so you didn't know the Fae existed. Xabian watched you grow up. He came to me for advice when your time drew closer; he even suggested I take you somewhere..." He scoffed. "Like that would change anything."

"Your parents believed they had found a way out of the bargain, a way to keep you. The day Sila took you, your parents were in turmoil. They both had severe regrets about making the bargain in their desperation. They warned everybody in the village to never form bargains with the Fae, to not even acknowledge them if they came near."

Orison sucked in a breath, hugging one of her knees to her chest as she listened and stared at the stone floor of the kitchen. Knowing her parents pleaded for her made her feel like crying, she blinked back the tears. It was a sacrifice they had made for her. It was a relief to know her parents regretted it; that they wanted her back and now resented the Fae. She wasn't angry anymore; she accepted that it had happened.

"Xabian helped me find the log about the bargain and I was devastated," she admitted. Bara nodded in agreement. "Though what they did is wrong, I've somewhat accepted this."

"You look beautiful as a Fae."

She smiled, looking up when she noticed movement in the entrance door. Xabian leaned against the door frame with a solemn expression on his face; Orison beckoned him over to them. Bara glanced over his shoulder as Xabian entered the shop. She stood up, allowing him to have her seat. Orison continued to roll out the dough, her hair falling into her face.

"Taviar is leading a mass evacuation of women and children," Xabian announced, his hands on his lap. "They will leave at sunset. Thought I'd give you a heads up."

Orison tensed, turning to face Xabian in shock, but then she relaxed—she had nothing to be shocked about; this was in the Luxarts' nature. She rubbed her face, watching as Bara checked on their cookies in the oven. They were cooking nicely from what she could see; they also smelt amazing.

"Alright, the children can have these cookies we're baking; they'll like those."

Bara sat back in his chair and rubbed his pot belly. "I'm glad they're doing it. Children have no place in battle. They don't need to experience it."

"I am too. It's for the best," Xabian replied, stretching out with a yawn. "Once they're evacuated, we're moving out of Torwarin and setting up a war camp."

Leaning against the table, Orison's heart started thumping in her chest at the possibility of a war camp. The concept was so new to her. As with most royal duties, she didn't know what to do to assist. All she knew was that they would have this battle, hoping they'd win. Then they could focus on breaking the curse.

Lightning forked across the night sky with a giant clap of thunder. Rain pounded the cobblestone path to Alsaphus Castle. Aside from the golden glow of candles in some windows, the castle sat in relative darkness; like a dormant volcano before an unexpected eruption. The horse's hooves clopped against the slick cobblestone as Kinsley walked it into the stables, glancing over her shoulder for any guards; to her relief, most were stationed at the castle entrance. Placing the horse in an empty stall, she rubbed its muzzle before shutting the gate; using her magic to dry the rain from its hair. The creaking sound of a door made her turn around to see Eloise in an exterior doorway to the infirmary, beckoning Kinsley towards her.

Her feet sloshed in puddles as she ran towards the castle, trying not to slip on the cobblestones; slinking through the door as Eloise closed it behind her. Kinsley's cloak splattered water onto the stone path, she was cold to the bone and each breath was visible. She let Eloise take the cloak from her and dry her rain-soaked dress with magic to make Kinsley warm up so she didn't get sick.

"Is the plan in place?" Kinsley asked, savouring the warmth of Eloise's magic in her veins.

Eloise looked around. "Yes, we have to meet Aeson at the king's office. We should probably make our way over."

The castle shook from the thunder—Fallagh wasn't happy about battles. The weather always took a turn for the worse when a battle was looming. Fallagh wanted peace, like any regular person. There shouldn't even be a battle, it was one out of sheer spite with Sila thinking he owned something he couldn't have.

The women held hands as they jogged down the dimly-lit passageway underneath the castle. They pushed open a door that led to the servants' staircase; which they would use later to get to the East Wing, undetected. The guards wouldn't bat an eyelid because they were familiar with seeing Kinsley around and roaming the empty corridors, but she still had to be careful.

It was an eerie feeling, ascending the deathly silent stairs; each turn led them higher up the castle behind the walls. The higher they climbed, the more Kinsley and Eloise's breaths grew heavier from the exertion. It would have been easier to Mist, but in a storm like the one raging outside, it was dangerous.

Eloise stopped when they got to the secret door that Aiken had told them about. She gently pried it open, blowing dust and cobwebs their way. She coughed while waving her hand to make the cloud dissipate faster; then she slipped through first with Kinsley on her tail. The walls were made of solid gold, a four-poster bed sat in darkness; near the window was a writing desk next to a large cast-iron fireplace.

"This is Xabian's chambers," Eloise clarified in a whisper.

Kinsley watched Eloise move to the bedroom door and crouch down to look through the keyhole before opening the door. They hurried along a corridor of gold-plated walls., but Eloise skidded to a halt when she heard voices. She checked through the veil of blackness to see who was interrupting their plan. After a few moments, the voices dissipated. They both slipped out from the veil before sprinting up the stairs to King Sila's office.

Both women knew the office was shielded so they didn't try to open the door. Instead, they made a shield of invisibility until Aeson arrived to guide them into the office. They stood in concealment for a while, before the sound of footsteps coming up the stairs echoed around the stone walls. An enormous shadow climbed up the wall like a monster, before the king appeared before them. Kinsley froze, thinking that the king had returned early, until he glanced over his shoulder and morphed back into Aeson.

Removing the shield, Kinsley smiled at him as he pulled her into a hug. "Are you ready?" he said. "Let's do this,"

Eloise kissed his cheek. "For luck."

In the blink of an eye, Aeson morphed back into King Sila. Looking at him this way truly unnerved Kinsley and Eloise, but they understood why he had to take on this disguise. Now the real challenge presented itself—getting the two women past the shield that surrounded the office, without any queries from the guards. Taking the spare key from his pocket, Aeson stepped towards the doors; giving both of them the cold shoulder like the king would, as he unlocked the door. It eased open.

"You might as well come in," he said, doing his best to trick the shield into believing it was Sila who passed through the door.

The shield couldn't tell that the king was an imposter, as all three of them entered with ease. Now their mission could be fully under way and they would uncover the secrets the office held, without the king's knowledge. No one knew what secrets they would find, but any information to pass on to King Idralis was better than nothing.

Forty-One

The trio separated into individual areas of King Sila's office. Still in his disguise, Aeson made himself at home as he sat in the leather chair, reading sheets of paperwork on the desk. Eloise looked through the chest of drawers built into the wall. Kinsley searched over the various maps spread out on the coffee table in front of the wrought iron fireplace.

"I found the logbook for Orison's bargains," Eloise announced, flicking through the book. "It's quite sad that her parents did this."

Kinsley sat back on the sofa. "That's why you don't make Fae bargains with a brute."

All three of them paused at the sound of approaching footsteps. Eloise fumbled to put the logbook back and closed the drawer before hurrying to sit next to Kinsley. She tensed when a knock sounded on the office door; Aeson used his magic to hide evidence of anything amiss.

"Come in," Aeson snapped.

A guard came in with a bow. "Your Majesty, have you found what you're looking for?"

"Not yet. Somebody has been through my things. I can't find Orison's contract to show to King Idralis. Do you know the thief who put their dirty hands all over it?"

"Is it in your box?" the guard asked, pointing to the desk.

Aeson opened the third drawer down on a whim. Seeing a wooden box with an intricate design, he forced himself not to react. He smirked at the guard. "Ah, here it is. Now get out. I have much to discuss with Lady Luxart and her father's treasonous ways."

The guard bowed, walking backwards as he left the room and headed into the dimly lit castle. Aeson inspected the box that was put away from prying eyes; his eyes lit up as he pulled it from its hiding spot. Waving his hand, it opened and revealed several unsealed envelopes inside. Thunder crashed outside as Aeson flicked through each unlabelled envelope and stopped at one with '*Contract*' scrolled on it. Pulling it out of the box, he turned it around a couple of times; it wasn't Orison's bargain—they'd just looked through that.

Slipping the sheet of paper out of the envelope, Aeson took one look at it and gasped with a hand over his mouth. He looked at his girlfriends in disbelief at what he had in his hands, then he started reading again. When accepting this mission, he never expected to find something so important for King Idralis.

Kinsley approached, holding his shoulders as she leaned down to read. "What does it say?"

"It says how to break Prince Xabian's curse," Aeson said quietly.

Eloise tensed, her attention immediately snapped to her boyfriend and girlfriend around the desk. They all exchanged glances. Sila had the answer to end Xabian's suffering all this time, hidden in a box in his desk that nobody would question. Now the triad knew the answer—it was information they would have to tell King Idralis immediately. Aeson stood up and slipped the envelope in the inside pocket of his blazer.

"Wait, what about the other documents in the box?" Eloise asked.

He started to check each one. It was only a collection of contracts from various enchantresses or wizards gifting him an enhancement on his powers. There was nothing else holding the power like the contract burning a hole in Aeson's pocket. They had found no other secrets for King Idralis.

"Let's clean up before the guards come back," Aeson suggested.

Each of them put everything back the way they found it, closing the box and setting it back in its rightful place. Aeson scanned the room one last time, ensuring everything was in its original spot. Once satisfied, he guided Eloise and Kinsley out, locking the door behind him. They made their way down the stairs, past King Sila's chambers, then down the forgotten corridor towards Prince Xabian's chambers.

Inside Prince Xabian's room, Aeson shifted back to his usual self as Eloise guided him to the servants' door. They would return to Cardenk, use the Teltroma to get the information to King Idralis, then await further instructions.

Kinsley paced in her room as the Teltroma dialled King Idralis. The golden disk device pulsated silently in a blue light as it tried to reach out to the receiver. The blue light turned yellow as Idralis answered, appearing in a wisp of white smoke. She sat beside Aeson, wringing her hands in her lap from nerves.

"King Idralis, a pleasure to meet you," Aeson greeted, bowing in his chair.

A smile grew across his face. "I received the envelope, thank you. Were there no other secrets you could uncover?"

"No, King Idralis; at least not in his office," Kinsley announced, holding her hands in her lap. "Just the one regarding Prince Xabian's curse."

They discussed the conditions of Xabian's Nighthex, going over the details of how to break it so he no longer had to suffer. It didn't surprise any of them of the effort it would take to get rid of the curse, but it had to be timed right. To break the curse would mean a major change in power.

King Idralis shuffled paperwork, looking off somewhere, deep in thought. "This is an enormous secret indeed, one that is understandably making Sila more brutal than normal." He dipped his head.

"Are my fathers with you?" Kinsley asked, shifting to the edge of the seat, glancing at the rain that battered the glass. "What about my brothers?"

"They are leading an evacuation of women and children to Yetnaloui in the north of Akornsonia; all of them are safe. When they get there, I will give instructions to call you," King Idralis explained to them all. He sat back in his chair, sipping from a glass.

Kinsley smiled as she took Aeson's hand. "Please give my fathers that message. Will Orison be joining that evacuation effort for her safety? I'm worried she may try to join in the battle untrained."

"She has refused to go; we will respect her decision."

It took every ounce of effort for Kinsley not to swear. She wanted Orison protected, not out on the battlefield; but at the end of the day Orison was determined to do what she thought best. Kinsley hoped Xabian would find his release if Akornsonia was triumphant in the battle. She nervously rubbed the back of her neck, watching the rain batter the windows as she tried to quell her nerves.

With a heavy shove, Saskia crashed to the floor in the bathing tent. Picking herself up, she held her skirts as she took in the space before her. A wash basin was next to a steaming hot bath. Some clothes and make-up, and a pile of towels with a razor on top were on a table.

Despite a black veil concealing her face, Saskia shied away from her reflection, knowing there would be days of stubble from Sila forbidding her to bathe. Since she had been in his imprisonment, this was only the second time he had given her this luxury.

With trembling hands, she clutched her dirty nightgown to her body. She turned to the guard standing at the entrance. "Do you want to see a lady bathe, or are you going to leave her alone?" she asked, trying to blink back the tears stinging her eyes.

"Apologies, Miss." The guard bowed and disappeared.

Ensuring she was alone, Saskia thanked Fallagh for giving her another opportunity to escape. She removed the veil and quickly shaved away the days of stubble that had built up. She tried to keep a steady hand so she didn't cut her skin, taking the extra time while she was by herself. Stripping off her soiled dress, Saskia sank into the deliciously hot bath with bubbles that smelled like flowers, enjoying the warmth.

Time went by in a blur while she bathed; she only got out when the water ran cold and her fingertips and toes had gone wrinkly. In silence, she put on a baby-blue dress that Sila had picked out for her. She sat in front of the vanity as she did her make-up—already feeling more like herself; with pink lipstick, blue eyeshadow and dark eyeliner. Saskia combed her short hair into a simple style; though her curls stuck out at odd angles.

Picking up the razor, she glanced over her shoulder for guards before prying out the blade, hiding it in her stay. Not a moment too soon, her tent flap moved and in the mirror, her eyes met Sila's.

"Is there a reason you burst in on a woman bathing, or are you just the usual disgusting pervert I've always known you to be?" Saskia snapped with a smile.

The king snarled. "Have some fucking respect."

She snorted, discreetly placing a sound shield around the tent. "That's rich, coming from somebody who just walked in on a woman bathing."

He was at the entrance one moment, trying to grab Saskia the next. With one quick movement, she grabbed the blade out of her stay and sliced a long line down Sila's face. She stepped backwards with her weapon extended. The king cried out as he collapsed to the ground, blood trickling through his fingers. Saskia quickly glanced over her shoulder, figuring out her escape path. She could escape through the back of the tent; guards weren't watching her there, and war camps were second nature to her.

"You fucking bitch!" Sila screamed, huffing like a bull ready to charge.

He staggered to his feet; blood trickled down his cheek as he stared at her with his one good eye. He tried to unsheathe his sword, only to be horrified when he discovered Saskia had taken it with her magic. She smiled sweetly as she held the sword.

With a war cry, he surged up to her, only for his head to snap back; Saskia had jammed the pommel of the sword into his face—along with a kick to his chest. It sent him flying back, smashing his head on the side of the porcelain tub, knocking him out cold. She was lost in her anger. When Sila regained consciousness, she swooped a long arc of the sword across his throat. His eyes bulged as he held a hand to his neck while choking. Unfortunately, the injury was not fatal for the Fae—it would heal in a matter of moments. Breathing heavily, Saskia crouched in front of Sila.

"Now if you'll excuse me, I have a family meeting to attend," she said with an authoritarian tone she hadn't used since losing her position.

Clicking her fingers, Saskia Misted to the horse tent. To her relief, when she landed, all of the horses were saddled up and ready for riding. Her only obstacle now was the fact she hadn't ridden a horse since her banishment from the castle. She had never ridden a horse in a dress either, though the other women in Cardenk made it look effortless.

Shaking her own doubts out of her head, she untethered the horse named Beakbul. She scratched behind the horse's ear in the way that she liked, giving Saskia a huff of warm breath in response. With nervous steps, she ascended the mounting block, mounted the horse and adjusted her dress a few times until she was comfortable.

"Alright, that wasn't so bad," she muttered to herself, petting Beakbul. "I hope you're ready, Beak."

With a small nudge to Beakbul's side, using the heel of her foot, she walked the horse to the open entrance of the horse tent. Once out in the open, it only took the cry of a guard for her to give Beakbul a kick. The horse broke into a gallop. Saskia struggled to stay on, the hold on the reins so tight that her knuckles were white. More guards shouted out a warning that she was escaping. For her freedom—she would do this, even with a barrage of arrows trailing after her.

Forty-Two

Torwarin seemed to close in on itself as Xabian ran through its streets. He pushed through the crowd of people as he raced towards the infirmary. Skidding around the corner, he used the walls for support before running through the open door. He gulped down air, staggering towards the desk.

"Where is she?" he gasped.

The nurse gave him an inquisitive look. "Who?"

"Saskia Kyle, I got word she's here."

The nurse looked through her book. "Oh yes, she arrived a couple of moments ago. Right this way, Prince Xabian."

With a sigh of relief, he followed the nurse through the ground floor of the infirmary. This was the first place he had arrived at in Torwarin; when he had the argument with Orison and again when he drank the Keres Waters. Today, most of the beds in the downstairs area were empty. Xabian's heart skipped a beat when he saw a couple of occupied beds concealed with white curtains; he was convinced Saskia would be behind one of them. It relieved him when the nurse led him upstairs instead.

He'd seen the stairs before, assuming they were for the staff instead of private rooms. The higher up the stairs he climbed, the stronger the smell of herbs became. It wasn't a pleasant scent, making his stomach churn whenever it intensified.

Upstairs, white plaster covered the corridor. The only separation of colour was the wooden doors. The nurse approached the first door on her right, knocking before entering; Xabian followed her into the room. He froze in the doorway when he saw Saskia on the bed, laying there in a white dress with a large bandage poking out of it.

"What..." He swallowed the lump in his throat. "What happened?"

"She got shot in the shoulder by an arrow and fell off a horse," the nurse replied.

Xabian swore under his breath. He sank into the chair by her bed, holding her hand. "The king will pay for this," he promised. "What's the bandage for?"

"Some herbs to make her relax," the nurse announced. "She'll be fine —you Fae, with your fast healing. We found Miss Kyle outside the gate. The trees insisted she receive sanctuary."

He shook his head and grimaced. "Thank you for rescuing her, she's like family to me."

Saskia had practically raised him behind his parents' backs, teaching him battle techniques in her spare time, especially how to hold a sword properly. She read bedtime stories to him on the nights when he had nightmares. He even knew about her desire to transition, way before she admitted it to anybody; he kept her secret until she was ready to divulge. When Sila placed the Nighthex on him, Saskia didn't hesitate to give him a room in her home; she gave him a roof over his head when nobody else would. Then, the plan to protect Orison came to fruition—an entire month of planning and then some.

"The trees also told King Idralis that Sila had held her captive for a week."

"Bastard!"

"I shall leave you both alone," the nurse curtsied and left.

Xabian held Saskia's hand as the door clicked, signifying that they were alone. She looked so fragile on the bed. He squeezed her hand gently, hoping she would know he was there for her recovery.

"Where am I?" she asked quietly as her eyes fluttered open.

"Torwarin. You're safe now, the elves rescued you," Xabian said quickly.

"Poppet!" she gasped, holding her hands out. Xabian stood up and held her close. "I never thought I'd see you again. You're here!"

Saskia looked around the room, her gaze lingering on the medicines on the bedside table with a jug of water. She reached for the jug with a wince, but Xabian took over by pouring her a glass.

Xabian helped her drink. "You're in the infirmary while you recover."

"Water has never tasted so good," Saskia said with a weak smile. "Sila refused to allow me a drink until I begged."

He helped her have another sip. "You're free now."

She nodded and relaxed, allowing Xabian to take care of her. He moved her hair behind her ears; the nurses had removed her make-up while she slept. There was a lot he had to say, but Xabian would keep it to himself until she recovered—he had a war to plan.

"Have you been training?" Saskia asked.

Xabian nodded. "Yes, when I can."

"Good, you need to tell Idralis that Sila plans to start the war tomorrow night. You must use tonight to set up a war camp." He froze and looked at Saskia. "Sometimes I would pretend to be asleep, then he'd talk battle strategies in my presence."

"You haven't had a chance to tell King Idralis, have you?" Xabian asked. She shook her head. "I'll relay the message; we've already evacuated the women and children. Riddle predicts this battle would be brutal."

"Go."

Xabian kissed Saskia's forehead before he hurried out of the room. He jogged down the stairs as his nerves amped up. He dashed through the infirmary, then out into the streets of Torwarin, towards King Idralis' cabin. Setting up a war camp in a night was going to take hours; way past sunset, when he wouldn't be able to help. He didn't care, as long as they had prior warning.

The drumming began thirty minutes before sunset. It felt like the sound was coming from the earth, only to settle in the pits of everybody's bellies. Akornsonian foot soldiers marched through the gate, armed to the teeth, with the cavalry behind; led by King Idralis. Despite the soldiers' confident stances, a heaviness weighed on everybody.

Orison was at the back of the procession, mounted on a horse beside Xabian, nurses from the infirmary and men from the bakery—including Bara. Idralis had decided that Saskia would join Taviar and Riddle in Yetnaloui.

Keeping her shoulders back, Orison tried to keep the façade that she was more confident than she felt inside. From the corner of her eye, she noticed that Xabian kept glancing at her. She was fine; she could do this.

Singing filled the air once they passed through the gates, though Orison couldn't understand the words—the song was in Elf tongue. After the first chorus, the soldiers joined in with them. Xabian smiled as he sang; it was like he was part of Akornsonia, despite coming from an enemy land. As she listened to the song, she noticed some soldiers had tears streaming down their faces and hands over their hearts as they sang with pride. It was clear to her that it had important meaning.

Orison turned to Xabian. "What is the song about?"

He stopped singing, looking at the Akornsonian soldiers. "It's to tell the trees to protect our men and bring them home to their families."

The singing ceased and they travelled on in silence as they made their way through the flat plain outside of Torwarin's gate. For Orison, being back in Fallasingha felt strange. She had grown accustomed to the peaceful life in Akornsonia; now she feared Sila spotting her in his lands and watching her every move.

"We'll be in a tent next to King Idralis," Xabian told her.

Orison looked at him. "That's reassuring."

"Sunset is coming soon," Xabian announced solemnly. "Will you be okay on your own?"

"I'll figure it out."

They kept travelling farther away from Torwarin. Some soldiers talked amongst each other, sharing hopes for the future. Orison had requested to help with the cooking. Being untrained in wielding anything other than an axe, she was thankful King Idralis didn't object.

Once they were at the war camp, the soldiers erected tents for their needs and the nurses set up a travelling infirmary. Xabian quickly Misted away; he must have felt the change coming. Seeing everybody so prepared for battle made Orison feel out of her element; she hung back, staying with King Idralis until he gave her a job.

"Are you well?" King Idralis asked. His crown was a band of wood with a crystal hanging down to rest on his forehead. "You look tense."

"To be honest, I don't know what I'm doing," she admitted.

"You'll be fine." He tapped her arm before guiding her through the maze of tents and wooden structures. "In a war camp, you get used to where things are pretty quickly."

He gave her a grand tour of the locations of everything, Orison took it all in. She could tell he was being patient with her, talking to her slowly so that the information could sink in. Idralis was correct, it was easy to remember where everything was. The men around them were too busy preparing for the battle to dwell on what was to come.

When word spread to Idralis that the royal tents were ready, he led Orison to her own tent, which she would share with Xabian. She gasped when she entered, seeing two large beds in the centre on a royal red rug. Akornsonian flags were hung proudly and there was a writing desk and a chest of clothes. Approaching one of the beds, she sat down, running her hand over the soft sheets. This would be her home until the battle was over.

"Thank you for providing this," she said.

"It is not a problem for a princess who we owe a life debt to," King Idralis replied. He bowed. "I shall leave you now."

Orison watched him depart, alone for the first time in a new bed. A roar in the treeline was her signal that the change had been a success—to her and Xabian's dismay. Both vowed they would get through this, no matter how terrified Orison became.

Within a circle of fire lanterns that illuminated the camp, Orison aimed the sword towards the dummy. Breathing heavily, she turned the sword as she went in for another attack. From the sideline, Nazareth was monitoring her technique, watching as she adjusted her grip, depending on the different blows. Orison was still tense, holding the sword in a death grip. Nazareth had to step in to help her.

"Stop," she announced, pushing her wheelchair towards Orison when it was safe to do so. Nazareth picked up a spare practice sword. "You need to relax; sword fighting is a dance." She held the sword in a handshake grip. "This is an extension of your arm. When you're in the fight, you are the blade."

She lunged the sword into thin air along with a series of other moves, showing Orison the agility expected when sword fighting. Nazareth was thankful that Orison gave her full attention; after a few moments, Orison started copying.

"Like this?" Orison asked, sweeping an arc in the air with the grace of a dancer.

"Much better." Pushing herself away with a smile. "Try it on the dummy."

Orison copied Nazareth's movements on the dummy. This time she held the sword with a looser grip and her muscles were relaxed. She looked confident and strong; this was only the first of many training sessions. When she finished, Nazareth clapped her approval with a huge smile, knowing she had helped Orison achieve this.

"Do you want a real target?" Feud asked, stepping into the circle of flaming torches.

Folding her arms over her chest and smirking, Nazareth said, "I think you're too advanced to battle a trainee."

Wincing, Orison looked at Feud and Nazareth. "Maybe another day."

Feud shrugged. Picking up a practice sword, he swung it a few times in the air, smiling at the two women. Orison gasped as they both watched him decapitate the dummy that she was practising on; its head rolled onto the ground.

"Someday, you'll be at that level," Feud said with a smirk.

The ground shook as Xabian landed nearby to watch them; he huffed out a breath and ruffled his fur. Feud looked at him with a smile, pointing the practice sword towards the Nyxite. Nazareth clicked her fingers and the head reappeared on the dummy; he knocked it off again.

"This dummy's head is what you should do to King Sila," Feud said with a laugh, looking at Nazareth and Xabian.

"I'll make him choke on my other leg," Nazareth retorted.

Orison clicked her fingers and a cup of water appeared; she was getting used to this new development in her magic. "If you don't mind me asking, how did you lose your leg?"

"The Battle of Vorex," she began. "King Sila stabbed me in the foot with a sword coated in what we believe was Necro's Kiss. My foot started to decompose; it was the worst pain I had ever experienced. When it reached my calf, the infirmary nurses told me they had to amputate right there on the battlefield to stop the spread." Nazareth rubbed her stump. "Me, the emissary, temporarily weakened because of that bastard's poison."

"But you aren't weak," Orison pointed out. Nazareth nodded with a smile as she hit the ground with her sword. "Having a disability doesn't mean you can't kick ass. I've seen you shoot arrows off a horse and decapitate training dummies."

Orison watched as Nazareth pushed herself towards Feud and pick up a training sword. "King Idralis said the same thing, obviously in different words." She swung her sword towards Feud who blocked it with a smirk. "Idralis helped me regain my confidence. He even went to Nallavaghn for a tinkerer to design my leg and chair." Swinging her sword again. "When you take the throne, I hope you're as compassionate as he is."

"Of course," Orison stated, moving to stand next to Xabian.

Feud lunged his sword towards Nazareth; she blocked it with a determined smirk. Pushing herself away from him, their swords clashed against each other; they burst into laughter. Orison noticed he wasn't going easy on Nazareth; he was fighting with her like he would any other person. A loud gasp came from Feud, Orison noticed that Nazareth had knocked the sword from his hand, with a laugh.

"Oops," Nazareth said, moving around him in a circle. "Are you distracted, Feud? The least you could give me is a real battle."

"I let you win," Feud smirked.

Nazareth paused in front of him. "Keep telling yourself that."

Orison covered her mouth to stifle a laugh when he picked up his sword, lunging it towards Nazareth, who blocked it. The sound of their swords clashing filled the campsite.

Feud knocked the sword out of Nazareth's hand, sticking his tongue out as he took it.

"We should rest before the battle tomorrow night, we'll be exhausted if we carry on," Feud said with a smile.

"You're just a sore loser," Nazareth teased him. Orison laughed. "See, Orison's laughing at you now."

"There's a campfire going; do you want to go there?" Feud asked.

"Let's go," Nazareth said.

Standing up, Orison joined the group. She glanced at Xabian as he huffed out a breath, as if telling her to go on. With a nod, she walked with Nazareth and Feud to the camp. The sound of music and drums grew louder the further they moved into the camp.

Elves danced around the fire, making Orison pause and her jaw to fall open. It reminded her of the fire dance in Parndore—except without the Fire Singers. People drummed their feet on the ground, using pots and pans as instruments.

Echo took Orison's hand immediately, spinning her around; she smiled as they started to dance. While twirling, she caught glimpses of Nazareth dancing with Feud, singing along with the others. Orison tensed when somebody started hollering in the Elf tongue, but everybody cheered.

The drumming and singing intensified; the dancing became more erratic. Despite the danger that everybody was in, this was a final celebration before all hell broke loose. War didn't exist amongst the camp; it was just the elves sharing their culture with the Fae. For one night, they would dance without prejudice.

Forty-Three

"This one is the Galormal Navistar," Riddle recited, as he crouched in front of a golden artefact shaped like a four-pointed star. The centre separated into the shimmering phases of the moon. "It acts as a compass for places in the Othereal that can enhance your powers. Supposedly lost in the great battle of Galorm, but it appears to have ended up here in pristine condition."

"Don't tell Sila that," Taviar said with a smirk as he leaned against a red painted wall. "He'll steal it."

Riddle scoffed. They had been roaming the old halls of Yetnaloui Palace for two hours now. The palace was filled with ancient artefacts, which were thought to have been lost to the power of time. Seeing them there had Riddle in his element. Through the open windows they heard children laughing as they ran into the sea, with the cool morning breeze flitting around them.

Roaming the corridor again, Taviar let out a laugh as his husband hurried to the next artefact to inspect it. The piece was a necklace with a mood changing pendant; it instantly turned green for happiness. He started rattling off its history as Taviar looked out at the waves crashing on the shore. Usually, Taviar loved hearing Riddle ramble on about the history of something; but today there was a lot on his mind with the battle for Orison's freedom. They had both accomplished the difficult task of evacuating the women and children, but would the men get to return home?

"Sweetie, are you well?"

Taviar turned to his husband. "The battle commences tonight."

Pulling Taviar into his embrace, Riddle held him close and rubbed his back. He understood the severity of this situation; both of them knew that not all of the men would come home to their wives and children. All battles meant sacrifices. While holding his husband, he looked over Taviar's shoulders and watched the children swim in the ocean, playing like they were on holiday.

Pulling away from Taviar, Riddle looked at the man before him. "Did you hear about Kinsley finding out about how to end Xabian's curse?" After a few moments, Taviar nodded. "Let's just hope it happens the way the contract says it does. Let's get some fresh air."

They guided each other down the corridor, bypassing all the artefacts that Riddle was dying to inspect. Instead, he pushed open the double doors leading to a balcony and they stepped out into the crisp, sea air. Sitting Taviar down on a wrought iron seat, Riddle sat on the next one. With a click of his fingers, a servant arrived with iced tea; a refreshing drink for the warm season.

"What do you think Sila would do if he won?" Riddle asked. It was a possibility nobody had thought of, trying to convince themselves Idralis would win. "I don't want to think of it."

"Sila would imprison Orison in the castle, never to see the light of day," Taviar announced, leaning back as he sipped his tea. "He'd probably invade Akornsonia and strip Idralis of his title."

Riddle shifted. "Which is why we need to win this, for these children and our own." He gestured to the beach. "They need their freedom. Sila would destroy all those artefacts in this castle if he invaded."

"While we're here, our duty is to protect the future of Akornsonia," Taviar announced. "We'll take it one day at a time."

The children laughed as they splashed each other. The mothers of Torwarin were watching with smiles on their faces. Saskia watched diligently while knitting some more of the blanket that she had retrieved from Cardenk. In front of the Luxarts were the children of Akornsonia and the future leaders of great things. If they didn't evacuate Torwarin, they might have had their existence wiped out. Their children were somewhere down there; both Riddle and Taviar knew something great would be destined for their twins. All of them deserved a chance.

Staring at her food, Orison was too nervous to eat. Aside from herself and Xabian, the canteen was empty; all the guards were out practising. Xabian was able to eat without any issues. Her cutlery clattered against the tray as she buried her head in her hands; groaning from frustration that she was letting her nerves get the better of her.

Xabian shifted. "What's the matter?" he asked as he ate some steak.

"I'm worried about you fighting today," Orison admitted, resting her head on his shoulder. He rubbed her arm and looked around.

"I'll be fine. You should eat something," he suggested.

Straightening up, she forced herself to eat some of her steak and mashed potatoes. Xabian nodded his approval. They sat in silence, Orison still filled with nerves. Movement at the entrance drew Orison's attention; she choked on her food when Kinsley and Eloise stepped through.

"Orison!" Kinsley hollered and ran up to her, throwing her arms around her friend.

She squealed until Kinsley pulled away. "How are you here? I thought you were staying in Cardenk."

Kinsley sat next to her. "No, King Idralis' services need me." She smiled. "During the battle, I'll help in the kitchens. Eloise will be a nurse, and Aeson a stable hand."

"This is amazing," Orison said, hugging Eloise when she came near.

They all sat around the table and chatted about the events since Orison came to Akornsonia. She explained about Xabian taking the Keres Waters and the mysterious message from Lioress.

The sound of a longhorn signal cut their conversation short. Each of them turned their head towards the sound; like it would hold the secrets in the message. The sound came again. Xabian stood in an instant and started to get ready.

"What's happening?" Orison asked.

Xabian looked up from lacing his boots. "Sila is about to strike."

"There's an hour until sunset!" Orison gasped, looking at Kinsley and Eloise.

He tied his hair up. "My brother has grown impatient. He wants to start early, meaning now." Xabian kissed Orison and held Kinsley, then Eloise. "For Fallagh we will rise."

The three women copied his statement, watching as he ran out of the canteen. They all looked at the entrance when they heard the sound of drums. The heavy beat of stomping rattled the earth and Orison felt it in the pit of her stomach. Men shouted orders; some ran past the tent entrance with fear in their eyes. Orison closed her eyes as her heart began racing. She hoped the enemy didn't have Fallasingha arrows which could injure Xabian in the worst possible way. She prayed that Xabian would be safe from Sila's grasp.

Orison couldn't eat anymore; the heavy booming of drums added to the already nauseous feeling and to her nerves. Standing up, she pushed her tray over to Eloise, who looked at her, puzzled. Orison was erratic as she smoothed out her uniform and scratched behind her ear.

"Kinsley or Eloise, do you want to bake with me?" she offered; her friends nodded as they stood up.

They walked from the canteen towards the baker's tent, dodging soldiers who were running around with armour and weapons. Most looked prepared and some looked terrified—especially the younger ones. They all paused and curtsied when King Idralis stepped out of his tent in brown armour. Tree branches adorned his metal helmet; he bowed before turning towards the horses' hitching pole. Nobody talked about what horrors the night would unleash, so they prayed instead.

When the sunset came and Xabian changed, he flew high above the trees, looking down at the vast battlefield where king met king on the frontline of battle.

The Fae outnumbered the Elves, the only advantage the Elves had was controlling Earth to level the playing field. They had trained well for this day. King Sila's men didn't have that luxury or the element. He had also made the mistake of only bringing half his fleet. Xabian landed with a heavy thud behind the cavalry; he watched King Idralis talk to King Sila—not as men with a mutual understanding, but as enemies.

"If you just allowed Princess Orison to have freedom, we wouldn't be having this fight." Xabian overheard.

He noticed another disadvantage for Sila; an eyepatch covered his left eye, making him vulnerable to attacks from that side. Xabian bristled his fur to indicate he was rearing to fight, trying to quell the fire that was building in the pit of his stomach.

"You should have given Princess Orison her liberty. Hence, why we need this day," Idralis corrected, unsheathing his sword and holding it steady in front of him. "For the future queen of Fallasingha, I'll battle and honour her from this life into the next."

"She is not the future queen, for I will rule long after I leave this field," he snarled. A trumpet cut off their conversation. "Charge!"

A barrage of arrows flew through the air, all brought down by gale force winds conjured up by the elves. The ground shook and thorny vines erupted out of the grass; slithering like vicious snakes towards enemy guards and leading them into a twisted, suffocating death. A clap of thunder erupted from Sila's hands, lifting elves off their feet before slamming them into the ground. Once that attack was complete, Sila charged the front line of elves, using his sword and what little sight he had to quench his bloodlust.

Beating his wings, Xabian conjured up enough wind to take down a small section of Sila's ranks on the right. With a big intake of breath, he exhaled a barrel of purple flames, severing a long perimeter through the left side of enemy lines. It had always been the weakest of the ranks, long before Sila started using enchantresses. All the cowards stationed on the left flank fled as soon as the fire graced their fellow men. They took off on horseback towards their camp. If Xabian was in his Fae form, he would have laughed.

With more blasts of purple flames and magic whipping around them as they fought, the air quickly became heavy with a metallic scent that stung the back of everybody's throats. Horses on the Fae side whinnied out of fear and fled, leaving their riders vulnerable. Men cried out as they lost their lives, others were shouting or screaming for assistance from other soldiers.

As time wore on, the once green grass became red with blood. The elves coaxed trees out from their resting places in the earth and made them topple over onto Sila's men; or they tore them from the horses that were tethered. With more purple flames ripping through the ranks, the Fae turned on Xabian and shot at him, attempting to make him fall from grace.

He dodged each arrow, despite exhaustion already kicking in—the Nighthex wasn't kind on his strength since he drank the Keres Waters.

Xabian expelled more purple fire from his lungs out of anger; he only had to last until sunrise, then he could join the elf army. Nazareth waved her arms in the air. He swooped down and she grabbed onto a tuft of his fur as he rose again. She mounted him, bow in her hand, firing arrow after arrow.

Are you well? he said to her mind.

"My bad leg hurts. That's why I'm assisting you," Nazareth said with a smile.

Using her magic, she made the group ripple like the ocean in a storm. The Fae toppled before her as she slammed her hands down, causing a sinkhole to open up and swallow the men. Now that Sila's army was cut in half, the battle finally had an even amount of both sides. Now it was every man for himself.

Forty-Four

By morning, it was Akornsonia who fared the best as they rested for the day to regain their strength, but the battle was far from over. King Sila always battled at sunset. With Xabian in King Idralis' ranks, it was a foolish move. If Sila wanted to fight his brother, it would be wise to attack when he was weakest throughout the day. The Fae King thought he was indestructible, even against a Nyxite—it was a laughable concept.

The surviving soldiers were ravenous as they lined up at the canteen in Akornsonia's war camp. Two enormous pots of stew were waiting with a large array of bread. Some soldiers came in covered in blood or mud. Orison had been told not to ask questions; they would get showers later.

Every single soldier looked absolutely exhausted from the previous night's battle. Each time a soldier approached, Orison helped ladle soup into a bowl and hand it back with a smile. Despite not participating in battle, the noise and rumblings of the ground made it difficult to sleep.

"May I enquire why Sila won't fight during the day?" Orison asked Kinsley, who also assisted in providing soup. "He's making himself weak."

Kinsley chuckled as she handed over bowl after bowl. "He's an egotistical prick."

"Yeah, Princess. He thinks he's more powerful than Xabian at night," a soldier said with a smile, as he took a bowl from Orison.

Orison laughed. "He thinks he's more powerful than a dragon?" Her friends nodded as they ate their soup. "Othereal above, what a dufflepud."

The soldier's laugh skittered across her skin. Despite exhaustion seeping into her bones, she focused on serving food to everybody, powering on with a forced smile. Each face that she met, she hoped it was Xabian. She hadn't seen him since yesterday before he went off to battle; Orison had woken up alone this morning. The line was continuous; it seemed endless while she was so eager to find him. She promised herself she would hunt for Xabian as soon as she could have some free time. Orison tightened her grip on the ladle. Through the gaps in the entrance, she saw the infirmary nurses bringing through an expansive amount of the dead—covered in white sheets in a wagon. She hoped none of those were Xabian.

"The funeral for the fallen is at noon." Nazareth pushed through to the front, her uniform covered in mud and blood, her helmet under her arm. "You should eat and get some rest after this is over."

Orison forced herself to focus on Nazareth; she'd never been to a funeral for the Elves or Fae before. She didn't know if it was like a mortal one where people sat in a church as they celebrated the life of the deceased; then buried or burnt the remains. She wondered if they required her to attend because of her new title as a royal. She was serving food on autopilot, worried about the wellbeing of the soldiers and her friends. It relieved her to see the last person in the queue—but it wasn't Prince Xabian.

After Orison finished serving the food, she was about to pack up, until Kinsley nudged her. Turning her attention back to the line, she stood tall, as King Idralis strolled up to her; looking as bad as Nazareth. She needed to get this over quickly to find Xabian.

"Good morning, Princess Orison," he drawled, sounding tired.

Orison put stew into his bowl, extending it to him. "I'm relieved to see you are well." He took his bowl with a tired smile. "Have you seen Xabian?"

"Not since sunrise," Nazareth replied from a nearby table.

She tapped her foot on the ground, growing impatient and nervous about his whereabouts. If he got hit by a Fallasingha Blade again, she didn't know if he would be so lucky to survive. Once the king and Nazareth left, Orison handed a towel to Kinsley as she got ready to head into Torwarin. As she was about to leave, Kinsley grabbed her arm to stop her, shaking her head in disapproval.

"Kinsley, please! I need to find him. He could be hurt," Orison groaned, trying to pull away.

"I am not letting you leave until you've eaten. You look like you're about to pass out." She rolled her eyes at the realisation that Kinsley was right. "Please eat something, then you can find him. Eat for me and Eloise."

Kinsley pushed a bowl into Orison's hands as she kept tapping her foot. Kinsley shoved her towards an empty seat, adding to Orison's short temper from being tired. All she had to do was finish this bowl, then she could search to her heart's content. She had to make a plan for ways to find Xabian.

"He's probably getting some rest." Kinsley grumbled in disapproval. "You barely ate your dinner yesterday; you must be starving."

Despite her protests, Orison's stomach growled loudly, telling everybody in the vicinity that Kinsley was right. Looking down at the bowl of stew, she glanced as Kinsley set down a loaf of bread next to her. Blowing on the stew, she forced herself to eat everything, despite having no appetite from the exhaustion weighing her down. She would sleep when her quest was over.

Panic grew in Orison when she couldn't find Xabian. She had asked the nurses of the infirmary to check death records, but he hadn't made the list. Orison pulled Eloise to one side while she was preparing to perform surgery, but he hadn't been checked in there either. Screams of pain filling the war camp didn't help her anxious state. She felt like she was losing her mind. Checking King Idralis' tent, he wasn't there either. Her last hope was their own tent.

She stepped inside, breathing a sigh of relief to see him sprawled out naked on his bed in a deep sleep; nothing seemed to be amiss. His hair was still damp, indicating that he had taken a bath to remove the battle grime. Moving towards his own bed, she pulled a blanket over his lower half to conceal from any visitors who may appear. Apart from looking exhausted, he was perfectly fine.

Climbing into her own bed, Orison settled down. She stretched and yawned; the bed so cosy she couldn't help but start to fall asleep. Just as she drifted off, Orison tensed when she heard Xabian move. Opening her eyes, she could see through the gap in the wooden wall that separated them; he moved in his bed and settled back down. He mumbled something incoherent as he pulled the blanket over his shoulder and cuddled the pillow.

Both of them went into a deep slumber, allowing Orison to dream of her time exploring the Othereal. Her dream turned to her dancing the night away; something she only wished she could do. She dreamed of a sunrise over the Visyan Mountains, of a future where they didn't fear a tyrannical king; where either of them would rise to the throne for a better future. It was a much better dream than the nightmares that occasionally haunted her.

Her eyes fluttered open when she felt her bed moving. She lifted her head as she looked around with a frown. Xabian was lying next to her. He rolled onto his back with a huff of breath, hand on his stomach as he stared at the tent's ceiling above them. Orison snuggled back into her pillow trying to catch up on the much-needed sleep that she had missed out on the previous night. However, the close proximity of Xabian made her lift her head as she looked up at him to see what he needed.

"Good morning," his voice sounded groggy from sleep.

"Morning," she said and snuggled into the blanket. "It worried me when you didn't show up for breakfast. I thought you got injured and..."

He cut her off and rolled onto his side. "No, I'm fine. The battle took it out of me and as soon as I changed back, I went for a shower and passed out here."

"And you have to do it all again tonight," Orison groaned.

Xabian nodded, rolling over as he grabbed a pair of his trousers from the chest of clothes beside the bed. When he stood up completely naked, Orison quickly averted her gaze. She stretched across the bed with a groan, squeezing her eyes shut; Xabian disappeared behind the divider to get dressed.

When he returned, she lifted her head up. "I'm glad you made it back in one piece. It was scary not knowing whether or not you were safe."

Fixing his belt, Xabian's hair fell in his face. "Get dressed. We have a funeral to prepare for," he explained as he shrugged on a shirt. Orison laid back down. "There were a lot of casualties, so the funeral may be long. I actually have something to discuss with you in the meantime."

Orison sat up and looked at him. "What do you have to talk about?"

"Do you remember when I said I couldn't find the tellage books back in the castle?"

She looked him up and down. "Yes... I now have a feeling you're going to say you lied about that. It was why Sila locked me in my chambers." Xabian closed his eyes with a nod. "Where are they?"

"Well, I wanted to say it now that we're close to freedom-..."

"Where are they?" she snapped.

He sucked in a breath and crouched beside her again. With a click of his fingers, they appeared in his hand. Three thick books, along with the single page from Xabian's last entry. Looking solemnly at them, he ran his finger along the spine of one book.

"At first, I took them because I wanted to get justice for my oldest brother, Neasha. It clearly didn't happen," Xabian explained sadly.

Orison placed her hand on his arm. "What happened to him?"

"Cleravoralis." She blinked a couple of times in confusion. "I wasn't the only Alsaphus brother to be cursed with the Nighthex. Neasha was cursed first for the same reason I was; trying to prevent your bargain from coming true."

"Taviar told me about Cleravoralis, but I didn't know it was about Neasha," Orison pointed out.

Xabian nodded. "Our oldest brother knew from the start that Sila would use you to gain power and alliances with countries he wanted to invade. Neasha tried to prevent him from making the agreement. Unlike me, when Sila cursed Neasha, he was allowed to remain in the castle. Banished to the stables at sunset, during the nightly torture that the Nighthex provides. What happened next is why I was the one banished when it happened again.

Our brother ultimately descended into madness from the pain every night. He had given up hope of ever finding a way to break the curse; he had the same condition as me. Neasha became so angry about the circumstances, he attacked Sila's favourite city—Cleravoralis. He caused mass destruction and loss of citizen's lives. The guards shot him down with twenty arrows of Fallasingha ore." Xabian pushed away tears on his cheeks as he recited the story. "All that and the king never learned. History repeated itself twenty years later."

Orison cried as she looked at Xabian. She was told Prince Neasha died in battle, but now she knew it was a fight he ultimately couldn't have won. Wiping away the tears from Xabian's cheeks with her thumb, Orison exhaled a breath. Anger replaced the sorrow she felt while he told the story. Sila was obsessed with her long before she was born and would even abandon his family to make sure she was his.

Knowing he needed the comfort, Orison pulled Xabian into the bed beside her, using his chest as a pillow. She couldn't believe Sila would betray his family in such a way, hence it was about time he got his comeuppance for what he had done. The major obstacle was how to take down a king who thought he was invincible.

At noon, the surviving soldiers of Akornsonia's ranks surrounded a lake in the centre of a vast mountainous valley near the war camp. It was a requirement for everyone to wear red velvet cloaks with the hoods pulled over their heads to conceal their faces. Each held candles in their hand for the fallen soldiers of last night's battle. Four burning torches encircled the lake in a ring of fire—a door to the afterlife. Some soldiers held Akornsonian flags instead of candles, while others beat drums as they sang a prayer. It was mandatory for everyone in the camp to attend, even if Orison didn't understand their customs.

Over the crest of a hill, people wearing black cloaks were in groups of four; each group carried a stretcher made of wood. All of them were silent as they neared the water. The drumming built to a crescendo; Orison felt the bass vibrating in the pit of her stomach. With one last thrum rattling off the mountains, everything went silent as the first group pushed the body into the lake before them.

Xabian held Orison's hand as the corpse floated to the centre. A white sheet covered their body and white stones with runes painted on them covered their eyes.

King Idralis stepped out of the circle of those who watched on. He plucked one of the flaming torches out of the ground and shouted something in the Elf tongue before he pressed the torch to the first body. The white fabric went up in flames, consuming the corpse underneath. Orison's grip on her candle tightened to stop her hand from shaking.

The black cloaked figures pushed the second corpse into the lake. The king repeated the process as the corpse joined its companion in the centre. Orison didn't know what would happen next, as she watched the flames grow higher and converge into one unified unit. Her eyes widened as the water swirled underneath the flaming wooden structures and swallowed them whole. Another shout in the elf language and the process began anew with two more fallen soldiers.

Idralis set fire to each and every fallen soldier, the lake consumed every worthy one. By the end, Nature had sorted all one hundred and eighty fallen; deciding on those deemed worthy or unworthy. More would fall in tonight's battle; this funeral process would continue daily until one side had won.

As the final body drifted to the centre of the lake, the elves dropped to their knees with their heads lowered. Orison was naive about the procedure, but she did her best to copy. She placed her hand in the soft black soil like everybody else around her as she listened to them shout a prayer. The air fell silent before a chant began in time to the low bass of the drum. Orison felt the vibrations in her bones. Although she didn't chant, she felt connected to the Othereal in a way she didn't know was possible. Orison could see why the elves loved nature, if this is what it felt like.

Each of the elves bowed when they rose to their feet, then they stood for two minutes in silence. They all lowered their heads as they sent a prayer to whichever deity they worshipped. While this was happening, the ancient voice of Lioress filled her head, which made her heart race. It was like a siren song guiding her to a body of water; but it wasn't a siren or a song. Lioress spoke four simple words:

Kill the Fae King.

Forty-Five

While the battle raged outside of the Akornsonia war camp, the earth shook at random intervals from cannon fire and Elf magic, causing the lantern hanging near Orison's bed to sway. The sky was alive with a spectacle of colours, as magic tore down ranks on both sides to expose their weaknesses. It would last until sunrise, like the night before.

As the sounds of cannons rattled the air, Aeson paced in Orison's tent. Eloise and Kinsley sat with Orison on the bed; no one could sleep, despite exhaustion. Scattered between them were Neasha's tellage books. Exhaling a breath, Orison smoothed out her baby-pink nightgown as she stared down at them. Her answers lay in these entries; she gave a brief glance at Xabian's last entry on her vanity table.

"There's three tellage books we have to look through. We'll take it in turns to go through the entries and find answers," Orison instructed.

Aeson sat beside Eloise. "We get transported into these pages. What happens if we find any useful information?"

"Pull me out and tell me," Orison said.

Kinsley ran a hand down her face. "This is going to be distressing. If it gets too much, we'll be here."

With a nod, Orison opened the tellage that she assigned for herself; the bindings creaked as she flicked to the first page. Age and disuse had yellowed each page. Running a gentle hand over the page, it felt cold to the touch, but most importantly, it felt wrong. It was like walking through a cobweb that covered a door—she shook off the goosebumps it gave her. The strange feeling intensified when her hand hovered over the black square in the centre. It was telling her not to face the truths that lay within; but she was determined to discover what they were.

"You've got this. Stop being silly," Orison muttered to herself.

Kinsley looked at Orison. "Are you sure you want to do this?"

"Yes, I need to do this."

Mustering up her courage, she reached out to the black abyss in the centre, but paused once again. Being near the tellage made her tremble and she was fearful of discovering something that she didn't want to know. It was like opening a tomb and stealing the treasure inside. Shaking the thoughts and hesitations away, Orison placed her hand down.

The war camp transformed into Alsaphus Castle; an area where she hadn't been in. Before her was an immense space, which reminded her of Sila's meeting rooms on a much grander scale. An opulent seating area in front of huge stone pillars led to an identical balcony.

She walked across the vast space towards two figures who were seated on the large round sofa. One of them was Sila, who didn't have a care in the world; the other one was a courtesan who fed him grapes. He gave the woman an occasional kiss as he smirked at his brother seated next to him. Neasha sat on the edge of his seat, wringing his hands together in his lap. Unlike Sila and Xabian, their oldest brother had short hair.

"I told you not to make that bargain," Neasha snapped.

Sila kept his attention on the courtesan. "I needed to make that bargain. Now I have two happy mortals."

With a click of his finger, a servant appeared, passing Sila his goblet of wine. Neasha glared at his brother, folding his arms over his chest as he looked at him with contempt. Instead of showing compassion, Sila grabbed his goblet of wine and toasted the air with a smirk as he took another grape. He loved this—Neasha's disappointment and his loathing of Sila over a foolish bargain.

"In twenty years' time, you are going to tear a family apart," Neasha explained sternly.

His brother waved him off. "I need the power."

"With a mortal?" Sila nodded. "Othereal above." Neasha said.

"There are ways and means to turn a mortal into a Fae. I intend to do that and make it my child for alliances that people have only dreamed of."

Neasha shifted, shaking his head with anger. "The bargain only says you take the child to the Othereal, not to make it Fae, nor your child. You are breaching your own bargain!"

He jumped when the Fae King slammed the goblet down on the coffee table; the wine inside sloshed around, splattering on the wood. Sila sat forward with a glare, taking his hands off the goblet as he stood over his brother like a terrifying beast.

"I am the king!" Sila hollered. Even in black and white, Orison knew his eyes flared. "I can use bargains however I see fit, and if I want to use it to create an heir for power, I will. Regardless of the wording, that child will be my heir."

"Whether or not you're king, that is not how bargains work!"

A loud growl cut through the air. Sila used his magic to pick Neasha up and slam him into one of the marble pillars holding up the ceiling. Orison screamed and covered her mouth as the pillar cracked from the impact. Neasha let out a strangled noise as he arched his back in a wide-eyed stare at his brother, a single tear rolling down his cheek. Orison looked at Sila in horror, then back to Neasha.

"You don't know a fucking thing; I will have power!" Sila retorted.

Orison tore her hand away from the tellage. She was breathless as she stared at the entry before her. The three friends who were also observing the entries looked at her with concern; they must have found something too. Orison wiped away tears. She knew it would be terrifying to face this, knowing that Sila would betray his own brothers in vain.

"Next entry," Orison said bravely, as she turned the page.

Her friends copied and went to the next entry. In unison, all three of them placed their hands on the black circle in the centre of the page, each transported to hell incarnate.

Neasha's tellages were a story of heartache, misery and hope. Orison, Aeson, Eloise and Kinsley scanned through the tellages. They had to keep diving into the happy memories to clear their heads of the hatred that Sila spewed. They all forgot about the battle wreaking havoc outside, as they jumped between the pages of time. At first, Orison thought it was the best novel she had ever read. However, she soon discovered that the book was a living nightmare. It relieved Orison that her friends had left the last entry of the final book for her to uncover—October sixteenth, her birthday. Sucking in a breath, she placed a hand on the black void.

It transported her to the throne room, where Sila sat beaming on his throne. He guzzled his usual goblet of wine with a smirk as he stared down at the dais. The sound of opening doors echoed around the walls. Orison watched as a procession of guards stormed into the throne room, dragging somebody bound in chains with a bag over their head. The guards shoved their prisoner to the floor at Sila's feet, tearing the hood off to reveal Neasha. They had heavily beaten him. Also, it was evident the guards had put something in his veins to prevent him from healing—just like the king wanted. He wanted his brother to suffer for his treason.

"The child has been born, brother, a healthy baby girl," Sila drawled as he sipped wine. "I have yet to see her, but she shall rise to power as Princess Orison Alsaphus on her twentieth birthday. On that day, we can rejoice in my new power!"

Neasha lowered his head. "She is not Princess Orison Alsaphus, no royal blood runs through her veins. She is Orison Durham, Maiden of the Earth. You do not own her."

"Treasonous talk for such a simple fellow," Sila spat, clicking his fingers. "And as it goes, I must punish all traitors."

Somebody wearing a black cloak emerged out of the shadows. Waist-length hair spilled out of the hood as they approached the throne. They held a leather-bound book; the colour of the book was unknown for the tellage was in black and white. They didn't push back the hood, but as Orison looked at Neasha, his facial expression had become one of terror. He was shaking and his eyes glazed over with tears.

"Brother, no!" he pleaded. "Please, I'm sorry. I'm sorry, please spare me."

The enchantress chanted in a foreign language. Sila sipped his wine with a pleased smile while he listened to his brother beg for his life. Orison winced when his brother arched his back with a blood-curdling scream of agony. She covered her mouth when fur sprouted across his entire body with the sound of his terror-filled howling. Neasha clawed at his face to try and get it to stop. The first snap of a bone made Orison jump. He screamed even louder when his arm snapped again, bending into an unnatural angle, yet the enchantress never stopped chanting.

"Brother, spare me!" he begged and begged, with breathing that became more laboured.

Sila guzzled wine and smirked as he watched his brother suffer. Nobody came to Neasha's aid. The guards kept their heads down, trying to ignore what was happening right in front of them, but as the screams grew louder, it was difficult. To Orison's relief, Taviar wasn't present to witness a life taken; to watch the king enjoy every prolonged minute of this fateful night.

As the enchantress yelled out the last of the spell, Neasha screamed so loud that Orison had to cover her ears as his voice broke. The glass windows around them shattered, followed by a blinding white light that filled the air.

The tellage slammed her back to reality, where she was screaming out of sheer terror. Tears were streaming down her face and her heart was beating rapidly against her ribs. Aeson was holding her close, rubbing her arm. Her screams gave way to great gasping sobs as she clutched a hand to her chest. Orison kept recalling what the king had done to Neasha. Along with Aeson's embrace, Kinsley and Eloise also held Orison close to them. Pushing them all away as her stomach lurched, she ran outside of her tent and threw up violently onto the grass, clutching her stomach.

Moments after sunrise, Xabian staggered into the tent. The battle was taking a toll on him; he was exhausted to the point where he was shaking. Stripping off his bloodied clothes down to his underwear, he contemplated going to the bathing chambers; but the exhaustion weighed too heavily on his body. He saw Orison sprawled out; sound asleep on her bed. Neasha's tellages were scattered around her, evidence that she had missed her morning duties with breakfast.

Xabian carefully removed the tellage from under her arm, noticing her tear-stained face. Frowning at her condition, he looked down at the dates of entries—Neasha's last moments as second-in-line to the throne, before the curse consumed him.

His mouth set in a grim line; Xabian placed the tellage down next to the chest of clothes. He placed his hand on the cover as he sent out a silent prayer to his brother. He looked at the sheet of paper containing his own last entry that was still sitting on the vanity table. He assumed she would read it later.

Just like the day before, knowing she needed comforting, he climbed into bed beside her. Orison stirred as he pulled her close. He didn't want to know how long she had stayed awake looking over the tellages, but probably well into the night if she had missed her duty to the king. Xabian looked down at her, moving her blonde hair from her face. She tensed and sat up.

"What time is it?" she asked groggily.

"It's four in the morning," Xabian replied.

Orison tried to get out of bed, but he held her firm. "I'm late, I have to..." Xabian interrupted her as he pulled her back to bed.

"You're fine, but you need sleep. King Idralis will understand. Go back to sleep before we have to attend the next funeral service," Xabian said as he lowered her back down on the bed with a reassuring smile.

Orison snuggled back into the pillow, allowing Xabian to place a blanket over her. "Xabian." He made a noise to acknowledge he had heard. "Why didn't you try to save your brother?"

"I didn't know until it was too late," Xabian admitted. "Sila sent me out on a mission with Taviar to Navawich. When I returned home, I discovered what Sila had done to Neasha."

She squeezed her eyes shut. "Have you watched it?"

"No, it's too painful."

"Don't."

Xabian pulled the blanket over their heads, creating a stuffy, humidity-filled artificial night. "Best to get back to sleep."

She snuggled into his chest as she closed her eyes again. He wiped away her tears. Whatever she had seen within Prince Neasha's tellage, made Xabian more nervous to dive into the pages. Xabian kept fighting to stay awake, wanting to make sure that Orison returned to her slumber. Her body relaxed as she dozed off and he rubbed her back in a comforting gesture.

Eventually, sleep pulled Xabian in where he dreamed of the battle he fought, wiping out entire lines of Sila's army with his flame alone. Nazareth rode on his back as she fired arrow after flaming arrow, using her magic to send the enemy back. It was like hell had come to life on the battlefield the previous night; the brutality had increased with Sila's temper. Xabian knew this battle would haunt his dreams—like all the battles he had fought in his life.

Forty-Six

The day went by in a blur. After the second funeral, Orison stayed in her cloak as she walked around the war camp in a daze. She had overdone it last night by consuming so many harrowing tellage pages in a short space of time and now her mind was officially a muddled mess. She kept recalling Neasha's final moments since she woke up in Xabian's arms.

"You didn't attend to your duty today, Princess. Are you well?"

Orison froze when she heard Idralis' voice next to her. She turned to him. "Please forgive me, I apologise profusely for missing the duties you set out."

His chuckle bounced around the tents. "It's perfectly okay. The trees have told me you're a hard-working individual and that missing your duties is out of character. Aeson explained the situation, saying you were asleep and he took your place at breakfast."

"Are you going to punish me?"

Another chuckle. "Othereal, no. You're mistaking me for the Fae King. I won't punish you for necessary sleep. Was it a good sleep?" Orison nodded, feeling strange that he wasn't upset. "Are you going to tell me what's on your mind and why you're acting how the mortals would say —*away with the Faeries*?"

She snorted with a smile at the irony of that saying, knowing she *was* away with the Faeries in a literal sense; given her recent change of appearance and her powers. Idralis smiled at her in a silent request for her to get everything off her chest.

"Let's take a walk around the forest. We can talk in private then," Idralis requested with his hands behind his back.

He led Orison to the nearby forest; the brightness of the afternoon light dimmed as they went deeper. When Orison was certain that nobody could overhear them, she revealed everything she had experienced the previous night with the tellage pages. She told Idralis about how she shared the encounter with Kinsley, Eloise and Aeson when going through each harrowing entry. Idralis heard that Neasha had tried to save her from this way of life and the endless arguments that she had intruded upon. Orison explained that they looked into the happy memories when needing to catch their breath; and that she enjoyed the scenario of Neasha travelling to Parndore with some guards and attending the Fire Dance. Finally, she told Idralis about the tragic incident, where she watched the king smile as they tortured his brother at his feet.

"And tonight, I'll have to watch Xabian's," she finished off.

King Idralis pouted as he took in the information, looking at his feet. "You don't have to watch Prince Xabian's tonight, Princess, especially because of how affected you are from Neasha's."

"No, I have to," she said sternly. "Maybe... maybe I can break the curse."

A daisy appeared in his hand, followed by another one, plus one more. "The Nighthex curse is dynamic. You'll have a difficult time trying to break it. The conditions are usually impossible to meet."

Orison came to an abrupt stop as he sat on a fallen log. She sat next to him and watched as he created a daisy crown, throwing in some twigs and leaves. He lifted it like a king who was familiar with crowning people, extending it towards Orison; she lowered her head as he crowned her. She placed a hand on the crown with a smile.

"Thank you, it's beautiful."

"You've never owned a crown or tiara before, have you?" King Idralis asked.

Orison shook her head. "King Sila said that was only for worthy royals."

"He's ridiculous. From what I've seen of you, you're more than worthy of being queen. You're compassionate, you can be firm and you can persuade people with your tone of voice alone," Idralis listed off with a grin.

"Pfft, no, I can't."

"The trees tell me that when you left, most of the castle staff quit in the following week." Orison's jaw dropped as she looked at the king. "If that's not queen material, I don't know what is. You will make an outstanding leader of Fallasingha."

Her cheeks heated at the compliment. "Maybe I should get out of these robes."

She stood up, shrugging off the funeral robes and handed them to Idralis. He held them close to him with a smile as they walked back to the war camp. Orison felt like a heavy weight had been lifted off her shoulders after speaking to Idralis. Although she had told Xabian about her feelings, he already had first-hand experience of Sila's brutish ways.

King Idralis escorted her back to her tent. He told her she could come to him if she ever needed to talk about anything, before he disappeared into his own tent.

Like the night before, the earth shook at random intervals from cannon fire and magic. Orison's tent groaned from movements in the ground. The sky illuminated with spectacles of colour from magic, enhanced by a thunderstorm to add to the things that could go wrong.

Lightning forked across the sky and thunder clapped. Rain smacked against the tent, causing the entrance to keep flapping open with gale-force winds.

Hugging her knees to her chest, Orison stared down at the lone tellage page of Xabian's last entry. It was like it was mocking her; saying she couldn't put her hand to that black void—like it knew that the horrors lying within would terrify her. Orison tugged on the hem of her baby-pink nightgown as she tried to pluck up the courage.

Just like the night before, she told herself, "I can do this."

Trying to calm herself and her nerves, Orison shifted on the bed as she got closer to the tellage. Holding it in her hand, she exhaled a breath. Spreading her hand out, she paused... no, she couldn't pause. She could and would do this—all she had to do was get it over and done with. Her hand hovered over the tellage page for a long moment as she squeezed her eyes shut, then slammed her hand down.

The colourful world turned black and white; Orison was standing in Sila's reflection room. She could see Taviar and Sila talking while drinking wine on the balcony. Sila appeared cheerful, but she could see Taviar was the opposite—forcing his laugh to please the king. Orison heard the entrance door open and she watched Xabian walk in. It surprised her at how furious he looked as he stormed past the reflection pools, standing at the doors to Sila's balcony with his hands balled into fists.

"Why is there a portal in the throne room?"

Sila stopped his laughter. "You know why. I am to collect my bargain."

"You made Orison's parents pay to remove the bargain, yet you still intend to take Orison away and tear a family apart?" Xabian spat, hands on his hips.

"I need money to take care of it."

"It?" Xabian scoffed. "It? You know Orison is not an 'it'."

Sila stood, drawing a sword and pressing it underneath his brother's chin. "Do not try to prevent me from taking what is rightfully mine," he snarled. "That mortal holds the power I seek and I desperately need that power."

She watched as Xabian stared down at Sila, a drop of blood landing on the blade. Ducking down, Xabian took a step back and drew his own sword. Even in black and white, she could see his eyes flaring with rage.

"I will stop you from going through with this," Xabian warned. "You're making a terrible mistake."

The brothers duelled, their swords clashing. Taviar watched from his seat, wincing when the metal sang. In one swooping arc, Xabian sliced a line down Sila's spine. As an act of retaliation, Sila administered a kick to Xabian's stomach; causing him to cry out as he slammed to the floor and skidded to the edge of the balcony. He Misted behind Sila, kicking him in the back of the knee and narrowly avoiding the sword that Sila hurtled in his direction. Their swords continued to clash together, both lost in a frenzy. Sila spat something out in a foreign language as he looked at Xabian with scorn.

In a flurry of black smoke, the same enchantress from the last time appeared next to Taviar. Once again, the enchantress kept their head down as they held the leather-bound spell book to their chest. Xabian glanced at the enchantress, but he continued to fight, grabbing Sila by the hair as anger boiled in his veins.

"Really? You can't fight your own battles, so you have to have an enchantress?" Xabian spat.

Sila slammed his foot into his brother's kneecap, making him fall as he let out an agonising scream. The king stood over him and they returned to duelling. Sila haphazardly jammed his sword; with Xabian blocking as he managed to regain his footing.

Xabian paused briefly when the enchantress began the first half of the spell. He continued to battle his brother as fur sprouted on his limbs. The prince winced in pain but wouldn't surrender, fighting until he was panting from the growing agony. His hair was slick with sweat, his eyes glazed over with tears as reality sunk in.

Another two hits, and his fingers bent back at an unnatural angle. He finally hollered in anguish; his sword clattered to the floor as he fell to his knees. King Sila sneered as he sheathed his sword. He stepped back from his brother, watching as Xabian's arm snapped in two, causing another scream to bounce off the Visyan mountains.

Taviar was as white as a sheet—Orison had never seen him look so horrified. She recalled Kinsley saying he looked as though he saw a Rokuba, Orison didn't know anybody who had looked into the eyes of one; she didn't want to, if this is what survivors looked like. Xabian began sobbing, letting out another cry of agony as his leg snapped in several places before he let out a remorseful scream.

He was panting as he collapsed to the cold stone floor in a trembling mess. His eyes were bloodshot as he stared at his brother in sorrow. Sila returned to his seat, sipping on his goblet of wine with a smug smile. Xabian's pain had paralysed him; he could only lay there and listen to the enchantress continue with their spell. Xabian screeched even louder as his spine snapped in several places. His eyes rolled to the back of his head as a phantom hand lifted him into the air. Just as it had with Neasha, a bright light shattered all of the windows near the balcony where Prince Xabian fell, ripping Orison back to reality.

Unlike the night before, Orison felt too numb to even have an emotion that could describe what she had witnessed—all she felt was cold, hard rage. A plan was forming in her head as she tapped her foot on the ground, biting her nail. She was too angry to cry after watching Sila turn Neasha into a Nyxite. It hurt worse watching Xabian, knowing that he fought it until it forced him to surrender. Her breathing was heavy as she tried to calm down. When the tent flap opened from the wind outside, she realised what needed to be done.

Clicking her fingers, a guard's armour appeared at the end of her bed, along with a pair of boots. She prided herself on perfecting that skill. She quickly stripped out of her nightgown and dressed into the armour. Orison had decided it was her time to enter the battlefield.

Weapons had always been Orison's downfall. Although she had small training sessions with Nazareth, she didn't have ample training to wield a sword. She had never been interested in learning how to shoot a bow—she had tried to learn archery, but never mastered it.

Looking around the weapons tent, she cringed at the swords that looked strong enough to maim a large ogre. Orison found a sword like the one she had trained with and sheathed it to her holster belt. It added substantial weight to her already heavy uniform. She ignored the vast array of bows and arrows—it would be useless to go into a battle with a weapon she couldn't handle; she knew that much. In the far back corner, she saw something that she instantly knew she could handle; a labrys axe.

Despite never handling a labrys axe, she had handled regular axes enough to know about weight distribution and how they moved in her hands. She had spent years helping her father chop firewood in the winter months. There were four axes on the wall, all labelled, but the one that called to her had a gold-plated handle with jet black blades.

"What are you doing?" Orison tensed at Kinsley's voice in the entrance. "Ori."

She looked at her friend. "Going into battle. If I'm going to get freedom, I need to go in there myself and fight for it."

Kinsley hurried over to Orison. "This is ridiculous. You can't wield a sword." She looked at the axes that Orison was eyeing, then the princess herself. "No, you are not going in there. What's gotten into you?"

"I received a message from somebody during the funeral yesterday. They assigned me the task of killing the Fae King. After watching Neasha's and Xabian's final tellage entries, I intend to do that."

Letting out an exasperated sigh, Kinsley watched Orison approach the golden labrys axe. Kinsley fell silent as she realised there was no way to convince Orison not to do this.

Kinsley watched her run a finger over the label that was above the axe she favoured. It said *Fallasingha*.

This was the axe that she would definitely take into battle. The blades were made from Fallasingha ore. It was perfect for taking down a king. Picking it up, it was heavier than Orison was used to. Regardless, she moved it in her arms a few times to get accustomed to how it moved.

"I'd do a couple of practice swings on a barrel over there, if you're serious about this," Kinsley groaned, leaning against a pillar, glancing at the entrance when a crash of thunder sounded.

Orison scoffed as she went over to a nearby barrel. Swinging the axe, she smashed it into the barrel. It was like the axe was made for her, an extension of her arm—just as Nazareth had said it should be with a sword. It sang a soft song as Orison let it fly through the air, crashing into the wood of the barrel and creating a rain of wood fragments. After a few practice swings, she had obliterated the barrel. It was ideal, as long as she didn't cut herself on the sharp blades.

"You, my friend, are perfect," she said to it, turning it around in her hand.

Kinsley shook her head, plucking a holster from the wall mount and handing it to Orison. She placed her new-found weapon inside and slung it over her shoulders. Leaving the weapons tent, the rain beat down on Orison as she made her way to the hitching pole. Pushing her way inside, Aeson baulked to see her adorned in the Akornsonian battle armour.

"Orison, you better not be doing what I think you're doing," Aeson spat.

"She is. I tried to talk her out of it," Kinsley said.

Catching herself in the reflection of a puddle, Orison admitted she looked terrifying, even in armour that was supposed to be for her enemies. She should have felt guilty for turning her back on Fallasingha, but tonight, Akornsonia was her ally. Her own kingdom was what she was fighting for; Fallasingha was hers if she ended Sila's existence. Ignoring Kinsley and Aeson's protests, she styled her hair into a tight bun to keep it out of her face. She looked like a warrior as she placed the helmet on her head. She knew it was foolish to go into battle without adequate training, but that voice at the funeral yesterday told her this was her destiny. For her kingdom, she would do this; she had to claim the crown.

"I need a horse," Orison requested. She watched Aeson hesitate. "I swear to Fallagh, if you won't provide one, I'll Mist there myself."

Swearing under his breath, he led a black horse. He started preparing it for a ride. "Please reconsider this. You're untrained. I've overheard that the Fae have Fallasingha blades," Aeson suggested, but she shook her head. Both looked at the thunder crashing outside.

"I need to do this. I'll be fine," Orison said with determination.

He ran a hand down his face. "You can't even create a shield."

"I have a Desigle, I'm fine."

Giving up a fight he couldn't win, he gestured for Orison to allow him to pick her up; she obliged. Aeson lifted her onto the saddle, looking at Kinsley with concern darkening his eyes. Orison reached over and petted the horse's neck with a smile.

"Are you ready to reclaim a kingdom?" she asked it.

The horse huffed out a breath, making her laugh. Aeson looked at her once more as he fed the horse an apple, which it devoured. Orison exhaled a nervous breath as the reality of what she was doing set in. She already had help from Kinsley and Aeson. What will happen when Idralis finds out about this foolish plan? She watched as Aeson checked over the horse; Orison knew he was only doing it to delay her from the inevitable. Petting the horse's neck again, she kept remembering what Sila had done to his family; while smiling his approval of the torture he was inflicting. The rage returned; she was raring to go.

The same ancient voice that Orison heard during yesterday's funeral filled her head; *Kill the Fae King.*

It was like a voice of reason. Everybody knew Sila wouldn't stop until he was successful at acquiring Orison; taking her back to a glorified prison where she may never get free. This was her time to claim the throne. It was her time to fight, not have others fighting the battles for her.

"Let me go, Aeson," she said sternly.

He hesitated but stepped back, looking at her with sadness. "Please return. May Fallagh bless you, my future queen."

A loud clap of thunder rattled the sky as she walked the horse across the threshold. Deep coldness settled into her bones, freezing the fear that was suffocating her of the fact that she was actually doing this. Giving the horse a kick of her heel, it bolted through the downpour, towards hell itself.

Forty-Seven

Hooves pounded the sodden grass as Orison unsheathed her axe when she neared the battlefield. Through the dense fog from the use of magic, she could see the silhouettes moving in the graceful dance of battle. The wind and rain took her breath away, forcing its way into her lungs and trying to push her back to the camp. As she entered the heavy atmosphere, Orison adjusted her grip on the axe handle. The battle came upon her like a tidal wave and she was a tiny boat out on a stormy sea. She cried out as she forced down her fear.

The noises of the battle became deafening as she rode through the final lines of the battle. She tensed at explosions that were timed perfectly with the clashes of thunder. Magic flew around in every colour under the sun and soldiers screamed orders or cried out for help. The sudden level of noise made Orison disorientated. She should have trained for this instead of going into it recklessly.

Noticing a Fae pinning down an elf, she swung her axe at the Fae's neck. In one clean swoop, the head went flying through the air and landed in mud. A spray of blood splattered over her armour—her first kill. Deep down, Orison knew she should have felt remorse or nausea. She was so desensitised from what she had witnessed in the tellages, there was nothing left to feel. As her horse continued to thunder through the battle, Orison carried on swinging, consumed by the frenzy of relentless rage.

A few moments later, she screamed. A cannon exploded near her, causing the horse to rear up, throwing her from the saddle. Landing with a heavy thud in a puddle of mud, she groaned. Lifting her head up, she watched the horse disappear into fog, lost in the night; leaving Orison on her own.

Even though she hadn't trained in battle, she knew staying down was the worst thing that one could do. Orison scrambled to her feet and took off running. She skidded to a halt when a sword hurtled towards her; she dodged it at the last minute. Smashing her axe against the metal, both pieces of weaponry screeched as they clashed.

Her eyes widened like saucers when Edmund emerged out of the fog with a sword raised over her head. Edmund baulked when he recognised Orison. He lowered his sword and bowed to her before dashing off to find his next target. Shaking off the experience, she fled in the opposite direction. Orison didn't know his motive for defying the king, but she was thankful Edmund had spared her life; when he could have easily taken her down for siding with the enemy.

Navigating her way through the battle on foot, she continued to swing her axe at the Fae who pinned down helpless elves; or those who tried to kill her. She killed so swiftly, none of her victims recognised that she was the one they were fighting for.

A barrage of arrows hurtled towards her; she dived to avoid them, throwing ice towards her assailants. The only sign that she had hit her target was a pain-filled groan through the fog. Her breaths came out in heavy pants. She tensed when a tight grip on her arm pulled her back. She turned around to find Echo glaring at her.

"Orison, what the actual fuck are you doing here?" he shouted over the battle.

She swung her axe at a Fae coming near them. "A prophecy told me to kill the Fae King," Orison gasped. "Please."

"Alright, we're partners. Back me up," he instructed.

Standing back-to-back, Echo and Orison walked in unison towards the throng of people fighting. Each time Echo struck out at a Fae, she blocked any enemies who tried to stage an ambush. Both mixed their different magics to rain down on their assailants. They were a force to be reckoned with and the enemy became terrified of them. Together they worked through the ranks, which had been utterly obliterated; getting lost in the bloodshed.

While making her way to the frontline, Orison noticed many of the Fae were avoiding her. They either backed away completely or picked a new challenge. Some went after Echo to isolate her, but she wouldn't let them near him; they were battle partners and she would do him justice.

Throughout the battle, Orison approached where Xabian was fighting the majority of Sila's ranks. His purple flame obliterated the rain-filled night, sending men screaming as he took their lives. She noticed that Nazareth was on his back, shooting arrows. It was the best vantage point of the battle; she could tear through the ranks without batting an eyelash, like death incarnate.

When an arrow grazed Orison's arm, she cried out. In retaliation, she conjured up more of her magic, thrusting it out at her assailant. She refused to get injured before having the sweet taste of revenge. Seeing a group of Fae bearing down on Xabian, she used her fire to take them all down. Xabian looked at her, purple eyes widening. The roar he gave upon seeing her shook the ground with such violence that it knocked Orison off her feet. She staggered up, crying out when a purple flame came just mere inches near her; and then she felt the hairs on her arms rise.

"There you are." The familiar voice made her blood run icy cold. She turned around to face Sila.

She swung her axe in fury upon seeing the king; the metals sang as Sila smashed his sword into her weapon. She winced as the vibrations through the handle made her bones rattle; it was a weird sensation. Groaning, she swung the axe again, coming up with the same resolution. Throwing her magic towards Sila, he was lifted into the air and was smashed onto the ground.

She walked around him, pushing wet hair away from her eyes as she pointed her axe at him. "I know what you did to your brothers," Orison snarled. "You smiled as you tortured them, you sick bastard!" When Sila tried getting back up, she slammed her magic down on him; he groaned in pain, staring at her.

"It was to keep you safe," Sila said as he staggered to his feet.

Orison swung her axe again, meeting Sila's sword; he used the opportunity to push her away. Tears stung her eyes, though she wouldn't let him see her cry; crying was like the sweetest wine for him. Throwing ice shards his way, he tried to dodge them, only for one to hurtle straight into his side. Sila cried out as he ripped it out, making it melt in his hand.

Her breathing became laboured as she kept swinging her axe, meeting Sila's sword; he was pushing her back. When Orison had thought of fighting Sila, she hoped to take him by surprise as a way to take him down, not fight him face to face.

"You never kept me safe. You kept me in your glorified prison!" Orison shouted.

Sila's yellow eyes flared with a clap of thunder. "Everything I did was to keep you safe!"

"No, you wanted nothing more than power and to take over empires, like Fallasingha wasn't enough. All you cared about was yourself, and still do. The only reason you started this battle was because I took a stand and you lost your trophy!"

With a holler, she swung her axe, only for Sila to throw magic towards it. She yelped when it blew out of her hands, landing in the mud. Orison smirked at the king, flexing her hands into fists before she clicked her fingers and the axe returned to her; like it was made for her. The trick made Sila's eyes widen in surprise. Throwing more ice shards at him, she made dents in his armour, another one impaling him in the arm, making him howl.

"My bargain only said I was supposed to live here, not that I was the next heir to the throne!" Orison shouted over the sounds of the battle, panting as she tried to compose herself. "You made me Princess Orison of Fallasingha and I have come to claim my crown!"

The sounds of battle ceased. Sila scoffed as he was brought to his knees, only to pale with what he was seeing. All soldiers had ceased fighting, forming a circle around the pair to watch Orison take on King Sila; they sorely outnumbered him.

A barrel of purple flame scorched the earth at his feet; he jumped with a yelp and glared at Xabian.

"You stay out of this; I will get my daughter..."

An arrow slammed into Sila's arm and he staggered back with a cry of pain. He looked down at it, then glared at Nazareth. Conjuring up a fireball, he threw it towards an innocent bystander. Orison jumped in the way at the last minute and it bounced off her, sending her flying backwards into the mud. The fireball slammed into Sila and he cried out as he went down. The impact tore off most of his armour as he coughed up dirt, glaring at Orison. Idralis picked her up, and she wiped the mud off her face. Orison refused to let King Sila win this time—she'd had enough.

"Are you well?" Idralis asked. Orison nodded, though she had a cut on her forehead and a split lip; both injuries were already healing.

Sila staggered to his feet, spitting mud into a puddle. He screamed as a frenzy of angry elves jumped him from behind; the Fae who also wanted revenge joined them. Orison watched with abject horror at the carnage until a strange satisfaction filled her veins.

The earth shuddered as Sila rose from the slaughter. He pointed a finger at Orison with fury on his face. "I guess there is no other way." With a clap of his hands, Orison cried out and fell into Idralis; when the cloaked enchantress from the tellage pages Misted onto the battlefield and came to the Fae King's side.

A deafening roar shook the battlefield as Xabian slammed his paw down near Sila. The Fae King dodged out of the way with a smirk and tried to swing his blade towards the Nyxite. Unfortunately for Sila, his brother picked him up like a doll and threw him across the battlefield. Sila landed face-first into the mud. They both knew what the enchantress was meant for—if Sila was going to try to force the Nighthex onto Orison, Xabian would pulverise the king.

On the ground, the battle had well and truly ended in a ceasefire as the Fae and elves united to protect Orison from Sila's wrath. The Fae King screamed as he tried to get up, but Xabian slammed his paw down, knocking Sila off his feet. The elven archers hollered in the Akornsonian tongue, raising their bows as they nocked arrows and aimed for the king.

The king regained his strength, staggering as he cackled. "Twenty against one? That's hardly a fair battle now, is it?"

He dodged Xabian's purple flame—whose purple eyes flared with rage as he lowered his head with a growl. In a protective embrace, Idralis cradled Orison. He shouted an instruction to his soldiers in the Akornsonian language, and one by one, they let their arrows fly. Sila cried out as he tried to use his magic to deflect the arrows; the magic worked and they disintegrated in mid-air. The Fae King tried to throw his flames at each of the elves, but shields deflected them back at him.

"You are not turning Princess Orison into a Nyxite! You have grown power hungry!" King Idralis shouted to Sila.

Sila chuckled, looking around the battlefield as if he hadn't a care in the world. He pointed a finger at Idralis. "That is not my intention."

With a low growl, Xabian inched closer to the king while he distracted himself with the enchantress, who stood there with their head down. Shooting fire towards the king, it hit Sila in the back. He slammed into the sodden ground, crying out as the fire ate away at what bits remained of his armour.

Rolling around in the dirt, the flames dissipated. Sila breathed heavily as he stared up at the stormy night. Without his armour, he was exposed—proving he wasn't invincible against the Nyxite.

Everybody screamed in protest as Sila ordered the enchantress to start the spell he had prepared. With a nod, the enchantress read from their book, speaking loudly so their voice carried throughout the battlefield. Orison winced; she had convinced herself that the enchantress was about to turn her into a Nyxite. However, her eyes widened when a portal appeared in mid-air. Nobody could see where it led—it was like a floating mirror, but instead of glass, there was nothing more than a swirling purple portrait. It attracted lightning, causing thunder to grow exponentially.

"If Orison won't come with me, I will drag her parents from the mortal lands. I will make her join me once again!" Sila shouted.

"No!" Orison screamed.

Sila cocked his head with a smirk. "Are you scared, Princess?"

"My parents don't deserve this; you've already destroyed my family enough!"

"I don't care!" he screamed. "I need the power!"

With the spell complete, the enchantress moved away from the portal, their head hanging low. Slowly, the enchantress walked towards King Idralis, turning to face King Sila where they finally raised their head to look at the person before them. They muttered something under their breath. Tucking the book into their cloak, the enchantress had their full attention on Sila, with a smirk spreading across their face. His face paled as he saw what the enchantress was doing.

"Mililkhm," was the only word they said.

The final command was in an ancient language, which made Xabian charge.

Forty-Eight

Xabian no longer had control of his body and he didn't know who he was either—not anymore. He roared loudly as he charged towards Sila. The Fae King paled when he looked at his brother, taking a couple of steps back before he turned and ran. Sila was fast, but not fast enough to outrun a Nyxite.

Xabian slammed his paw down and pinned the Fae King on his back; the scream that tore through Sila ricocheted around the field. Unable to control his own body, Xabian threw the king around like a ragdoll, making him squeal like a pig as he struggled to get out of the Nyxite's grasp.

Growing bored, the Nyxite threw Sila across the field, who narrowly missed the portal. He skidded through the mud, landing face down in the rain. It suddenly hit Xabian that it was the enchantress' last command that made him lose control. The enchantress was his puppeteer. All he could do was sit back and watch the events play out like he did with a tellage.

Sila staggered to his feet, spitting mud onto the ground and staring his brother down. He moved his hands around, creating flames. Sila bellowed as he threw the flames towards Xabian. Anticipating his move, the enchantress blew fire towards King Sila. He shrieked as the fireball slammed into him, bringing him down again.

"You can't defeat me. I am unbeatable!" Sila shouted, blood pouring out of his mouth.

Xabian wanted to walk away when he heard the sinister laughter coming out of Sila, but the enchantress' hold had him planted to the ground; he growled at the restraint. He could feel his heart racing the more he tried to fight the enchantress' hold on his freedom.

War cries filled the battlefield as the elves charged up to Sila. Despite his injuries, the Fae King grabbed a sword from the ground and got ready to defend himself against the onslaught of bloodthirsty creatures. He cried out as he swung his sword in a frenzy towards his assailants, sending some to their graves as he worked his way through the lines. Then he collapsed to his knees. Xabian could see the fear growing in Sila's face—even smell it. It was satisfying to watch Sila lose hope.

Another roar came from Xabian's mouth, making the elves break away as he spat a purple fireball towards Sila. This time, the Fae King dodged out of the way, looking at his brother and heavily panting. Exhaustion weighed tediously on Sila as the reality of losing everything started to sink in.

He had lost his army, the staff at the castle, even his loyal enchantress. His worst fear came true; the Fae King had lost his power.

Orison walked up to him, sword in hand. "Power is like a sword. It's only lethal to its owner when the owner loses control," she said. Xabian kept a close eye on Sila. "It doesn't feel nice, does it?"

"You bitch! You caused this!" Sila screamed.

He grabbed his sword and was about to swing at Orison, until an arrow was shot through his wrist. Sila screamed with rage, glaring at an elf. He thrust his hand out at Orison and a gale-force wind picked her up, throwing her through the swirling purple portal, screaming. The elves gasped as they looked at the portal. Xabian fought and fought against the enchantress' hold; in his head he was screaming for Orison, but the enchantress held strong. The enchantress had taken away his only form of communication. Now he was truly a prisoner in the Nyxite form.

Another roar came from Xabian, who charged up to Sila, picking him up by the foot and throwing him high into the raging storm clouds. The Fae King's scream bounced around the electrically charged clouds. Losing momentum, Sila plummeted back to the ground.

Xabian took flight, beating his wings heavily as he tried to catch up to the raging king. At the right moment, when Sila was just mere inches away, he opened his mouth. The Fae King tumbled into the deep abyss of the Nyxite and

Xabian swallowed his brother whole. The hold on his free will snapped like a frayed rope; his eyes widened as his muscles seized. Xabian tried to beat his wings, but it was a wasted effort and he began the long descent back to earth.

He smashed into the drenched ground like a meteorite, creating a crater in the centre of the battlefield. Xabian couldn't move as he began convulsing, eyes rolling to the back of his head. His breaths were coming out in pants. He roared loudly when both his wings snapped and disappeared from view—those were the first to go when he changed back to his Fae form. His heart pounded against his ribs; he yelped when his leg snapped. It was too early in the day to change back. Xabian couldn't move because of the debilitating pain—paralysed in the mud, all he could do was lie there.

Mounting a horse, King Idralis rode over to him, crouching down beside him, but as soon as his hand rested on Xabian's body, an eruption of white light threw him back.

Xabian was still shaking as he regained consciousness; tears streamed down his cheeks and his eyes stung. Looking down, he cried out when he noticed there was flesh instead of fur.

He touched his face, but even that was as smooth as silk. Sunrise wasn't for another few hours and he hadn't drunk the Keres Waters again. He didn't understand.

Standing on shaking limbs, he staggered around, trying to take in what had happened. He had killed his brother, the brother who had placed this curse on him. Xabian climbed out of the crater, remembering the way Sila had thrown Orison into the portal. He fell to his knees.

"Orison!" he shouted as he got to his feet. He tried to run but fell flat on his face. "Orison!"

"The portal's about to disappear. You won't be able to make it in time," King Idralis said, returning to Xabian's side.

He looked at the portal with determination; it was, indeed, disappearing. "Tell Taviar and Saskia to uphold royal duties until we find a way back."

"You aren't going in there!" Idralis baulked. The prince didn't listen as he staggered to his feet, the world swaying like a boat out at sea. "Xabian!"

Ignoring all the shouts of protest, he Misted to the portal entrance; diving into the unknown at the last minute, before it sealed off the connection to the Othereal.

Coming Soon

The Fallasingha Chronicles Book 2

L.J. Kerry hopes you have enjoyed your time in the Othereal.
If you liked what you read, please leave a review wherever you like.
By leaving a review, you help L.J. Kerry get this book into the hands of more readers.

Thank you for reading.
Have an awesome day!

Acknowledgements

Well, that's my first Fantasy published and in the hands of readers! I hope you enjoyed it.

Thank you so much to my team of beta readers for reading through the horrible early drafts and crafting it into what it is today. To Z.K. Dorward who not only made my amazing map but also read through the book, pointing out my silly errors and ensuring the plot flowed. I'm so glad you took a chance on this new adventure in my publishing career and I hope you enjoyed every minute of gearing up to the launch.

To my awesome attentive editor Dianne M Jones. I thought the final draft before edits was good, but no... Dianne blew it out the water and I'm so thankful for her help and assistance. I learned so much and this book would not be where it's at without her.

For everybody on social media who kicked my butt and told me to write this.

Thank you to my mum, Margaret. Thank you for always encouraging me to become a huge bookworm from an early age. A huge thank you to my sister, Emma, for also supporting me and helping me come up with plot points.

To you, the reader for taking a chance on a small author.

Glossary

Animunicate (*Ani-muni-cate*) - A type of Fae who can communicate with animals through the mind.

Aquaenix (*A-queen-ix*) - legendary creature from the Phoenix family. Possesses water instead of fire.

Carchaol (*Car-kale*) - A mythical creature which is a snail with eight appendages. Causes adverse effects on the Fae when it eats them.

Charmseer (*Charm-seer*) - A type of Fae who can see enchantments

Desigle (*Des-idgel*)- A powerful protection spell. Prevents enemies from coming near somebody who has a desigle placed on them. It also

binds the spell creator to the subject, so when they are in immediate danger the spell creator gets Misted to their location.

Eryma (*Eri-ma*) - A mythical creature of a pig with poisonous flowers which grow out of its back.

Fire Singer - A type of Fae who can manipulate fire to their will.

Illusage (*Ill-you-sage*) - a type of Fae who can create illusions, making people think they see something which isn't actually there.

Mindelate (*Mind-el-ate*) - A type of Fae who can read and manipulate minds when directly touching somebody.

Mist - Type of Fae magic which allows Fae to travel from one destination to another over long distances.

Nighthex (*Nigh-thex*) - A curse placed on the people of the Othereal. By day they're fae, by night they're Nyxite; a rare form of dragon.

Othereal (*Other-eel*) - The magic realm where the Fae, elves and other magical creatures live in isolation from the mortals.

Projeer (*Pro-jeer*)- A type of Fae like an Illusage who has the ability to create hallucinations.

Rokuba (*Rock-ooba*) - A mythical creature which resembles the snake but has the head of a beautiful mortal woman.

Shifter - A type of Fae who can change into various animals or people.

Tellage (*Tell-age*) - A magical diary for Fae royalty which contains all their memories until their demise.

Teltroma (*Tell-troma*) - A golden disk used to project one user to another for communication.

Tearager (*Tear-age-er*) - A type of Fae who can tear down shields.

Traquelle (*Track-elle*) - tracking spell watch her every movement through a mirror.

Viren (*Vi-ren*)- A sub species of Siren, but they lure mortals into forests instead of water.

Pronunciation Guide

Characters

Aeson *(Aye-son)*
Aiken *(Aye-ken)*
Alsaphus *(Al-sa-fuss)*
Aragh *(Ah-rah)*
Eyam *(Eem)*
Idralis *(Idra-lis)*
Nazareth *(Naz-a-reth)*
Neasha *(Knee-sha)*
Orison *(Or-eye-son)*
Sila *(S-eye-la)*
Taviar *(Tave-ee-yah)*
Xabian *(Zabe-ee-an)*

Places

Akornsonia *(Akorn-zo-nia)*
Braloak *(Brah-loak)*
Cardenk *(Car-den-k)*
Cleravoralis *(Clair-ah-for-alice)*
Fallasingha *(Fal-la-singer)*
Irodore *(Irrow-door)*

Karshakroh (*Car-shack-row*)
Nallavaghn *(Nal-la-van)*
Old Liatnogard (*Old Lee-at-no-guard)*
Parndore (*Parn-door)*
Torwarin (*Tour-war-in)*
Tsunamal (*Zoo-nah-mal)*
Yetnaloui (*Yet-nal-we)*

More by L.J. Kerry

The Listed Duology

Listed

Rebound

The Fallasingha Chronicles

The Stars Plot Revenge

About

L.J. Kerry is an author based in England. She's an avid reader turned author with some of her favourite genres being Fantasy and Dystopia.
Kerry likes to spend her free time playing video games and travelling.